To Sun

(To Bill who so loves
the lake)

Robert Dean Anderson

2008

and to our dear Susie
and Syle and

Paula + John

ASHES

THE YEAR THEY BURNED
OLD LINN CREEK

Continuing the story of
LIMB OF THE JUDAS TREE

Robert Dean
Anderson

Aux Arcs Novels
26183 Indian Creek Lane
Barnett, MO 65011

E-mail bdanders@socket.net

www.AuxArcsNovels.com

First Edition 2004

ISBN: 9720680-3-1

Set in Palatino
Front Cover: From a photograph hanging on the wall in the Camden County Museum in Linn Creek, Missouri. Used with permission of the Camden County Museum.

Printed in the United States of America by
Central Plains Book Manufacturing, Winfield, KS

Dedicated to the memory of the brave and valiant people of Old Linn Creek who fought the good fight in the battle against power and corruption and lost, but won in the end the spoils of that war, the magnificent Lake of the Ozarks.

PART 1

ONE

The last thing you want to find when you're looking for a man who has been missing for three days is a dead body. I'd seen a dead man before, but it's not something you get used to. What I was looking at was a figure that appeared to be a man lying prone with his head at the edge of a flowing creek of clear water tumbling over hat sized rocks, his legs drawn up and hands placed between the knees as if trying to stay warm. And, just like the last dead man I'd seen, I knew who it was and I was the first one to find him. The shock of dead men still and unmoving does not diminish, and does—with time—wear a crease in your mind.

The warm April morning with the sun rays growing stronger between the basswood trees that lined the creek was otherwise pleasant. Spring flowers were sprinkled along the bank and somewhere nearby an oblivious robin sounded happy. The day was a day you waited for throughout the winter months if you lived in a place where winters were cruel and confining and made you long for the unencumbered freedom of the great outdoors and all the sights and sounds that were here with me now. Except for the dead man.

The man wore brown gabardine pants and a tan light-weight jacket. The gray felt hat with the black, two inch band was still on his head with graying brown hair sticking out from under the brim. His face, what I could see of it, was placid and pasty.

We were supposed to signal with a policeman's whistle, but the sight of the man's body froze me to the spot. I stood staring, remembering, agonizing all over again. The sound of footsteps crunching turned me to Maynard Freeman coming toward me in his shuffling gait, trying not to trip over the foot in front. Maynard stumbled over a rock when he got within six feet, righted himself and grinned. Maynard had been the first person I'd seen after alighting from the motor car that brought me from Jefferson City to start my new job in land acquisition in Linn Creek and I freely admit he had made a lasting first impression as I was sure at the time he was the prototype of all the other people in that small town.

"Takin a rest?" Maynard inquired, the grin holding while he pulled his floppy felt hat off and drew a sleeve across his forehead.

Maybe it was the fact that I didn't answer that dried up the grin and made him regard me with a quizzical look. He was accustomed to being ignored. How could he know I was in a condition where it would have been impossible to speak or even to point to the dead man? I stared at Maynard until he grew uncomfortable and looked down at his worn brogans that had weathered several Missouri winters.

When I was able, I turned my head, closed my eyes, then opened them slowly, making sure the man's body had not gotten up and walked away. Maynard's eyes must have followed mine because I heard him catch his breath behind me and heard him say, as only Maynard could, "My . . .my . . . G-G-God a mighty. . . what, what is it?"

Blood began to flow to my brain and anger replaced the paralysis that fright and consternation had forced upon me.

"It's a dead man," I said. "You never saw a dead man ?"

"I . . . I . . . No, I . . . I guess . . . uh uh, I never did."

"Well, take a good look, Maynard, and hope you never see another one," I said.

Maynard, like me, had not moved since first sighting the body. He didn't look at me, his eyes drawn to the body as if it was a magnet and his eyes were iron filings.

"What . . . what can we . . . are you sure?"

"Maybe you better blow your whistle," I said. "Tell the others."

"Who . . . who . . ."

"Happy Meens."

"Didn't he . . . wasn't he . . ."

"My boss."

"Well . . . he was the one we was . . . he was the one lost."

"Yeah. Go ahead, blow your whistle, Maynard. Better tell the rest of the search team. And the sheriff."

"Will we . . . I mean, are we witnesses or something?"

"Just blow the whistle, will you, Maynard. I'm tired of looking at him."

"Are you . . . I mean, he's dead? For sure?"

"He's dead."

"Well, that is . . . how can you tell?"

"God dammit, Maynard, are you going to blow the whistle or not?"

"I . . . I can't."

I found the shiny, silver whistle in the pocket of my twilled, city trousers and stuck it in my mouth and blew as hard as I could. Maynard jumped back from me and his eyes got big and his hands began to shake as he searched his bib overalls for his own whistle, found it and began to blow in a steady, loud, ear shattering blast that drowned out my own signal. The peas of both whistles rattled against the whistle bodies in shrill warbles that drove the robins from the trees and pierced that peaceful day like a dagger to the heart.

6   ROBERT DEAN ANDERSON

Once we started, we couldn't seem to stop. I blew and blew with my face growing hot and stiff and a pain began in my chest as I struggled to keep the air coming, but I couldn't. The pea rattled in the whistle one last time and was still while I gulped in fresh oxygen. Maynard couldn't—or wouldn't—stop. The sound became one like grating glass and annoyed me greatly. I reached out and placed my hand over Maynard's and jerked the whistle from his mouth. A look of surprise came over him as if I had slapped his face. I could see a question there, but I ignored it.

"Hadn't we better . . . what if they don't hear us?"

I sat on the ground—my knees unable to hold my body erect any longer—and propped my chin on my hands. I knew Maynard was looking to me for direction, but I was all done for the time being. We waited, me sitting with my head propped up, Maynard standing over me, all six foot two of him, a look of puzzlement dominating his long, stringy face. Sheriff Doyle Savoy and two townsmen found us that way some time later. They came from the opposite direction and approached the body before they saw us.

Sheriff Savoy was a couple of inches short of six feet with a heavy chest and an almost square face that was creased deeply and seemed to perpetually wear a slight grin. Only, now, the grin was gone as he knelt on the bank of the creek and with his one good arm, turned the body over on it's back. It was then the pool of blood under the body was visible. The side of Happy Meens tan jacket was stained so red it was almost black.

Maynard said again, " My . . . my God a mighty . . ."

I was close to vomiting at the sight of the blood.

Even from fifty feet I could hear Doyle Savoy say in his low, gravely voice, "Damnation. Deader'n a stomped snake."

The two townsmen—Everett Grimm who was a mechanic at the Linn Creek Ford garage before we bought them out, and

Arnold Engberg, the janitor at the Linn Creek school— approached cautiously and peered over Sheriff Doyle Savoy's shoulder.

"That's him, ain't it? That's ol Happy," Everett said.

He looked at Arnold who bent over Doyle to get a closer look, then straightened and said, "By God, who you figure done this, Doyle?"

"Coulda been anybody, considering the job he was doin." Savoy looked hard at me when he said it.

Maynard started gesturing with his hands. "Could'na been me . . . could'na Doyle . . . I only seen him. Smith here . . . Smith, he was here. Could'na been him, Doyle . . ."

Doyle looked at me. "You find him Mister Beauchamp?" (pronouncing it Bo-champ.)

I nodded.

"How long ago?"

"I don't know, half-hour maybe."

"You and Maynard together?"

"Maynard came along later. Maybe ten minutes."

"You check to see if he was dead?"

"I knew he was dead."

"How'd you know that? How close was you?"

"No closer than I am right now. Fifty feet, I guess."

"How'd you know he was dead?" he asked again.

"I've seen a dead man before. I just knew, that's all."

"He was your boss at the land transaction office wasn't he?"

"Yeah, Happy ran the office for Elmer Byron. I came in about two weeks ago."

"Helluva way to get started, huh? You and Happy get along all right?"

"In two weeks, nothing came up worth killing him for if that's what you're asking."

"You come down from St. Louis I believe."

"I was hired in St. Louis. Worked in the office there for awhile. Got transferred to Jefferson City, then here."

"What do you know about Happy?"

I shrugged. "Nothing, I guess. Saw him each morning in our office up at Bagnell. We would drive down here and he went on over to the west side where the lake's supposed to go over the farms. He handled most of the farms and it was my understanding when I was hired that I was to write up the deeds, but then Happy said I was to buy up all the houses and lots in Linn Creek that were below the six hundred and sixty foot mark."

"Was this farm part of what he was buying?"

I shrugged again. "I'd have to check at the office. I'm not sure where we are or who owns the land here."

Savoy looked around. "We're still on ol Hayden Joost's farm looks to me like. Done some fishin and huntin around here."

"I don't recognize the name," I said. "Have to admit I'm not very familiar with the area. Is he someone who could have shot Happy?"

"Uh huh," Savoy said. He scanned the ground and the trees around us with a curious eye. "Meanest son of a bitch in Camden County is who he is."

"Would his place be in the path of the lake when it rises?"

"Probably, but it's a hard scrabble fifty acres or so. Wouldn't be worth much."

"Maybe this Hayden Joost thought it was," I said. "If I've learned one thing in this job it's that most people think their property is worth more than it was before somebody else wanted it."

"Ain't that the way of it, though."

"Was he shot?"

"Once with a deer rifle it looks like," he said. "Probably somebody hiding behind one of those trees over there." He pointed to a grove about thirty or forty feet behind and to my right. There was a lot of underbrush around the trees that had just started greening up with new leaves.

"Did you know Happy?" I asked.

Savoy shot me a look like what was I doing asking the sheriff questions.

"Yeah, went to school with ol Happy. He cheated at marbles, that's what I remembered about him. Went off and got a business degree at the university. Guess he was pretty high up in the electric company in St. Louis. Then he got this acquisition job. Sounds like real estate to me."

"Was he the kind of guy somebody would want to shoot?"

Savoy answered without hesitation. "Hell, anybody who'd spent any time at all with Happy would want to shoot him." He gave me another long and hard look.

"What about his wife?" I asked for good reason.

"You know her?"

"Met her. Had a pretty high social standing in St. Louis, I think. She didn't stay in Bagnell. Jefferson City, either. You'll probably find her in St. Louis."

Everett Grim and Arnold Engberg along with Maynard had been standing around the body of Happy Meens talking in hushed tones. Everett Grim came over to where Savoy stood talking with me.

"Reckon we better get the undertaker or somebody, Doyle?"

"Better go get Mary Little," Savoy said. "She's the only undertaker left in town since Romer sold out. Mary's doublin as the coroner so the county'll pay for her trip out here."

"You be needin us anymore after we fetch Mary?" Grim asked.

"You can go. See if you can find the rest of them and tell them about findin Happy," Savoy said.

"You reckon it was ol Hayden shot him?" Grim asked.

"What do you think?" Savoy asked.

"Wouldn't want to say," Arnold Engberg said. He smiled a little at the corner of his mouth. "Wouldn't want ol Hayden Joost after me."

"How long's he been dead?" Grim asked.

Savoy shrugged. "Hard to say. Rigor mortis hasn't set in yet. Blood's still wet. Not more'n a few hours, I'd say."

"I'd kind of like to leave," I said.

Savoy looked hard at me again. What the hell's he thinking? That I killed my own boss?

"Stay around awhile. You got a stake in this. I'll see you get back in town all right. Where you staying?"

"Bagnell."

"There's a good boardin house in Linn Creek. Rose Minton's place. I'll get you a room there. You'll like the food."

"I'm not a favorite person in Linn Creek," I said. He should know why.

"Rose won't bother you. She's good folk and you're going to have to talk with her sooner or later anyway when you buy her out."

"Thanks, but I'd feel compromised."

"Well, I kind of insist. Stick around for a few days. Don't leave town, stuff like that. I'm sure you understand,"

"Are you saying I'm a suspect?"

"Well, right now everybody's a suspect but me. I'm the only one I know for sure didn't kill old Happy, though if I'd had to spend much time with him I might of."

The first time I'd met Happy Meens he told me I would have to kick twenty dollars a month out of my salary back to him. I knew then Happy Meens was not a man of high moral standards. I could have objected since he hadn't had anything to do with hiring me for the job, but I didn't. It never occurred to me until sometime later that Happy's demise meant a twenty dollar raise in pay for me.

I'd never heard of Linn Creek, Missouri, before accepting a job with the Land Acquisition and Development Company in St. Louis. It was shortly after I graduated from law school where I'd spent the last nine months on a subsistence of bean soup and cornbread in return for sweeping out the "Droppin' By Diner" every night. Getting my law degree was about the only good thing that had happened to me after I had happened upon the other dead man I mentioned. A story I don't wish to tell about at this time.

Working at the Land Acquisition office had seemed like a good enough job. I would have taken it even if it hadn't been because jobs were scarce in 1930. The talk around the office was about the dam some electric company was building in the hills of the Ozark highlands in south central Missouri. I had never been farther west of St. Louis than Wentzville so I had no idea about this Bagnell Dam. At first I helped prepare land transactions coming in from little towns like Eldon, Mack's Creek, Zebra and others not even on the map. I envisioned the area where the dam was going in as barren wasteland. I worked for Elmer Byron and when he came back from a trip to the dam location, he was ecstatic about the structure and what was going to happen to the area.

"It's going to be the biggest lake man ever created in this country," he said. Then, as if he was giving me the biggest Christmas present ever, he said, "I'm sending you down there, Smith. We've been hired to do all the transactions for the electric company."

I thought about ticks and chiggers and snakes. But I needed a change, I needed to get out of the town where I'd spent all of my twenty-five years.

"You'll love it," he said. "You'll be helping Happy Meens. Happy grew up down there in that country so he'll know his way around. What you'll be doing is giving those people more money than they ever saw before in their lives. They'll love you for it. That country down there isn't good for anything but a lake."

I helped Happy close a few deals and, like Elmer Byron had said, the people were as glad to see the money as a kid seeing a full stocking on Christmas morning.

Then we went to Linn Creek. It was a scenic little town with one main dusty gravel street and all the businesses lined up facing the creek. One well-placed, high-power rifle shot through the end store had the possibility of penetrating every business establishment in town.

I detected right away that I was in a different world. Happy introduced me around and told me about the shootings that had occurred in Linn Creek in '29. I met the prosecuting attorney, Joel Dean Gregory, a man not much older than myself, but he looked for all the world to be someone with the weight of the universe on his shoulders. I would not say he was rude to me, but I could see that he and I were never going to be great friends.

The first people we called on were the banks because Happy said they would be the hardest to deal with. Both banks wanted new buildings erected in a new Linn Creek, to be built farther up the rock-strewn stream from which the town took its name. Happy didn't close the deal with the banks. He sent a report to Elmer Byron who told us to sit on the deals for awhile and let the banks sweat. That's what Elmer said about all the deals we kicked up to him.

Happy said the townspeople wouldn't give us that much trouble, but the first door I knocked on flew open with a man holding a pistol in his hand.

Then Happy disappeared three days ago and the whole county had been searching for him the last two days.

And here I was accompanying the one-armed sheriff who

seemed bent on asking the meanest son of a bitch in the county if he had shot Happy Meens.

The road to the Joost cabin quit on us on the opposite side of the creek, which had a French name of Auglaize, but it wasn't much of a stream to someone used to the Mississippi. I'd heard people here refer to it as the Glaize. We got out of the sheriff's black Chevrolet under a canopy of new oak leaves that locked out the sun. I stood on the other side of the car just in case this Hayden Joost might take a notion to resent our intrusion.

Savoy tugged his hat brim down and said, "Come on, lets go see if ol Hayden is home."

Reluctantly I followed him down to the creek bed which was mostly rocks with a foot of water running over them. Savoy found a couple of large, flat stones to step on and he crossed the creek in two strides without getting his boots wet. I stepped across the same way.

From the creek bank I noticed a steep climb going to the cabin which was constructed of logs on the right half and boards rough sawn from native timber on the left side.

Savoy looked around to check that I was behind him.

"Be hard to sneak up on that cabin from the creek," he said, sounding like an answer to a question I hadn't asked.

I was out of breath when we got to the top of the rise, but Savoy wasn't even breathing hard. A flat area of about thirty yards lay between us and the cabin with a half-dozen hogs rooting in the dirt around the cabin. Three spotted hound dogs slunk out from the crawl space under the cabin and started toward us.

Savoy yelled, "Hayden. Hayden Joost. This is Sheriff Doyle Savoy."

I glanced around at the place while we waited. If anyone who lived in the cabin cared about the overall appearance of the Joost homestead, it was not evident. Except, that is, one small spot about a hundred feet from the cabin and under the branches of a spotted-trunk sycamore where a patch of wild flowers bloomed profusely in a pattern on the ground that was too deliberate to have occurred without human assistance.

If ever a man could be said to resemble a bear, it would be the man who came out of the cabin and began walking toward us in animal-like strides. His body was massive, but stood a good half-foot short of my six-foot height. Savoy moved toward the man as if to assert some authority, but this man I guessed to be the meanest son of a bitch in the county clearly would dominate any group he was in.

He stopped eight feet short of Savoy and said, "You're on my land, Savoy."

Doyle Savoy said, "I'm the sheriff of this county investigating a crime, Hayden. I go where my job takes me."

"Nobody comes on my land without me saying so," Hayden Joost said.

"What do you do to someone comes on your land without your say-so Hayden, shoot them?"

"What do you want?" Joost asked. His arms hung nearly to his knees. Each hand, ending in knurly fingers, was ample enough to cover a dinner plate.

"This here's Mister Beauchamp," Savoy said, gesturing toward me with his withered right arm. Without taking his eyes off Joost, he added, "Mister Beauchamp, this here is Hayden Joost."

Hayden Joost showed no interest in me whatsoever. I nodded, but he never took his eyes off Savoy. He wore denim bib overalls that could have used a good scrubbing and a flannel shirt of indeterminable pattern and color that was frayed at the cuffs and collar and looked to be handmade. But, then, what store carried shirts of a size to fit a man who must have been 80 inches around in the chest?

Savoy took his hat off, then put it back on. "Mister Beauchamp here works for the Land Acquisition Company," he said. "Him and Happy Meens have been buyin up all the land that's goin to be under water when they get the dam finished. You know Happy. He grew up in town."

Hayden Joost said nothing.

"You been talkin with Happy about sellin your land?"

"My land ain't for sale," Joost said.

"What do you reckon your land will be worth when it's twenty feet under water, Hayden?"

Joost's face flushed a deep red under the grizzled stubble. I thought for a moment he might charge Savoy and I think Savoy thought likewise because he took a step away from Joost and his good hand went to his holster.

"I'm tellin you one last time, Savoy, get off my land."

"And I'm tellin you I'm investigatin a crime. You can answer my questions here on your land or you can go to town and answer them on my land. You make the choice."

"What crime you talkin about?" Joost asked.

"I'm talkin about a dead man no more'n a quarter mile from your house on your land. And I want to know how he got there and what you know about it."

Joost blinked and for a moment, what would have been a look of fright in a normal man, took over his face.

"What dead man you talkin about?"

"Happy Meens."

Joost jerked visibly. He spoke nothing as Savoy waited for something from him. I became uncomfortable in this strange standoff.

"Did Happy Meens approach you about buying your land, Mister Joost?" I asked and Doyle Savoy shot me a glance like what right did I have to be asking questions he should be asking and Hayden Joost looked at me for the first time. I detected no malevolence in his face nor none when he answered.

Merely anger and a bit of sorrow.

"I talked with him. I run him off. My land. Damn your souls to hell, you ain't got no right takin a man's home and ever thing he owns. Runnin a man and his woman and all his offspring, dogs and chickens and ever thing he's worked for, off land that belonged to his own pappy. His pappy before him."

"Just when did Happy Meens come by here, anyway?" Savoy asked.

Joost's voice was subdued. "This mornin. About an hour 'fore noontime, I reckon."

"So you threatened him?"

"I told him not to be comin around here no more."

"And what did Happy say?"

"He said he would flood me out. Then my woman, she pulled me away 'fore I could hit him. I never touched him."

"He had the law behind him, Hayden," Savoy said, speaking down to him now like he was a school child. "The courts done said the dam people have a right to be on your property, to make a lawful contract with you . . ."

"He said all that. I didn't kill him if that's what you come to find out."

"Now who you s'pose killed Happy Meens on your land, Hayden? Who would have reason to do that?"

"I mighta had reason, but I didn't kill him. Go ask my woman, you don't believe me. She's a church raised woman, she wouldn't lie."

"Intend to do that," Savoy said. "Where's them two boys of yours? Grant and what's the other one's name?"

"My boys ain't got no part in this."

Joost moved his body as if to block Savoy from the house, but Savoy hadn't moved or even looked like he was going to. Joost spread his feet wide and took a stance that would have taken an army tank to break, and I'm not too sure that the tank could do it. He and Savoy stared hard at the other, two men who would ask no quarter nor grant one. I saw the steel in Savoy then and decided he was someone I wanted on my side.

Joost turned and stomped back toward the cabin. By this time three people had come out of the door to stand in the dirt in front of the cabin. One of them was a growing version of Joost without the girth and the heavy, whisker-covered jowls. The other male was a boy, probably mid-teens, and stood near my height. His face was lanky compared to Joost and the other man. The woman near him stood tall and straight. She appeared to need every ounce of meat on her bones and maybe a few pounds more. Her face gave away the measure of the life she'd lived. The three of them watched Joost as he approached them, making it apparent they would do nothing, say nothing that Joost didn't tell them to.

His voice, when he spoke to them, was low and gruff. "He wants to talk with you," and with that he turned sharply and came back to stand before Savoy. His manner and the appearance on his face carried a dare, perhaps a threat, and he never took his eyes off Savoy.

The woman stopped in front of Savoy, her back straight as one of the rays of sunlight that sliced through the hickory and ash leaves around us. She was tempered; I knew that here was a woman who would not break.

Savoy appeared somewhat put off by the rigid pose she struck. He rubbed his mouth with his hand, looked at the ground, then put his one good hand at his belt with the elbow extended. And smiled. I had not seen this side of him. His tone, his words and the smile told me he was a man who not only knew how to talk with women, but enjoyed it.

"Hello, Eleanor." He removed his hat momentarily as a sign of respect, then replaced it on his head. "Pleasure to see you. Hayden hasn't had a chance to tell you what this is about, but I wanted to know if you all had seen Happy Meens today and, if you did, what might have transpired between you."

She snapped her head around, presumably to get instructions or clearance to talk from Hayden, but he never looked at her, just kept his eyes glued on Savoy.

"Tell him the truth of it, woman," Joost said in a low, flat voice. "Tell him all of it."

"He was here, Sheriff," Eleanor Joost said in clipped tones. "Late morning. We was through morning chores and started on day work. Happy came walking up this here bank. He was grinnin and breathin heavy like he wasn't in no shape to be walkin."

"He wasn't drivin a car?" Savoy asked.

"No sir, he was a walkin like I said."

"What did he say to you?"

"He just said howdy and asked was Hayden around. I told him Hayden was in the barn sharpenin the hoe and the sickle. He started toward the barn when Hayden, he come out to see who was talkin."

"How long was Happy here?"

"Not long atall. Him and Hayden begin talkin and Hayden didn't like what Happy was a sayin and he run him off."

"What exactly did Happy say to Hayden if you recall."

Eleanor hesitated. She wanted to look at Hayden again, but thought better of it. She could have been worried by the question as if the wrong answer could fetch reprisal. But she threw back her head a bit, looked Savoy in the eye and said, "He was agitatin about our land again. He's been out here twice before and each time he gets a little more aggravatin. When he told Hayden he would flood us out with his dam water, Hayden started walkin toward him real fast with a sickle in his hand."

"That scare Happy any?"

"You might say it did. He backed up three or four steps, then turned around like he was goin to run, but after I took ahold of Hayden's arm, they both stopped."

"You worried Hayden might use that sickle on Happy?"

"No sir, I wasn't worried about that atall. Never seen the man Hayden would need a sickle with."

The truth of that statement settled on Savoy. He walked a few feet past Eleanor Joost to face the son who would soon be as big as his father. His features resembled Hayden's to an uncanny degree. He stood calmly watching Savoy approach him.

"Grant, did you see Happy here this morning?"

"I seen him," the son said.

"Where were you when all this talkin was takin place?"

Grant jerked his head in the direction of the barn. "I was throwin hay out of the mow when he was here."

"You hear any of the talk?"

"Heard it all."

"Anything you can add to what your mama said she heard?"

"No. I heard it just like she said. Pa might of popped ol Happy one if ma hadn't stopped him, but that wouldn't've hurt him none, except maybe scare him half to death."

"Why you think I'm askin these questions?" Savoy asked, looking around to include all three of the Joosts.

The son called Grant said, "It's likely he's lodged some kind of complaint against us."

"He's dead," Savoy said and Eleanor and her sons showed genuine surprise if I'm any judge of people's composure. "Shot dead with a deer rifle."

He centered his attention on the other, taller son. I guessed him to be near sixteen. "How about you, son? Where abouts were you when your daddy and ol Happy were exchangin words this mornin?"

"Name's Eldon," the son said. He let that sink in for a moment. "I was drivin a heifer over to the Lewis place. She was comin fresh and I reckoned she was ready."

"So you woulda been where when this was takin place?"

"Reckon I woulda been at Lewis's. You can ask Harvey."

"I will," Savoy said. "Hayden, you got one or is it two deer rifles on your place?"

"We ain't got but one," Hayden said.

"I'll need to see that rifle."

That didn't go well with Joost. He and Savoy had another stare down for a few minutes before Hayden looked at Eldon and jerked his head toward the house without a word.

Eldon came back from the house carrying a lever action rifle that was a heavy caliber from the looks of it. He stood holding it until Hayden motioned his head again and Eldon handed it over to Savoy. The sheriff levered the chamber open and stuck his nose down to it and sniffed. He turned it end for end and sniffed at the barrel.

"When's the last time this rifle's been fired?" he asked, swinging his eyes from one to the other of the Joosts. None of them spoke.

"Somebody help me out here," Savoy said. "Hayden, when was the last time you shot this rifle?"

"Last week, I reckon."

"Grant?"

Grant shrugged. "Sure wasn't today. I don't remember when."

"I shot it yesterday at a coyote," Eldon said. "Three shots. Up on that ridge across the creek."

"You clean it after?"

"We always clean our gun after we use it," Hayden said. "I taught them boys that."

"This rifle's been fired recently," Savoy said. "And the barrel's dirty. Nobody cleaned it after the last time it was fired."

Hayden looked at Eldon who pointed a sharp, defiant chin right back at his father.

"I cleaned the damn gun," he said, looking down.

Savoy held the rifle, barrel down, lever halfway and the chamber jacked open. He walked a few steps away from them, levered the chamber closed, aimed the rifle across the creek with his one arm and pulled the trigger. The hammer snapped down with a sharp metallic click. I was the only one to flinch. The Joosts stood as motionless as an oak.

"Eleanor," Savoy looked straight at the woman, "did someone take the rifle out of the house this morning?"

The shock of the question did cause her to flinch. Hayden and both the sons sensed their mother's hesitation and turned their heads toward her.

She did not answer and did not appear as if she would answer. We were all staring at her now and her composure began to slip. Her hands came together in front of her and one hand gripped the other in an iron-tight clinch.

"Who took the rifle this morning, Eleanor?" Savoy asked, his voice soft and friendly and the woman looked at her hands as if she only now noticed they belonged to her.

She glanced over at Hayden. "Well, Meren took it, but she wouldn't shoot nobody."

Hayden Joost's face turned black in anger and he took one short step toward his wife.

Grant said, "Shit," and his brother Eldon looked at the ground and shook his head. "Jesus," he said.

"Is Meren around?" Savoy asked.

"She's gone out to the timber somewheres," Hayden said, his anger filling each word. "You know damn well she ain't shot nobody."

"Not on purpose, no," Savoy said. "But there could have been an accident. She could have thought he was a deer. I'm going to have to talk with Meren, Hayden. You know I am. A man's dead on your land and this rifle's been shot. Now you know I can't let it drop."

While Savoy was facing Hayden Joost, the rifle hanging

from his one good hand, I detected a movement by the tree where the wild flowers had been planted by someone's hand and looking there I saw the top of a person's head and the eyes. Though it was too far away to be sure, I thought they belonged to a girl, probably in her teens.

"You ain't talkin with the girl, Savoy, and that's my final word."

"Hayden, I have a job to do. The people of the county voted for me and pay me to keep the peace and find out who shoots people. I'd do the same if it was one of yours that was shot."

"One of mine gets shot, I'll take care of it myself," Joost said.

"What do you want, Happy Meens' wife to take a gun after the person killed her husband? That ain't the way it works, Hayden. We got laws and I'm hired to keep them. You want to live where there ain't no laws, go live in China or someplace."

"Where's your damn laws when people come around to take my land away from me?"

"When we have disputes, we settle them in court. Each side has their say and then the judge decides. Happens the judge said more people depend on the electricity coming from this dam than need the land the water's goin to cover."

"I didn't get no say in court," Joost said.

"Well, see, that's part of the law, too. Joel Dean Gregory went to court and spoke for all of us. And he gave a right good speech too, how we didn't want the dam and the people like you want to keep their land, but the judge didn't see it that way."

"Rich folk own the courts," Joost said.

"I'm halfway inclined to agree with you on that, but it's been carried as far as we can carry it and the dam is comin in."

He handed the rifle back to Eldon and turned and walked

toward the creek. I sneaked one more look at the spot where I'd seen the girl, but she was gone. I felt like I ought to say something to the Joosts in parting, but they offered nothing so I offered nothing in return.

I retraced the way across the creek behind Savoy, stepping on the same rocks we had stepped on going over. Savoy was in his Chevrolet and had the engine started before I got in on the passenger side. He wheeled the car around and we drove back over the rock-covered road toward the spot where I'd found Happy's body. Neither of us spoke. When we got there and he stopped the Chevrolet, I saw three men and a woman loading Happy's body into a hearse.

Savoy was shutting the door on his side of the car when I asked him, "Who's this Meren?"

"Hayden's daughter," he said. "She ain't right."

"I saw a girl up by the flower bed," I told him.

"Yeah, I know. I saw her."

"Could she have shot Happy?"

"Not likely."

The hearse pulled away with Happy's body inside, the two of us watching it out of sight.

Savoy said, "Where was Happy goin three days ago when you last seen him?"

"He dropped me off in Linn Creek at the courthouse and said he was going over to the west side. North of Mack's Creek if I remember right."

"What was he doin over here this morning?" Savoy asked, seeming to talk with himself. "Where's he been the last two days? And where's his car? What was he doin walkin on Hayden Joost's property instead of drivin?"

"Looks like you got work to do, sheriff," I said.

"Yeah," stroking his chin. "Looks like you got some work to do, too, Mister Beauchamp. With Happy dead, you're the one goin to have to make a deal with ol Hayden on his land."

That thought had occurred to me and I wasn't too comfortable with it.

"I wouldn't want to be you," Savoy said, walking off to where I'd first spotted Happy's corpse.

"Then again," he continued without looking back, "I ain't exactly lookin forward to bein me the next couple of weeks, either."

TWO

A brown-boarded, two-story house standing just off Main Street in Linn Creek had a two-foot diameter forged iron ring hanging on a front porch which ran the length of the house. Just as Sheriff Doyle Savoy pulled his Chevrolet up to a foot-thick log rail running horizontally across the front, a man well into his years rose from a rocking chair on the porch and, taking up a six-inch long iron pin suspended with the forged ring, began whipping the pin back and forth inside the ring banging out notice that echoed back off the limestone walls of the courthouse down the street.

"Looks like we're just in time for supper," Savoy said as he stepped out of his car and slammed the door closed. I took that as my signal to disembark. No sign adorned the front of the house, but I had a feeling this was where the sheriff intended for me to "stick around" as he put it.

"I'm not a rich man, Sheriff," I said, following him onto the rambling front porch. "I'm already out rent in Bagnell at one of the cabins for the dam crew."

"You have trouble meetin your bill here, let me know."

Savoy opened the front door and walked in without knocking so I assumed this was a legitimate business establishment. He held the door for me and when I entered, a woman leaving middle age came forward, a greeting smile on her face. She wore an apron over her dress and held a small towel in both hands, drying them.

"Rose," Savoy said, stepping ahead of me, "this here's Mister Beauchamp. He's goin to be stayin a few days with you if you got room."

"Glad to meet you Mister Beauchamp," the woman named Rose said, offering her hand which was soft and warm and still slightly damp. "I can put you up in a private room with meals for $30 a month, or a dollar fifty a day."

Before I could open my mouth, Savoy said, "Why don't you go ahead and make it by the month. He has business here in town and he don't own an automobile. Isn't that what you said, Mister Beauchamp? You don't own a automobile?"

I could only shake my head, stunned as I was at him contracting my living arrangements without consulting me.

"Good, then," he said. He hung his hat and jacket on the hall tree just inside the door and stood waiting for Rose to lead us inside. I followed suit like some kind of tin man or puppet. "We'll be takin supper with you Rose if you'll remind me where we can wash up. I've got some news that concerns everyone here that I'd like to share and sort of introduce Mister Beauchamp around."

Rose led us to a wash stand in a hallway off the entry and poured water from a pitcher into a china basin. I washed my hands thoroughly to cleanse myself of any contaminant from the corpse of Happy Meens, though I had been no closer than thirty feet of the body. She handed me a towel and while I dried, Savoy poured fresh water and did his own washing up. He took a little longer than I did because, I suppose, he did touch Happy when he turned him over.

"Where you from, Mister Beauchamp?" Rose asked with a smile and I barely got out that I was staying at Bagnell when Savoy interrupted.

"I'll just go ahead and introduce him when we're all seated, Rose. Save Mister Beauchamp the trouble of tellin it twice."

Rose led us to a large table where nine people were already seated. With a hand in my back, Savoy guided me to a place at the table directly across from the elderly man who had rang the meal announcement on the ring outside. Next to him was an equally elderly lady looking very proper and elegant in a lace trimmed dress of 1890's vintage.

"Ever body, I want you to meet Mister Beauchamp," Savoy began. He was wearing his talking-to-women smile and a politician-running-for-office voice. "He's goin to be stayin with you awhile."

He introduced everyone around the table. The elderly man was Uncle Billy Jack Cummins and the woman next to him was Jane McGann. After that the names got a little hazy. There was Jack something-or-other who ran the ferry, Volly New-something who owned the Shell filling station and a smiling, skinny, Lonnie who worked for Volly. Doc Hardesty looked like a doctor, staring business-like down his nose over his gold-rimmed spectacles. There was a man named Joe Collie— a name easy to remember—who led a crew that cut trees on land the lake would cover.

I was relieved to note that I would not be the only person staying at Rose's house who would be involved with the dam. I did note that a good many of the people at the table would be out of business once my assignment was complete.

As conversation went around the table, I caught the Indian woman's name on my right, Oma Thornbush, and the man with a woman's name of Ruby who Savoy introduced as a real estate man from the town of Lebanon to the south of Linn Creek.

Everyone respectfully waited to begin passing food while Uncle Billy Jack offered up a prayer that pleaded with God to intervene in the dam building so that Linn Creek would continue to loll by the creek in sunshine and moonlight and not be cast to a watery grave.

Quite a welcome.

After all the dishes had made it around the table and the diners had begun to eat, the quiet at the table made it quite clear that everyone was waiting for Sheriff Doyle Savoy to speak.

He started by saying how everyone knew the dam was coming and there was nothing that could stop it now. He said most people welcomed the promised prosperity a filled lake would bring, but, dammit—with apologies to the ladies at the table—why couldn't they let Linn Creek live.

"But it's not to be," he said. He chewed thoughtfully for a minute or two and added, "You all know Happy Means, he was raised here. Happy had a job to do and he set about doin it. Not ever body liked Happy and he could get downright abrasive at times—tellin people to sell out or be flooded out—and that was bound to make some enemies."

Here Lonnie interrupted. "Arnold Engberg says somebody shot ol Happy deader'n hell. Reckon that must have been one of them enemies you're talking about."

Savoy looked irritated at Lonnie's interruption.

"Reckon it was, Lonnie. But I don't aim to see somebody shot in my county and the killer get away with it."

"Reckon it was ol Hayden?" Volly asked.

"Joosts are mostly trash," Uncle Billy Jack chimed in. "Knowed old Hayden all his life and his daddy, Rothman, too. And his granddad, Old Hayden Joost the first, I guess he would have been. Mean people. Keeps to themselves. Them boys are probably going to top Hayden for orneriness. Only one worth saving is the girl. Born innocent and treated indecently. Poor girl."

Doc Hardesty peered down his nose at Uncle Billy Jack. "Uncle Billy Jack, you're too quick to judge. I've doctored the girl. She's about as retarded as you can be. The way she is, she couldn't help it. And you don't know everything about it."

"Well," Uncle Billy Jack said somewhat chastised, "I do know Hayden and all the other Joosts. But, you're right Doc, I don't know much about the girl. They keep her hidden; she has hardly ever come into town since she was no more'n belt high. Pretty little thing, but Hayden and the rest of them treat her as if she was an imbecile."

"Unfortunately, they aren't far off the mark," Doc Hardesty said.

"Was it old Hayden who shot Happy?" Volly asked again.

Savoy shoveled the last of his dinner onto his fork and ate it. While he chewed he watched Volly while everyone else at the table watched Savoy, including me. I was fascinated by the man. The first time I had met him I wrote him off as a small town, small time sheriff maybe a notch above Maynard. But there was depth to this man and I had already seen his steel.

"I'm workin on that," he said.

"All right," he balanced the elbow of his good arm on the table's edge and pointed his fork in the general direction of Volly and Lonnie. "With the dam comin and with Happy dead, you're all going to have to deal with someone else. Now, the company could send some real tough character to make a low offer to you for your property and your business and say take it or leave it."

Volly and Jack, the ferry man, nodded their heads in agreement. Savoy went on, "Or the company could send in someone who might show a little compassion and be on your side in trying to relocate you and get the property transferred."

"Fat chance," Lonnie said.

Savoy jabbed the fork at Lonnie alone, now. "Maybe not," he said. And I began to get this really sick feeling. That son of a bitch. He's setting me up. Telling these people how I was going to deal with them without giving me a chance. My face burned in anger and I barely heard Savoy say, "That someone's going to be Mister Beauchamp, here."

The silence almost roared it was so heavy and dominating. I knew every eye in the room was on me except for Savoy who was helping himself to an apple cobbler. He passed it on to me and as I took the the hot pan with the toweled mitt that came with it, I dropped the dipping spoon onto the table, then onto my trousers, and finally, onto the floor.

I was embarrassed, angry and even felt guilty, surrounded by people who I was employed to put out of their homes and businesses. Rose appeared at my side.

"Here, Mister Beauchamp, let me handle that for you. It's hot." With a clean spoon she heaped a good-sized portion onto my plate and went on around the table with the cobbler.

The elderly woman, Jane McGann said, "Beauchamp (pronouncing it like the French, Bo-shawmp) I believe is of French derivation, is it not? Where are you from, Mister Beauchamp?"

"St. Louis," I muttered around a bite of the cobbler.

"Yes, I suppose there are quite a few French still in St. Louis," she said. "After all, they did found the city a couple hundred years ago."

"My father was French," I found myself saying. "My mother was English. Her name was Smith. That's my first name. Smith. Smith . . ." I hesitated, then went ahead and said it like Savoy had introduced me, Bow-champ. I knew I would never be known as Beacham (as my mother insisted on pronouncing it) or Bo-shawmp as Jane McGann and my father's family had articulated it.

Lonnie said, "Well, I guess me and ol Volly and Jack here, and Rose, too, are goin to have to be real polite and nice to you, Mister Beauchamp, since you're the one going to say how much we get for our property."

I had regained my composure and most of the anger and embarrassment had dissipated. I said to Lonnie, "You can call me Smith. But I'm sure the company will replace Happy with a more experienced person than myself. I've only been with the company nine months."

The real estate man named Ruby showed real interest in me, saying we could sure do some business together with him selling property in Lebanon to the people for the money I gave them for their homes and businesses in Linn Creek. Maybe, he suggested, if I offered a little more to the people, he could charge more for the property and then suggested it would be better for everyone, including me.

This job was full of kickbacks.

Other than him, for the remainder of the meal, the rest of the people treated me as if I'd brought smallpox into the room.

Once when I visited my grandmother on a farm outside of Hannibal, I woke up with a chicken staring at me. The room Rose set me up in was small, but considerably cleaner than the one at grandma's. And it had screens over the windows.

The decision I had to make was one that didn't really have to be made. I mean, only an idiot would continue working at a job after his boss was shot and killed doing what he would now have to do. So, the bed was soft, the sheets crisp and clean, outside I could hear the frogs down on the creek getting back in voice after a winter layoff, and no thought entered my mind about continuing to work for the Land Acquisition Company.

Except I couldn't sleep.

To say that I liked Happy Meens would be a statement without truth, but he didn't deserve to die. Seeing him lying there in death brought terrible memories back to me, memories I had never wanted to enter my mind again.

But there they were.

Unfamiliar as I was with the house, finding the stairway in the dark was like finding stars on a stormy night. How I got down them and out onto the expansive front porch without waking the whole house could qualify as a minor miracle. The moon in its second phase provided enough illumination to guide me over to one of the rocking chairs. Seated, I tried to concentrate on the frogs, hoping to keep my thoughts off things I didn't want to think about. I'd learned the trick several years ago; focus on the moon and you can't see the stars. Focus on the traffic noise and you can't hear people yelling.

But it wasn't working because I kept hearing a grating sound that rose above the croaking frogs. It took me a full minute to realize someone else was on the porch and that someone was rocking a chair and making the boards of the porch creak.

"I often come out here when it's warm and calm and listen to the sounds of the night," someone said. I recognized the voice of the elderly gentleman who sat across from us at supper, Uncle Billy Jack Cummins.

"Pretty soon you'll hear some coyotes up on the ridge and some owls hooting up a storm. They have any of these sounds back in St. Louis?"

"No sir, they did not" I said.

"Never been to St. Louis. Wanted to go to the World's Fair, but had to work the farm. Spent three nights in Springfield once. Noise all night long with automobiles coming and going. The hotel was across the street from a speakeasy. Police came there four times in three nights. Made me think prohibition was never going to work. Just as well, I guess."

"Sounds like downtown St. Louis," I said. "I lived over a tavern once."

"I suppose when you're born to the city, it's the quietness of the nights that make it difficult to sleep."

"Actually, every time I closed my eyes I kept seeing my boss lying there beside the creek with blood all over him, his eyes still open, staring at nothing. I came out here hoping to hear the peaceful sound of the frogs, thinking maybe they could help me erase that sight."

"Tomorrow they will bury Irvin Meens and say good things about him. And that is as it should be. When a man dies, the good things he did should be what is remembered."

"You knew Happy?"

Uncle Billy Jack did not answer for a time. A match flared and he touched it to a corn cob pipe releasing a cloud of smoke to drift past the half-moon and disappear into the cool spring night.

"I have to cut down on my smoking," he said. "If Rose caught me she'd hide the pipe and the tobacco. She's hid three of them now."

I could hear him chuckling softly in the night.

"Last bout of consumption nearly called me home. Doc and Rose keep their eyes on me every hour of the day. So I sneak out here at night and have a drink of Ernest Raines smooth mash whisky and smoke my pipe. Say, would you join me in a drink tonight?"

Though I'm not a drinking man, I found myself saying, "Yes, I would like that."

Uncle Billy Jack passed over a quart jar and I unscrewed the zinc lid and took a drink. Whatever it was in the jar burned all the way down and momentarily stopped my breath somewhere between my nose and lungs. Then a mellow warming slowly spread throughout my body and entered my mind, changing my mood so quickly I momentarily forgot my surroundings.

"Goes down pretty smooth, doesn't it?" Uncle Billy Jack said.

I glowed from the inside and all of a sudden a fence surrounded my brain and outside thoughts that bumped up against it were repelled.

"Would you believe that the law has made that illegal?" he asked.

When I didn't answer, he said, "Go ahead, have another drink."

So I did.

"You know," Uncle Billy Jack was talking now farther away from my mind and with a deeper sound. "When you showed up tonight, I was prepared to despise you on sight. You see, I love this town. There's been talk about a dam on the Osage River for twenty years or more. Nobody thought it would ever happen. And if it did, nobody ever thought it would wipe out the whole town."

I had another drink of the whisky and Uncle Billy Jack sounded even farther away. I heard the frogs again, and a howling up on the ridge behind the town. No automobile noise, no people arguing. I had found the peace I had searched for.

"But it happened and now, nobody can stop the dam. When the waters start coming, nobody can stop them, either. They say before summer's over the town will be covered with water. I don't want to see that. So why should I stop smoking and drinking whisky just so I'll live long enough to see the town I love disappear before my eyes like it never existed."

"I know," I said. "Some things I've seen, I wish I hadn't."

"Happy Meens was a dishonest man." Uncle Billy Jack sounded as if he was up on the ridge with the coyotes. "I guess I'm the hair shirt in this county. I remember too much. I should just talk about the good things a man did after he dies, like they do at funerals, but somebody has to keep the history of this county and tell the truth about it. And the truth is, Happy Meens has always been a dishonest man. So was his daddy."

I had another drink, my fourth. Or maybe my fifth. Or sixth.

"I've come to live with the fact the dam can't be stopped. But the thought of a man like Happy Meens cheating the people out of the houses they've worked for all their lives is more than I could bear."

"I had to kick twenty dollars of my salary back to Happy each month," I said, and had another drink.

"But I saw in you, an honest man, Mister Smith Beauchamp. And the people of this town have the right to expect to be dealt with by an honest man."

"I'm quitting my job tomorrow, Uncle Billy Jack," I said, feeling sad of a sudden.

"Do you believe the Lord works in mysterious ways, Mister Beauchamp?"

"I'm Catholic, Uncle Billy Jack. I believe what they tell me to believe."

Another drink.

"I believe you're the man the Lord sent to help the people when they have to sell their homes. I see kindness in you, Mister Beauchamp. And honesty."

I tipped the jar up for another drink, but got only a few drops.

"I can help you out, Mister Beauchamp. I can tell you about each family and probably what you ought to pay each one. It's a blessing, your being here . . ."

Uncle Billy Jack's voice faded till it was hidden behind the croaking frogs and the howling coyotes. The last clear sound I heard was an owl, not too far away, saying, "Who. Who."

You talking to me?

Leah was there. Savoy had placed a telephone call over scratchy wires, but coherent enough that she understood. Happy Meens was dead.

She smiled at me in a bit of a patronizing way when I

made my way down the stairs and into Rose Minton's parlor.

"You poor dear, I understand," she said, laying a hand on my shoulder. "With Happy's death and all, it's understandable you would want to stay in bed until eleven. But, life goes on"

"Uh huh," I said. God, I felt awful. The whisky Uncle Billy Jack fed me last night may have slid down my throat like silk, but this morning it was like a loose cannon inside my head.

"It was awful, wasn't it?" Leah said, being Leah and tearing up. "I mean, I was the one who had to tell Happy's wife. Elmer's in St. Louis but he'll be back for the funeral. Which, by the way, is now scheduled for tomorrow in Jefferson City. Vivian wanted him buried there."

"But Happy's from this town," I said. Then, rethinking the burial issue, let it drop.

"Well, there's going to be a memorial service here tomorrow morning at eight o'clock at the Methodist church."

"Eight o'clock? Who goes to funerals or memorial services at eight o'clock."

"I was under the impression you and Happy weren't that friendly," she said, surprise showing in her face.

"He was my boss. I owe him some loyalty."

Even if he did appropriate twenty bucks from my paycheck.

Rose Minton came into the room to see if we would like some lemonade or maybe just a drink of water, looking directly at me. I introduced her to Leah, but she said the two had introduced themselves.

I gulped the lemonade down in one drink, slaking my immense thirst from the whisky hangover, and stood.

"We need to talk, Leah," I said. "Would you like to take a walk with me?"

"Yes, of course, Smith," she said. There was the patronizing smile again.

Leah was three years my senior, but ages my senior in class and worldliness. She ran the Land Acquisition Division office in Jefferson City, though officially Happy drew the supervisor's pay for it. Truth was, Happy deferred to Leah on all office decisions. When we stayed in Bagnell, Happy would call Leah almost daily on the telephone and rail away at the inefficiencies of the telephone company about times he couldn't get through. Happy spent a great deal of time either talking on the telephone or trying to talk on a balky telephone. I never knew who he talked to, other than Leah, but I remembered one time he told someone that he would have his ass.

Remembering that, I thought I should tell the sheriff.

"What is it you want to talk about, Smith?" Leah asked, coming up beside me and snuggling close as we walked in the chilly, cloudy April day.

Her body felt good to me, warm and soft. I always had the feeling since the first week I worked in the Jefferson City office with her that Leah could be my girl if I wanted her to. But, my God, she was essentially my boss, older than me, and I was certain that if I kissed Leah, she would consider us engaged to be married. She was pretty, smart, tough as nails with a velvet covering and very much involved in the beliefs of the Presbyterian Church.

"Listen, Leah, I can't go on with this job. You're going to have to tell Elmer to get someone else. I mean, with Happy getting shot by who knows who, and me inexperienced in buying land, it just wouldn't work."

"But I'll be right there for you in Jefferson City. Just call me anytime you want. Happy did."

"Okay, call me a coward if you like, but I don't want to get shot. Why do you suppose someone shot Happy? It was a warning, see. You think they wouldn't shoot the next person to come around trying to buy them off their land?"

"Of course, I understand your feelings, Smith. But we don't

know who shot Happy or why. And they wouldn't be foolish enough to shoot two people."

"Leah, you don't know these people. They hate my guts. This Hayden Joost would as soon shoot me as look at me."

"That's the man who owned the farm Happy was trying to buy?"

"Hayden Joost. Yeah. Hayden ran Happy off, but says he didn't shoot him. He seemed to be telling the truth, but somebody shot him."

"Are there other Joosts on the farm?"

"Yeah. A wife tough as scrap iron. Two sons who don't seem smart enough to shoot anybody and an imbecile girl who doesn't talk. Take your pick."

"We have to get this done, Smith. Don't walk out on me now."

"We? I have doubts about my future with the company when this job is over. So, I'll take my leave now. While I can still walk away instead of being carted back to Jefferson City in a hearse like Happy."

"They're closing the gates on the dam next month. The water will start coming up and the electric company has got to have ownership of this land before it does. Otherwise, the electric company is facing a flood of lawsuits. We'll have lawyers so thick in Jefferson City you could walk on them all the way to the dam."

"Maybe that's where my future is, filing suit against the electric company."

"Smith, you have no legal experience. It would take you a month to file a suit."

"If I'm so incompetent, why are you asking me to stay with the company?"

"Because I'll be there to help you. Listen, I thought you might want to walk away, what with Happy getting shot on the job, so I have it on my list to take it up with Elmer. I know he'll want to keep you on at all costs. And I know he'll be getting some help for you."

"What did you mean, 'At all costs?'"

"He'll give you a raise."

"How much?"

"How much would it take?"

"Double my salary."

"Be reasonable, Smith. I'm sure he would give you a hundred a month increase."

"Double and you stay here and help me until Elmer sends someone else."

Leah stopped in mid-stride. We were opposite the big limestone courthouse in Linn Creek and the big redbud tree now leafing out with heart-shaped leaves and losing the purplish-red, tiny flowers. The tree Happy referred to as the Judas Tree where a hanging almost took place.

"There's no one to handle the office in Jefferson City and besides, who would sell their land to a woman?"

"Another woman," I said. "And you have a secretary in the office, you can call her every day like Happy called you."

"Hmm. Maybe it could work"

"I'll bet Elmer would agree with you."

"The two of us could get it done, couldn't we?"

I nodded my head slowly. "Yeah, if you aren't scared of taking Happy's place."

"Smith you should know by now I'm not scared of anything."

"Yeah, I did notice. But, I didn't hear Happy saying anything about being scared either."

"Anyone but you I'd say let Elmer get someone else to do the buying. But, I've always thought you and I could work well together, Smith. We'll do it, then. The two of us, we'll do it."

She tapped me on the arm with her small fist. Firm lines of determination were visible in her face and her smile was more like one a cat might wear regarding a cornered mouse. I thought, Good Lord, what have I wrought?

"When does my double salary start?" I asked.

"Come on, Smith. Is money your number one priority here?"

"No. That would be staying alive."

THREE

I'll tell you how efficient Leah was. By three o'clock we had an office in the back room of one of the banks, a telephone and a sixteen-year-old girl named Mary with long blonde hair and more freckles than flies in a stable to type up contracts and answer the telephone should it ever happen to ring.

Leah, to initiate her reign as self-appointed supervisor of land acquisition in Linn Creek, elected to begin where Happy had failed. The banks. At the Missouri State Bank across the street from our newly founded office, she waltzed through the front door like a New York socialite and went directly to the president's desk and took a seat across from him. Mister Lane Lindall looked up from the fat sheaf of papers in front of him, saw a stunning brunette sitting in one of his Windsor chairs uninvited, wearing a cheery smile I might add, and he could not prevent doing likewise.

"Hi, I'm Leah Turner," she said, and extended her hand across his walnut desk. He was severely taken aback at first at her effrontery. He did an executive throat clearing and asked in a somewhat supercilious tone what it was he could have someone take care of for her.

"I'm here to buy your bank," she said with an increasingly clever smile.

He straightened into a rod-like posture and said, "And what led you to believe this bank is for sale?"

Lindall was fifty or more, steel-colored hair and a chin that resembled the square end of an anvil. But those all melted into ordinary features when Leah said, still smiling like the Harvey girls in Union Station, "Because, Lane, in about 90 days the Osage River is going to start running in under your front door and it won't stop until you're thirty feet under."

Mister Lane Lindall's face turned the color of the gray limestone walls of his bank.

"Who are you?" he demanded.

She produced a calling card from her small purse and, with a flourish, plopped it in front of him.

He looked at the card and took his time moving his eyes back to her. When he shifted his gaze to me, Leah said, "Smith Beauchamp, my assistant."

We had met before, of course, but he didn't seem of a mood to acknowledge that.

"I, uh, yes, I believe a Mister Meens came by to see us about the move. We gave him the particulars, of course, on what our needs would be . . . "

"I've read your list Lane. A new building on a lot of your choosing, but purchased by us. Five thousand square foot building, I believe you said. Cost of the building to be at least one hundred and fifty thousand dollars. No competing bank within three blocks in any direction. Seven thousand dollars for moving and miscellaneous expenses. Four thousand dollars for furnishings. Marble floors. Walnut desks and counter. Latest stainless steel vault by Moser guaranteed unbreechable. Two thousand dollars for lost time in moving. Have I left anything out?"

"You have the list I believe, Miss Turner . . ."

"Indeed. A grand total of $301,000. I have a counter proposal, Lane. One hundred twenty five thousand. Find your lot. Build your own building. Pick out your own floors, furniture and vault. Take it or leave it."

Lindall's face went from gray to red in a flash. His features hardened like concrete on a summer day.

"You'll have to talk it over with your board of directors, of course," Leah said, her mouth full of sugar. "So I wouldn't expect a decision from you until closing time one week from tomorrow. My offer will expire at that time and you're on your own. You can sit and watch the water coming in your door."

I tried to keep up with her long, stepping strides as she left the bank lobby, but had to break into a trot outside the door to catch up with her.

"My God, Leah, you don't have the authority to do that, do you? I mean, Elmer told Happy to delay in hopes the bank will soften up. You just threw down the gauntlet in there. No way Lindall is going to take that, especially from a woman."

"You men are too soft. Look, in two months they're closing the gates in the dam and thirty days after that, you're going to be standing knee deep in water if you stay where you are. Elmer said get the job done and that's what I'm doing."

"What about the Ozark National where our office is?"

"We're cutting them some slack. Missouri State Bank said they had no room to spare for our office. Their loss."

"Elmer's not going to go for this," I said, genuinely concerned.

"Elmer's not here. Elmer's down in Ironton writing up a deal to sell the electricity to the lead mines down there. If he fails at that, there won't be a need for the electricity this dam generates. So you think he's going to worry about what goes on in Linn Creek? He never has."

Miniature dust whorls puffed from the heels of Leah's pounding patent leather pumps. How women could even stand straight in those scientifically unbalanced boats that women strode about with feet strapped inside puzzled me, but here she was outstriding me and doing so with a cadence I couldn't maintain in Florsheims that were perfectly designed to maneuver in. I was about to inquire about our next call when to my incredulous eyes, she made straight for the front door of the courthouse.

I called, "Leah," but if she heard, she chose to ignore me as she passed through the doors. Inside, her hard, leather-stacked heels clacked against the oaken boards in the floor as they headed her to the county judges' office.

Just as I reached the doorway, Presiding Judge Cargrove was rising to his feet in a chivalrous move while the two associate judges looked up sleepily and a bit incredulous at the bold young, attractive woman who stood before them.

"Gentlemen," she said, "I am Leah Turner of the Land Acquisition Company in Jefferson City. I came to inform you that all negotiations between the county and our office will cease in 30 days. You have that long to make a final accounting of the county property that will revert to the electric company upon the closing of the dam gates."

The three of them, of an age every one to have possibly been a grandparent to the woman now giving them a deadline to end their business with the electric company, looked as if she had hit them over the head.

Cargrove himself was the first to recover from her threatening statement of extortion.

"Why, young woman, whoever you are, you surely are in no position to make such a statement to the people of Camden County."

"Thirty days, your honor," she said, confusing the title shown on his nameplate in front of his chair with the standing of a circuit judge. "That should give you sufficient time to get your accounting of the affected property listed."

"Well, perhaps you would do well to tell that to the judge in the federal court in St. Louis where the county's case is now being heard," Cargrove said. The other two judges' heads bobbed up and down in almost perfect unison.

"I can't hurry up a court action," she said. "It will be mute, however, in about 90 days because I can't stop the water that will be coming in your front door at that time."

"Then my advice to you, young lady, is to slow down the water." Judge Cargrove said. He rose to a pompous height on his elevated platform and stared condescendingly down at Leah. "Court decisions are never mute. A judgment against your company by the court and the people of Camden County could end up owning that electric company and you could be working for us."

"There have been three court rulings in the electric company's favor so far, judge, and none for the county. The score at this point is three to nothing against you and we're coming up on the seventh inning. In sixty days this ball game is over."

Joel Dean Gregory, whom I had met before, strolled into the county court room, no doubt drawn by the bombastic tones of Judge Cargrove. He was a tall, slender man well dressed in a suit of fine cloth with hair parted down the middle, but with a perpetual air of sadness about him. Some said it was because his best friend and then his sister had been killed a short time back and he had shot and crippled the father of the woman he was about to marry. Enough to paste a sad countenance on any man's face.

Gregory introduced himself to Leah and nodded to me. As I said before, I liked the man, but being friends was something that was not about to happen.

Leah passed her ultimatum on to Gregory who heard her out without interruption or change in attitude. Then he explained to her how the county had many claims against the electric company, such as who was going to pay for all the county roads that the lake waters would wash out and cover up. And what about the schools that would have to be moved? And the courthouse itself along with the jail sitting a mere fifty yards away? The voters would have to approve moving the county seat, but where were they to go? The electric company had pledged to build replacement schools and pay fifty thousand dollars on the construction of a new courthouse and jail. This matter couldn't be settled until a neutral third party—the federal court—heard all the facts in the case and gave a just and fair ruling.

Leah, unfazed, said, "It looks to me like there's a lot of stalling going on here. The construction of the dam goes on. Hundreds of cubic yards of concrete are being poured every day. Does no one believe that the water will actually rise to cover your town once the gates are closed in the dam?"

Joel Dean Gregory said, "Of course we believe. Even the most rabid non-believers of six months ago now see the futility of further resistance. The water is coming. But these matters I speak of take time."

"Take all the time you want," Leah said. "The electric company is ready to pledge fifty thousand dollars to your courthouse. And to build a new, modern school building for you. Just tell them where you want it. The demolition crew will be here in a matter of days and this courthouse is sitting right in their path. But you people don't even know where you want your courthouse."

Gregory stuck his hands in his pants pockets and stared at his shoes. "What you say is true, we haven't decided on a location for the new county seat yet. This isn't something you decide in a few days. It affects a lot of people and the decision has to be a right one for everyone concerned."

"Well, you're going to have to grow gills if you don't decide right away. The banks want their buildings in a new town of Linn Creek about two miles upstream. Near a place called Easterville. What about building the courthouse there?"

"It's under consideration," Judge Cargrove said in a manner not belying the irritation showing on his face.

"There are several candidates for the county seat," Gregory said. "The state has to move both highway Five from Versailles and highway 54 coming from Bagnell. They might intercept at the new town or they might not intercept at all. The state may just terminate Highway five at Versailles. We have no control over where the state decides to locate highways. And there's the town of Mack's Creek that wants the county seat relocated there."

"Interesting," Leah said. She walked to the door of the judges' office where she turned and looked back. "Thirty days, Gentlemen" she said. "Thirty days."

Rose had no rooms left that night. She told Leah she would fix something for her, not to worry. Around the dinner table, Leah was—well, the word for it would be chatty, I guess. The ultimatums she had thrown at the Missouri State Bank and the county judges had made the rounds, with embellishments, I'm sure, and from the set of Uncle Billy Jack's jaw, her bold actions were not going to be well received.

As we were beginning to enjoy the beef and noodle dish Rose had served and while listening to Leah's account of the yards of concrete being poured at the dam site, Uncle Billy Jack blurted out, "Why is the electric company coming in here where everyone's life is already disrupted and telling the people of this town they have just days to put their life in order and pack their belongings and get out."

Leah halted the fork on its way to her mouth, licked her lips and, knowing her, put her brain to work trying to figure out just why no one wanted to hear about the marvelous new dam being built and just why this one man seemed to find her so disagreeable.

"Why?" she asked. "Because there's this big rock rolling down the hill and it can't be stopped. What we're trying to do is help everyone out of its path."

Lonnie Harper said, "Seems to me the electric company is the big rock rolling down the hill."

"Okay," Leah shot back, "Listen, Volly, what do you want for your Shell station?"

"I'm Lonnie," he said. "Volly here owns the station. I only work there."

"Oh. Okay. Volly," turning to him, "The Land Acquisition Company is prepared to be most generous to you and to all the people in Linn Creek. Name a price."

Volly looked at her as if she had horns coming out of her head. He said nothing.

I was moved to say, "Don't you think we could save this for tomorrow, Leah. I'm sure Volly needs some time to think about this."

"But, no," Leah came back. "I want to show everyone just how lenient and generous the Land Acquisition Company can be."

"Save it for Lane Lindall and Judge Cargrove," Volly said, looking straight at Leah.

"Leah, dear," Rose said from her end of the table, "we try to keep the conversation light and pleasant at the table."

"Oh," Leah said and began shoveling food into her mouth at a rapid pace.

"Anybody think it's going to rain," she asked, smiling.

No one did. Or, if they did, they weren't of a mind to discuss it.

I gave up my small room to Leah and moved in with Lonnie and Volly. I got the bed against the wall, the one Joel Dean Gregory used to sleep in, Rose told me. Lonnie and Volly sat on their beds with a small table between them and a checker board on it. They looked up and Lonnie said, "Gave your bed up for the Duchess, eh. Did she try and buy it from Rose, yet?"

"Leah takes some getting used to," I said.

"Guess we don't have much time to get used to her," Lonnie said.

"Just how much was she prepared to pay for my station?" Volly wanted to know.

I shrugged. "Leah always surprises me."

"What's your job going to be here in Linn Creek?" Lonnie asked. "Doyle Savoy seemed to think it would be you who was going to be doing the buying of property here."

"Like I said, I've only been working for Land Acquisition nine months. I don't have much experience at this."

Volly said, "Neither do we."

I needed to be alone. I stashed my belongings which had been delivered to Rose's by one of Doyle Savoy's deputies while I'd been backing up Leah as she delivered her demands to the town's most influential men. I considered it another mark in Sheriff Savoy's favor that he had sent a deputy all the way to Bagnell to pick up my things.

Late evening had brought on darkness when I stepped off the porch of the rooming house. Enough light filtered out of windows, aided by the growing half-moon to make my way down the darkened Main Street.

I felt betrayed by Leah. She had hard ways. I knew how arduous she could be, I'd witnessed it before. As the dam neared completion, Leah would become more edgy. My future was even more uncertain with Leah in the picture.

I veered off the street to go up a shorter, one block street with six houses on it. In the near dark, I looked the houses over and tried to decide how much I was going to offer the people for the sum of their life's work. Me, a newly admitted-to-the-bar lawyer.

At first, the company had hired experienced, local real estate people to buy up the towns in their path. What went wrong with that plan was the real estate people wanted to assess each piece of property for its actual value and negotiate with the owners with a price close to that. But the company was not interested in buying these properties that would soon be under water at market value. After several meetings with the electric company, a figure was set for purchasing the entire lot. Don't waste time setting prices on each property, set prices on each town, divide it up by the number of properties, tell the property owners to take it or leave it and move on. The local realtors quit. Happy was left. And me.

Leah had given me the background when Happy and I first started buying the properties. I had asked Happy about it and he said, don't worry, he would be doing the buying. I was to be the legal end, tying up the deeds and purchases and delivering them to the main office in St. Louis. But it wasn't long before Happy had me out buying properties.

So I could see what Leah was doing with the banks and the county, but I wasn't the person Land Acquisition was looking for to do business that way. Tomorrow, I would come back to this street—no more following Leah around—and I would start the project of buying out Linn Creek by offering people what their property was worth. If that didn't suit Elmer or the main office in St. Louis, so be it.

When I got back to Rose's, I could see the glow of Uncle Billy Jack's pipe and heard the creaking of the boards on the porch. He invited me to sit with him and I did.

"Ernest Raines made it by with another jar of his mash whisky," Uncle Billy Jack said.

"Better not," I told him. "I apologize for drinking up the whole jar last night. I'm afraid I abused your hospitable generosity"

He chuckled. "You needed some relaxation after what you'd been through yesterday. Not everyday you see someone who's been shot."

"Seems like I do," I said without explaining. "I suppose I should apologize for Leah, too. I guess the company is starting to put the pressure on her to get things taken care of."

Uncle Billy Jack took the pipe from his mouth and pointed the stem at me. "I'm real disappointed that she got involved here. I thought it was going to be you dealing with the people in town. Why she's no better'n Happy Meens was."

"Happy sort of took his lead from Leah," I said.

Uncle Billy Jack rocked back and forth, puffing on some aromatic blend in his corn cob and finally said, "We've got to think of some way to get rid of her."

"Well, the thing is, Uncle Billy Jack, I'm sort of responsible for her being here. There wasn't any way I was going to do this job all by myself."

"Hmm." Floorboards creaking, frogs croaking, coyotes howling.

I could see a conspiracy developing here with Uncle Billy Jack and me against my boss, Leah. But then, was Leah really my boss? She hadn't said that Elmer had promoted her to Happy's job.

How was I going to get out of this town? No railroad and no buses. I could talk with Volly, he should know how I could get a ride back to St. Louis. Start all over. Get a government job, maybe. Anything was better than getting shot by Hayden Joost's imbecile daughter.

"I know how to get rid of her," Uncle Billy Jack said. "In a couple of days, you'll be the only one buying property here."

"You want to pass that jar over?" I asked.

Lonnie punched me in the side.

"Breakfast in fifteen minutes, Mister Beauchamp. Better get down there. You'll need your nourishment if you want to keep up with Queen Victoria today."

The headache was milder, the taste in my mouth muted and my stomach was more agreeable than yesterday morning. Maybe I was getting used to Ernest Raines mash whisky.

Leah was already seated at the table wearing the same clothes, of course, but making them look fresh. I could not imagine Leah ever looking anything but fresh and shining.

After Uncle Billy Jack's prayer and before Rose started passing the first bowl, she asked for everyone's attention.

"I've made an agreement with Leah and the land company on the price of the boarding house. We will close it in thirty days so everyone should make plans about where they want to go after that."

I glanced at Leah and she was smiling again like a Cheshire cat. While I had been forming a conspiracy with Uncle Billy Jack against her, she was negotiating with Rose without me present. Now, I really felt betrayed.

The meal was finished in silence. Leah tried several times to get a conversation started, but no one joined in. After the meal, I waited on the porch for Leah. She came out of the door following Volly who was asking her about pricing his station.

"I already made a promise to you, Volly. You name the price. We're anxious to make it easy on you and on everyone in town."

"I'll take an inventory," he said. "Maybe we can agree on a price by tomorrow. I'll have a chance to get started on my new garage in the new town."

Then Leah said something to Volly and Volly said something to Leah and the two of them walked right on by as if they didn't notice me leaning against a post on the porch. Lonnie came out behind them.

"Boy, Mister Beauchamp, it looks to me like you won't have anything to do, what with Queen Victoria there buying out the town. Why, you all and that electric company will probably own the whole she-bang by noon."

He walked on past leaving me alone with my thoughts of returning to St. Louis.

Contrary to my thinking, the Methodist Church was packed for the memoriam for Happy Meens. I thought it probable that the small town atmosphere was responsible for anyone who ever knew Happy or any member of his family to attend the service. Elmer Byron wasn't there. Maybe he would attend the funeral in Jefferson City. I was hoping to see him, hear him say officially that Leah was in charge.

I rather enjoyed the program the minister had put together. I mean, I can't say I enjoyed Happy's condition, overlooking the $20 raise it gave me, but it was a solemn, simple ceremony that people honored, maybe as much for the thanks and gift of life as honoring Happy. A cousin who seemed to have stature in the county, gave a eulogy for Happy and I learned that my old boss had been an all-conference football player at Missouri University and that he sponsored a program for youth football in Jefferson City and donated liberally to athletic equipment in the school and town of Linn Creek. Everyone from Rose's Boarding House was in attendance.

After the service, I walked in the direction of the houses where I had gone last night. I heard the hard clacking of heels on the walk behind me and my thoughts told me it could only be Leah coming toward me. She caught up with me in front of the Earnhardt General Store.

"Ah, Smith, ready to go to work?"

"I'm headed toward those houses right around the corner. I thought I would start there. You don't need me following you around today."

"Start right here," she said, indicating the general store. "I understand the daughter runs the business for her father who's bedridden. They own half the town, but he lost a lot of money in some land up on the hill where he thought the new Linn Creek would be. They're pretty desperate for money, so you should be able to make a good deal with them."

"You've been doing all the talking so far. You sure you don't want to be in on this?"

"The daughter is young and very pretty, I hear. I think you could do this better by yourself."

"Where will you be?"

"You won't need me. I'm looking the rest of the town over."

She was gone on her way, walking with an air of great importance. I had created a monster. I entered the general store and was shocked at the young woman behind the counter. Though she was engaged with another customer, her eyes lifted to mine and momentarily my heart just stopped in my chest as I took in the beauty before me.

The customer paid his bill and left and the young woman turned her attention to me.

"Mister Smith Beauchamp," she said, her smile like sunlight entering a darkened room. "I've heard about you. My goodness, you look so young to have such an important position with this electric company."

I was so taken by her beauty I forgot for a moment just what my important position was and why I was here. I stammered about, saying something, as best I remember, about what an honor to be here and some other schoolboy gibberish that branded me as a fool forever, I feared, in her lovely blue eyes.

She smiled even bigger, or perhaps she was laughing, and she extended her hand which I took daintily as if I feared breaking it and that seemed to amuse her even further.

"I'm Estelle Earnhardt, you can just call me Estelle, and I just know we're going to get along famously. You're here to see about the businesses my Daddy owns, I'll bet. I've been anxious to get that over with. We won't be selling the house, of course, because it's not in your magic six-sixty figure, whatever that is. My goodness, just everybody is talking six-sixty, six-sixty. And here, silly woman that I am, I don't even know what this six-sixty is."

"Elevation," I blurted out. "It's the height the lake water will be at full pool. I mean, when, you know, the dam is closed. I mean, the gates to the dam . . ."

"I'm afraid you're just talking right over my head, Mister Beauchamp. All this technical talk and the details, I don't know a thing about. Would you like to inspect the property?"

"Well, I suppose that would be in order, that is, if you don't mind, I mean . . ."

"You go right ahead, Mister Beauchamp, look all you want. We have the store here and the hardware store next door and we have the mill just up the hollow and there's the power plant and we have some mortgages in town and, well, I can't even remember what all Daddy owns."

"Uh, maybe you have a list, or something . . ."

"If we did, I probably couldn't find it. I'm not that good of a business woman, I'm afraid, Mister Beauchamp."

"You could call me Smith, if you don't mind. I mean, Mister Beauchamp sounds like you're talking to my grandfather."

Her laughter was an infectious chiming, as lyrical as a swiss music box.

"I'll bet you've already met Joel Dean Gregory over at the courthouse. He's going to be representing my interests in Daddy's affairs. You see, Daddy is confined to bed most of the time and he's rarely rational enough to carry on any business, so Joel Dean will be doing it for him and for me. Only, Daddy has a lawyer in Lebanon name of Mister Bickers. Now, when you talk with Daddy, if you do—or maybe you won't—you have to say you've talked with Mister Bickers because, see, Daddy won't have anything to do with Joel Dean because Joel Dean shot Daddy and paralyzed him. But you won't actually conduct any business with Mister Bickers."

I was so enraptured with the sound of her voice—like the rising and falling notes on a well-tuned piano—and in watching her small mouth with red blooming lips that I never caught much of what she said.

After mumbling that I would look up Joel Dean Gregory and how sorry I was about her father and that I did like Linn Creek and I hated like everything to have to be putting her out of her father's businesses and all the people out of their homes and after blabbering on and on, I finally regained some portion of my intellect and bid her good day.

And she smiled the sweetest smile my heart could ever remember seeing. I fled out the door aware of her amusement and of my extreme embarrassment.

Joel Dean Gregory looked up from his desk in the courthouse and gave me a cursory nod and said, "Mister Beauchamp."

I sat in a straight, ladder-back chair beside his desk without being invited and started right in, taking a cue from Leah, perhaps. "I've come from Miss Estelle Earnhardt and she tells me that you will be handling all of her father's business interests."

He looked straight into my eyes without answering for some moments, then, "She tell you about Mister Bickers?"

"Well, she did bring the name up, but I'm afraid I didn't quite catch the connection."

"Simple. You deal with me, but if you ever talk with Yawley Earnhardt, then it's important to say you dealt with Bickers."

"Ah. Well. It could get difficult when it comes time to sign off on the property."

"Let me worry about that."

"Yes, well, all right then, suppose we get to it. Buying the businesses, that is. Miss Earnhardt seemed to think you had a list of properties her father owns and . . ."

He retrieved a file of papers from his desk drawer while I talked and handed it to me. I flipped through the papers and caught my breath. It was a thorough and complete listing and went on for almost 20 pages. I caught headings of lost business, employee compensation for job loss, health considerations for the Earnhardts and on and on. I was speechless. I wished Leah was here instead of me.

"This, uh, certainly is a complete listing," I said, stumbling through my words. "Some of the items, well, to be frank, Joel Dean, I'm not sure the company can recognize all that you have listed here."

"Such as?"

"Well, there's the matter of lost business, I was specifically instructed not to compensate for lost business . . ."

"It's not the Earnhardt's fault that they have to close up and move their business somewhere else. That's a loss in revenue. Any court would tell you that. If not for lost business, just what is it that this electric company instructed you to compensate for?"

"To be real truthful, Joel Dean, I'm just the lawyer who was told to handle the transactions of property. I'm doing this now only because Happy Meens was killed and there is no one else except Miss Turner and myself."

"So the company thinks so little of the people in this town they don't even prepare you people to equitably handle the transfer of property that folks in Linn Creek have spent their life acquiring?"

"I think we're expected to take care of these things through negotiation," I said.

"How are we expected to negotiate with a rude woman and a green lawyer just out of law school if they don't know anything about what they're supposed to be doing."

"I regret to tell you, Joel Dean, but you really don't have a choice in this. We're all you've got, so let's begin the negotiation."

"We've got the property, Mister Beauchamp. I represent more than fifteen people in the sale of their property here in Linn Creek. So, if you want the property, begin the negotiation by recognizing the rights of these people."

"We do want to recognize the rights of all the people. What is it that you want? Do you want all of the money that has been allocated for the purchase of property to go to the few who are retaining you to represent them? And where would that leave the ones without the means to pay your legal fees?"

"My legal fees are considerably more fair than are your offers to buy out the homes and businesses that residents of this community have spent lifetimes accumulating and building."

Joel Dean Gregory was becoming an irritation to tire of. I said then, as I rose from the ladder-back chair, what I never wanted to say, but what Leah and Happy would have said to Joel Dean Gregory in the beginning.

"We have the water, Mister Gregory. And it will be coming here to your town in 90 days."

As I left through the door to his office, he said to my back, "See you in court."

FOUR

Not all the boarders took lunch at Rose's. Uncle Billy Jack was there with Leah and me, Jane McGann and the Osage woman. Rose had cooked up some fresh greens—dandelion, I think—and some fried apples and beef stew with a lemon meringue pie.

"How's the real estate process going?" Uncle Billy Jack wanted to know.

Leah said, "It's going well. Maybe we'll have the whole job completed ahead of time."

"Oh," Uncle Billy Jack said, "You've bought Hayden Joost's farm, then?"

Leah looked at me and I looked at her.

"Well, we thought we'd let Hayden alone for a while," I said. "Let him get used to the idea of moving."

Leah said, "But why? Maybe we'll call on Mister Joost this very afternoon. It would be fitting to have his name on a deed in time for Happy's funeral."

Uncle Billy Jack had a very slight smile on his face and I knew then what his plan was to get rid of Leah.

"No," I said, slicing into the lemon meringue pie with my fork. "It would be wise to leave Hayden Joost alone for a few weeks."

Leah did not expect me to challenge her. Now, perhaps, she would admit that Elmer hadn't really promoted her to Happy's job. Still looking at the pie, I waited for her next move.

"We shall see," she said, reaching for the pie herself.

I walked outside and stood by the porch post after finishing lunch—which Rose and the rest of her boarders called dinner—and was leaning against it when Leah joined me.

"Smith, don't challenge my authority again in front of the other residents. With Happy dead and Elmer off to southeast Missouri, someone has to assume the leadership or this whole project is dead and you and I are out of a job."

"Elmer didn't really appoint you to take Happy's place, did he?"

"I've been in the office for two years now. You've just barely started with the firm. I was there in the beginning, me, Happy and Elmer. Who else would be in charge?"

"Does Elmer know about Happy?"

"He does now. The sheriff got hold of him this morning by telephone. I talked with the sheriff. He said it would be all right for the two of us to drive up to Jefferson City tomorrow for Happy's funeral. He even offered us a ride in his automobile."

"So I didn't really talk you into staying here since you intended to do that all along. And Elmer will grow wings and fly before he doubles my pay."

"I'll put in a good word for you."

Across the main street from the boarding house, along the banks of the creek, the dogwoods had exploded with brilliant, four-petal white blossoms and the leaves on the cottonwoods and sumac were peeking out of their buds.

"Leah, I hate being played for a chump. Even when I am a chump. Why would I want to stick around here and get shot at and maybe killed. Happy was shot trying to buy the land of the meanest son of a bitch in the county. That's from the sheriff who ought to know."

"That's why I called the sheriff just now. He's going out to Hayden Joost's place with us this afternoon."

If Uncle Billy Jack thought he was going to outwit this woman, he had better start getting up pretty early in the morning. And the same went for me.

"All right, Leah," I said. "But tomorrow when I ride up to Jefferson City with the sheriff, I'm taking all my belongings. I'm taking the train back to St. Louis and look for another job."

She was silent for a long time and I didn't bother to look at her. I didn't want to look at her. I felt her hand through the bend of my arm and she maneuvered me down the steps into the street.

"You'll feel differently in the morning," she said. "I'll see to it."

Hayden Joost was standing across the creek from us when Sheriff Doyle Savoy stopped his car in the spot where he'd stopped it before. I could swear he was expecting us, but how, I had no idea.

"Hayden," Sheriff Savoy said, raising his voice above the sound of the trickling stream, "I brought the person they sent to take Happy Meens place. She would like to speak with you."

Hayden Joost said nothing.

Savoy stepped across the creek the same as he had the last time and Leah, watching, raised her skirt a foot, took a long stride to the first dry rock in the creek, then skipped a long stride to the next and landed nimbly on the rocks lining the creek bank. Savoy looked embarrassed that he hadn't thought to help her, but Leah was unfazed and walked right up to Hayden Joost and stuck out her hand.

"Leah Turner, Mister Joost. I'm from the Land Acquisition company and I think you will like what I have to say about your land."

Hayden Joost was clearly caught off guard. He found himself taking her hand as if he was in a trance and didn't know what he was doing, then, quickly dropped it like it was a hot coal and said, "The only thing you could say I would like is you're not going to be botherin me again."

"And I'm not," Leah said. "When we get through transacting business today, nobody from the Acquisition company will ever cross your path again. Unless, of course, you need us."

"Not likely," Joost said. His eyes were dark and close together and squinted a bit as if he held us all in contempt, which I'm sure he did.

"Okay," Leah began, pulling several papers from the purse she had swinging from her shoulder, "You own fifty-three acres here. It's a nice little farm and you've improved it quite a bit. So we're prepared to offer you twenty-five dollars an acre plus five hundred dollars for your livestock, five hundred dollars for the house and outbuildings and three hundred dollars for moving expenses. And the good part is, you can keep your house and the land around it that won't be in the water, the livestock if you want, and the five hundred dollars. Good farm land just a couple of miles down the road is selling for twenty dollars an acre. So you would be walking away from this deal with two thousand six hundred and twenty-five dollars in your pocket."

Leah had clearly caught Joost's attention with the dollar figures. Chances are, Hayden Joost had never even dreamed of seeing anything like two thousand dollars, let alone having that much money in his pocket.

"I never said I wanted to sell," he snapped back at her, but without the bite in his words that had been there when Savoy had talked with him.

"I know, I know," Leah said. "Nobody wants to move and we don't want people to have to move, but the truth is, Mister Joost, you have to give up your land. Neither of us can do anything about that. So, my job is to make it as easy for you as possible. Twenty-six hundred dollars is not too bad, now, is it, Mister Joost?"

"How come they sent a woman?" Joost asked, looking over at me with the question like maybe I wasn't up to the job or something.

"Because I'm smarter," Leah said. "And a woman understands better than a man what it's like to leave your home and all the things you're used to."

"Uh huh," he said, still looking at me.

"Mister Beauchamp here will work up the papers for you to sign and I suspect you would prefer we bring your money in cash rather than a check, wouldn't you?"

Leah was clever, all right. Ending her statements with a question so Joost would have to commit himself.

"I ain't saying I'm sellin, yet," he said.

"I know, I know," Leah came back as sweetly as she could present herself. "But planting time is already upon you, isn't it? And you do understand if you plant anything on this farm, it will be under water by harvest time. Be a good time to get situated on that new farm before the choice properties are grabbed up by the other farmers we'll be buying out."

Leah had turned and was poised to leap to the first rock in the creek crossing when she turned and said, "Mister Beauchamp will be out in a week or so with the papers and the money. Good afternoon to you Mister Joost."

Joost was stuck with no words for her. Savoy asked him about the girl Meren and Joost, jarred out of the spell Leah had put him under, shot back that the girl wasn't at the house.

"I'll be in Jefferson City attending the funeral for Happy Meens tomorrow, Hayden," Savoy said. "The day after that I want you and the girl in the sheriff's office or I'll have to put out a warrant for both of you."

"You misuse that girl of mine and, sheriff or no sheriff, I'll be squarin accounts with you."

"You've known me a good many years, Hayden, and you know I don't misuse anybody, man, woman or child. I have a feelin that girl knows something about Happy Meens gettin shot and if she won't tell you, she's goin to have to tell me."

Before I knew it, just me and Hayden Joost stood on his side of the creek. Whatever bad feeling he had from Leah and Savoy, he summed up in his look at me. I had nothing to say to the man, so, I too took my leave, crossing the creek in two quick leaps and crawled into the front seat of Savoy's Chevrolet.

On the ride back into Linn Creek, Leah, from the back seat, questioned Savoy about the town and about who would be the hardest residents to deal with in the purchase of their land. Savoy answered that probably the most difficult would be the banks, the county and Joost. And he mentioned the Earnhardt holdings because he said Joel Dean Gregory would be the one we would have to do business with and that he would be a hard one to satisfy.

"Well, then," Leah said, "We're practically through all the hard ones, aren't we Smith. After Happy's funeral we'll both call on this Joel Dean Gregory."

I still hadn't spoken and I did not intend to. My mind was clear on what I would be doing and where I would be going after Happy's funeral.

Later, I would look back and not be surprised that it was a female who changed my plans and for the oddest of reasons.

In the office, Leah told Mary she could leave for the day.

That left the two of us sitting on straight chairs, pulled up to the one and only table which served as a desk for us both. Leah looked very pleased with herself. I had to admit, but only to myself, that I was impressed with her.

"See how easy it is, Smith. Start talking money, mention a price and what they think about is having all that money in their pocket. Chances are, old Hayden will spend that money and never buy another piece of land. How many times in their life are these people going to have that much money?"

"Didn't seem to work that way at the bank with Lane Lindall."

"That's why he got the bulldog approach. Look, Smith," Leah transformed into the sweet young thing on a high school date, "Joost is taken care of, the banks will come around, I'll take care of this Joel Dean Gregory. What's the problem. You know I can't do this without you. By the time Elmer hired another lawyer who learned how to wrap up the deeds, our 90 days would be over. I need you. Don't quit on me."

"Who do you think shot Happy? You forgotten him?"

She shrunk back into the demure young thing. God, there were so many Leahs I didn't know which one to expect next.

"Happy gambled a lot," she said, so quietly I barely caught her words. "I don't know if you knew that or not. He was in a lot of card games in Jefferson City and probably down here, too. And I overheard him talking with someone about whisky one day. He got mixed up in something, gambling, whisky, something illegal. He owed someone some money, he didn't have it, they shot him. That's the way I have it figured. We—you and I—don't have anything to worry about."

"You tell all this to the sheriff?"

"Well, I haven't had the chance, yet. We're going to talk tomorrow. I think he wants to hear from you, too. When they get the Jefferson City police involved, they'll find out who killed Happy."

Her words had no meaning to me. I didn't know if she was lying or guessing, but it made no difference to me.

"Joost said Happy made three trips to the Joost's farm. On the last trip he was shot. Why?"

Leah thought about it and her face took on a hard and determined look.

"What have you told the sheriff about Happy?"

"Nothing. I mean, I don't know anything to tell him. I'm a suspect in Happy's shooting, he says. I can't afford to be withholding information."

"You're a suspect?" she asked.

"He suspects everyone. Probably even you now that he's met you."

"That's interesting," she said. "I've never been a suspect in a murder case before."

"Somehow, Leah, that surprises me," I said, starting for the door.

Dinner conversation was all Leah. Uncle Billy Jack grimaced all the way through, even with dessert. Oma Thornbush, the Osage Indian, asked Leah what the Land Acquisition Company was going to do with all the land they bought up. Leah said they were going to resell it to the electric company. What happens to your job then, Oma Thornbush wanted to know. Leah said Elmer would move on to some other location where a dam was being built or some powerfully big highway to accommodate larger and larger motor cars. Maybe California. Or New York. Could be anywhere there was land to be acquired, she told Oma Thornbush with a flourish of her fork-holding hand. First time I'd heard about California. Or New York.

Maybe California would be good for me. But, no, tomorrow was to be my last day at this job. Besides, I was stuck in St. Louis and I knew it.

I sat on the porch with Uncle Billy Jack for an hour or two in the dark. Rose came out and caught Uncle Billy Jack smoking his corn cob pipe, but didn't chastise him about it. Then she found the whisky jar sitting on the porch beside his rocking chair.

"I'll get some glasses," she said and came back with three kitchen glasses that she poured two fingers worth in each and passed them around. She seated herself in another rocker, raised her glass and said, "To the old boarding house, Uncle Billy Jack and Smith. And to a new life for us all."

"I'm too old to start a new life, Rose," Uncle Billy Jack said, his voice slow and easy like someone saying goodbye.

"What will you do?" Rose asked.

"Reckon I'll go to the county farm. They feed tolerably well, I hear."

"You are not," Rose said with conviction. "I'm not going to see you at any county farm. You're coming with me to Lebanon."

"I'd just be a burden, Rose. I'll be fine at the farm. I couldn't abide it if I was to place a load on someone else."

"They have some nice retirement places in St. Louis, Uncle Billy Jack," I offered. "I could probably get you in one of them."

Uncle Billy Jack puffed on his pipe for a moment in time and said, "The truth of the matter, young Mister Beauchamp, is that I don't have any money. Rose has been generous with me for the piddling pension I've been getting from the railroad and from the government for serving in Cuba, but St. Louis, my goodness, you're talking probably a hundred dollars a month. I don't have that kind of money coming in."

"I could spare some," I said.

"Why would you do that?" he asked.

"Because you need it. And I could spare it."

"That's mighty generous of you Smith," Rose said. "But I'm taking him to Lebanon with me. I'm buying a large two-story house there, if I can find one, and I'm going to take in boarders. I couldn't stand to just sit around doing nothing."

"Both of you are overly kind," Uncle Billy Jack said. "But I'll get by. And I don't want any worrying done about me, you hear?"

"We'll see," Rose said. "We'll see."

We shared a few more drinks, all of us melancholy with the thoughts of each of us getting ready to start a new life. Rose got out of her rocker after three drinks, poured one more for each of us—twice as much for me as for Uncle Billy Jack— and left the porch with a "Good night," and, taking the Mason jar with her, she stopped at the door, thought better of it and brought it back and set it by my chair. She gave me a look that said I was to watch that Uncle Billy Jack didn't overdo it. Uncle Billy Jack and I sat for another quarter hour, I finished up the jar by myself, and both of us went inside without exchanging another word other than "Good night."

I was feeling slightly tipsy and I stumbled a bit going up the stairs and down the hallway to the doorway of the room I used to have by myself. I opened the door and immediately, even in my inebriated condition, discovered my mistake. Leah was propped up in the bed with papers scattered all over the top quilt. She looked up in fright, then replaced it with a pleased look and a smile.

"Ah, Smith, I was hoping you would drop in to . . . well, to go over the work we have to do. Please," she climbed out of bed in her nightgown and pulled the one chair in the room out from the wall, "have a chair. We'll go over some of this . . ."

"I'm sorry, Leah, I wasn't thinking . . .I thought for a moment I was still . . ."

"It's okay. Listen, I'm glad you're here. Go ahead," taking me by the arm and pushing me down in the chair, "just sit there and I'll sit on the bed and we'll discuss some things and we'll. . ."

"It's not right, my being here," I said. "Or proper. I don't want people getting the wrong idea about you and start talking . . ."

"Oh pshaw, they're already talking. Might as well give them something else to gossip about."

She smelled of lilac and roses and the whole flower patch and I could tell she had taken a bath this evening. And brushed out her brown hair which now glistened. But it was her body beneath the gown that I was having trouble keeping my eyes off. Her breasts were about to pop over the top when she bent over me and I could see the outline of every curve she owned, the material was so flimsy. I thought of how smooth and soft her skin would be after the bath.

"It's about time we got together like this, don't you think? You've probably guessed that I kind of take a liking to you, Smith. I mean, well, you're a handsome man and . . ."

I was kissing her. I don't know who started it, did she or did I?

It was hot, I was sweating and all of a sudden we were sprawled on top of the papers spread out on her bed. Things were happening too fast, I couldn't stop it, nor did I want to. Then, as quickly as this thing started, it stopped. Or rather, I did. The whisky, the heat, Leah, all combined to start my head whirling and I was aware of being back in the chair.

"You've been drinking," Leah said and I recognized her disapproving tone.

I got out of there as fast as I could. My embarrassment weighed a ton on my mind. I stumbled into the common bathroom we all shared and I lost all of Ernest Raines fine smooth mash whisky.

Time passed and I knew I had to leave the bathroom before someone else wanted to use it. I opened the door a crack, saw no one in the hall, and stumbled into the room I shared with Lonnie and Volly, disrobed in the dark and sneaked into the bed by the light of the half-moon coming through the window curtains. I went to sleep before I had time for remorse.

I am sitting in a straight-back chair and facing me are Happy Meens and Langston Beauchamp. Happy has a bullet hole in his tan jacket and blood is spurting from it. Langston Beauchamp has a round black hole centrally located in his forehead. They both are rocking away in their rocking chairs, saying nothing. Happy is smiling and Langston looks solemn in his unique, aloof manner.

Happy says, "You keep drinking that whisky Smitty my boy and you won't get anywhere with the women." And he laughs and laughs.

Langston regards me without approval and says, "A gentleman always holds his drink. No Beauchamp has ever passed out while intimately engaged with a lady."

Happy laughs even louder and slaps his leg. "Did you see it? I mean, the kid lost it. He has no business drinking if he can't do any better than that. How many ladies want a man passing out on top of them."

"A learning process, I'm sure," Langston replies. "He's a Beauchamp. Don't worry, he'll do all right, you may be assured of that."

Happy cackles some more and says, "What the hell's a Beauchamp? Hell, they ain't no better'n a Meens. When it comes to whisky and women, a Meens takes a back seat to nobody."

"The Meens are uncultured ruffians," Langston says. "Don't you worry about my son. He's a Beauchamp."

"Better ask the lady about the Beauchamps," Happy says. "Leave it to the Meens to finish up this job."

Langston rises from his chair and slaps Happy across the face with a glove he holds in his hand. Happy shuts up right away and doesn't smile again. The blood continues to spurt from the bullet hole in his jacket.

"Get up and be a man," Langston says to me. "Be a man."

"Be a man," I said aloud and Lonnie, sleeping six feet away, rose from his pillow and said, "You speaking to me?"

Joe Collie said, "Surprised to see you up this early. Thought you was a city boy."

Joe Collie was built like a sculpture in the St. Louis Museum of Art: hard, bronzed, big and powerful looking. His shock of reddish-blond hair stuck out in all directions from under his cap. He walked past me in the early morning light and down the steps of the boarding house into the street.

"I'm going over to the jail house for some breakfast if you want to join me. Rose won't set her table for another hour and a half."

I fell in beside him. "You really eat breakfast at the jail?"

"Best breakfast in town, except maybe Rose's. Doyle won't mind. He likes company and the prisoners would probably like to meet you. Doyle'll turn you in for feeding and collect a dollar off the county. Sheriff'n don't pay much in a town like this."

"Never ate in a jail before," I said, but that wasn't quite true. I'd eaten in a jail before as a guest.

"You'll like it. Birdie's a great cook. Only rules are you don't leave until the prisoners do. And they don't leave until Doyle's through eating. So you better keep an eye on him and don't fall behind."

"I'll remember that."

The jail was a two story limestone building similar to the courthouse only smaller. At the doorway, Joe Collie turned and said, "Besides, since you're buying the place you need to get a look at it."

Inside, a man with a generous growth of all-white hair and a large mustache greeted Collie.

"Noah, this here's the Smith Beauchamp you been hearing about. He's here to look over the jail house and see how much it's worth. And maybe work in some breakfast."

The man Noah was probably in his late fifties and had creases everywhere his skin was exposed. He was deeply tanned and the corrugations of his face stretched into white lines when he smiled.

"Hi, Mister Beauchamp. You don't look nothin like the devil you been made out to be. And as far as this old jail house is concerned, I wouldn't give the county more'n a hundred dollars was I buyin it."

"I'll keep that in mind."

Noah unlocked a door and led us into a large room with an enormous table almost in the center of the room. Sheriff Doyle Savoy, sitting at the head of the table, looked up and my presence seemed to catch him unaware.

"Mister Beauchamp," he said, "pleasant surprise to see you in our jail house. Have a seat."

I walked to the nearest empty chair and started to sit, but Sheriff Savoy said, "The other side of the table if you don't mind, Mister Beauchamp. That side's reserved for our prisoners."

Four men already seated in chairs adjacent to the one I had started to occupy, snickered, then broke out in guffaws.

Red faced, I went around the table and selected a seat beside Joe Collie who was already helping himself to a half-dozen slices of bacon. I was the last one present to start eating and, keeping in mind what Joe Collie said about keeping up with the sheriff, I started helping myself to the bacon, biscuits and a bowl of peppered gravy.

Savoy, around a bite of jellied biscuit, said, "Gentlemen, this here is Mister Beauchamp who is buying up the land for the electric company that is building the dam over close to Bagnell. If any of you have acreage that is going to be covered up by the water after the dam is finished, then I expect you'll be doing business with Mister Beauchamp."

He shifted his gaze to me and said, "Our semi-permanent residents of the quarters upstairs are Mister Frank Truesdale here on my left" (a tall, ruddy-faced man of about fifty), "George Tubman" (a short, dark eyed man with one outcropping of black hair sticking straight up), "Glen Colwell" (thirty or so, tough looking with small ears that stuck straight out), "and Billy Bross" (a small teenager who looked scared to be here). "Frank and Glen took a liking to George's chickens. George was a little too vigorous in taking exception to their liking and put some shot into their rear ends. He also took a shot at Noah when he went out to investigate. When they tell me they've worked it out, I'll let them go. Billy there is another case. He was driving around with a coupla cases of somebody's dynamite in his automobile and about five gallons of really bad whisky."

"There ain't no law against havin dynamite in your car, Sheriff," Billy said, a sneer on his face.

"Depends on what you had in mind to do with it, Billy. I'll let the judge sort it out."

"And that wasn't no whisky. That was paint remover."

"Well that's sure enough what it tasted like, Billy. The taste alone may get you off if you can get the judge to take a snort."

George Tubman said, "What's the electric company payin for acreage?" looking at me.

"Depends," Remembering Leah's offer to Hayden Joost, I said, "Maybe twenty, twenty-five dollars an acre."

"T'aint much," George offered. "I got thirty acres close to Stoutman. That wouldn't be but $800. That ain't much money for a lifetime of hard work."

Joe Collie said without looking up from the two fried eggs

he was cutting up with his fork, "Your place ain't even close to lake water, George."

"Never said it was," George said. "Just sayin it wouldn't be much for all the work I've put into it."

Frank said, "You'd take half that for your rundown place. Them chickens was near starved to death."

"Well, it didn't stop you from wantin them," George shot back.

"I was just inspectin 'em. See if I wanted to make an offer."

Sheriff Savoy said, "No use either of you pleading your case here. Save it for the judge."

I asked Joe Collie if he knew where the water was going to be when the lake became full.

"Pretty much. Have to. My crew's cutting trees between 625 and 660. I've got a surveying crew working so we should be able to put a map together."

"So you mark it down on a plat map or something?"

"Yeah. I keep a map after they do the surveying. I go cutting trees down on land the electric company doesn't buy up, I could be in trouble."

"So you cut the trees on land before we buy it?"

"Sometimes."

"I didn't see any trees cut on Hayden Joost's farm," I said. "Is that on your plat map?"

"Don't know. I'd have to take a look at it. Survey crew's out that way right now."

Sheriff Savoy said, "Guess you heard Happy Meens was shot out there yesterday."

Joe Collie stopped eating and seemed to reflect on that for a moment. "Yeah, heard that. Reckon my survey crew's in danger?"

Savoy thought about it. "Maybe I better take a drive out there this morning."

"I'd like to go with you, Sheriff," I said. There was no reason to say that. Or maybe there was, just to avoid Leah.

"Sure," he answered. "Glad for the company. Maybe ol Hayden will invite us in for a cup of coffee."

That brought a chuckle from everyone at the table.

Noah said, "If he does, I wouldn't drink it if I was you. They used to tell that Hayden poisoned his daddy just to get the fifty acres he's on now."

"You ever find Happy's Buick?" I asked Sheriff Savoy on the way out to the Joost farm.

"It turned up down in Lebanon. Sheriff down in LaClede County telephoned me yesterday afternoon. The car had been parked in front of the courthouse down there for three days."

"Happy sure didn't walk from Lebanon to Hayden Joost's farm. That would be more than fifty miles."

"About that," the sheriff said. "The sheriff down there asked around the courthouse, but nobody workin there had talked with Happy."

"What's your best guess about what happened out there on the Joost farm, Sheriff?"

Savoy didn't answer right away. When he did he said, "I want to talk with that girl of Hayden's. Have a feelin the Joosts are mixed up in it one way or the other."

"Uncle Billy Jack says the girl can't talk."

"She used to talk when she was nine or ten years old. I heard her."

"Will Hayden bring her in to see you tomorrow?"

"Well, it was a gamble on my part. If he doesn't I'm not sure what I'll do about it. Hate to swear out a warrant on a simple-minded girl who can't speak up for herself."

"You think she could have shot Happy?"

"Oh, I doubt it. But, then, who can say. She's a Joost and I wouldn't put it past any of them to shoot somebody. I haven't seen the girl for about six or seven years. They just don't bring her around anyone."

"How old is she?"

"I'd say eighteen, maybe seventeen. She was a real pretty little girl last time I did see her. Don't look nothing like the Joost side, that's for sure."

We rode along for several minutes with neither of us speaking. After thinking it over, I said what was on my mind. "I thought Hayden Joost was awfully different yesterday from what he was the day before. I mean, he wasn't belligerent or threatening. I can't believe Leah would have that kind of effect on him."

"She's quite a gal," the sheriff said. "She the boss now?"

"I guess," I said. I didn't want to get into it. In fact, I didn't want to think too much about Leah today. I mean, who could blame me after last night.

Joe Collie, driving a Ford with a bed on behind loaded with axes, saws and other various woodcutting tools, pulled over to the side of the road and stopped.

The surrounding trees resembled a solid wall of green moss with a hole here and there thru which the sun shot a blinding stream of light.

"Is this the Joost farm?" I asked the sheriff who pulled his Chevrolet in behind Joe Collie's truck and killed the engine.

"I'm not sure," he said. "I think the Joost farm starts at that fence you see up ahead of us."

We got out of the car and Joe Collie walked toward us.

"My surveying crew has been through here already. I'm going to look for some stakes over here."

"I'll tag along," Sheriff Savoy said.

"Where did we find Happy's body from here?" I asked.

"Up the road about 200 yards and back to the right through the trees, close to the creek," the sheriff said.

"I think I'll go up there." For some reckless reason I wanted to see the spot again where Happy died and I wanted to see it before they buried him.

Savoy didn't like the idea. "Well, I better stay with Joe, him being the one who cuts down the trees. I'll walk up there with you when Joe's through with what he's doing."

"I'll be all right," I told him.

"Don't get shot," he said, bringing up a possibility I hadn't given thought to until now.

I walked up the narrow dirt road, mostly covered with rocks, with the edges of the road greening up and wildflowers springing up in various spots. The trees alongside the road had leafed out to full foliage, but the leaves were still young in size. For the first time it struck me what a truly and naturally beautiful country this was. People were right, I suppose, about the snakes, chiggers and ticks that resided in these woods, but the downright beauty of it reminded me of a sunset amongst the clouds that promised a storm. You shouldn't overlook the beauty of the sunset just because of the threat in the clouds.

I could understand the Joosts and all the others who didn't want to pack up and leave this spot on earth.

I angled off to the right about where the sheriff had told me to, and pushed my way through the undergrowth until I heard the sound of trickling water. Blackbirds merged over the trees and at some unseen, unheard signal the whole amalgamation set off for a more fruitful site amid a clamoring flutter like bedsheets flapping on the line. I stopped where the sheriff said the person might have been who shot Happy and looked in the direction of the creek until I was sure of the spot I had first seen the body of Happy Meens. The question now sprang to mind, what was I doing here? Was it the dream I'd had of Happy spouting blood that brought me here? Was the killer of Happy Meens waiting right now for Happy's successor to show up?

Who stood here, if they had, and looked toward the creek

and saw Happy Meens standing there and decided to end a man's life? For what reason? And what was Happy doing there, on that spot? And how did he get there from Lebanon?

When I got to the creek, to the ground beside it where Happy's blood had spilled and stained the grass and rocks where he had lain, the revulsion I had felt that day returned. Dizzy and sick at the core of my stomach, I knelt and scooped both hands full of water and splashed it on my face. I was about to scoop up some more cold, creek water when I picked up an image in the clear stream, an image that hadn't been there before. A shock ran through me as I realized what I was seeing was not something but someone, not six feet away, across the creek from where I was kneeling.

I raised my eyes to a face that was tanned and slender and bore the look of a frightened fawn. The eyes were wide and white around soft, brown pupils and the nose was slim with a slight upturn on the end. A pretty face. I knew who she was right away.

"Hello Meren," I said.

Some of the fear drained out of her face, but not all. Her eyes focused on mine. Her brown hair was clean and brushed, but fell away from her head onto her shoulders like cascading water onto rocks. Her body was slender like her face and I knew that, standing up, she would be near her mother's height and shape. She was dressed in a brown frock that looked to be shapeless and made of a sackcloth that would have come from the cheapest bolt in the dry goods store and sewn by hand without a pattern.

We stared at each other for long moments until I said, in a low tone not to frighten her further, "Your flower garden by the tree is very pretty. I see that you like flowers as much as I do."

The only indication that she may have heard me was a slight flickering of her eyelids.

"My name is Smith Beauchamp. I'm staying in Linn Creek

now. I'm supposed to come back later with some papers for your father to sign."

Her eyes roamed over the rest of me then as if she was committing my appearance to memory. When they came back to focus on my eyes, the fright was gone, replaced by a childish curiosity.

"Did you see the man who was here yesterday?" I asked.

Her eyes snapped downward and her body visibly flinched.

"The man who was shot, do you know what happened to him?"

She did not look up.

"He was my boss. I would like to know what happened to him."

Slowly, she raised her head and looked again into my face. Big, double-sized tears ran down her cheeks and the fear had come back to her eyes.

"Did you see?" I asked. "Did you see what happened to him? Were you here?"

She raised a hand and brushed the tears from her cheeks. When she rose to her feet, I saw then she was even taller and slimmer than her mother. Tall, almost, as myself. I raised from my kneeling position and we again stared wordlessly into each other's face and through the eyes into that private, inner person inside.

I wanted very badly to know this Meren Joost. Was it possible she held within her some terrible secret about Happy Meens?

Her eyes shot over to the grove of trees where Sheriff Savoy had thought the killer might have hidden. She was frightened. Her eyes flickered nervously and when she brought them back to bear on me, the enlarged pupils of her eyes glistened from more tears that were reforming.

"Maybe I could be your friend," I said.

I held my hand out to her, palm up. She looked at it and backed away from me.

"Do you have a friend?"

She shook her head. Her mouth and her lips moved and the word they formed I would have known, even if the whisper-like sound had never come through them.

"Goodbye," was the word and she was gone. Only afterwards, when I was standing alone and her deer-like form had slipped out of sight over the bank of the creek did I realize that one hand had gripped a rifle exactly like the one Sheriff Savoy held yesterday at the Joost cabin.

"Goodbye," I said after her, but whether she heard me or not, I had no way of knowing.

What I did know was I had to see Meren Joost again.

PART 2

ONE

Happy's funeral came off in respectful style. Vivian Meens wept like a good widow on my shoulder while pressing her ample breasts into me. I told her about Happy's Buick which I judged to be no more than two years old and worth probably $500 and she asked if I wanted to buy it. Well, no, I told her my financial condition was such that owning an automobile was not within my means. But she seemed to really want me to be the car's owner, offering it for $300 to be paid off at $20 a month. The same amount Happy had been extorting from me. Before I knew fully what I had done, I held the deed to Happy's Buick in my hand. I suppose the best way to look at it, justice had been done between Happy and me.

I avoided Leah. I learned from Elmer she would be staying in Jefferson City for a few days to iron out some problems at the office. He never said she was in charge and he never said she wasn't. He did tell me that he had hired Ruby Elam, the kickback-offering real estate man from Lebanon who was also staying at Rose's, to assist me in purchasing property in Linn Creek. He exhibited a complete lack of interest in my opinion about Ruby having a conflict of interest. Elmer was vague about how it would work out among me, Ruby and Leah, and who would decide which one of us was to do what, so I knew

Leah would be aggressive enough to step forward and assume command. Unless I beat her to it.

I maintained silence, even to Sheriff Savoy, about meeting Meren Joost. I wanted to see her again, but didn't understand exactly why. Meanwhile, my plans to quit the Land Acquisition Company and head back to St. Louis had flown from my mind.

Back at Rose's I told Uncle Billy Jack about the funeral, who was there, who wasn't. And enjoyed Ernest Raines sour mash whisky while doing it. At the time, I would have scoffed at anyone who dared suggest I might be growing too fond of the stuff.

I started the next day with a new exuberance. The hangovers were milder, Leah was not present and a more amiable atmosphere had settled on everyone around the breakfast table. I had told Uncle Billy Jack that Leah would not be around for a few days and the news seemed to spark a new life in him. And the new life spread a contagious mood of good will amongst the others. Lonnie joked—Volly even smiled —Jane McGann told about the time she had visited Paris, wisely choosing not to come home on the Titanic, and Oma Thornbush told a story her mother had related to her about how the Osage taught the French trappers how to carve long bows out of the hard, yellow-tinted wood called Osage Orange.

"It's how the Ozarks got their name, you know," she said. "The French called it land of the bows. They had two words for it, Aux Arcs." She spelled it out for me and said that's how the French trappers pronounced it. "We come to call it Ozarks and spelled it different from the French," she said.

Ruby Elam announced to everyone he would be joining me in purchasing the properties in Linn Creek. Uncle Billy Jack looked sharply at him, then at me with a question on his face. I grabbed that opportunity to assert myself in the position of authority before Leah returned.

"Ruby," I said, "you're to work with me until I get the as-signments straightened out."

Ruby didn't care for that; Elmer must have told him some-thing different. But Elmer wasn't here, was he?

We started at the house closest to Main on the side street I had walked several nights before in the dark. It belonged to Ira Bell. He introduced himself to me when I told him who I was. Ruby shoved his way in front of me to introduce himself and began a speech of how he was sorry Ira had to sell, but he, Ruby, could put him in a good place in Lebanon. I placed a hand on Ruby's arm and when he turned to me, I moved him gently, but firmly aside until it was I who faced Ira Bell.

"Mister Bell, we would like to make your move as pleasant as possible," I told him. "We would like to pay you more than your property is worth, but if we did that with everyone, we would soon run out of money. Tell me what you think your property is worth and I'll tell you what we can afford to pay. The difference is negotiation. Friendly negotiation."

Ira Bell said that sounded fair to him. He said he had al-ready bought a lot where the new Linn Creek was going to be and had paid down on it. And he had contracted with the Rasher brothers who were going to move his house. How did eight hundred dollars sound to me?

I said I could close the deal and have his money in his hand in three days if he wanted to take seven hundred and fifty. We shook hands on it.

Ruby started for the next house, determined to beat me to the door.

"Just a minute, Ruby," I called to him, still standing in the street. When he looked around at me, I motioned for him to come out into the street with me.

"Look," I said when he had, "we're not here to sell prop-erty. We're being paid to buy these people's homes and land. If you want to sell property, then quit this job and work that one. Don't be trying to do both. You're on trial here. I'm going to see how you do and if I don't like it, you're out."

"Elmer didn't say anything to me about taking any orders from you."

"Maybe you want to drive down to southeast Missouri and ask him about it because that's where he was headed today. So you got three choices, do that, quit or do it my way."

Ruby didn't like it worth a damn. He got a little red in the face and the jolly man who wanted to sell everyone a house in Lebanon turned into a sullen grump.

"All right," he finally said. "We'll do it your way until I can talk with Elmer. I wouldn't a took this job if I'd a known you was going to boss me around."

"Everyone's got a boss, Ruby. Now just follow along and listen. When I think you've learned something, I'll put you on your own."

"Hell, I've sold more property than you've seen, bud. I've been doing real estate for twenty years. Maybe you ought to watch me for awhile."

"See there, Ruby, you haven't learned a thing. We're not selling, we're buying."

I started for the next house and Ruby tagged along, but he didn't hide his displeasure.

We made a deal at the next house, too, but the older couple said they had no place to go and didn't know what to do. I could see Ruby barely containing himself, but he kept his silence. I felt really bad for the couple. They owned a nice little three-room bungalow, well painted and cared for. Not every house in town had seen paint and few of them were as well cared for as this couple's. The attention that had been given it was obvious. Flowers had been planted with some already in bloom. The others probably would never make it to the blooming stage before the lake water came.

After we closed the deal, the woman asked if she could

take some of the flowers with her. I told her she could take anything she wanted to. She asked what would happen to the house and I told her it would probably be torn down or burned. Her eyes teared over and she said she wouldn't want to watch that.

When we got back to the street, Ruby said, "Look, Smith, I could have helped that couple. They got no place to go."

I softened some. He had a point. But I couldn't back down. I said, "Why don't you go down to the newspaper and put in an ad. I saw a lot of real estate ads in their last issue. Or you can quit this job, like I said, and sell houses full time. But you're not going to do both and that's final."

I couldn't reach agreement with the next owners, a German man and his wife. The man, in a heavily accented tone, wanted two thousand dollars, a lot more than I paid the last couple, and the house hadn't been cared for nearly as well. I was determined they weren't going to get as much money as the couple who had lavished a lot of care and love on their little bungalow.

"So vhat ve do now?" the German fellow asked, his tone gruff and demanding.

"Have you looked at other houses and priced them?" I asked.

"Ya, I look some. Eldon, other places."

"Then you know you're pricing your own place way above the market. I'd like for you to get a high price, too, but it's not possible. I can't even offer you within five hundred dollars of what you're asking."

He drew himself up to full height and said, "Then I don't sell to you."

"I'm sorry then, sir," I told him. "You are welcome to find another buyer."

"Damn you electric people," he said. "You t'ink you so high and mighty. Somebody take you down a step or two."

On the way to the street, I turned back and said as calmly as I could make it, "You can get a lawyer if you want. Joel Dean Gregory is representing a lot of people here in town. Or you can take my offer. The other thing you are free to do is sit on your porch and wait for the water to come. It will be here in about ninety days."

"Damn you electric people," he kept saying as I left, heading for our office. I'd had enough property buying for the morning.

Ruby said, "See, what I would have done, let him name the price, then I would have sold him another house and added the difference onto the price. He would have been happy, the electric company would be happy and we get the job done. What's wrong with that?"

"What's wrong is the electric company ends up paying an inflated price and you pocket the difference. That's dishonest, Ruby."

"That's business, Smith," he said, "and you don't know a damn thing about business."

"Tell Rose I won't be there for dinner today. I'm going over to the cafe and see what everyone is saying about us. I'll be at the sheriff's office afterwards so you can go out and sell property this afternoon if you want. Just don't try and do any business for the Land Acquisition Company while you're doing it or you're through."

"You know, Smith, I could teach you things you need to know about business," he said.

"I know, Ruby. But I'm a lawyer. I don't need to know anything about business."

"Well, you should be satisfied then because you don't."

The restaurant was crowded and everyone looked up when I came in. Talk stopped, the waitresses stood still and the short order cook froze with his spatula hoisted above the burning morsels steaming and smoking on the grill. I sat at a stool at the counter and took a menu propped between the salt and pepper and the catsup and the sugar. The blue plate special of fried chicken, mashed potatoes and gravy sounded good to me. I told that to the short blond waitress who copied it down and turned it in at the window to the kitchen. Talk resumed, but in subdued tones.

"You're that fellow, ain't cha?" the blond asked when she set a glass of water and utensils on the counter.

"Which fellow is that?" I asked.

"The one who's buying up all the property."

"Smith Beauchamp," I said. I smiled my friendliest smile and asked, "who are you?"

"Uh, Juanita. Juanita Green."

"Nice to know you Juanita."

"We got a place outside of town. You buying that?"

"If you're in the six-sixty," I said. "A list is posted somewhere in the courthouse, I believe."

"But the list ain't right, is it?"

"What makes you think that?"

"Hayden Joost's farm ain't on it. But old Hayden shot Happy Meens anyway. So why'd Hayden shoot him if his farm ain't even on the six-sixty list?"

"Who says Hayden shot Happy?"

"Everybody knows it. Doyle Savoy, he knows it. You know it too, don't you?"

"I don't know that. I don't think the Sheriff knows it ."

"Hmmph. Doyle Savoy ain't no fool."

She made her way on down the counter to take another order. The man to my right said, "Name's Paul Lightgood. I guess you'll be around to my place soon enough. Uncle Billy Jack Cummins says you're a fair man so I don't see we'll have any problem. I know I got to move out before the water gets here, so all I want is to be treated fair."

"All I want, too, Mister Lightgood."

"Reckon you got a right smart job, buying up all that property before the water gets here."

"That I do. Tell me, where's everyone planning on moving to?"

Paul Lightgood was finishing up a cream pie and he waited to answer until he'd scooped the last of it into his mouth. "Depends," he said. "Me, I'm planning on moving up the creek where the new town is going to be. Reckon it'll be the county seat. I do some work for the county, so that's the most convenient place for me to be."

The man on the other side of Lightgood, a short, bald man of fifty or so, said, "Don't be too sure about where the county seat's going to be. Rumor going around is the highway department's looking further south to bring the two highways together."

"Why, that'd be plum foolish," Lightgood said. "There ain't even the start of town in that direction. Have to go all the way to Mack's Creek if they was to do that."

"Just sayin that's what I hear. I ain't got no stake in it anyway, the water ain't coming close to me."

The fried chicken dinner was nearly as good as Rose's. While I ate, a large man with big rough, red hands took Lightgood's place next to me. The short man called him Phil. He looked around Phil and said to me, "Ask Phil, here. He drives the highway all the time between here and Mansfield. He ought to know where they're going to move it to."

Phil looked at me. "You figurin on buying some property where they move the highway to?"

"No, I'm Smith Beauchamp. I'm buying up property so the electric company can fill up the lake."

"Uh," Phil said. "Heard they wasn't goin to pay nobody nothin. Just flood 'em out."

"Where'd you hear that?" I asked.

"I hauled a load of wooden stakes out to some pasture land belonged to a man named Fergus. Man told me he was starting a town out there so they could build a new courthouse."

"That's interesting," I said. "Judge Cargrove says they haven't made a decision on where the courthouse will be?"

The short man asked, "Who paid you to haul them stakes, Phil?"

Phil said, "Well, that's the part worries me. The man hired me ain't paid me and don't guess he ever will. Somebody shot him the other day."

I laid the piece of chicken I was eating down on my plate. "You wouldn't be talking about Happy Meens, would you?"

"That's the guy," Phil said. "Damn shame."

"That's true. Happy wasn't such a bad guy," I said.

"Yeah," Phil said, "that too."

Her radiant face was looking through the glass right at me. I walked into the store and she turned that face of beauty toward me and said, "Well, well, I'm honored by another visit from Mister Smith Beauchamp. How is your stay in our fair city that has such a short time to live?"

"Good afternoon, Estelle. I hope I'm not being too forward in believing we are on a first name basis."

The thing I liked about this beautiful woman was she did not try to hide her feelings. The smile was one she could not contain, which meant she must hold some feeling of enjoyment at my being in her store.

"Smith," she said as if she was feeling the texture of my name in her lovely mouth. "You must tell me sometime how you came to have two last names."

"I would like that opportunity. Not everyone in your fair city is as gracious as you. Some, in fact, treat me as if I was sent by the devil himself."

"Perhaps they haven't been given the chance to know the real you."

"I would like to give that chance to all the citizens here."

"I hear that sooner or later, you will."

"In a business way, yes. A social setting would give me a better occasion to present my best qualities."

"Of which I'm sure there are many. How are you progressing on the matter of my daddy's properties with Joel Dean Gregory?"

"I did speak with Joel Dean about your father's holdings. We seem to have a few basic disagreements."

"Would you like to meet my daddy?"

"I would, yes."

"If you come to our house at six this evening, you can meet him. Don't expect too much, he's not well. And please don't forget about Mister Bickers."

"Ah, yes, Mister Bickers. I shall see you then at six. I suppose anyone can direct me to your house."

"My goodness, Smith, if you're going to buy property, you have to know where people live."

In the office of the recorder of deeds, I found stack after stack of cardboard boxes. People were removing files from sturdy steel cabinets and placing them into the boxes. The recorder, who doubled as circuit clerk for the circuit court, was quite pleasant. She was, she said, preparing the office and records to be moved. I inquired about filing some deeds and she said that no recording of deeds had been made for several months and none would be made until the office was relocated. To check on a particular plot or under a particular name would require opening up already sealed files.

Did I really have to do that at this time?

I waived that right for the time being and asked about a posting in the courthouse of the properties that were included in the six-sixty zone. She directed me to the entryway where the list of papers were tacked on a board along with tax notices, auction bills and various other notices. Juanita was right, Hayden Joost's name was not on the list. I assumed the list came from the electric company and therefore might not agree with Joe Collie's survey. Happy would have had the portion of the list that pertained to the farms he was supposed to buy out and specifically Hayden Joost's farm.

Where were Happy's files?

I walked back to Rose's where I had parked the Buick that Happy had left in Lebanon and searched it again, under each seat, took the back seat out, but nowhere did I find any of his papers or even notes he might have made.

I made my way to the jail house where I found Sheriff Savoy manning the front office. After a close to cordial greeting from him, I told him about the information I had gotten from Phil.

"What do you think Happy meant about building a town on this man's farm?" I asked.

"I've heard rumors about buildin a new county seat just about everywhere in the county, even on the Fergus farm," Savoy said. "One of the rumors is bound to be true. I'll take a drive out there tomorrow and ask Fergus about it."

"What about Meren Joost? Wasn't Hayden supposed to bring her in today?"

Savoy gave me a look before saying, "The girl, yeah. I sent Noah out to fetch them figuring Hayden wouldn't get riled at

Noah like he more than likely would if it was me comin to get her."

"Word down at the cafe is that you know that Hayden shot Happy."

"Two places in town you can't believe what you hear. The cafe and the barbershop. Both places, everybody feels they know something nobody else knows. That's where the rumors start."

"This waitress down there, Juanita, she asks a good question. If Hayden's farm isn't on the six-sixty list why would Hayden shoot him? And what was Happy doing on his farm?"

"I reckon I ought to go pin a badge on Juanita. She's got all the questions and none of the answers. Those are questions you ought to know more about than I do."

"That's just it," I said. "I don't know. And I should. I should have Happy's records, what farms he has bought, who he has talked with and what price he has offered each one. But I don't. I can't find Happy's files in his car. He would have had them with him the day he was shot, it seems to me."

"Maybe he did. Maybe whoever shot him, took the files and left old Happy lying there beside the creek where we found him."

The door opened and Noah came inside and held the door wide. Meren Joost came in next, looking lost and scared. Her dress was white and brown striped with a brown sash and bow at the waist. It was probably her best dress. She saw me and her eyes went wide. Eleanor Joost was next. She too wore a dress more intended for a church gathering than a visit to the sheriff's office. Eleanor Joost had a determined look on her thin face and I knew she was not going to be cooperative.

Savoy stood. "Eleanor. Meren. I'm pleased that you came. I'm sorry to impose on you both. A man is dead on your farm and it's my job to find out who shot him."

Eleanor said, "And you're sure it was a Joost, ain't you?"

"No, Eleanor, I don't know who shot Happy Meens. But maybe somebody at your farm saw something that might help me find out who did shoot him."

Eleanor Joost took Meren's arm and led her over to a chair beside the rolltop desk. Meren sat in the chair and Eleanor took up a post behind the chair and looked hard at Sheriff Savoy who sat in the swivel oak chair at the desk and turned it around so that it faced Meren. She stared into his eyes as if trying to figure out who he was, though I was sure she knew.

Savoy, looking at Meren, asked, "Meren, can you talk to me?"

"She can nod yes or no if you ask her that way," Eleanor said.

"Did you see Happy Meens day before yesterday? The day he was killed?"

"No, she didn't see him," Eleanor said before Meren could nod yes or no.

Savoy looked up at Eleanor. "Eleanor, how am I going to find out what she knows if you answer for her?"

"Go ahead and tell him," Eleanor said, but Meren didn't move her head.

Savoy asked her again. Meren didn't move her head. Savoy looked up at Eleanor again. "Why isn't she answering?"

Eleanor shrugged. "Maybe she don't know who you mean."

Savoy stood up. "Eleanor, I need to talk with Meren alone. Why don't you and Noah and Mister Beauchamp go on into the kitchen and have a cup of coffee."

"I can't leave her alone. She'll be scared to death. She scares easy."

"It'll be all right," Savoy said.

"I'm her mother. She ain't but just a girl. And she ain't like any other girl."

"I know this girl, Eleanor. You know I couldn't hurt her."

"You could scare her, though."

Savoy showed exasperation with the girl's mother. "Why don't we give it a try. Maybe it's time you let her grow up, Eleanor."

Eleanor didn't care for that. She pressed her lips together in a thin line. Savoy waited. She finally broke the silence when she leaned over Meren to look into her face.

"It'll be all right, Meren. I'll be in the other room. You just go ahead and answer the sheriff's questions."

Meren rose quickly to her feet. Her eyes shot around the room like a scared deer. I had seen that look on her face before. I felt this desire to help her, tell her not to be afraid, but I could only watch.

The three of us went into the large kitchen and Noah shut the door. Eleanor stood not two feet from the closed door, each hand gripping the other. Her face was lined and worried and now the years behind her showed through.

Noah brought her a cup of coffee and she started to refuse it, then thought otherwise and took the cup in both hands. But she did not drink.

Noah said, "It'll be all right, Eleanor. Drink your coffee. Doyle'll treat your girl okay."

"She can't be alone with a man," Eleanor said quietly. "It scares her."

"It'll be better if she tells what she saw," I said. "Then maybe it won't bother her so much."

Eleanor Joost turned to me showing disapproval. "You're the one saw her the other day, ain't you?"

"Yes."

"Don't see her again."

"Why?"

"You frightened her."

"I don't think I did. She spoke to me. She said 'Goodbye.'"

"She can't speak. She's got something wrong with her."

"People say they have heard her speak when she was younger."

"She used to be able to speak. Something happened to her. Maybe a sickness. I took her to the doctor. He don't know."

"Is she deaf?"

"She ain't deef," Eleanor snapped, showing anger. "She just needs to be left alone."

"I only wanted to help."

"She's got me to help her."

Eleanor walked over to the table and raised the cup to her mouth. Her hands shook so much I thought she would spill the coffee. Noah set sugar and cream down by her and gave her a spoon. She put both in her coffee and stirred with vigor.

When I sat next to her, she said, "You the one bringing Hayden the two thousand dollars?"

"That'll be up to Miss Turner, I guess."

"He's countin on it."

Let Leah straighten this out. Was Hayden Joost's property on the six-sixty list or not.

Eleanor drank some more. "Will that end it then?"

"You mean the land purchase?"

"That and . . . and, this."

"The questions?"

"Yes," quietly. "No more questions. Ever body leavin us alone."

"That'll be up to the sheriff."

"That'll be up to me," she said and meant it.

We finished our coffee and sat quietly at the table, not talking, not looking at the other. Noah had taken leave somewhere and I was alone with this strange, strong woman. I could not help but wonder what her life was like, had been like, living with a man like Hayden Joost who clearly was in control of everything that took place on the Joost farm. Did this woman fight back? Had her spirit been broken? She was probably not much over forty, but the years stacked up on her and some of them had a terrible effect because by appearance I would judge her at closer to 60.

Sheriff Doyle Savoy opened the door from his office and came inside. Eleanor looked up at him, no anger showing now, just questions.

"I don't think I scared her too much," he said. "I thank you for coming in, Eleanor. I know how difficult it was for you. And for Meren. I don't think there'll be any need for me to bother either of you again. Noah will take you back to your place."

I looked over his shoulder and saw Meren looking at me and seeming by that look to be blaming me for her being here. I wanted desperately to talk to her, but how could I?

Noah left with Eleanor and Meren and I was alone with Savoy. He went to the stove and retrieved the coffee pot, poured himself a cupful, then replenished mine.

"How did it go?" I asked.

"The girl can't talk."

I didn't bother disagreeing with him.

"So you didn't find out anything."

"Not for sure. But I have a hunch."

"What's your hunch?"

"That girl knows who killed Happy Meens."

From the top of the hill, the little town appeared at peace, but the scene wasn't real. I mean, peace is the absence of outside agitation and aggravation and they had plenty of that. One nice thing though about living way up here on the hill, none of that showed.

Smoke from cooking fires and fires to warm the evening chill curled upward and dissipated before rising to the level of the residents on the hill. The late spring sun shone from the horizon with a faded brassy glow and a few clouds daring to give promise of a warm spring rain, spread themselves across the pale blue sky like lace on a pretty girl's dress. Nothing showed of what lay ahead for the town and it's inhabitants, yet inside each home thoughts about what was to come had to be festering in people's minds.

I climbed to the porch of the big, impressive house and, looking back at the town, I had the feeling of somehow being in charge of what took place down there, as I'd been told the owner of the house once had felt.

Yawley Earnhardt had been a robust man, back when the town had a future. What took place in Linn Creek in those days was whatever Yawley Earnhardt wanted to take place. But he had lost his wife to a man lesser in his eyes than himself and it was something he never came to live with. Eaten up with jealousy and hatred, he stepped beyond the bounds of decency and because of that he now lay an invalid inside the big house.

All this according to Uncle Billy Jack Cummins who filled me in on the Earnhardts just before I drove up the hill to keep my appointment with Yawley's daughter.

A colored woman answered the door and was not happy to be doing it.

"Yassuh," she said, her hand holding the door in a way she could slam it shut before I could get a foot in it.

"Miss Earnhardt," I said. "She's expecting me. Smith Beauchamp."

"Hmmph," she said and slammed the door in my face.

I stood there, wondering what I should do, when the door opened again and Estelle Earnhardt stood there. The glow of the interior light formed a halo around her head and her face, partly in shadow, had all the allure and heavenly features of an angel.

"Good evening, Estelle," I said, my voice weak and totally captivated.

She smiled greatly and for the life of me, at that moment, I could not remember why I had come.

"One thing I'll say for you, Smith Beauchamp, you are a prompt man."

"I have other attributes," I said.

"I'll bet you do," she answered. "Well, why don't you come in, you made the trip all the way up here. My goodness, is that your automobile parked out there?"

"Yes, it is. Well, actually, it did belong to Happy Meens and his wife, his widow, but, well, she offered me such a good deal . . ."

"I hear she's very pretty," stepping back and motioning me inside.

"Some might say that. Some might say they have seen prettier."

She caught my meaning and I was again rewarded with that angelic smile.

The room would have been well furnished anywhere in St. Louis. In Linn Creek it was no doubt considered extravagant. A mohair sofa, several wing chairs bracing the sofa, tables with glistening finishes and lamps with shades of expensive looking material with lace dripping off the edges. Embossed wallpaper and heavy drapes over the windows decorated the walls. When my attention came back to Estelle, she stood attentively holding out a hand.

"I was about to take your hat, but I have noticed you don't wear one, Smith. Every man in Linn Creek wears a hat. Why is it you don't? My daddy always said you could tell a man by the hat he wore. Now, how are we to tell what kind of man you are."

"I always heard you would know men by their deeds."

She found that quite amusing. "Ah, a biblical scholar, I believe. Can we expect to see you in one of our churches in Linn Creek before you tear them down and burn them?"

"I, uh, hadn't really thought much about tearing down the churches."

"But you will, won't you. And the schools. And the boarding house."

Her mind this evening was full of all the bad things I might have to do and none of the good. That wasn't going to favor me in any way that I could think of.

"Someone will eventually tear them down. Joe Collie probably. Try not to think badly of him. Nor of me."

She continued to be amused, at what I was not sure. I began to wonder just why this beautiful and rich woman had invited me here to her home. She said to see her father, but was that the real reason? Or did she want to hold me captive for her amusement while she tormented me with her beauty?

She changed of a sudden and said, "It was not my intention to be rude, Smith. Forgive me. My goodness, I guess I can be mean without really intending to be. I just had to get to know you better. I have this awful curiosity about people, especially dangerous people, and I only mean to see what makes them what they are. Like, why on earth would you take a job like this. Tearing down people's businesses and houses. You seem like such a sensible and nice man. Uncle Billy Jack says considering the town has to be torn down, you're a good choice to do it."

"I just never looked at it that way. I took a job to record property transactions and somehow ended up buying people out. Do you suppose if I was to just leave your town, that it would survive?"

One part of my mind was saying senseless drivel while the other part was admitting to myself what I had been thinking the other times I had seen her: this is the most attractive woman I have ever met.

She parted her full red lips and breathed a long sigh. "I know our little town is doomed and we must learn to live with that. And maybe Uncle Billy Jack is right. Maybe you are the right person to see it torn down."

She walked away from me and at the large arched doorway leading out of the room, she turned back.

"Come along, Smith. Come meet my father."

We walked through the house to a room at the back where she opened a door and motioned me through. Inside, the colored woman was tending to a man in the bed who was covered to his neck with quilts so that I could not tell what size of man he was. His hair was completely white and the lines in his face were shadowed clefts with eyes sunken so deep he must have had a difficult time focusing them.

Estelle walked in front of me to the bed and stooped to place a hand on the man's forehead.

"Daddy, this is Mister Smith Beauchamp. He's in town to buy up all the property the electric company means to flood when their dam is finished. Mister Beauchamp, this is my father, Yawley Earnhardt."

He did not extend a hand, in fact, looked too weak to even extract one from under the covers. His eyes bore into mine and I knew I was fortunate in one way that I would not have to deal with a healthy Yawley Earnhardt.

"Smith you say?" he asked in a gruff, gravely voice that lacked any real force behind it. "Smith? Is that your name? I don't know any Smiths."

"Smith Beauchamp, Mister Earnhardt. I'm glad to make your acquaintance."

"Well, you won't be. Not at all, you won't be. I'm a hard man to deal with. Your damn electric company is about to drive me into bankruptcy. I'll see you in court for that. You know Bickers?"

"Ah, Mister Bickers. Your lawyer, I believe."

"Mean son of a bitch. He'll tie you in knots he gets you in court."

"I'm a very easy person to deal with, Mister Earnhardt. I don't think it will be necessary to go to court."

"Bickers will get you, he will. That's what I'm paying him for. What'd he tell you?"

I glanced over at Estelle who wore a small grin and a telling expression.

"We haven't exactly discussed your property yet. But, I suspect we will soon enough."

"Well, we got plenty of property. There's the store, then the hardware business, the furniture store, a feed store and . . . what else is there, Stell? Tell Mister Smith here what all we own in this town . . ."

"He has the list, Daddy. He'll go over it with Mister Bickers."

"That damn Bickers, sometimes I don't trust him. He never reports to me . . . "

He started coughing, a racking sound that rattled around inside his lungs and escaped through his mouth in a heaving sound. Estelle rubbed her hand gently across his forehead. I'm no doctor, but I thought right then that Yawley Earnhardt would likely never live to see his town torn down.

"Shoo, you two," the colored woman said, lifting Earnhardt's head from his pillow and holding a handkerchief over his mouth. "You done caused this man enough worry for one night. Now git before he cough himsef to def."

I felt myself being led out of the room by Estelle's firm hold on my arm. She led me back to the parlor where I had entered and sat me down on the mohair sofa. She took a wing chair across from me and turned it slightly so that she faced me .

"Daddy's very sick. The paralysis in his arms and legs is spreading to his lungs. Doc Hardesty says he only has several weeks to live."

The light from the lamp sitting next to me on a small, round table, reflected off tears in her eyes.

"I'm very sorry," I said, and meant it.

"Daddy loved my mother and he loved me. It seemed at times he hated everyone else. He was a man of extremes. He either loved or he hated. The hate was his undoing."

I nodded my head. "I've heard the story. Do you want me to proceed with the property before he's . . . well, while he's still alive?"

"Deal with Joel Dean Gregory, I trust him. And thank you for the Bickers thing. I just couldn't stand for him to know Joel Dean's handling his property."

"Your father holds a lot of property. And I hear he has some in the new Linn Creek."

"No, he made a mistake. He bought property here on the hill where he thought the town would move to. He gambled on the highway going through his property and he could sell the lots or lease them and have as much influence as he had before. But the highway didn't go through Daddy's property. Instead, it's going close to where the new town is going to be. Daddy was double-crossed by a man who was supposed to have influence with the highway department. The man wanted half of Daddy's property and when Daddy wouldn't give it to him, the highway was changed."

"Sounds like someone with a lot of power on a pretty high level. Who was this man?"

She leaned forward and looked straight into my face.

"Happy Meens," she said.

The next morning was different from any morning before. I chatted like a magpie to Lonnie and Volly while getting ready to go downstairs for breakfast. Lonnie cracked a couple of jokes then he told some more and I laughed a little bit louder with each one until Volly laughed at me laughing at Lonnie and that's the way we entered the dining room.

The mood went around the table faster than a plate of hot biscuits and even Jane McGann and Oma Thornbush grinned. Maybe they were starting to like me.

Ruby Elam was not at breakfast. Rose told me he had given her notice the night before and when she arose in the morning, he was gone. My good mood climbed even higher. That had to mean he had quit the job at Land Acquisition and I was free of the problem he caused me.

I drove my Buick automobile to Volly's Shell station where he put five gallons of gasoline in it while Lonnie checked the oil and aired up the tires. Another car pulled into the station across the pumps from me. I looked over to see Joel Dean Gregory getting out of the car.

"Good morning, Smith," he said, then told Volly to fill up his tank. Lonnie made some joke about the man tearing down the town driving a better car than the man trying to save it. Joel Dean Gregory didn't laugh.

"I hear you gave a report to Yawley Earnhardt last night on your progress with Mister Bickers," Joel Dean said.

"I went along with the pretense. No harm in it."

"Well, I expect Estelle was grateful for that. She knows how to be grateful."

I couldn't come up with an answer for that.

"Look, Smith, Estelle wants to get on with disposing of the property. She has some rather large expenses to cover for the care of Yawley and she would like to get it over with. Come by my office this afternoon and let's open the negotiation."

"Consider it open. I'll come by and see if we can complete the transaction. I imagine you'll both be happy when it's over."

"It's difficult for her. She's nostalgic about selling the businesses. Two things I'm not anxious to see happen either, but both are inevitable. Yawley dying and the businesses gone.

Only good thing about them is there will no longer be a reason we can't marry."

I nodded, understanding his meaning. He glanced up sharply at me and his eyes locked onto mine.

"Will there?" he asked.

Ruby Elam was there, in the office, smiling hugely, saying good morning so enthusiastically I barely heard Mary's greeting.

"Leah telephoned," Mary said. "She won't be back in Linn Creek for another week. She wants you to continue on. When she gets here, she said she would like to, let's see how she put it," and Mary referred to a note she had written, "wrap it up."

"Thanks."

I took a chair at the table looking across at Ruby glowing and grinning. What was he up to?

"Rose said you moved out. Thought you might have gone back to Lebanon."

"Me? No, I think I'm going to like this job. What's in store for today?"

Ruby's red, wavy hair, freckles and boyish small nose offended me today. The upbeat feeling carried over from my visit with Estelle, the camaraderie at the breakfast table and the small-though-it-may-have-been, but showing nevertheless, jealous display of Joel Dean Gregory vanished with his presence.

Knowing I wasn't being fair, but doing it just the same, I said, "Ruby, I have a new job for you today. I want you to appraise the churches and the schools and bring me back a realistic price on what they are worth. It won't be necessary for you to talk with anyone, just look them over and tell me what they're worth."

Radiance blazed in his face. "Sure thing, boss. Consider it done."

Suspicion filled me with contempt. What was he up to?

Mary said, "Mister Elam, Lonnie down at the Shell station brought this telegram by for you while you were talking with Mister Beauchamp. He said it came to the boarding house this morning."

Ruby took the telegram from Mary's hand, unfolded it and read it. His face looked as if it had suddenly bleached out behind the freckles. He crammed the telegram into his pocket and without a word, hurried out the door.

"Must have been bad news," I said.

"It was only two words," Mary said. "A strange message. It said, 'Let's meet'"

"Somebody telling Ruby let's meet? Meet where, I wonder. Did you see who sent it?"

"Not for sure, but it looked something like Fergus."

"Ruby Elam, Clifford Fergus and Happy Meens. Wonder what the three of them were up to," Sheriff Doyle Savoy was saying as we drove along a narrow dusty road that skirted a dome-like hill I learned later was referred to as a savanna. The hill was devoid of trees and underbrush but lush with long-stem, dark-green grass. Spotted Shorthorn cows grazed the hillside showing no curiosity whatsoever to the black Chevrolet with SHERIFF OF CAMDEN COUNTY painted on the doors.

"I don't think Fergus is going to be here," I said. "He wouldn't have sent a telegram if he was at home."

"Those are his cows," Savoy said. "He may be gone, but he'll be back."

Rain clouds were rolling and tumbling in the western sky, though the sun, halfway to the noon position, was intensifying its heat production as if daring the black-edged clouds to come closer.

Savoy leaned forward and peeked up at the sky. "Could

be caught in a Spring storm here if we're not careful. These roads get pretty sticky with red clay when they get some water on them."

"Let's meet" I said, repeating Ruby's message. "Ruby's a pretty shady real estate dealer. Maybe this Fergus—if he was the one who sent the wire—wants a real estate man in on his highway deal. I wish the county recorder's office was open for business. I'd like to know if Ruby bought or sold some property for this Fergus."

"Does Clifford Fergus have land that's going under the lake waters?"

"I don't know for sure because I can't find Happy's plat book or his records, but we passed the line about five miles back where Joe Collie's crew was cutting trees."

"That's his house up ahead. Let's see if anyone's at home."

We pulled off the dirt road onto a curving lane that had been spread with creek gravel. The farm looked prosperous with sturdy outbuildings and a large, two-story house recently painted with a good roof on it.

"Clifford always kept a respectable looking place," Savoy said as he stopped the Chevrolet at the edge of the graveled drive. "Always seemed to have plenty of money, too. Can't imagine him getting mixed up in some scheme with men like Happy Meens and Ruby Elam."

We got out of the car and stood a few minutes giving anyone inside the house time to decide whether they were coming out to meet us. When no one came, Savoy walked up to the house, across the front porch and knocked on the door. He repeated the knocking twice more and when no one came to the door, he walked back off the porch and started around to the back of the house.

"Maybe they're busy back here."

I followed him through a wire gate that had a leaf-spring latch. Chickens roamed the backyard, a goat chewed away at the limb of a tree in a small lot behind the yard and across the way, behind the red-boarded barn, four milk cows stood in the thin shade of a cottonwood chewing their cud. Appearance wise it was a perfect working farm.

"Probably gone into town for groceries or something," the sheriff said.

The edge of the black clouds had gained on the sun and it was now just a pale yellow disc behind them. The shadows were gone and the chickens began heading for the chicken house which sat forty or fifty feet from the main house. The sun made one more appearance through a tear in the cloud cover and a brilliant flash of light shot out of the small window in the garage that was next to the house.

"There's a car in the garage," I told Savoy, but he had seen the flash just as I had. We both went over to the garage and opened the side door. A tan Model A Ford coupe sat inside. There was no one in it.

"I guess that ought to mean someone's around here. You wouldn't think they would go far without taking the car," Savoy said.

We went back up on the porch and the sheriff began hammering on the door again. When there was no response, he tried the door and it swung open.

"Maybe you better stay here on the porch," he said and entered the house.

I waited four or five minutes before sticking my head inside and calling, "Sheriff?"

I saw him coming down the stairs and he walked on outside and closed the door.

"Nobody home," he said. "That's strange."

We searched the barn, then we walked back to a grove of locust trees a couple of hundred yards behind the barn and called. When no one answered, Savoy said it looked like nobody was home.

A few drops of rain began to fall, spotting Savoy's felt hat. He looked at me and said, "Where's your hat?"

"I guess I'm going to have to buy one. It seems it's expected of me."

"You can tell a man by his hat," he said.

"I've heard that."

The rain began to pelt us pretty good and I broke into a run for the sheriff's car, but Savoy just tugged his hat brim down closer to his eyes and turned around a couple of times searching the farm and outbuildings. Nothing stirred except the last of the chickens making for the hen house and the four milk cows wandering slowly toward the barn. Savoy and the goat ignored the rain as if it was not really happening. When it started coming in slanting streams of water, Savoy trotted the last few steps to the car and came inside with a gust of wind-blown raindrops. He slammed the door and leaned forward peering through the cascading water over the windshield.

"Look at that damn goat," he said. "Ain't got sense enough to come in out of the rain."

Sheriff Savoy was sure enough right about the clay-dirt roads. We got a mile or so from the Fergus farm when the Chevrolet got mired in the stuff all the way up to the axles. The rain was still coming down like it had some lost time to make up, so we sat in the front seats looking out through rain-streaked glass.

"My guess is," I said, breaking a long absence of words between us, and loud enough to come out over the sound of the beating rain on the roof, "Happy, Ruby and this Fergus was involved in some kind of scheme to influence where the two highways were going to meet."

"That would mean somebody in the highway department would be in on it."

"Or the county judges. Or some politician."

"Or the governor."

"How high would it have to go?" I asked.

"That's something I'm going to have to find out."

"What's this do to your theory about Meren Joost?"

He turned in his seat and pinned me with his eyes. "Seems to me you're awful interested in Meren Joost, Mister Beauchamp."

"Everybody who likes me calls me Smith," I said.

He nodded his head and turned back to stare out the windshield. "Smith it is, then."

"You're right, I am interested in what happens to the girl. I saw her the other day down by the spot where Happy was shot. The day I went out there with you and Joe Collie."

"Uh huh. Now that's interesting."

"I hope you don't use this to prosecute her in any way, but she spoke to me. Not loud. Just one word, but she said 'Goodbye' loud enough for me to hear."

Sheriff Doyle Savoy said, "Next to the last thing I want is to prosecute that girl. The last thing I want is for whoever killed Happy Meens to get away with it."

"When I asked her about Happy she cried," I said. "I agree with you, I think she knows something. Maybe not who killed him, but enough that you might be able to figure it out."

"The question is Mister uh . . .the question is, Smith, how do we get it out of her?"

"I'd like to see her again."

"Hayden Joost catch you with his daughter and I'd have another killin on my hands."

"Why're the Joosts so protective of her. Uncle Billy Jack says she hasn't been to town in years."

"Something's wrong with the girl, no doubt about that. They're not sayin what it is. Doc Hardesty knows, but he ain't sayin. Some kind of mental handicap. My guess is, the Joosts, though they don't look it, are a proud people. I guess they're ashamed of the girl, but don't want to say that."

I stared off down the road, watching the rain, thinking about Meren Joost and waiting for Sheriff Savoy to restart the conversation. When the rain slackened, he said, "I guess I'm the one going to have to find somebody to pull us out of these ruts, seeing as how you don't have a hat to keep the rain off your head."

He got out of the car, hunched his shoulders against the fine mist now falling and tugged his hat brim down as he set off across the domed hill. I watched until he was out of sight. I was alone with my thoughts. Happy Meens. Who killed him and why? Happy's papers. Where were they? Meren Joost. What did she know? Ruby Elam. What was he up to? Joel Dean Gregory. Was he threatening me?

My mind could not roam freely without centering on Estelle Earnhardt. Her face, those sparkling blue eyes, the little heart-shaped mouth, the soft, musical voice that at first sounds innocent, frivolous and trivial, but turns out to be quite knowing and intelligent, made it difficult for me not to be thinking about her. Sure, Joel Dean sends out a warning, but she may not be as committed to forming a union as he thinks. While she was occupying my mind and the vision of her occupied my visual thoughts, I saw that the rain had stopped and that Sheriff Savoy was coming back across the savanna with a man leading a team of mules. One of the mules was plain brown, but had a white nose that set him apart from the other one which had no markings at all. They looked strong enough to extricate Savoy's car from the mudhole.

I tried to avoid the mud, but couldn't as I walked to the front of the mired Chevrolet while the tall, lean man in overalls looked the situation over. The mules had no interest in the car, in the mud or in us. The man put the mules in position to hitch onto the front of the car and they went along with him, their features placid.

Savoy said, "This is Ed Gentry. Mister Gentry, this is Mister Smith Beauchamp. Smith is the man buying up the land for the electric company."

Ed Gentry gave me a cursory nod, then went about hitching the mules to the undercarriage of the Chevrolet with a clanking log chain.

"Is she out of gear?" he asked Savoy. I was curious about why Gentry chose the female gender for the stranded and helpless Chevrolet. Then I realized that in Gentry's mind, my question probably answered itself.

The sheriff opened the driver's door, moved the shift lever until it was in neutral, closed the door then stepped aside. Gentry snapped the reins and the mule without markings lurched ahead in the harness while the other one was of a different mind. Ed Gentry slapped a rein against the recalcitrant mule who of a sudden found himself being dragged along with the car by the unmarked mule who came here to do a job and get it over. Together they extricated the car from the red colored mud and pulled it another 20 feet until it was on more solid footing.

Savoy tried to give Gentry a couple of dollars for his trouble, but the farmer refused it, saying he might need help himself sometime.

"Ed's looking out for Fergus's farm," Savoy told me, loud enough Gentry could hear. "Says they were in a rush to leave. Told him they were visiting relatives in Westphalia"

"How'd they go?" I asked. "Their car's in the garage."

"Ed says they were in a black car with someone. It was a big car."

"Looked like a Packard," Gentry said. "Saw one in Lebanon couple of weeks ago."

"Looked like two men in the car with the Fergus's?" Savoy said. Gentry nodded.

"Big men," he said. "Wore fancy looking felt hats."

I looked at Savoy. "You can tell a man by the hat he wears," I said. He didn't appear to appreciate the comment.

"The Fergus's say how long before they come back?" I asked Gentry.

"Couple days, they said. Acted kind of nervous and in a hurry. The men in the big car never did shut off the engine."

Savoy said, "Ed noticed something else. According to the license plate, the car belonged to the State of Missouri."

"Well, well," I said. "Big car. State license plates. Two men with fancy felt hats. Don't suppose it was the governor do you?"

I directed my meant-to-be humorous question to Sheriff Doyle Savoy, but it was the farmer Ed Gentry who answered.

"No, it wasn't the governor. He drives around in a Buick. I seen him out here last week."

TWO

"Why, Mister Smith Beauchamp, what an honor to have you calling at our store today."

Estelle Earnhardt looked especially glamorous this afternoon. She had done something different with her hair and she wore makeup that emphasized the eyes and mouth like movie actresses do.

"I couldn't help noticing you look extremely attractive this afternoon," I said. "Something on the order of a movie star."

"My mother's a movie star," she said.

I didn't know whether she was being serious or not, this young woman who, I decided, could be anything she wanted to be.

"I'm not surprised," I told her. "What's your mother's name?"

"Her real name's Margaret, but her movie name is Mona Dearing."

A chime went off in my head and I realized that from the first I had been enchanted with her because of the likeness to one of my favorite screen actresses, Mona Dearing.

"She's one of my favorite movie stars," I said. "Are you telling me the truth or just trying to kid me a little, because I really do think you look like her."

Estelle came out from behind the counter and for one rare moment there was no smile on her face.

"She really is my mother. It's something I don't talk about much. Few here in Linn Creek know it except Joel Dean and Daddy. And Daddy doesn't know that I know."

"I feel privileged that you would share that with me. There must be a long story behind that fact. How long since you've seen her?"

"I was six when she ran off with an escaped prisoner. Daddy faked her death and there's a grave and a tombstone in the cemetery with her name on it. But she's not in the grave."

"You know that for sure?"

"She's my mother. I would know."

"It must have been very painful over the years, knowing that."

"It's been painful knowing my mother ran off and left me, but Daddy's been good to me. As I told you before, he has always loved me and that has seen me through. So I will never leave him even though he did shoot Joel Dean's sister Addie who was the sheriff at the time."

"A woman sheriff? What a progressive little town you have here."

"Yes, and only a real meanie would tear it down." The smile was back on her face in a flirtatious way. "So, I've told you my deepest and darkest secret, tell me yours."

"I have secrets so deep and dark I would have trouble reaching them."

"Well, don't you think it's time you did? It's supposed to be helpful to talk about your problems. Or is it because you don't quite trust me as someone to tell a secret to?"

"I think I do."

"I'm right here waiting to hear it and console you about your problems. Go right ahead and tell me."

"Maybe I will," I said. "Someday."

"Okay then, if you're going to be that way, Smith, no more secrets from me. Now then, you didn't come in here to hear my secrets anyway, and you didn't come in here to buy my property so tell me, what can I do for you?"

"I came to buy a hat."

"Ooohh." Her red rose-like mouth formed a perfect letter O. "Caught out in the rain without a hat, weren't you?"

"That and the sheriff thinks I need one. Tell a man by his hat, he said. Someone else told me that, too."

Her smile got bigger. "And just what kind of hat is it you're looking for, Smith?"

As she talked she led me over to the shelf where the men's hats were displayed. She took an overly large gray felt with a crease down the middle off the shelf and put it on my head.

"Take this hat, now, it's your standard businessman's hat. And that's what you are is it not? A businessman?"

I looked in a small mirror hanging from the shelves. "I don't think that's me," I said.

She took a black hat with a wide, stiff brim circling a round crown and set that atop my head. Her smile was getting close to being a giggle. She was enjoying this too much.

"Makes me look like a gambler," I said. "People are not going to trust me in this hat."

A derby was her next choice to adorn me with and this time she couldn't contain the laugh, though she tried to hide it behind her hand.

"There you are," she said in between the giggles. "The perfect look for you. Smart, educated young professional from the east. People will like you in that one."

"I look like I just fell off the turnip truck," I said and she busted out in the most infectious laughter I have heard. I could not help but join in. When I turned she pointed a finger at me and great peals of musical laughter rolled out of her.

She whipped the derby off my head and replaced it with a

brown, pedestrian model like every other man in Linn Creek was wearing.

"There," she said, "that will make you look like you belong here."

I turned to her and in all seriousness said, "I'm not sure I do."

"You're getting closer."

I called on all three churches and no one had seen Ruby Elam. Mary said that Ruby did not come back into the office nor did he contact her. I assumed Ruby was history as far as the Land Acquisition Company was concerned. Mary did, however, have a message for me. Leah had called and instructed Mary to instruct me (Leah's exact verbalization) to drive the Buick I purchased from Vivian Meens to Jefferson City and transport Leah back to Linn Creek since she was unable to locate a taxi there that would bring her here. I was to do this as soon as possible, no later than tomorrow.

While I tried to think up a suitable answer that would let Leah know that I had placed myself in charge of the Linn Creek office, I remembered the state automobile that had picked up the Fergus's. In Jefferson City I could find out why the governor was on the Fergus farm and who the people were who had caused the Fergus's to flee their farm. And to see what someone might know about Fergus wanting to meet Ruby Elam.

It wasn't my job to find out who killed Happy Meens or why. It wasn't within the scope of my job to figure out why Happy hauled a truckload of stakes to the Fergus farm to start a new town or who it was that whisked the Fergus's off their farm and what the governor had to do with it all. Nor was I concerned that Ruby Elam was going to meet somebody. Good riddance. Give me a choice of what all of this meant and

I wouldn't have chosen one reason over another. I just didn't care. Curious, yes. Concerned and involved, no. So what drove me to solve this mystery? Why was it always at the front of my mind? Why did everything that happened make me try and fit it in with the murder of Happy Meens and the puzzle that centered around the Fergus farm?

Because the face of Meren Joost and the whispered, "Goodbye," haunted me and I could not turn my back on that vision and the softness and sincerity in a young girl that day by the creek. The spot where Happy Meens had died a violent death at someone's hands, perhaps her very own.

So it was that I walked to the end of Main Street, to the jail house where I found Sheriff Doyle Savoy inside sitting at his desk.

"I'm going to Jefferson City tomorrow," I told him. "I'm going to find out who was in the state automobile at the Fergus's and why they were there and why the governor was there."

"You're getting to be a pretty good detective, Smith. Is that why you're going to Jefferson City?"

"I'm picking up Leah," I said, knowing I didn't appear too happy about it. "But, it's a chance to get that information. I'm trying to find out who killed my boss and what happened to Ruby Elam who works for me."

"So am I," Savoy said. "Go ahead and see what you find out. See if it jibes with what I found out just now in a telephone call up there."

"Oh," I said, somewhat deflated. "I wasn't trying to do your job or anything like that . . ."

"No, no, that's all right. I appreciate your help. From what I got, the men in the car were George McDermott and Carl Graves. McDermott is head of the Highway Department Commission and Graves works for the department. I didn't get to talk with either one of them, but McDermott is in the process of laying out the highway route for Highway 54 and Highway

5, if the state decides to extend it. Right now it don't look like they will, but Versailles and Camden County has started a law suit to get it done. At the governor's office, I was told the governor was in the county to inspect the progress of the dam."

"You didn't find out anything about the Fergus's?"

"No, I didn't. Maybe you can."

"Maybe," I said. "Maybe I could do better if I was deputized."

Savoy smiled. "I don't think so."

I nodded knowingly. Why did I think he would do that? And why did I really want him to?

I had started out the door when he said, "Smith?"

I turned back.

"Nice hat," he said.

I met Maynard outside the courthouse door and we spoke. Maynard was of good cheer and seemed to have forgotten when last we saw each other—on the bank of the creek where Happy Meens died—but it was another grim reminder for me.

Joel Dean Gregory looked up from his desk and showed his usual lack of enthusiasm when he recognized me.

"Okay, Smith, let's begin the act of negotiation. I'm willing to reduce the lost business by ten percent and the personal loss by a like amount."

"Not necessary," I said. "I'm paying the asking price. Why don't you go ahead and prepare the deeds. Estelle can maintain ownership as long as she likes, but I advise her to have everything she wants to retain moved out no later than 90 days."

Joel Dean Gregory was clearly surprised.

"So the green lawyer gives in before the negotiation begins." he said. "And what reason would you have for doing that?"

"Actually, it's a favor to you, Joel Dean. Estelle thinks highly of you, so I therefore take it that you are a person of good character. Tomorrow Leah will be back. Now, you don't have to deal with her."

"You don't think I'm up to it?"

"We don't have to find out," I said. "Count yourself as fortunate."

"I was rather looking forward to the challenge."

"She is the Jack Dempsey of negotiations," I said. "Undefeated."

"Even by you?"

"Especially by me."

"Well then," he said, "I suppose there will no longer be a need for you to be visiting Estelle or lying to Yawley about Mister Bickers."

"Only if I'm invited," I said. "Again."

Uncle Billy Jack was saying, "I don't like it, that woman coming back here. Her mind is full of schemes. Should be something we could do about her."

I had a long drink of Ernest Raines smooth mash whisky.

"Don't worry, Uncle Billy Jack, I've put myself in charge of the office here. I can handle Leah."

Uncle Billy Jack puffed reflectively on his corn cob and after a long silence said, "I wonder if anyone can."

We both maintained our silence for some time. Rose came out carrying three glasses from the kitchen. She poured three well proportioned drinks from Ernest's glass Mason jar and the three of us drank as we listened to the quiet of the night.

"Do you suppose Leah will bring a check to me for my property?" Rose asked, breaking the stillness among us.

"I'll make it a point to see that she does, Rose," I told her. "Have you located a place in Lebanon yet?"

"Ruby Elam had a place picked out for me to look at. But he hasn't been around since he moved out."

"Maybe you ought to do some looking on your own," I said. "I don't think Ruby will be coming back."

Then I had to tell them all of it. About the wire to Ruby from Fergus's wherever they ran off to. Or were taken to. About the governor, the highway man, McDermott, and about Happy Meens starting a new town on the Fergus farm. And I threw in the attempted extortion of Yawley Earnhardt by Happy. I ended by asking what they thought it all meant. Uncle Billy Jack was the first to respond.

"I never knew Clifford Fergus very well. He came here from somewhere up north, Iowa I think. Whether he's an honorable man or not, I couldn't say. Happy Meens seemed to be in everything where a dishonest dollar could be made. I don't know why all the talk about starting a new town. There's going to be a new town just a few miles up the creek where the Easters own property. They're an honest family. Of course, Yawley Earnhardt tried to get control of everything he could, just like his family did when they moved here. If Yawley hadn't started up the Klan chapter, he probably would own everything. But he got greedy and he got mean. He tried to hang that Gowan boy whether he needed it or not and he ended up killing Addie Gregory. Things went bad for him after that, as well they should have."

Rose said, "Sounds to me like the governor and the highway department is trying to ram a new town down the county's throat. Shouldn't wonder it became political. But our own county judges will be the one's to decide where the county seat is going to be. Have you talked with Judge Cargrove and the others?"

"Leah kind of muddied the water for me there," I said.

"She's good at that," Uncle Billy Jack said.

"Don't be so hard on her, Uncle Billy Jack. You never accepted the fact that a woman could do a job as well as a man."

"That's not true, Rose. There's not a man in Camden County could do what you do even one-tenth as well as you do. And I'd take a cane to the man who said you're not as good as any man. Addie Gregory did a good job as sheriff. Not as good as her husband had done, but as good a job as Doyle Savoy is doing. And the women on the city council, well, I can't see that they've hurt the town any. But this Leah person, she's a runaway train. I just hope she doesn't try and renege on any of her deal with you, Rose."

"She's not going to renege, Uncle Billy Jack. She gave me all I asked. And she's offered to give Volly all he's prepared to ask for his station. She's been good to the people of this town, seems to me."

"All the same, I'd feel a lot better if you'd made the deal with Smith here."

"Doesn't mean I don't trust Smith, too," she said and laid a hand on my arm. "You two go ahead and enjoy the evening. And not too much of Ernest Raines' fine whisky. I've got to get up early and fix your breakfast."

After we bid Rose good night, I told Uncle Billy Jack I had better get to bed also since I had a lot of driving to do tomorrow going to Jefferson City and back.

"Don't worry about Leah," he said. "I have a new plan for her."

And that started me to worrying.

"You're not an honorable man," Langston Beauchamp says to Happy Meens.

Happy notices the blood spurting from the hole in his

jacket and holds a hand over it causing the blood to turn into a fine mist that clouds the air and turns everything except Langston Beauchamp a bright, scarlet color.

"I'm not a well man," Happy says. "Cut me some slack."

"Look at the trouble you've caused my son. And look at the courthouse you've built. It's a disgrace."

Happy looks at the structure which becomes visible behind him. It's constructed entirely of short, wooden stakes. Any kind of wind would knock it to the ground.

"I didn't build it. The electric company built it. Your son gave away all their money to that girl he's been trying to court."

"If you make another accusation against a Beauchamp, I'll skewer you."

Langston Beauchamp pulls a long, slim sword from the scabbard on his belt. The blade of the sword winks in the fire-light from the ramshackle courthouse which just now has turned into a roaring inferno. He thrusts the sword forward and the length of it passes through Happy Means' body and then the blood starts spurting from multiple holes in his jacket. He looks helplessly at the wounds, but they seem to cause no further harm to him.

Off to one side, a young girl appears. The fire from the courthouse licks at her brown sackcloth dress, but does not burn. Her face comes closer and two tears can be seen running down the cheeks of Meren Joost.

Lonnie said, "Man, you are getting to be the hardest person to wake up I've ever roomed with. If you're not down to break-fast in ten minutes, you'll get nothing but cold biscuits and hard-cooked eggs."

THREE

Leah was ebullient. I wasn't sure what to expect from her at our first meeting since the disastrous night in her room.

"Smith! Boy am I glad to see you. I couldn't have taken another day in that office. The paperwork is mounting up to the ceiling. I hired another secretary to handle just the stuff coming in from the electric company. They're so afraid of lawsuits. God. We have to get signatures from everyone saying they won't sue the electric company. And Elmer, well, let me tell you, he's going mad I think. Some of his instructions are just outrageous . . ."

She kept up the running chatter all the time I was making multiple trips to her apartment room and back to the car with suitcases, files of papers, dresses on hangers and cases of woman stuff that they put on their face and skin at night. When we finally got into the Buick, I started for the capitol building on High Street and she kept up the blabber which I paid no attention to until I realized she had stopped. I looked at her.

"Why are we going this way?" she asked. "This isn't the way back to Linn Creek. Did you read the sign wrong? This street runs into the capitol. If you turn . . ."

"I'm going to the highway department," I told her.

"Why?"

"There have been some developments. I'll fill you in on the way back to Linn Creek."

"Maybe you should tell me now."

"Nothing urgent."

"But I'll need to know."

"You will know."

I found a place to park and as I left the Buick she was right beside me.

"This isn't some secret is it? Because if it is, you shouldn't keep it from your supervisor."

I let that pass.

"Does this have anything to do with our job?"

"No."

"Then, let it go for another time, Smith. We've got to get those properties wrapped up. That's what all the correspond-ence from the electric company is about. They're going to be closing the gates on the dam in less than two weeks. We're running out of time. We can only afford to attend to the busi-ness at hand. If you. . ."

I went through the door first and left her standing outside. She didn't like that. She caught up with me at the door into the highway department.

"Smith, I demand to know. . ."

I left her standing again outside the door as I went through and approached the man standing by a row of file cabinets large enough to hold maximum size blueprints.

"I need to see Mister McDermott," I said to the man who turned to regard me through dark, horn-rimmed glasses on a skinny face with a mustache and a pipe stuck between his teeth.

"Who are you with?" he asked, his bow tie and Adam's apple bobbing with each word.

"Smith Beauchamp. I'm with the electric company building

the dam down in Camden County. The Bagnell Dam? I need to ask some questions. . ."

He interrupted. "Oh, yeah, sure. Have a seat, I'll go fetch him."

After he departed through a door at the rear of the room, Leah said, "What are you doing? You're not with the electric company."

"Close enough," I said.

"Well, I don't intend to be a part of this," she said.

"Wait in the car, Leah."

"What? What are you saying?"

I turned to her, looked her straight in the face and said as firmly as I could, "Wait in the car Leah or keep quiet."

She could not control the look on her face. Surprise at my audacity still resided on her face when a tall, bulky man with sandy hair and goldrimmed glasses came through the door at the back followed by the bow tie man.

"Mister Beauchamp, was it?" the sandy-haired man said, coming up to me but withholding his hand until he had appraised my worth. He moved with a slow and easy, yet assertive walk that went with the title, I suppose.

"Smith Beauchamp. My assistant, Leah Turner." I nodded my head in her direction and from the edge of my sight I caught the still bewildered look on her face. "We've come about the Fergus property in Camden County."

Both of his hands went to his belt akimbo style, he cocked his head to one side and put a scowl on his face that he had worked to place there.

"I'm not sure I follow you Mister Beauchamp."

"You follow me all right," I said. "You and your assistant Graves picked up Mister and Mrs. Fergus yesterday at their farm. I need to talk with them."

"What's your interest in the Fergus's?"

"We have interest in their land."

"The electric company? What's your interest?"

"What's the highway department's interest in the Fergus farm?"

"I'm not at liberty to say."

"Look," I said, "I understand that highways 54 and 5 are to meet on the Fergus farm. A promoter name of Happy Meens plans to start a new town there to become the county seat. The electric company is committed to building a new courthouse for the county."

McDermott wasn't buying it. "I heard that Happy Meens was dead."

"Yes, I know."

"Who do you work for at the electric company, Mister Beauchamp?"

"Carter," Leah said. "We work for Elmer Byron. He reports to Carter."

"Yeah, I know Carter," McDermott said. "You don't mind if I check with him?"

"Not if you don't mind if we check with the governor," I said. "I understand he was at the Fergus farm last week."

McDermott didn't like it at all. He turned to the bow tie man and said, "Get Carl."

"I'll take this up with Carter," he said, after returning his attention to us. "We'll get this ironed out."

"I'll need to see the Fergus's," I said.

"Fine, if you can find them. We dropped them off on High Street. Going to see some relatives I believe they said."

"Maybe I could see Ruby Elam, then."

McDermott put a big grin on his face. "Ah, Ruby Elam. This is beginning to make a lot more sense now. Anything Ruby Elam is mixed up in is bound for complications. See, Ruby follows us around trying to guess where the highway is going. Then he tries to buy up all the land and when we condemn it, well, there's Ruby and his lawyer from Kansas City.

So if you are unlucky enough to find Ruby, tell him the highway is going around all the property he owns or has leases on. We just can't afford to do business with him anymore."

A man as tall as McDermott, but with a lot more bulk came through the back door, sliding sideways to get his shoulders through. He was mostly bald with the hair on the sides of his head cropped so short and was so white I didn't think at first there was any hair at all on his skull. He had narrow, small black eyes and a mustache no more than an inch in width. And he looked mean.

"Carl," McDermott said, "This is Mister Beauchamp who says he is with the electric company that's building a dam down at Bagnell. He is asking about the Fergus's."

Carl said, "Who are they to you?"

"Take it up with your boss," I said.

Carl moved between McDermott and me. "I'm taking it up with you."

"No," I said, "you're not."

I turned to go, but Carl reached out to take hold of my sleeve. McDermott watched with barely a smile on his face.

"You can't come in a state government office and threaten the employees," Carl said. "My job is to see that you don't do that."

Leah swung her purse, catching Carl in the chest. She swung with might, but it was the complete surprise of the blow that caused Carl to drop my sleeve and show consternation as his brain tried to figure out what was happening.

"Keep your hands off my boss," Leah said. "Come on, Smith, let's get out of here." She grabbed my arm and shoved me through the door. Still pushing and dragging, she made for the Buick while I, like Carl, tried to figure out just what was going on.

"Drive," she said, shoving me toward the driver's side of the Buick.

As we departed the parking lot, Carl was standing in front of the door to the highway department staring after us.

"What the hell did you mean, your assistant? Since when have I been your assistant?"

"Since you didn't know why I was there."

"And I still don't. Why were you there?"

So I told her. I told her everything: Happy Meens and Yawley Earnhardt; Ruby Elam and Clifford Fergus; George McDermott, Carl Graves and the governor.

We were several miles on down the highway before Leah said, "What's all that have to do with us? Elam? We don't need him."

"Are you forgetting, Happy Meens was our boss. What he was involved in, we're all involved in."

"No, what Happy was involved in, Happy was involved in. Forget the rest of it. We have a job to do."

I didn't answer. She had a point, of course, but who killed Happy and what was going on with the highway department and the governor was important to me.

"Look, Smith," she said, finally ending another no-talk stretch. "Let's show Elmer, the electric company, Linn Creek, the world that we can do it. I don't want to fail. I don't want you to fail. If we don't wrap this up in two weeks, Elmer's going to send in a crew of real estate professionals from St. Louis."

"They set us up to fail," I said. "That was the plan from the beginning."

"What do you mean, set us up to fail."

"They gave us a dollar figure. Don't go over that, they said. Use your own judgment. Don't make enemies. Keep us out of court. How could we do all that and get the job done in 90 days?"

"I could have done it."

"How? You gave Rose what she asked. You were going to give Volly what he asked. Then you play it tough with the bank and the county. Both of them are taking the electric company to court. So how much of our budget is left?"

"I don't know. I don't have Happy's list of purchases."

"Where are Happy's purchases?"

She looked surprised. "Don't you have them?"

"No. I looked in the car, but they weren't in here. The sheriff gave all of Happy's belongings from his apartment in Bagnell to Vivian and she gave me a few things that belonged to the company. But his records of what lands he bought and what he paid for them are still missing."

"No problem. We'll have to go down to the courthouse and get them."

"Can't do that either. The recorder is packing all the records in boxes so they can be moved. She hasn't recorded any real estate transactions since we started buying land."

"Happy, that son of a bitch," she said and beat her fist against her leg. "Well, we'll just go over each one again. The ones Happy already bought, the people will tell us. Just waste more time, but we can still do it. You take Linn Creek, I'll take the farms around it. How are we doing with the Earnhardts?"

"Taken care of," I said.

"How much did you get Joel Dean Gregory to come down?"

"Paid the asking price."

"What?" I was aware she was sitting over there in the passenger seat staring in disbelief. "Why?"

"Get it over with."

"So the pretty young thing got to you, huh? It was supposed to be the other way around."

"It's done. I thought you would be pleased. I bought the churches, too. The electric company is taking care of the schools. We're almost through."

We were going through a pass between two rock cliffs, then across a creek. I was glancing back and forth between the highway and Leah to catch her reaction when a black car went roaring past us in the left lane. It was so close I could have stuck my hand out the window of the Buick and touched it. Before the car was all the way around, it cut back into the right lane. I caught a brief glimpse of a big man at the wheel of the black car as I slammed on the brakes, tried to keep the Buick on the road, but went off the edge of the highway, then the shoulder and after that we were going down a steep decline.

Leah screamed.

A tree came at us and I whipped the steering wheel as hard as I could to the left, but the tree got the front of the car, scraped the door on Leah's side, twisted us around and my side of the car banged into a rock outcropping, spinning us again until finally we came to a stop.

I felt something sticky running down my forehead and a red film formed over one eye.

"Leah, are you all right?" was all I could think of to say.

She was crying. I put a hand on her face and turned her to me. She had one small scratch on her cheek and a lump on her forehead.

"Are you all right?" I asked again.

She looked at me and screamed once more. I couldn't remember anything after that.

The cut only took six stitches to close. The headache lasted longer. I came around in time to feel the last jab of the needle.

"Here's a dozen tablets. Take a couple when you can't tolerate the pain any longer. Go home and rest for a couple of days. Might have been a concussion, might not."

The doctor finished washing his hands and dried them. "I'll

need five dollars," he said. "You can pay my assistant on the way out."

"What about Leah? The young woman who was with me?" I asked.

"Bump on her head, scratch on her cheek. She didn't have a steering wheel to run into like you did."

The room smelled like raw alcohol. The examining bench I sat on was well-worn and everything else in the room looked as if it had been around as long as the 60ish doctor had been. He left the door to the room open when he left and while I was deciding whether it was time to take a couple of his tablets, Leah came through the door. She had a small bandage on her cheek and the lump on her forehead was beginning to discolor.

"My God, Smith, you look terrible," she said. She was at the examining bench before I could make up my mind to rise. She ran her hand over my face and around the stitches on the side of my forehead showing real concern.

"How's the Buick?" I asked.

"I don't know. They towed it to a repair shop and brought you in here to the clinic. How do you feel?"

"I'm not up to running any foot races," I said. "How did we get here?"

"After we hit the tree, you looked at me and asked if I was all right, then you leaned over and passed out. Blood was running down your face and I just knew you were dead. Scared me to pieces."

"Who found us?"

"I walked back to the highway and waved a car down. They drove back into town and an ambulance and a wrecker brought us here."

"Best I remember, a big black car forced us off the highway. I think it was Carl Graves, the guy you hit with your purse."

"He did that because I hit him with my purse?"

"He did that because there's something going on out at the

Fergus farm and it's pretty clear they don't want us to know about it."

"They?"

"The highway department. The governor. Ruby Elam."

"So we're so important now they're trying to kill us?"

I said, "How many times has someone tried to kill you, Leah?"

That wiped the mocking grin off her face.

"I have the feeling if they really wanted to kill us, we'd be dead," she said. "All the more reason to keep our noses out of their business and get on with our own. Now, you sit there while I try and find a telephone and I'll see if my landlord will let us spend one more night in my old apartment."

"See if the Buick is okay to drive," I said.

"You can't be thinking of driving on to Linn Creek tonight. It's almost dark."

"The Buick has good headlights, if they weren't broken. Go check on it."

"We can't drive tonight. You've had a concussion or something. You're not fit to drive."

"I guess it'll be up to you then, Leah."

Leah was right, it was a bad idea. One fender was crumpled and a wheel was bent on the Buick. The shop had straightened the dents on the fender out pretty well, but didn't have enough time to paint it. They sold me a new wheel and tire and tube. Leah slept most of the way after voicing her displeasure the first twenty miles. We got to Eldon about two a.m. and stopped at an all-night station where I swallowed two more of the doctor's tablets with a bottle of Royal Crown Cola. Leah never woke up.

We got to Rose's about the time she was putting breakfast on the table. We drew a lot of attention as we walked by,

Leah in her crumpled dress and bandaged cheek, me with the stitches prominent on my head and a skinned nose.

When we returned to get something to eat, we told the tale of being forced off the road, going to the clinic, driving the road at night from Jefferson City and downing 12 pain tablets in the 50 mile run.

Lonnie put our ordeal in perspective when he asked, "So you two spent the night together in the car, huh?"

I couldn't believe that was the area of concern here until I saw Jane McGann look at Oma Thornbush and shake her head.

Doyle Savoy was the only person to see the incident for what it was.

"How sure are you it was Graves driving the car?"

"I didn't see his face, but from the back, the quick look I got before we went off the road, it sure looked like him."

Savoy looked off down Main Street as if he was seeing the town for the first time. The mid-morning sun cast shadows of the bass trees lining the creek on one side of the street and glanced off windows of the store fronts across from them.

"Joe Collie will be cutting down those trees in a couple of weeks," he said. "And burning the store buildings. First time I came to this town I was five years old. I remember those trees. I went into that store over there, Yawley Earnhardt's store, and got a penny's worth of candy. About all the money my daddy had."

I wasn't going to interrupt his reminiscing. Seems it was what everyone in Linn Creek was doing these days, now that the time grew near when the town would go down.

"My name's carved into one of those trees," he said.

"I wish there was some way I could save the town," I said. "It seems such a waste to tear it all down and burn it."

"It ain't the buildings and the trees so much as it is the people. You know these people grew up around each other, became friends, went to school together, church, borrowed from each other, married their neighbors. Now they'll be scattered to the winds. Some of them won't ever feel like they belong anyplace again. Guess I'm one of them who'll feel that way."

"Too bad the town's not thirty feet higher, then it wouldn't be flooded out."

"I suppose fifty years from now rich people from St. Louis will be drivin big boats right over the top of where we're standin and think nothin about what used to be on the bottom of the lake."

"You may be one of them, Doyle."

"Not me. If I'm around fifty years from now I'll be sittin on a park bench somewhere thinkin about the days when this was a town."

"I see you sitting on the bench telling stories about the good old days to your grandkids."

"I won't have any grandkids. I was married once, but it didn't work out. I loved Addie Mitchell, but she loved someone else. That was my luck with women. That's the way life goes for some of us. How about you, Smith? You and this woman, Leah, everbody says you spent the night on the road with."

I laughed. "She slept all the way here from Jefferson City. And I don't think telling that around town will do much for my reputation."

"A man don't own his reputation. That's something somebody else makes up for you."

"What do we do about Graves and McDermott?"

Savoy was a long time in answering. "Smith, I want you to let it drop. If it was Graves who tried to run you off the road, it means they're willing to kill somebody for something they don't want anyone to know about. They might have already killed somebody."

"You mean Happy?"

"Could be. So let me handle the detective work. You don't know what you could be getting mixed up in."

"Does that mean I'm not a suspect any longer?"

"Yeah, you don't have to worry about me any longer," he said. "You might want to keep your eye on Joel Dean Gregory, though."

Estelle Earnhardt saw me coming into the store, but no smile, no greeting. I went up to the counter and stood across from where she was writing a list on a paper. She looked up.

"Well, well. Mister Beauchamp. I heard you had an interesting trip last night from Jefferson City."

"News travels fast in Linn Creek."

"You and this Leah Turner is all anyone talks about. 'Did you hear they spent the night together?' 'Did you hear they were kissing and ran off the road.' My goodness, how many of these stories about you and Miss Turner are true?"

"I'll bet you were never the object of gossip around town."

This time she did smile. "You'd lose your bet. Joel Dean and I spent the night in a cave once. People gossiped right in front of me about that."

"How much of the gossip was true?"

The smile grew bigger. "Some of it. Most of it. Not all."

"I suppose you know by now I have closed the deal with Joel Dean. We purchased your property at the asking price."

"I'm most grateful to you. Seems a real sad way for my life in Linn Creek to end. I mean, with Addie Mitchell getting killed and Daddy being shot. All for nothing. I suppose you'll be burning my stores down now."

"Something else to be sad about, but that's what's going to happen to them."

"Well, you didn't turn out to be such a bad man after all, Smith Beauchamp. Fact is, you've been kind of fun to know. I hope you won't stop coming around just because we don't have anymore business to take up."

"Surely I can think up some reason to come into a general store before it goes out of business."

She was looking down at the list she was preparing when she looked up without raising her head, peering out from under long lashes with a sultry look in her eyes.

"I'll be expecting it," she said.

She was old. Probably older than the wood in her house. The porch listed to the north and had for quite some time from the looks of it. The floor boards were grooved and uneven. When she rocked, two of the boards squeaked at the nail holes and the ends of them rose and fell in cadence with her movements.

"How long have you lived here?" I asked.

She was puffing on what looked to be a homemade clay pipe. She removed it from her toothless mouth and looked seriously at the smoldering tobacco in the bowl. "I don't rightly know," she said. "I remember being in the house before I started to school. But, then, I don't rightly know how long I had to wait to get into the school. There was no teacher for several years. One came down by boat from Jefferson City, but he was always so drunk we only had school one or two days a week. I reckon I was eight or nine."

"There weren't many people in Linn Creek, then, I guess," I said.

"There were a good many. Maybe thirty or forty. But there was only five of us kids. I remember them all. The last one of them, besides me, of course, died ten year ago. All five of us stayed right here. It seemed to be as good a place to be as any."

"How far away have you traveled?"

"My family went up to Jefferson City on the boat about twice a year until I was growed. It was a big occasion for us kids. Then I've been to Lebanon a few times. But they're all too big. I never wanted to live around so many people. If I don't know everybody I live around, I don't want to live there."

"Where do you think you'll go now?"

She put the pipe back between her gums and puffed to get it going again. "I don't reckon I'll be going anywhere. I'm too old. I'll just stay here in this old house and see my last days here."

"You know they're building a huge dam up near Bagnell, don't you? And when it's finished the water in the river will start backing up until it's thirty feet over the top of your house."

Her face took on a hard set. The lines in her face were ridges of strength. The eyes, watery and pale, glared at me as if I had offended her greatly. Then she looked off to a spot on the river where a fishing boat was anchored with two men sitting in it casting lines into the river.

"I reckon my Lord will be beside me," she said. "He ain't never deserted me yet."

"But how is he going to save you in thirty feet of water?"

"I don't question how," she said.

"Look, Grandma Harris, I can give you enough money for your house and property here that you can move to the new town up the creek where most of your neighbors are going to live. You'll have a nice new house and all your friends will be there. Your church will be there. After you're settled in, you'll be at home again."

She rocked away as if she was pulled by a string. You

would think she never heard me. Smoke curled up from the pipe and drifted off to the north where the porch listed. She got up from the chair with surprising ease. She waved her hand for me to follow her as she started inside. I climbed the steps and went inside. The house was a single room, but a blanket hanging from the rafters divided off a bedroom. A stone fireplace stood in the center of the room with an opening on each side giving heat in the cold weather to the bedroom end and the kitchen-sitting room end.

She was standing at a round oaken table with curving legs that ended in lion's growling heads.

"My second husband was the load manager on a boat that ran between here and Jefferson City when the river was high enough. It usually dried up in the summer months and the boats couldn't get down this far. His name was Gilbert. On one trip from Warsaw, he brought this table. A family had started down river with it, but when they got to Warsaw, they didn't have enough money to pay for their freight and passage so they gave this table to Gilbert. It's a fine table. You can see where the legs are all scarred up from kids kicking it. And the top has cuts from the boy's knives and scratches and dents where they brought rocks in they found in the creek or the river. This old table's been sitting here for probably sixty years. It's been the center of all the family's activities. I wouldn't want to do without it. There was a lot of livin done around this old table."

"You can take the table with you," I said. "Do you have any relatives living here?"

"Not here. I got a great-granddaughter living in Springfield. She hasn't been up here since five year ago when her daddy died."

"And that's the only relative you have?"

"Well, she has a husband and some kids."

"Would you want to go and live with her?"

"I don't know her that well. Only seen her two or three times. Her husband is some kind of store manager down there. Land no, I wouldn't live in that big a town for nothin."

Four chairs sat around the table. The legs were carved spindle type and had been painted at least twice. The last time, as near as I could discern, was a pumpkin color. The seats were made of embossed cardboard held in place with a row of tacks with decorated heads around the edge of the seat. A table against the wall held a water bucket and a copper basin. A bar of lye soap lay in a saucer by the basin. Above the table was a towel hanging over a roller held in place by two brackets. The brackets probably had been there from the beginning. A window over the table was clean with chintz curtains hanging on each side on a draw bar. The walls had been plastered over the logs and were as uneven as the logs themselves. But everything was clean.

On the other wall two Morris chairs sat with naugahyde covered seats. She pointed them out to me.

"Them chairs floated in during one of the floods. Always a lot of stuff floatin in here off the river during flood season. People usually come around lookin for their stuff and we'd say, yes, it's out back or it's here on the porch. But nobody ever came for them chairs. My grandson lived with me for a spell until he went off to war in France. He loved to sit in those chairs. He died five year ago. He got gassed by the Germans and he was never in good health since he came back."

Two family pictures hung on the wall over the chairs. One was a fading metal print of a dashing union captain in an oval frame. The other one was a family of three children and a stern looking man with a large mustache and a much younger Grandma Harris.

"My first husband," she said, indicating the Union soldier. "I was standing outside in the back yard when that band of rabble calling themselves the State Guard come ridin into town shootin up the place and lootin whatever they could find. I wasn't a bit scared of them. They rode through town whoopin and hollerin until one of them yells out, 'Here comes the Yanks,' and they all hightailed it out of here. One of them rode right into my clothesline out there in the back. He went flyin off his horse and hit the ground hard. His horse kept on goin. He heard the Yankees comin and ran in the outhouse and hid. This handsome captain in the Union army rode into the back and he asked me, 'Are there any Rebs here, ma'am?' and I told him there was one in the outhouse and he turned and fired a shot into the side of it up high, you can still see the bullet hole if you want to look for it, and that rebel came out of there with his pants down around his ankles and his hands as high as he could get them. It was a comical sight."

Her face broke into a smile at the memory.

She led me to the corner where the bed stood. It was made of heavy posts, cedar from the looks of them, and had a quilt on top that was of a pattern I had never seen before. A series of broken circles, each of a different color, were linked.

"That belonged to my mother. I think she said she quilted it back in Virginia about 1860. I've always taken good care of it and took it off the bed before I retired. That's why it's never wore out. That old dresser against the wall was another piece of flotsam, I think they call it. My second husband put the marble top on it. He worked at the quarry for about ten years. One day a tram full of marble slabs turned over on the track and he wound up underneath it."

"That Union captain who fired his gun into your outhouse, did you end up marrying him?"

That brought a really big smile to her face.

"Yes. After he run the rebel off, he rode back and asked if I wanted him to walk through the house with me to make sure there wasn't any more dangerous rebels around. I knew what he really wanted. So I ended up courting him. When the war ended in a few months, he came back to live here and we got married. My pa had already drowned in the river and ma had died of consumption. I was all alone until we got married. He was shot and killed two years later by a man holding up the store. They never did catch the man that done it. There was a lot of bad men traveling around the country then."

"With all those memories here, I can understand why you wouldn't want to leave the house," I said. I waited before I said what I had to say. "But you know you have to leave, don't you?"

"No," she said. "I'll stay here. I wouldn't want to live anywhere else."

"I'm afraid you'll have to."

"What are you going to do, carry me off."

"It would be for your own safety."

"I won't accept any money because I won't sell. I reckon if I won't accept any money, that means the house still belongs to me. And I reckon if I want to stay in it until it's all under water, then I can."

"The water will be here in 90 days."

She walked back to the front porch and lowered herself onto the strands of hickory splits woven into the seat of the rocker. Reaching into her smock, she brought out a few twists of tobacco and tamped the bowl of her pipe full, then snapped the head of a sulfur match and stuck it to the pipe. With her toothless mouth she drew a draft through the tobacco and expelled a cloud of all-blue smoke.

"I'll be right here," she said, and looked off toward the river again.

The lowering sun was in line with the length of the river and the filtered rays shooting through the strings of variegated clouds bounced off the glass-smooth watery surface and lit up the age-worn lines of her face.

The sun setting on a life well-lived.

FOUR

Grant Joost lay flat on his back on the examining table leaking blood like a busted vase. Doc Hardesty bent over him, sopping up the blood with off-white towels and probing with a flashing, metal instrument. Doc looked up at me with a "You still here?" expression.

"She shot me, the bitch, she shot me," Grant wailed. He had a wild look in his eyes and his skin was losing its natural color with a yellowish pallor taking over.

"What's going on here, Doc?" I asked. Doc Hardesty's clinic was one small room over the bank where Leah had secured the office of the Land Acquisition Company. Coming out of the office I had encountered Grant half falling off a sway-backed horse of some indistinguishable shade of brown. I had helped him up the stairs to Doc's office with Joost blood dripping on each step.

"Well, hell, he's been shot it looks to me like," Doc said. "I don't know why he ain't dead the way he's losing blood. I'm going to need some help here. My nurse has gone for the day. You want to hold this towel while I probe."

Maggots, vermin and all kinds of repulsive rotten refuse have failed to move my stomach to revulsion, but blood will do it every time. I held the towel over the lower part of Grant

Joost's stomach where Doc had cut away the clothing and watched as Doc probed with the instrument with all the care and tenderness of a axe-swinging railsplitter. I had to look away finally and hold one hand over my mouth while attempting to stifle the bloodletting with the towel.

"Oh my God, I'm dyin ain't I Doc?" Grant asked with enormous eyes. "She shot me. God dammit, she killed me."

"Who shot you, Grant?" I asked, but Doc shot a look at me to keep the patient quiet.

Grant moaned and moved from side to side with Doc doing his best to hold him still. He raised his head up and Doc shoved it down so that it bounced on the table and Grant passed out.

"Is he dead?" I asked, but Doc wouldn't say.

Doyle Savoy came through the door and walked over to the examining table and looked down at Grant.

Doc said, "What the hell is this, a town meeting? I got work to do here."

Savoy looked at me, but all I could do was shrug. Doc pulled an object out of the inside of Grant and put it in a metal basin. It was covered with blood, but I could see it was a bullet.

"Who shot him?" Savoy asked.

Doc said, "Doyle, give me that bottle of alcohol on the shelf there. I've got to get this man cleaned up or he's a goner."

Savoy handed him the requested bottle and Doc began to swab away at the wound.

"Smith, you know what happened?" the sheriff asked.

"All I know is I was coming out of the office downstairs and saw Grant sliding off a horse there by the stairway. I helped him up the stairs and he never said anything until Doc got him stretched out on the table here, then he said she shot him, but didn't say who she was."

Doc ordered Savoy to get some bandages for him out of a

drawer and he laid them beside Grant. Then he began to thread a needle with some clear-looking thread and he proceeded to sew up the wound in Grant's side. I had to walk over to a chair by the wall and sit down before my knees buckled on me. Savoy continued to assist Doc until the wounded man was all sewed and bandaged back together. Doc felt for a pulse several times in Grant's neck and kept on working so I guessed that Grant hadn't died yet.

"He gonna make it?" Savoy asked Doc.

Doc was cleaning the blood off his hands in a wash basin and while he was drying his hands, he motioned me over to the basin to clean up.

"Not that I care, but he'll live if he don't get infection," Doc said. "Bullet didn't hit any vital parts. He'll come around in a few minutes I imagine."

"What are you going to do with him?" Savoy asked.

"Velma Tucker has some recuperation beds in her house. He can stay here on that bunk for tonight if he's too weak to move."

"I want to talk with him when he comes around," Savoy said.

"Suit yourself," Doc said. "I'm going over to Rose's." He glanced at me. "Supper'll be on the table pretty soon."

"I'll stick around here for awhile, Doc," I said. "I'll help Doyle get Grant situated for tonight."

Doc put his hat on, picked up his bag and went out the door, stopping in the doorway long enough to say, "Never seen a Joost worth missing supper for."

Grant wasn't too comfortable with Doyle Savoy being there when he woke up. But, then, Grant wouldn't have been comfortable even if Savoy hadn't been there. We finally got him moved over to the cot in Doc's office. I checked the bandage after he was moved and didn't see any sign that the bleeding had started again.

"Who did it, Grant?" Savoy asked him. "Who shot you?"

Grant closed his eyes and tried, I guess, to make us think he had passed out again. We both waited and after a few minutes he opened his eyes again.

"She did it," he said. "The little bitch. She shot Happy, too."

"You talking about Meren?" Savoy asked.

Grant turned his head to the wall. "Yeah," he said. "She did it."

"Why'd she shoot you?" Savoy asked.

"Well, hell, I wasn't doin nothin. She was down there in the creek taking a bath where she always goes, but I didn't know she was there."

Savoy said, "Uh huh, course you didn't."

"Well, I didn't. I just walked up on her and when she saw me she just went crazy. Crazy is what she is, anyway. I turned around and I was gettin out of there when she just grabbed the damn rifle and pulled the trigger."

"You got shot in the front," Savoy pointed out.

"Damn, this is hurtin. Doc ain't goin to give me anything for it? I can't stand this."

I went over to a cabinet on the wall and opened it. I looked along the shelf until I found the labeled bottle I was looking for and opened it, shook out a couple of tablets, got a glass of water and took them over to Grant. I didn't know if it was the right thing to do or not, but at the moment, I really didn't care whether I saved him some pain or caused him some more.

"I can't talk any more today, Sheriff," Grant said, fluttering his eyes like he was on the verge of passing out. Which he may have been for all I knew.

"How far away was Meren when she shot you?" Savoy asked.

"Hell, I don't know. Can't you see a man's in pain?"

"What did you mean, she shot Happy Meens, too?"

"She did. Damn right she did. I seen her."

"That's not what you told me the other day when I was out there."

"Pa wouldn't let me say she did it. He don't want you interfering."

"Tell me about you seeing Meren shoot Happy."

Grant lay there for a few minutes breathing heavily. He peeked over to see if we had left yet. I guess he decided we were going to stick around until he finished what he started to say.

"I was in the hay mow in the barn. I heard this shot. I looked out and I seen her runnin from that spot where Happy was shot. I went down the ladder real fast. I called for Pa, but he wasn't in the barn. I ran down to the creek and saw Happy layin there on the ground. And I seen the rifle layin in the grass. I figured Happy for dead. I picked up the rifle and took it back to the house. I didn't see her around anywhere."

"Who'd you tell about it?"

"Nobody. I didn't want you arrestin her."

"Uh huh," Savoy said. "I'll talk with you later, Grant. I notice you got some powder burns on your shirt there. Don't look to me like you had your back turned or that you were runnin away."

Grant squirmed some more and it was pretty obvious he was in pain. I mean, how could he not be? Savoy didn't look too sympathetic.

"Listen, Sheriff," Grant said in between his moaning. "If Pa comes here lookin for me because she lied about me, don't tell him where I am. I couldn't take nothin from him right now, condition I'm in."

"Why would she lie about you? What would she say?"

"Liable to say anything, little bitch."

"I thought she couldn't talk," I said.

"She'll make him believe it. She's always wanted to turn him against me."

"Why's that?" Savoy asked.

"I ain't talkin no more," Grant said, turning his head.

We walked out and closed the door to Doc's office. Savoy told me to come on over to the jail house, that I could eat with the prisoner tonight.

"Nobody left in jail except Billy," he said. "And I don't know what the hell to do with him."

When we got to the jail, Savoy sent Noah over to Doc's office, telling him to watch Grant, though he didn't think Grant would be going anywhere, and to see that Hayden Joost didn't come to town to cause trouble.

Noah stroked his bushy white mustache. "Tell Birdie to save me a pork chop," he said. "That's what's she's cookin up. With mashed potatoes, corn bread and greens. You sure them Joosts are worth missin that kind of supper?"

"Wouldn't hurt you to miss a meal now and then, Noah," Savoy told him.

Savoy went up to the jail cells and brought Billy Bross down for supper. Billy had long black hair and he kept it greased with some kind of pomade. He complained about being late.

"Ought to be a law requiring prisoners to be fed on time," he said. "What if you never showed up, Doyle? You mean I'd starve to death?"

"If you don't be quiet, Billy, I may just forget about you come breakfast time."

The supper was as good as Noah said it was going to be, but I wasn't hungry. I'd left my appetite up there in Doc's examination room where Grant Joost had fouled it up with his blood. I didn't believe Meren had shot Grant, or at least had shot him the way he said. And as for shooting Happy, I knew that wasn't the way of it. Grant was a liar I believed, but just how much of a liar was unclear in my mind.

"What do you make of Grant's claims about Meren?" I asked Savoy while we were eating.

"Concerns me," Savoy said. "Fits in with what my suspicions were, if you remember."

"I don't believe it," I said. "Grant's lying. Meren probably shot Grant, but not the way he tells it."

"You been in this job long enough, people stop surprising you," Savoy said. "You haven't acquired enough experience to know what kind of people shoot other people."

"I know more about those things than you think," I told him.

"What happened?" Billy Bross wanted to know. "You mean that Joost girl shot her brother?"

"All I have to do is feed you, Billy," Savoy said. "I don't have to keep you informed on all the latest news in town. I bring you the *Reveille* every week for that."

"I'll be damned. So she finally did it. That's what she used to threaten to do when we was in school together. He was a great big ol kid then and she was this little tiny thing. Cute, too. Grant would come around and lift up her dress and she'd pick up a rock and sling it at him and cuss him out, sayin she was gonna go home and get the gun and shoot him. He was an ornery cuss. Always slapping me around, too. Course he was five or six years older'n me and he could do it then."

"You went to school with Meren?" I asked.

"Sure did. She was smarter'n a whip and was always nice to me. Course, I didn't pull her dress up all the time like her brothers did. Once they come to school and both of them had welts on their asses and on their backs so they could hardly sit down. She said Hayden had used a rawhide whip on them because he caught them bothering her. They sure didn't bother her none at school for a long time."

"What happened to her that she stopped talking?" I asked.

"I don't know. She just stopped coming to school one day and I ain't seen her since. For awhile, we all thought she had died. The whole family stopped coming to school then. They're a secretive bunch of people. Nobody knows what happened as far as I know."

"Billy," Savoy said in a flat voice, "I never know how much you're sayin is true and how much you're makin up."

Billy said, "Nobody's ever caught me in a lie yet, Sheriff."

"What was the speculation?" I asked Billy. "What did people say happened to her?"

He looked at Savoy. "At school, we thought she died. Other people said it was scarlet fever. Some even thought she'd run away from home."

Nobody said anything for awhile then Billy said, "So ol Grant's dead, is he? I'll be damn."

"Grant's still breathin in and out last I saw him," Savoy said. "Doc sewed him up so he'll live till next time."

"Till the next time she shoots him?" Billy asked.

"Till somebody does."

"What're you going to do?" I asked Savoy.

"Don't know." He helped himself to a large slab of chocolate cake. Birdie brought a pan of vanilla pudding from the stove and poured a large helping onto the cake.

"Why don't you leave that little girl alone," she said.

"I have to enforce the law, Birdie."

"Somebody been enforcin the law when they shoulda, nobody wouldna been talkin about that girl now."

"What'dya mean?"

Birdie pointed the spoon at Savoy. "What I mean is somebody been messin with that little girl. That's what I mean. And it's time for her to be let alone."

She walked back to the stove taking the pan of pudding with her. I ate my cake without it.

I told Uncle Billy Jack about Grant and Meren while we drank some smooth whisky on the porch looking out at an almost full moon. The night was calm and cooler than usual and the frogs less boisterous. I could tell Uncle Billy Jack was agitated.

"I don't like it," he said. "Doyle's not going to try and arrest that girl is he? I mean that's crazy. Nobody would ever thought he would even think of doing that."

"I imagine he's just going to go out and talk with her, Uncle Billy Jack," I told him.

"Well, how's he going to talk with her," he said. "He can't talk with her. How? That poor girl can't talk. She never shot Happy Meens."

"Grant said she takes a bath in the creek. Maybe Happy walked up on her, scared her and she grabbed the rifle and shot him, just like she did to Grant."

"No, Smith, the girl never shot Happy. She may have shot Grant, and if she did, he had it coming to him, but she never shot Happy."

Uncle Billy Jack was so disturbed about it and so adamant that I decided not to discuss it further. He knocked the fire out of his pipe and rose out of his rocker and left the porch without a 'Good night,' which was unusual.

I was alone on the porch with thoughts I couldn't unscramble. Doc came walking up onto the porch out of the dark carrying his bag. I figured he'd been over to check on Grant.

"Still alive," Doc said and kept walking toward the door. "Damn shame."

Leah's door opened and she was standing there just as I walked by, outlined by the dim light behind her, making me think she had been waiting for me. I noticed right away she was dressed in a skimpier gown even than the last time I'd been in her room.

Quietly, she said, "Smith. Come in. We have to talk."

I looked up and down the hallway, not so much to see if anyone was watching as to let her know I shouldn't be seen entering her room at night.

She grabbed my sleeve and pulled me inside and closed the door. Her arms went around my neck and she was pulling my face down and kissing me before I could move to help her or to stop her, if I wanted to. And I didn't know at that moment if I did or if I did not.

She had a seductive odor about her that sent my head to reeling. Every breath I drew in was filled with her and my chest grew thick.

"Listen, Smith, don't worry about the other night. It's all right. I've been thinking about it and maybe when this is all over, we could go ahead and get married. So, it's all right if we spend—you know—time together."

She kept kissing me, pulling me, pushing me, and before I knew it the backs of my legs were against her bed and she was forcing me down.

"Wait a minute," I managed to blurt out, leaning my face away from her and taking her wrists in my hands. "I don't want to get married. My God, Leah, give me a chance, will you. I mean, this is too quick. Let me think."

"What's there to think about?" she asked, her voice still a whisper. She continued to lean into me.

"Leah, we need to talk about this . . ."

She turned limp and stepped away from me and I released her wrists.

"You're right of course," she said, and brought a hand up to fingercomb her hair. She turned away from me and began straightening some clothing that lay in a chair.

I realized I had hurt her and I was immediately sorry. I

liked Leah. I didn't want hard feelings between us. I doubted that we were compatible, at least not enough for marriage, but to love her for one night, well, I wanted to think about it. I wanted her to give me a chance to do that.

But she didn't. She walked to the door and held it open for me.

"Good night, Smith," she said, not looking at me.

I left, sorry, confused and regretful. I somehow knew I had just made a big mistake.

They just kept stacking up on me.

Langston Beauchamp is talking with a small boy that I decide must be me.

"Don't let people push you around. Especially a woman. A woman will try to push a man every chance she gets. A man can't let that happen. I want you to promise me right now that you won't ever let a woman push you around."

I don't think you talk in your own dreams. The boy doesn't talk, he just stands there. I'm lying there in the night, trying to push up an answer, an answer to Langston Beauchamp, squeezing my brain for words, the words he would want to hear. Even after I wake up, I'm still trying to find a reply. I'm listening to Lonnie breathing slow and easy and I hear Volly snoring softly, yet the fear goes on.

What to say.

Minutes go by with Volly's alarm clock ticking annoyingly. A dog howled down by the courthouse, it sounded like. And then, only then, with all that time gone by, did I realize it had only been a dream and I didn't have to answer him.

Breakfast at the jail again. Birdie squeezed my shoulder as she put a large stack of pancakes on my plate. Billy was silent for a change. After we finished, Noah took Billy back to his cell. I was having a last cup of coffee with Savoy when he began to talk.

"I have to go speak with the girl again. You seem overly interested in her, so you should know."

"I'll go with you."

"Why?"

"I don't know. Would you arrest her?"

"Maybe."

"You'd be making a mistake, Doyle. What would you do with her, keep her upstairs with Billy?"

"I might be able to take her to Jefferson City and get some help for her."

"What kind of help?"

"The kind she needs. The kind she'll never get livin out there with Hayden and them boys."

"What's wrong with those idiots, treating their sister that way?"

Savoy drained his cup and went over to the stove and brought back the big granite ware pot and filled his cup again. I waved it off.

"Grant ain't her brother," he said.

I didn't understand and looking at me, he could see that I didn't.

"Look, Smith, this is a small town. Things are different here than they are in St. Louis."

"Tell me about it."

He drew a long breath and looked down the length of the long table as if the past was down there and he could reach it.

"My folks brought me here when I was five or six. I grew up here, but when I got back from the AEF in 1918, I took off for Sedalia. I worked for the police department up there for a couple of years. I even got married up there. I married a prostitute. She was a good woman, didn't want to do it anymore and I felt comfortable with her and with our life."

I wasn't sure I wanted to hear Doyle Savoy's life story. But he wanted to talk, to tell it. He said he never had, that I was the first person he had ever told this story to. He felt a need to tell it, so he did.

They had been married for only a month. They rented a little house a block off the main street and three blocks from the railroad where the first Texans drove their longhorns in 1865 right after the war. Six blocks away Bloody Bill Anderson and most of Quantrell's gang of bushwhackers ambushed a troop of Union soldiers and shot them down. Some of the old timers claimed the blood of the soldiers could still be seen soaked into the railroad ties on the siding. Doyle wasn't sure about that, but he did know that on moonlit nights when he was on foot patrol in the area, he swore he could hear distant gunfire.

His wife had saved a little money, he didn't know how much, but he told her early on he didn't want any of it. He wasn't paid much and they didn't live well. He didn't want her working outside the house; too many men coming to town knew her in a way he didn't want to be reminded of. They were in love, he thought, and life as a newly wed couple went well. They didn't need money.

One day he noticed a set of new curtains in the kitchen, but he didn't mention it. The next week it was something else new. Finally, when the new things showed up in bunches, he asked her about it. She admitted to using her money. It was their first argument. The next day they went together to the bank where she drew out all of her money and closed the account. They went to the park by the train station where a preacher was raising funds for the orphan train that was coming to town in a few days. Doyle's wife gave all of her money to the preacher.

After that, there was something between them that hadn't been there before. He came by the house several times after that, in the night, while he was on duty, and saw a light inside. Maybe she was up reading. She wanted one of the new radios, but he didn't have the money. The third time he came by the house a Dodge car sat outside. And the next time.

The night he stopped and went inside, he found this man undressed, in the bedroom on top of his naked wife. The man clamored off and pulled a black, army Colt automatic pistol out of his pile of clothes on the chair by the bed. The wife screamed at Doyle to watch out. While the man used his other hand to pull the slide back on the automatic, Doyle shot him through the heart with the revolver he carried. The man was also a deputy with the Saline County Sheriff's Department and had never gotten along with Doyle. Doyle walked out of the house with his wife calling him and crying behind him.

"That's an interesting story, Doyle. It has something to do with Grant and Meren, I guess," I said.

He shot me a look, then shifted his eyes to gaze down at the end of the table again. "I got sent to the penitentiary in Jefferson City, sentenced to twenty years, but the governor pardoned me after serving two. When I got out of the pen, my wife had divorced me because she didn't want to wait for twenty years, and she got married again. She married a man who's wife had died and he wanted someone to help him raise his son and take care of the house. He did the same thing I did, married a prostitute. The same one I married. That man was Hayden Joost."

I was too surprised to even remark about that. Eleanor Joost was Savoy's ex-wife. I never did think of anything to say before he started talking again.

"They'd had Meren and she was carrying Eldon when I got out. I didn't know it for a long time. You know how the Joosts keep to themselves. It was five years before I met her out there. I couldn't talk and she didn't either. Fact is, we've never talked about it. Never."

"Does Hayden know?"

"No. I'm sure she never told him. He'd probably try and kill me if he knew."

"But didn't he know she was a prostitute?"

"Yeah, but I think he looks at it different."

"Quite a coincidence," I said.

"That's what I meant by being different here. Thing like that wouldn't happen somewhere like St. Louis where there's a thousand times more people."

"Probably not."

I filled up my coffee cup again wishing I had a shot of Ernest Raines whisky.

"You can't arrest Eleanor's daughter," I finally said. "You owe her that."

"I don't know who owes what to who."

"Besides, if you arrest his daughter, Hayden will kill you."

"He'd probably try."

"You shoot your ex-wife's husband it wouldn't look so good. Who knows about you and Eleanor?"

"I never told anyone till now. I'm hopin you'll keep my trust."

"Why did you tell me?"

"I had to tell somebody. At last. I just had to. You worry about the girl, so, somehow, it seemed that you ought to know."

"I don't know how this changes things, but it does," I said. "I can't tell you what to do, Doyle. I wish I could."

"Yeah," he said, looking at the other end of the table with a vacant stare, "I wish you could, too."

Trucks and wagons full of furniture and household items passed the courthouse headed out of town. The late April sun, brassy bright, bore down with mid-spring intensity, slicing through the dust cloud behind the trucks and turning the street into a sepia toned morning scene. Down the street in front of Ira Bell's neat little house, he and his wife were loading up an old Ford truck that said Rasher Brothers on the side. The fruit trees in the back of the house were in full bloom and neat rows of planted flowers flanked each side of the stepping-stone walk in front.

Savoy looked at them with concern showing. Reading his thoughts, I said, "I gave Ira and his wife a good price. They'll be all right."

"Hate to see people movin," he said.

We walked over to the bank where the Land Acquisition office was, the dust from the trucks leaving a residue on my newly shined shoes. A small locust tree by the corner of the bank was covered in blossoms and the sweet smell permeated the air. I looked through the door to the office to see if Leah was inside. She wasn't. We went up the stairs and opened the door into Doc Hardesty's office. The smell of ether and alcohol hung in the air. Doc came around a screen, saw us and grimaced.

"Grant lit out. Or else he died and the undertaker came and got him before I came in. Don't much care which way it was."

Savoy nodded. "Just as well."

Back on the street he said, "I'm goin to get the Chevrolet. You want to go out to the Joosts with me, come on."

I followed him back to the jail and we both started to get in the Chevrolet. I noticed Lonnie standing under the big redbud tree. He reached a twig on the lower branch and with a pocket knife he cut the twig from the limb.

"What do you need with that switch, Lonnie?" Savoy asked.

Lonnie walked over with the twig in his hand. "Hope you don't mind, Doyle, but I'm going to stick this in the ground and get a start off the Judas tree."

"Where you planting it?"

"I'll stick it in the ground until they build the new court-house, then I'll plant it right in front."

Savoy thought about it. "It ain't one of my better memories."

"It's our history, Doyle. We should save it."

With his good arm, Savoy opened the door to the Chevro-let and got in. I knew he had to be thinking about the tree, about the night he lost the use of his right arm and the life of a woman he loved. He didn't need a twig off the redbud tree to remind him. It wasn't something he would likely forget in his lifetime.

On the way up to the Glaize he talked about it. About get-ting shot by a mob of men he knew, except their faces were covered up with sheets. About the near hanging of Champ Gowen, the killing of Addie Mitchell and the paralyzing bullet in Yawley Earnhardt.

We drove through grove after grove of white covered dog-woods and the reddish-purple redbuds. It was so incongruous listening to the tale of killing and hate while being surrounded by such beauty. The air smelled of raw grass and wild violets. Crystalline drops of dew on petals and leaves looked like dia-mond dust scattered by the wind.

"What did it feel like to you to kill another person?" I asked. "What went through your mind?"

When he answered his voice could barely be heard. "A lot of hatred."

"Where did it come from?"

"Pride, I guess. Jealousy." Then, after a few minutes, he added, "Ignorance."

"Would fear make someone kill?"

"Yeah, it could, I guess. But I wasn't afraid when I shot that man. I was angry, but at the moment I thought it was what I had to do. Who would I be if I came home and found another man in bed with my wife and just turned around and walked out."

"Were you afraid of what others would think of you or what you would think of you?"

"Both, I reckon. Why you asking all these questions?"

"Something I'm trying to understand. It's one of those things most people would never do. But, no one's ever sure, are they?"

"Probably not. You thinking about the girl?"

"No. I'm thinking about someone else."

The trees and shrubs along the Glaize were in full foliage today and were so dense I could not tell where we were. When we came out at the location where we crossed on the rocks to the Joost house, it looked entirely different from the last time we were here.

We crossed over the creek and walked all the way to the house and knocked on the door.

"Means Hayden ain't home," Savoy said while we waited for an answer.

The flower patch under the tree was better groomed even than it was before. A string of rocks had been placed in a circle around it. Eleanor Joost watched us from the doorway to the barn. I didn't say anything, knowing that Savoy would already have noticed.

He walked toward the barn, ducking under a low hanging limb on an oak sapling. The ground was bare all the way to the barn except for the small patch of flowers. Eleanor Joost never stepped out of the barn to greet us.

Savoy removed his hat. "Morning, Eleanor."

"Doyle," she said in a flat voice.

"Grant was in town yesterday afternoon with a bullet in him that Doc Hardesty had to dig out and sew up the hole. You know anything about that?"

"Whatever Grant told you was probably a lie."

"Why don't you tell me what happened,then."

"I wasn't around when it happened."

"Well, see, Grant says it was Meren shot him."

"You're bound to pin something on that girl now, ain't you Doyle."

"Not if she didn't do anything."

"What law would she be breaking if she caught him spying on her and she shot to scare him off?"

"Is that what happened?"

"I'm just askin is all."

Savoy leaned up against the worn boards of the barn so that he and Eleanor were both staring at the house.

"Where is she, Eleanor?"

"I never know where she is all the time. She runs free."

"If she shot Grant under the circumstances you said, it might not be against any law. But that's not for me to say. Grant's been shot. I can't turn my back on people getting shot in my county. If the court says it was justified, then that's all right. But I don't have that authority."

"You're talking about taking her to jail and locking her up. You know Hayden would never allow that. Nor would I."

"If she will talk with me, tell me what happened, then I won't take her in this time. I'll talk with the judge and I'll talk with Joel Dean and see if they want to prosecute. If they don't, it's all over."

"Hayden'll be wantin to talk with Grant, too. Maybe Grant was mistaken. Maybe he'll tell you the truth of it for once in his life."

"That could happen. But till it does, I need to hear Meren say what happened."

"Now how you think she's going to do that?"

"She can write it if she wants. She went to school to the sixth grade, the way I heard it from Billy Bross. People went to school to the sixth grade know how to write."

Eleanor came out of the barn carrying a pitchfork. She didn't threaten with it, but held it loosely in both hands. Her hair was drawn back severely and wound in a knot at the back of her head. All the lines of her face went toward the knot and it was as if the hair had been drawn so tightly it pulled all the skin of her face toward it.

"What are you trying to do, Doyle Savoy? You trying to get at Hayden?"

"You know better than that, Eleanor."

"Do I?"

She faced him down and he wasn't comfortable with it. He shifted his feet in the dust we were standing in and he looked off toward the creek.

"Is that where she is? Down by the creek? Where she was the day Happy Meens was shot down there?"

"Damn you, Doyle. It's been twenty years. Can't you ever forget?"

"It ain't about twenty years ago, Eleanor. That's in the past."

"Then leave it there."

"This is about now. This is about Meren. Maybe I can get help for her in Jefferson City. It'd be terrible for her to have to spend the rest of her life like she is now, Eleanor."

"So what do you want to do, arrest her or help her?"

"I'm not here to arrest her. If the judge signs a warrant, I won't have any choice. I just want to talk with her. Grant has made some pretty serious charges against her and I want to hear her side of it."

Eleanor stood as still as a post. Her eyes locked on Savoy and he stared back at her. I watched the two of them for what seemed minutes, wondering which of them was the stronger. Which one would break first.

Eleanor said in a voice I could barely hear. "Doyle Savoy if you're lying to me I'll kill you with this pitchfork."

He said, "If I was lyin to you Eleanor, you'd have a right to kill me."

"I ain't forgot them days, Doyle," Eleanor said. She looked at me as she said it, wanting to know, I guess, if I knew what she was talking about. It was time they talked together about it. I didn't need to be there, didn't want to be there. Walking away I heard Doyle answering her, but I didn't catch the words.

I wanted to go down to the creek, anyway. To the spot where Happy had been killed. Where Meren might be.

I guessed at the direction, but I didn't need to. A well-worn path led through the knee-high brush where I saw footprints in the dust. About two hundred yards ahead the trees thickened and a blanket of green was spread over the path and beyond. When I got to the high bank over the Glaize, a stump rose out of the ground with the plants trampled around it showing someone had used it for a stool. I sat there and looked toward the creek. The spot where Happy's body had been found was visible through a hole in the overhanging branches. A hole large enough to poke a rifle through.

Meren knelt with her back to me on her knees, looking into the clear riffles floating by in the Glaize. I made no effort to be quiet as I approached her, but she never looked up. I knelt beside her and we were looking into the reflections of each other's eyes.

"Hello Meren."

She smiled and touched my hand.

"Why do you like it here at this spot?"

She reached over to the edge of the water and picked a rich yellow buttercup and handed it to me. I returned her smile.

"It's beautiful," I said. I held it up beside her face. "Like you."

She shook her head and ducked her eyes as she waved a hand over her face. I leaned over and looked at my face in the water. I pointed and she moved her head over the stream and her face appeared beside mine. I pointed at her image.

"See."

She could not suppress another smile.

"You put rocks around your flower garden. It looks even prettier than before."

A silent smile.

"Would you like to be able to talk?"

Her face was a question.

"Maybe you would like to go to a special doctor who could help you . . ."

She was shaking her head violently from side to side.

"It's a choice for you to make, not anyone else."

She looked away.

"Is there something you would like, more than anything else? Something I could help you get?"

She looked at the plain brown dress of hopsacking and lifted a piece of it in her fingers and looked at me.

"A new dress?"

Another smile.

"What color? Red?"

I had a blue necktie around my neck. She picked up the end of it and held it.

"Blue?"

She nodded.

"You shall have it then."

She squeezed my arm.

I didn't want this interlude to end. There was a pleasantness about it that I had not known for a long, long time. The lot of memories and the lot of problems I was inclined to march out of my head every morning and confront throughout the day had vanished. I placed my other hand on her hand

and held it there. I didn't want to ask what I had to ask, but if I didn't, Doyle Savoy would. And I knew that would upset her more than what I might say to her. Once again I found myself standing square between Meren and Sheriff Savoy.

"Grant came in to Doc Hardesty's office. He'd been shot."

Trouble came into her eyes. She blinked them rapidly and what had been there before was gone.

"He said you shot him."

Her eyes shot fire at me.

"Doyle wants to hear what really happened. If you want to tell me, you won't have to talk with him."

She rose from the ground, still with a hand on my arm, and began to walk along the stream, leading me with her. We stepped over rocks, around stumps, ducked under low hanging branches until we had gone about a hundred yards along the Glaize. We had passed around a slight bend in the creek which had taken us out of view of the spot where we had knelt. In front of us was a wider pool of water, twenty or thirty feet across. The surface was dotted with air bubbles from tadpoles and water bugs while the bottom was alive with catfish fingerlings. The pool here was perhaps five feet deep. A clump of short willows was beside us. Meren took her dress in her fingers and tugged at it, then motioned toward the clump of willows.

She had placed her dress on the branches of the short trees.

She made motions of bathing, bending over as if to splash water with her hands. She pointed up on the bank where a string of ten-inch oaks grew. She made a mocking face of Grant, peeping around a tree. Then she mimicked him skulking down the bank, She turned around sharply, feigned surprise, and began to thresh with her arms. Then she reached the rifle she had propped against the bushes and she jabbed it at me.

While she was frozen in that stance, I nodded. The anger

left her face and she placed the rifle back where it had been.

"He attacked you?"

She didn't nod nor even acknowledge that she had heard me. Her face was inscrutable, her breathing heavy, her eyes downcast.

I took her hand. "I understand. Doyle will understand."

I could almost feel her fear and despair through her fingers. I wanted to take her in my arms, console her against my chest, but that would have been a very risky thing to do. I had no idea how she would react to that, what she might think, how she might interpret the action.

"Did Grant do this often? Has he done this in the past?"

She turned her back to me and I knew the answer. "Meren, would you like to leave here? To go someplace where Grant nor anyone else will ever molest you again?"

She turned loose of me and sobbed into her hands. I could not hold back, I took both her shoulders in my hands from behind and gently leaned her into my chest. She turned herself and the grief and the sobs shook her body and I could feel the wetness of her tears through my shirt. I held her there for minutes, then took a handkerchief from my pocket and began to dry her tears with it. She took the handkerchief from me and held it over her face.

"You could leave with me now, if you want, Meren. I could find a place for you. A place where you would be safe."

She began to shake her head from side to side.

"Are you sure?"

She nodded once.

She held on to my handkerchief and picked up her rifle in her other hand.

"You wouldn't have to carry that rifle around to protect yourself with," I said.

I stood, looking at this brave, strong young woman, the strength in her arms and in her legs. The iron will in her face.

No one, not Grant, not anyone, would violate her again. The look on her face, the way she stood, said that.

"I'd better get on back and tell Doyle or he'll come looking for you."

But I didn't move. She looked down at the rifle and wiped an imaginary spot of dust off the barrel. The rifle was her protector and she would care for it.

I walked away. I heard a sound, a small sound.

"Smith."

I turned back.

Whispered, "Thank you."

FIVE

At dawn, the spell of a tropical spring had abandoned us and left a cold, gray presence that set the mind to gloom. Until, that is, you laid eyes on the likes of Estelle Earnhardt.

"Good day to you Mister Smith Beauchamp," she said. A yellow dress with fine lace winding around and around, a pale purple hat and a pearl necklace enhanced a face the law of chance creates too infrequently.

"Estelle, that smile could turn night into day."

"You're a real darb, Smith. I'm so glad you dropped in."

"I've got sort of a favor to ask of you."

"A favor? Me? Goodness, I don't get many chances to do favors. Tell me more."

"I know this young girl. She needs a friend."

"I see. Well, well. A young girl. Would this be the same young girl who spent the night inside your Buick automobile with you?"

"It's Meren Joost."

"Hayden Joost's daughter? I don't think I've seen that girl for five years. Whatever is the situation there?"

"She needs to leave there. She walks around carrying a rifle to keep Grant and maybe the other brother from molesting her. It's happened in the past."

"My goodness, have you told Doyle and Joel Dean about this?"

"Doyle knows. Grant came riding into town with a bullet in him. She says she did it because he tried to attack her. I told Doyle and he's accepting her version. He's talking with the judge and with Joel Dean about her. But the fact of the matter is, she has to leave that place. Can you help her?"

"Of course I'll help her. But what's Hayden Joost going to say about it. He scares the living daylights out of me whenever he comes into the store."

The bear-like man had been in the back of my mind since first meeting him. Now, I had to focus on him. A man with the need to control people and the will and means to do it. What would happen when Hayden Joost found out the woman he was married to had been married to Sheriff Doyle Savoy? And what would happen when Hayden came back from his trip to Sedalia with Eldon to "teach the boy to be a man," meaning, presumably, introducing him to one of the Sedalia prostitutes, and found out Meren had shot Grant because Grant was attempting to molest her again? And what would happen if he came back and found out I had coerced Meren to leave his home and come to Linn Creek.

"I could ask Rose, but Rose would be a mother to her. What she needs is a friend. Something she's never had."

"Are you in love with this girl, Smith?"

"She's a child, Estelle. You'll see that when you meet her."

"Let's see, she would be eighteen or nineteen now, wouldn't she?"

"Something like that."

"Hardly a child, Smith. I'll do it. She can stay at my house. I need a friend sometimes, too."

"One more thing. Do you have a blue dress in your store that would fit her?"

She removed her light purple hat and laid it on the counter.

An older woman came into the store carrying a basket. Estelle greeted the woman and guided her to some stock on a shelf. I noted that the shelves were practically empty. The store would be closing in less than two weeks. I was aware then of not having the courtesy of asking Estelle about her plans for closing her businesses and if she planned to open new ones in the new town.

She came back with a folded dress of blue material. She held it by the shoulders and let it fall to full length as she looked at me for approval.

I took the cloth between my fingers and compared it to my tie.

"Close enough," I said. "I'll take it."

"A man doesn't buy a dress for a woman because she's a friend," Estelle teased. "A man who would buy this dress for me would be more than that."

Mary worked on a reluctant typewriter. Leah sat at the table that served us both as a desk. She had a plat map spread out before her and was making notes on a sheet of paper. She looked up as I sat in the chair on the other side of the table.

"Where the hell have you been?"

Leah, the tough-as-a-man boss, exercising her self-appointed authority.

"Around town, buying property."

"I hear you've been spending a lot of time at the Joost place, which, by the way, has already been handled by me, and at the store run by the pretty young thing, which, by the way, you practically used our whole budget to buy out. Elmer's not going to go for that."

"Where is Elmer?"

She drew her face into hard lines and the realization of how she was taking my rejection of her proposal dawned on me. My actions had made her the woman scorned and the thought made me apprehensive about what was ahead.

"Our budget is shot, you know that? We've already paid out more money, thanks to you, than the electric company allowed us to complete this job. My God, we're not here to make these people rich. We're here to legally compensate them for the rights to their land. We have the power of Eminent Domain, you know. We don't have to deal with these people at all if we chose not to. Let the court set the payment."

"The court owned by the electric company?"

"The court elected by the people of this state. Who's side are you on? You're acting like you worked for the property owners instead of the electric company. Look at your pay check, see who signed it."

"I remember Elmer saying, let's treat these people right. We don't want a lot of hard feelings against the electric company. I remember you saying that, too, when you bought out Rose Minton and offered Volly whatever he asked for his station."

"I got it started," she said. Her face was really screwed up now into a knot. I had never seen this Leah before. Had I created a monster? "It was up to you to continue. Instead, you fawn all over the pretty young woman and you're going out offering this old couple and some old woman more money than they would even ask for. You're not even letting them tell you a price, you're making one up for them and it's costing the electric company a fortune."

"The company has a fortune. And when they get the generators in the dam running they will have several more fortunes. These people worked their whole lives for one little piece of property they can call their own. Along comes the electric company and they're going to flood them out. The people have a right to enough money that they can get started over again and continue on with their lives. How would you feel if someone came to take your home away from you?"

"I don't have a home."

"I did once. And it was taken away from me. With one shot."

I parked the Buick in front of the jail house. The light rain had brought a chill to the air, making me glad for the jacket I wore. I got out of the Buick and popped open an umbrella as I walked toward the front of the limestone block building. Before I got to the door, Savoy opened it and stood waiting for me.

I stopped outside the door and peering under the rim of the umbrella, said, "I'm going out to get Meren and bring her back here. Estelle Earnhardt says Meren can stay at the house with her."

Savoy studied me in a way he hadn't before. "You're askin for trouble," he said. "Hayden Joost is coming back from Sedalia tomorrow."

I nodded. "I know. That's why I'm here. I need you to protect her."

"Why are you doing this?"

"She needs help. You said so yourself. She needs to be living a life where she doesn't have to carry a rifle with her everywhere she goes to protect herself. I was hoping you would do that. I thought it was your job."

"She's still a child. She ain't twenty-one. That's the legal age. It's up to her parents to protect her."

"Then why's she carry that rifle everywhere if they're doing such a great job?"

"Leave it alone."

"If you won't protect her, give me a badge. Deputize me, I'll do it."

Savoy snorted and looked away. He lifted his revolver out of his holster and dropped it back, checking that it didn't stick. "You're sure fired certain to get a badge, ain't you? What do you think this is, some kind of game?"

"Ask her if it's a game."

"Damn," he said and kicked the door sending it swinging farther into the room. "All right, but you better do it today. You go out there when Hayden Joost is there, he'll kill you and there won't be anything I can do about it."

"Just do your job," I said and turned and went back to the Buick, got inside and drove away.

Puddles were forming in the road headed toward the Glaize, but I wasn't paying attention to them or to anything along the way. I was thinking about how I was going to get Meren to come into town with me, thinking about it so intensely that I was completely unaware of just how my life was about to change.

SIX

Meren was by her flower bed pulling weeds. She stood as she watched me approach. The clouds had drifted apart and a subdued sun shone weakly, spilling mottled light over Meren and her garden.

"I have a place for you in town, Meren," I told her. "Estelle Earnhardt wants you to stay with her. She picked something out to give to you."

I handed her the dress folded nicely as Estelle had given it to me. Meren took the dress and looked quizzically at me.

"Go ahead," I said, "Look at it."

She unfolded it and held it up. She could not suppress the glee that came to her. She pinched the cloth between her fingers and mouthed the word, "Blue," to me.

"Blue, just like you wanted. Estelle has more dresses in her store that she has to get rid of. The store will be torn down in just two weeks."

I wasn't sure what she knew about the dam, about Hayden's land that might be in the path of the lake. Something to talk about with her later.

"Let's go talk with your mother about you going to stay with Estelle."

She wasn't sure, I could tell that. I could see the fear in her, in her eyes, in the way she gripped the dress with both hands. Slowly she began to shake her head, but I reached out to take her arm and when she looked at me, I nodded my head up and down.

"It will be best for you. You won't have to carry the rifle around to protect yourself. You will have a friend. Estelle is looking forward to having you in her house. You don't have another girl for a friend now, do you?"

She moved her head from side to side. Her eyes went behind me and I knew Eleanor would be standing there.

"Estelle Earnhardt has a place for her in her house, Eleanor. I told her I would bring Meren back to town with me."

Eleanor came up beside me. Her face looked somewhat more relaxed than usual. She stood straight and tall, her hands locked together in front of her. A mother being ripped right down the middle of her soul.

"Doyle put you up to this?"

"He knows. I told him. He said Hayden would try to kill me."

"Likely," she said.

"You know it's best for her. What kind of life will she have, staying here, carrying a rifle everywhere; to bed with her, to take a bath with. Has Hayden ever tried to stop Grant?"

"Gives him a beatin every time he looks at her. Last time, Grant said his pa wasn't beatin him anymore. Now I don't know what'll happen."

"You want her to be here when it does?"

"This is her home."

"When it's time, all birds leave the nest."

"How I know I can trust you?"

"You look at me do you see somebody who would ever hurt her?"

"I don't know you."

"Ask her if she trusts me."

She had been standing silent, her eyes moving back and forth. She understood what I said. The moment had come for her. She looked at her mother and the wet eyes spilled over onto her cheeks. In a surprise move, Eleanor stiffly put her arms out and folded Meren to her chest. From the look on Meren's face, I knew it was the first time her mother had ever taken her in her arms since she was a child. They both had their answer.

Eleanor stepped back and tried to turn her face so the tears wouldn't show.

"Go on," she said with a wave of her arm. "Go put your stuff you want to take in that old carpetbag on the shelf. And I expect you to behave yourself in that town. Girls have to be careful in town like that. You ain't used to it."

Meren was a child on Christmas morning. She touched her mother on the shoulder, looked at me, trying to hold the smile from stretching all the way across her face, and she began running toward the house, the blue dress flying behind her like a festive banner.

"This Estelle Earnhardt is a rich woman," Eleanor said. "Why does she want to mess with a ragamuffin from the country like Meren?"

"Because she has a good heart," I said, and just now realized the truth of that remark.

"What will you tell Hayden?" I asked.

She took her time in answering. "I won't be able to stop him from coming."

Five minutes later we had crossed the creek and stood by the Buick, ready to leave. Eleanor let loose a flood of tears, streaming from her eyes like a water pipe had cracked. She wiped away with both hands, gave Meren a kiss on the cheek and stepped back from the car. Meren was smiling and crying at the same time. I got in the Buick and motioned her inside, but she turned at the last minute, walked to her mother and handed her the rifle she had been carrying everywhere, then flew inside the Buick in her all-blue dress and a carpetbag full of the fewest possessions any teenage girl had in the Ozarks.

Meren Joost was breaking away.

Both young women had an experience unlike any they'd had before or likely to have again. In telling about it later, Estelle admitted her reluctance to the project, but no hint of that was ever shown to me. She delighted in telling about that first night and the next day as if she was rewriting *Little Women*. And listening to the way she told it, with the expressions, the hand gestures and, best of all, Meren, giggling behind her hand like a third grader on a sleep over at her best friend's.

When we came through the door to the store, Estelle could barely conceal her amusement at Meren's bug eyes at all the shelves—never mind that they were one-fifth their usual stocked level—and the way she picked everything up and smelled it.

After being introduced to each other, Meren held back, not knowing what to do, but Estelle blurted out, "Well, for goodness sakes, let's don't just stand here google-eyed so Smith Beauchamp can stand there and make fun of us."

So Estelle, half a head shorter, light and fair against Meren's tanned, willowy body, threw her arms around the taller girl and hugged her tightly.

Meren at first fearing she was being attacked, held back, but when she felt the warm, friendly body against her, she tried her best to respond without knowing exactly how.

Estelle led her through the store, telling her what each item in stock was. When she got to the underwear section, Estelle held up a pair of satin panty underwear to Meren who shrank back until Estelle lifted her own skirt, showing the pair she wore. She picked out seven pairs for Meren.

"One for each day of the week," she said, but Meren looked bewildered so Estelle named off the days, laying down a pair of the satin panties for each day. Meren looked as if she still didn't get it.

The brassieres completely mystified her. Estelle started to show her, but with customers in the store, thought better of it. Later.

Nell, the colored housekeeper, frightened Meren. So Nell hugged Estelle, showing she meant no harm to either of them. Estelle showed Meren how to hold the napkin on her lap, how to use each utensil, how to cut her meat, eat her soup, drink gracefully from a glass.

Bath time brought moments of great humor. Estelle filled the bath tub full of warm water, poured in a generous amount of bubble bath and told Meren to sink herself up to her neck in the bubbles. She introduced her to shampoo, then pushed her head under water from which Meren came roaring up out of the foam like a whale, spouting water and bubbles.

She taught Meren about clothes, how to wear them, how to care for them and about the colors they came in. In just a few short days Meren turned from a naive, unknowing young female to a graceful young woman.

But she still didn't speak.

Estelle sought out Doc Hardesty who Uncle Billy Jack told her had been the last doctor known to examine Meren. Doc Hardesty told her that Meren's vocal chords had been crushed, either by a severe blow to the throat, attempted choking or perhaps some childhood illness. Only a specialist could help her, if she could be helped, but Doc had not been able to talk Eleanor nor Hayden into seeking one for Meren.

The two women communicated by Meren mouthing the words and before long Estelle could understand her. Nell taught Meren to cook and Estelle taught her how to count money and soon she became very good help in the store. Estelle taught her about womanly affairs, how to cope with her once-monthly occurrence and how to have confidence in herself.

It was a very short conversion, lessons crammed in day after day. Estelle grew very fond of Meren and her role as big sister to the younger girl, added to the necessity for her to learn Yawley's business, turned Estelle into a completely different woman from whom she had been just months before.

Meren worshipped Estelle. There was nothing she wouldn't have done for her. No tension ever developed between the two. Life was completely different for them both and their enjoyment of this new situation seemed as if it would not end.

Until the day Grant Joost walked into the store.

SEVEN

Sheriff Doyle Savoy said, "Ruby Elam is dead."

He took off his hat and the sun glinted off his short, black hair that twisted in loose curls on his head like finely woven wire. He slapped the hat back in place and while I was forming questions in my mind, he said, "They found him south of Westphalia about a hundred miles east of here on the Maries River. Ruby's car went over a rocky bluff and was half submerged in the water. They had to pull it out with a crane."

"Westphalia, huh. Isn't that where the Fergus's were going?"

"Believe so."

"How'd he die?" I asked.

"Well, it wasn't old age, you can bet on that."

"I mean, was there any reason to believe someone forced him off the road and over that bluff?"

"Like what happened to you?"

"Something like that, yeah. Where you suppose Carl Graves was about the time Ruby went over the bluff?"

"Drivin the same highway mindin his own business is about all we'll get out of him. Looks like Ruby was leavin town. He had twenty thousand dollars in a suitcase in the car."

"He have personal belongings with him?"

"Yeah, he did. Thrown all over inside the car like he'd packed by just throwin his things inside.

We were standing outside the courthouse the day after I brought Meren to stay with Estelle. The street that day was strangely deserted as if everyone in town had been in the three moving trucks that drove through here yesterday. The dust normally flying about in the street had been wetted down by the rain yesterday and small puddles looked like chips of ceramic blue as they reflected the cloudless sky.

"What are you going to do?" I asked.

"Right now I'm goin over to the cafe where everybody knows everything. Two cups of coffee and a doughnut and I'll be told by Juanita who killed Ruby and what I ought to do about it."

Savoy walked off with the sort of gait that comes from having music in your makeup. I'd been told that he was a good guitar player before he lost the use of his right arm. Now, according to Uncle Billy Jack, the sheriff took a trip to St. Louis about once a month and went down to the part of town where they played jazz and he sang some blues and upbeat tunes in the bars. Uncle Billy Jack said Doyle had a flat singing voice but it moved people.

I bought three properties before noon. They were all from people anxious to get moving to the new town. The Rasher brothers wanted more to move their houses than they thought they could build new ones for. I was Santa Claus when I wrote out the checks and they were kids pulling their stockings down from the mantle.

I should have taken lunch at Rose's as it was one meal when I didn't have to face Leah across the table, but I wanted to hear the town gossip at the cafe about Ruby Elam.

Juanita said everybody knew what happened. Ruby and Happy was in it together, running off with the cash that was supposed to be used to buy up property for the electric company.

I said we pay by check. Juanita said they forged the checks. I said, who you think killed Happy? Juanita looked at me like I was sitting at the counter playing with a rag doll.

"Hell, everbody knows Ruby killed Happy and the guy they worked for—what was his name? Al? Bill? Elmer? Yeah, that's the guy, Elmer—run ol Ruby off the highway."

"How you know it wasn't me?" I asked.

She threw a hand to her hip, shoved the hip sideways and regarded me as if I'd asked about the tooth fairy.

"Come on, Smith, be serious. What you gotta do is help Doyle find this Elmer. You ask me, that woman, the one you spent the night with in the car, is in on it too."

"But I didn't . . . Elmer's not even here . . . Leah's out buying up the farms . . ."

"You decided what you're gonna have today?"

"Uh, no, I . . .just dropped in to see how you're doing. I guess I'll eat at Rose's today."

"Liver and onions," she said.

"Gives me gas," I said. "I'll see you, Juanita."

The Bailey boys were the only twins in Linn Creek, they told me. They'd started building the house three years ago when they were nine, right after their father had fallen from a tree he was trimming for Yawley Earnhardt and couldn't walk. Their mother had died when they were three, so the boys got by doing odd jobs around town. Yawley let them build on a lot he owned, but they never got a title for it and Yawley's lot was now the electric company's lot so the boys had nothing to sell.

The house was put together with scrap lumber the sawmill had given them for cleaning up around the mill. The corners weren't square, the roof sagged and the windows were slanted down at the bottom and up at the top. The doorway was a trapezoid and the door opened to the outside so that it would cover up their mistake. At the end of their building, the boys were starting to learn something about carpentry and the north side of the house looked as if professionals had put it together.

"We always meant to go back and fix up our mistakes, but I got a job down at the Ford garage learning to be a mechanic and my brother, Eddie, works at the cafe learning how to cook," the brother named Tom said.

Standing at the north side of the house eyeing the plumb lines there, I said, "You boys sure did learn your carpentry. Maybe you ought to go into that field. I'm sure they need carpenters up at the new town."

"We already tried," Eddie said. "They said we were too young. To come back when we're sixteen."

"What are you going to do?"

"Good question," Tom said. "We got to be out of the house in sixty days so maybe something will come up."

"Well, listen," I said. "Maybe you can tear the house down and move the lumber up to the new Linn Creek and build on a lot up there. And when you do, you can build it right like you did on the end there."

"Well, that's a right good idea, Mister Beauchamp," Eddie said. "But see there's a couple of catches there. One, we ain't got a lot to build on and two, we ain't got any money to buy one or to pay to move the house."

The boys didn't really look like twins, but who was I to doubt their word. Tom was two or three inches taller than Eddie and he looked to be considerably stronger, his muscles almost splitting the seams on the arms of a striped chambray shirt. He wore an old felt hat, probably his dad's, over hair so fair it was almost white. Eddie was stocky with red hair and wearing his white pants that belonged to the cafe and a white shirt, he looked almost professional. Both had a good crop of freckles and overly large ears.

"Well, you have to move because of the dam, right? And you own personal property inside the house. We've paid other people to move personal property so seems to me the Land Acquisition Company owes you some money."

The twins looked at each other and began to smile.

"How much, you reckon?" Tom asked.

"Let me see. I hear for a hundred dollars down you can get a lot at the new Linn Creek. And I think the Rashers will move the boards in your house and your personal property, so I think two hundred dollars ought to be about right."

The Bailey boys were so happy I thought they might start crying. Eddie said, "Thank you, Mister Beauchamp, we won't forget how good you were to us. You come over to the cafe and I'll slip something extra on your plate and I'll tell Juanita not to charge you for it."

"Won't be necessary, Eddie, but thank you just the same."

Tom said, "So if we wait thirty days to start tearing the house down, and we have it tore down in thirty days, then we'll be out of here before the water comes into town?"

"Should be about right," I said.

Eddie asked, "When you reckon we might get the two hundred dollars?"

I pulled the company checkbook out of my back pocket. "I don't see why you can't get it right now."

I handed the check over and Tom took it, looked at it and showed it to Eddie.

"We never had two hundred dollars before," Eddie said. "I feel rich."

They both laughed and Tom stuck the check in his shirt pocket.

"There's a man over at the Missouri Bank selling the lots in Linn Creek. Better get over there with that check."

"Yes sir," Eddie said.

I walked back to the Buick, got in and started the engine. When I drove off, the boys were walking toward the bank.

I felt about as good as I was ever going to feel in Linn Creek right then.

But, of course, I didn't know that.

The next week was hectic. I still had properties in Linn Creek to close on before the job was complete. I would buy a property and the people would start right away packing their stuff to move. Five moving vans from Lebanon, Eldon and Jefferson City plied the town for business. One mover from Eldon offered me ten dollars a name if I would tip them off as soon as I purchased a property. I wasn't about to give in to kickbacks.

The Methodist Church was getting ready for demolition. Parishioners were examining the inside of the church looking for something they had missed. Almost every day at least one house was moved.

Rumors of a new town springing up out on the Fergus farm grew stronger.

"Aren't you concerned about the Fergus's?" I asked Savoy as he was coming out of the cafe, a toothpick in his mouth.

"Nah, Clifford dropped by the jail the other day. Said they were all right. Didn't understand what all the fuss was about."

"What were they doing with McDermott and Graves?"

"Goin along for the ride, they said. Just like McDermott told us."

"Well, are they building a new town on their farm or not?"

"Wouldn't commit to that, either."

"How come you're taking all your meals at the cafe, now?"

"Birdie quit. She's working for the judge down at Marshfield now. I let Billie out. Joel Dean couldn't come up with anything to charge him with. So when you goin to buy the jail house? It's ready."

"I'm not. I've got every place in town except the banks and the county property and a few houses. There's ten places so far that won't deal with me, so guess they'll go under the water."

Savoy stopped dead in his tracks. he took the toothpick out of his mouth and pointed it at me.

"Almost forgot. Got some news from Juanita that ought to make your job a lot easier."

"Comes from Juanita it must be official," I said. "What is it?"

"They just finished the dam. First car went across yesterday. She says they're closing the gates next week."

Hayden Joost had a terrible stomach ache when he got back from Sedalia. Eldon said Hayden had been complaining for two days before they decided to leave and come on home. Eldon drove the automobile from Versailles and had no trouble until they came to the swinging bridge over the Osage where he almost crowded two cars off the bridge and came close to going off themselves.

When they got home, Hayden went right to bed and asked Eleanor to fix him up with a tonic out of some unknown herbs they had gotten from an old man who lived in the woods close to their farm.

"Maybe you caught something from that whore up there," Eleanor said. Hayden roared at her, but he was too weak to get out of bed.

Eleanor didn't think it was a good time to tell him about how she let Meren go live with Yawley Earnhardt's daughter. She'd been dreading the time when he would ask where the girl was and she would have to say. Eldon didn't even miss

Meren, but he did ask about Grant.

"He's gone. Same as the two of you, only he ain't come back yet," she said. Hayden had grumbled some before going back to sleep. Whatever was in the herbs the old man had gathered, they made a person sleep.

After a week in bed, Hayden began to regain his strength. The chores around the farm had gone unattended except for what Eleanor did. Eldon spent most of his days and even some of his nights over at the Lewis farm where the family contained three girls from thirteen to seventeen. Eldon had let the work slip as he seemed to have gained a lot of interest in the female sex since his trip to Sedalia with his father.

When Hayden got out of the house and saw what shape the farm was in, he went into a rage about where the hell Grant had gotten off to and when the hell was he coming back. And when he did, Hayden just might take a whip to him. It never occurred to him, apparently that Eldon could have picked up the slack. He'd always coddled the younger of the two boys.

Several days later he discovered that Meren was also gone. Eleanor had covered for Grant a lot of times when she shouldn't have, but Hayden could be cruel when Grant wasn't doing what Hayden thought he should be doing.

"Damn funny both of them gone all the time I was gone. That girl's always around here. You sure something hasn't happened to her?" he asked Eleanor at the breakfast table.

"She's in town," Eleanor told him. "She's staying at a safe place there."

"What do you mean a safe place? What place you talkin about?"

"I can't say," she said, her words quietly spoken, but firmly, too.

"What the hell you mean you can't say. By God you better say."

"I couldn't protect her any more."

His face turned liver color and his whiskers, unshaven during his illness, looked grizzled over the strange looking skin. His eyes, screwed down to marble size and black as midnight, stared a hole through her. She knew she was on dangerous ground with him, but she had been there ten million times before and she was suddenly tired of it.

"Grant got after her down at the creek when she had her clothes off taking a bath. She shot him in the side. Doc Hardesty sewed him up."

"By God," Hayden said.

"You mean she was necked down at the creek?" Eldon asked, suddenly interested in their conversation.

"You a man now?" Eleanor asked him. She was disgusted with the whole lot of them. "You think you laid with some whores up there you're a man now?"

She brushed some hair back behind her ear that had escaped from the knot at the back of her head. God, what had she become. Talking with Doyle Savoy the last time he was out here made her realize how she had messed up her life. How stupid of her to try and continue her whoring after Doyle had gotten her out of the business and had been good to her, except for the money part. She guessed that was why she did it, because he had given away her whoring money. She had settled for Hayden Joost after Doyle went to prison and she thought he would be twenty years getting back to her. But she had suffered because of her mistakes. It hadn't been so bad here, except for what had happened to Meren and occasionally when Hayden got drunk or got in a rage over something and slapped her around some. She couldn't leave him because of Meren, whom she had no idea what to do with.

"Leave him alone, woman. You're a fine one to be talking down whores," Hayden said. "Grant ain't dead is he? She didn't kill him did she?"

"Not yet, but something was bound to happen. You knew that. You knew the day would come nobody could protect her from him."

He roared angrily and shoved the table from him, spilling contents from some of the bowls. He stood up from his chair and his powerful chest filled with air.

"Hell you say. The day ain't come yet and it never will that I can't take that pup down a peg or two. I told him to leave the girl alone and by God I meant it. I'll take that rawhide strap to him until his hide is bleedin all over. He better damn well listen when I talk to him."

"Grant said he ain't takin the strap from you no more, Pa," Eldon said.

"We'll see. We'll see," Hayden said. He put both hands on his hips and stared hard at Eleanor "Where is he, damn him."

"I don't know," Eleanor said. "Savoy came out here to talk with the girl. Grant claims she's the one shot that Happy Meens. Savoy said he would talk with the prosecutor and the judge. He might have to arrest her."

"Hell he will," Hayden shouted. "Ain't no Joost bein arrested. Not as long as I'm drawin a breath. Where's the girl?"

"How'm I going to protect her if ever body knows where she is?" Eleanor said, still using her firm voice. "She's safe and she ain't in jail. That's all I'm sayin."

"That's not all you're sayin either, by God."

Hayden slung the chair he was sitting in up against the cupboard where she kept her flour in a bin and her dishes over the counter behind glass doors. A piece of furniture she had insisted Hayden buy her before she would marry him. The glass in one of the doors shattered and fell to the floor, but Eleanor had the feeling that more than the glass had broken in the house. She was relieved at last that it had.

"Get up out of that chair and by God you tell me what I want to know or I'll knock you clear up against that wall."

"Savoy said if you was to beat on me again, I was to tell him," she said, using her calm voice.

Eldon stood up at the other end of the table.

"Savoy? What's he got to do with this anyway. He ain't in this family and he better not be buttin in to our business."

"It's about time you knew," she said. "I was married to Savoy before I married you. He went to prison so I divorced him."

"What the hell you sayin?" Hayden was completely perplexed. "Married? To Savoy? By God, I don't understand you, woman. He come around here and I'll kill him."

"No you won't," she said and began to pick up the articles that had spilled off the table.

"Woman, I ain't beat on you for some time, you know that. But, by God. Married. To Savoy. By God . . ."

He started toward Eleanor with his fists doubled. Eldon stepped in front of him.

"No, you ain't going to hit Ma. There's been too much hitting around here, Pa. You hitting Grant. Grant hitting me. Grant hitting Meren. You hitting Ma. You hitting everything you don't like. That ain't no way to live, Pa. That ain't how the Lewis's live. Stop hitting people."

Hayden whipped around and pointed a finger at Eldon.

"By God, boy, I can't believe you're turnin on me like this. All I've done for you and you turn against your own Pa. I ain't never took the strap to you. Looks like I mighta made a mistake."

"Like Eldon says, Hayden. You're all through hitting people," Eleanor said.

Hayden's rage was momentarily stifled by his confusion. "What's goin on here?" he demanded. Eleanor and Eldon stood silent, their defiance written on their faces as easy to read as storm clouds.

"Eleanor?" Hayden calling her name for the first time since

she could remember. "Eleanor, what is it. What am I supposed to have done. I ain't hit you for months. And the boy there, I never laid a strap on him. Just why you treatin me like this?"

"It's what you done over the years, Hayden. Treated us all like we was pups and you owned us," she told him. "People get tired of it after awhile."

"I never used the strap on the girl, even when she needed it."

"You know what you did to her. So do I. And I hate myself for allowin it. I shoulda paid more attention, but I didn't have no courage. You said she was tetched in the head and she heard you say that time after time. Remember when you asked me to marry you so I could keep your house and help you care for your son. And I did. And I never got more than that from you. Never."

Hayden kept rubbing his hand on his whiskered chin, his eyes going from total bewilderment to hatred and finally resignation. He sat back down in his chair, his stare against the far wall, his hands dragging between his knees. He looked old and weak and disoriented. The sickness had taken a harsh toll on his body and now, Eleanor and Eldon had siphoned off the sharp edge of his mind.

For a moment, just a moment, Eleanor felt pity for him. She had lain beside him every night for over twenty years, though, truth be told, she had felt resentment half those nights. She had succumbed to his animal instincts and sexual appetite half those nights, too. Still, she felt degraded for what she was doing to him.

Eldon looked at her with blame, forgetting his part in the conflict. He showed how very much he wanted not to be there. He scooped up his straw hat, slammed it on his head and walked out of the kitchen to the outdoors. Eleanor was all alone with Hayden and she was numb with apprehension.

Without thinking of what she was doing, she walked over

to him and laid a hand on his shoulder. He never noticed. She
went to bed early that night. Eldon was out of the house and
Hayden still sat in his chair, his mind and his eyes transfixed
on a spot on the opposite wall.

Toward morning Eleanor heard loud voices in the kitchen
and raised up from bed to listen. One voice was Grant's and
she heard the sharp bark of Hayden's reply. She covered her
ears with both hands and lay back in the bed, isolating herself
from the dispute raging in the other part of the house.

The sharp crack of a rifle shot penetrated her muffled ears
and fear grabbed every nerve. Her body began to shake.

Minutes passed before she drove herself to walk to the
doorway leading into the kitchen. A small lamp glowed in the
center of the table. Hayden sat slumped in his chair, a red
splotch covering most of his shirt front.

Grant, one hand on the door leading outside and the other
holding onto the rifle, looked at Eleanor with wild eyes.

"Damn him," he said. "God damn him. He won't never
raise his hand to me again. He won't never lay his strap on me.
And I'll be the one to deal with her when I find her, not him.
He's in hell where he belongs."

Grant walked out, leaving the door open behind him.

For the first time since she had married Hayden, she felt
free. She went back to bed and slept peacefully.

That was the way Eleanor Joost told it to Sheriff Doyle
Savoy the next day in his office in the jail house. Then she
hung her head and cried, proving herself wrong once again
when she thought she had no tears left.

EIGHT

Joe Collie wasn't at the breakfast table on that Wednesday morning and I might have thought that strange if I'd thought about it. He couldn't have been eating at the jail as there wasn't a breakfast being served there anymore. We had a good breakfast, though, even without Joe.

Rose said she was using up her stored food because she didn't want to have to move it. She'd gotten the house in Lebanon and was taking Jane McGann, Oma Thornbush and Uncle Billy Jack with her. Though Uncle Billy Jack insisted he wasn't going to be a burden to anyone.

Leah, in a red dress with blue and white trim and sitting across the table from me beside Uncle Billy Jack, eyed me like a hawk eyes a sparrow and said, "Uncle Billy Jack, don't you own some property that Smith could buy from you and you wouldn't have to be a burden to anyone?"

"Sold the last of my property ten years ago," he said without looking at her. "And I'm afraid the money from that has long ago petered out."

"Well, now, Jake Martin down at the Ford garage says the car our company bought from him was the one he loaned you a couple weeks ago. Said you wanted to go look at some property."

Uncle Billy Jack gave her a sharp look. "I just told him that. Just wanted to look at places you folks going to flood out."

"Blame old Smith there," Leah said, her voice and the look on her face taunting me. "He's in with that electric company, lot, stock and barrel."

"What about you?" Uncle Billy Jack said. "Farmers outside town say you're offering them low dollar for their farms, then threatening to flood them out if they don't take it. That was the way Happy Meens did business."

"You saying somebody might shoot me?"

"Just saying it, that's all."

"Well, I got a budget to keep, Uncle Billy Jack. Smith there, I don't guess he's got a budget. He's paying high dollar for everyone's property. Why, I hear he even paid a couple of twelve year old boys two hundred dollars just to move some boards."

Everybody looked at me.

"The Bailey twins," I said. They all nodded.

"Seems a Christian thing to do," Uncle Billy Jack said.

"Well, it is. It is. Only thing wrong is it wasn't Smith's money he gave away in a charitable cause. It was company money. So, what he gives away, I have to cut from the prices I give legitimate property owners to stay on budget."

"Why don't we talk about this down at the office, Leah," I suggested.

"The office," she said, getting really wound up now. She was leaning over the table with her chin stuck out. "Last two times I try to find you at the office I'm told you're at the sheriff's office doing what I have no idea because he doesn't own anything the company wants. The other time Mary says you went over to see the poor little rich girl and the poor little retarded thing you dragged in to let the little rich girl clean up and make a pet out of."

"Meren's not retarded," I said, my cheeks burning from Leah's onslaught.

"She doesn't even know how to talk," Leah said, her scathing tongue lashing across the table at me.

"Leave the girl alone," Uncle Billy Jack said.

"Oh," Leah said, looking around the table, sizing the situation up. "Okay. Listen, everybody, here's some good news. Cars are driving across the dam now. It's finished. Tomorrow or the next day they're closing the gates. Then you'll see the water coming into town in a few weeks."

Lonnie said, "You know what, Leah? You really know how to liven up the day. I think I'll go out and kill me a half-dozen snakes this morning."

"Well, there you are," she said. "Snakes need killing."

Volly said, "Exactly my sentiments."

Breakfast had just ended when Joe Collie showed up. The sound of large engines and heavy machinery came through the walls from the street.

"There comes Joe," Lonnie said. "Just like he said he was goin to do."

"Don't blame Joe," Volly said. "Man's got a job to do. Just like the rest of us."

"What in the world is he moving?" I asked.

"Looks like a couple of those big tractors without wheels on them," Lonnie said. "They been using them over at the dam site."

"What's he need with tractors?" I asked.

"Joe says the tractor company calls them bulldozers."

"Doesn't sound right," Uncle Billy Jack said. "It's bad enough tearing people's houses down without using something called a bulldozer."

"Well, it's startin today."

"What's starting?"

Volly stood up from the table and set his rose colored coffee cup on the tablecloth. His face looked like he was announcing a hanging.

"Joe's starting to level the town and burn it down," he said. "Starting down in Old Town."

Old Town was several hundred yards from the courthouse toward the river. I'd bought up all the property down there including a half-dozen houses on the verge of collapse. One big warehouse that hadn't been utilized for twenty years, had a sagging roof and a foundation that had given up years ago, belonged to the German who wouldn't sell his house. He thought the warehouse had appreciated from the fifteen hundred dollars it had cost him to construct in the 1890's. I offered three hundred dollars. Before the day ended it would be worth nothing.

I left the table as quickly as I could and went out into the chill of an early May morning—Uncle Billy Jack called it a blackberry winter—carrying only the hat Estelle had picked out for me and that I hardly ever wore. Joe Collie had stopped the trucks with the flatbed trailers on behind and loaded with large crawling type tractors painted green and with HOLT printed on them. They had wide, destructive-looking blades mounted on the front. As he started the tractors and backed them off the flatbed trailers, a crowd formed, in a line at first, then clustered as people began to talk.

Joe and another driver drove the tractors down a narrow street all the way to the river where one good wharf still stood alongside three so run-down they would have been unsafe to walk on. I had paid the owner a hundred dollars apiece for them and three hundred for the useable one. Joe's tractor nosed into the standing wharf while the other driver lowered his blade and started across the lawn toward a small house. The sound of splintering boards reached the crowd and as the house collapsed, a hush settled over the gathering of Linn Creek citizens. A rumble began, rose in volume and as Joe leveled the wharf with the boards buckling, ends rising and posts splintering, the crowd became angry and the men began to shout at Joe and the other driver.

Two small boys picked up some quarter-sized rocks and hurled them like baseball pitchers at the ugly bulldozers. Larger boys joined in and a hail of rocks flew at the bulldozers. One struck Joe on the shoulder and he stopped the tractor.

"Y'all better stop throwin them rocks or I'll have to get the sheriff," he yelled, then ducked as another fusillade of rocks zeroed in on his location and he ran for cover on the other side of the tractor.

"Frank, Ezra, better stop them boys from rockin us or I'll get Doyle after them," Joe called from the far side of the tractor.

"Go to hell, Joe, you traitor," a tall man with a peaked hat yelled.

The Dutchman who ran the town barbershop shouted, "Joe, you and Earl, don't come to my shop no more for a haircut. By God, I scalp you."

The crowd roared in laughter and they all began taunting Joe and the other driver, Earl, with the women joining in. The crowd grew and the boys gathered to one side where the rocks were more plentiful. The older boys, high school age, were getting their accuracy refined and the pinging of rocks hitting metal became a chorus of sound.

Earl called out. "Stop your damn rock throwing. I'm leaving. Joe, I ain't staying around here and be killed by a rock."

Joe, roaring like a bear in the woods, yelled, "I'm warnin you people. I'm havin the sheriff arrest ever damn one of you. Women and them damn boys, too."

Earl made a dash for the truck and took two rocks on his legs and one on the hand he held over his head. He jumped and yelped, jerked the door open and dove inside the truck. A barrage of rocks clattered off the side of the truck.

Joe yelled as loud as he could, "Earl, you damn coward, get your ass back here," but Earl was finished with the new thing called a bulldozer. The engine on the truck started and the sound of grinding gears rose over the crowd's shouting. The truck swung around and Earl headed across a lot where an old log cabin stood, half it's roof already collapsed inside. The women in the throng started screaming as Earl and the truck bore down on the log cabin. Through the windshield I saw the fiendish look on Earl's face and knew for sure the cabin was a goner.

The logs flew in the air and the splintering sound of wood and the crunching sound of metal was loud enough it would have drowned out thunder. Earl's truck didn't even slow down. Gathering speed, he swung around and aimed straight for the crowd of people. They scattered like a flock of chickens running from a hawk. Earl had a murderous look in his eyes and I thought, My God, he's going to kill somebody. The truck came to a sudden stop and the trailer, trying to pass the truck which had one front wheel down in an old well casing, came flying over the cab of the truck and landed on top of the bulldozer, only feet short of the women, running with their dresses and bonnets flying in the wind, their screeching sending chills up my spine.

Leah appeared beside me and when I turned to her, she wore a smile that covered half her face.

"And they said in Jefferson City nothing ever happens in a small town."

"Miss German?"

She was a small woman compared to Leah and Meren. She appeared to have twice the hair of any other woman in Linn Creek as it engulfed a small face with large brown eyes set too close together. Her lips were so bright red I honestly thought at first they were bleeding. Her smile was more patronizing than sincere.

"You must be that Beauchamp fellow everyone in town's talking about," she said, and offered her hand. "I'm Nita German. I reckon I'm the last person in town to meet you. I do own property, you know."

"Yes, ma'am. That's why I'm here."

"Oh, none of that ma'am stuff now, you hear. We don't say that in little ol' Linn Creek. They say you're from St. Louis and your manners show it. I like a man with gentleman-like manners. It appeals to me."

"Thank you, Nita."

"I'll bet you just can't wait to get out of Linn Creek, we're so small and so provincial."

"Actually, I've come to like Linn Creek very much. It's a nice little town and I like most of the people I've met here. It's too bad the electric company has to tear it down."

"Well, it certainly makes it difficult for a business person, I do say that."

"What business are you in, Nita?"

Her gasp was audible and genuine. "Why, I just assumed you knew, Mister Beauchamp. I mean, being a man and all and moving around town the way you do. But, you know, I'm going to be real honest with you. I do favors for men."

I could feel my face flushing and my mind raced for words to say. I remembered all the talk at the cafe about the German woman, but just now connected that to a name instead of a nationality.

"I see," was the best I could come up with.

She pushed the huge gathering of hair on the right side of her head back and I saw a flash of gold and diamonds hanging off her ear on that side.

"Well, I guess, we're ready to do business," she said, and angled her head to one side and showed me all of her teeth.

The whiteness of them contrasted with the layers of makeup on her face and I thought of Eleanor Joost and I was struck with pity for this woman.

"What would be your assessment of what your property is worth?" I asked.

"Why don't you come inside and have a sip of white wine with me and let's talk business."

I didn't see a way out unless I was rude and I'd had few lessons in that except what Langston Beauchamp had displayed and which I had always found so distasteful.

The inside of her house was all glitter and glamour. Everything in sight was the biggest, brightest and most expensive piece of that pedigree I had ever seen. The gaudy surroundings put me ill at ease, but I accepted a seat on a bright red, mohair camelback sofa. Tiffany lamps hung about, backed up by gold and silver embossed wallcoverings, large paintings that were cubist in art form, bold in color and sexual in content. Another painting that was clearly of a couple copulating, though abstract in form, hung above a short bar with lavish crystal pieces sitting in a silver tray. A lot of money had been invested in this room.

Nita German began pouring a clear liquid into one of the crystal goblets, matched it with another full one, then brought one to the sofa, handed it to me, and seated herself beside me, our hips touching. The heat of her body was scorching and I could feel the heat inside my own body rising.

"This is the finest French wine you can buy," she said. "It came from the Brittany region and it sells for fifteen dollars a bottle in Jefferson City."

She clinked her glass against mine and put it to her lips. I followed her lead. I remembered the taste from the bottles Langston always kept in the house and poured small portions weakened with water in my glass at mealtimes against my mother's objections.

"A chablis, I believe," I said. "Perhaps from the vineyards in Issodun. Very good selection."

"Oh, my goodness, you know about French wine," she said. "I've never met another gentleman in this part of the state who knew an excellent French wine like this from a jar of vinegar. I'm so impressed."

"Beauchamp," I said, using my father's pronouncement. "It's French."

"Oh, my goodness," she said again, sounding like a high school girl thrilled by her prom corsage. "I've never known a real Frenchman."

"I broke a record I guess"

"I've heard Frenchmen are great lovers." The eyelids with the enhanced lashes and with added color that fell into every crease under the eyes, fluttered and flashed and her body was suddenly closer to mine, burning with a fever from us both that was steamy.

"How's the Vin de Chateau Chirac?" she asked and I, holding the goblet by the stem as I was taught at the age of three, sipped at the wine, saw that she had devoured the whole glass she held, her chubby fingers wrapped firmly around the globe, so I tried to catch up, sipping the French way, and my glass was quickly full to the rim again—giving me pause to consider that Nita German was not first rate on wine etiquette—and the glasses were clinked again and empty again and filled again and emptied so quickly my head started feeling out of focus and the bottle was in her hand and we were both standing and I closed my eyes and opened them and she was undressed except for a red chemise with garter straps attached and all that whiteness of her body sent me to the wine again until I lost track of time and glasses of wine and even where I was.

At some point she asked if I was having a good time.

"*Oui, oui,*" I said, and laughed so loudly it hurt my ears.

"I better go," I think I said, but she was all of a sudden undressing me and I watched as if it was a motion picture filling the screen and I started laughing and spilling the wine and pretty soon she was lying on the sofa holding the chemise in her hand twirling it around and around and I was laughing, then pawing at her and on top of her and while I was thinking about another glass of wine, it was all over and she had me encircled with her short, stubby arms and I was out of breath, sick at my stomach and a low, soft groan turned out to be me.

"I was thinking the house was worth ten thousand dollars," she said, her voice silky smooth and coming from a long distance away followed by an echo.

I was sitting on the hump of the camelback sofa with my feet on her bare stomach, holding the bottle of French wine in one hand. She was looking up at me with three eyes at first, then only two, and I said, "Sounds about right to me," because at the time I could not recall any previous selling prices with which I could compare her figure.

"Would you pour us some more wine," was the last thing I remember her saying.

I like to think I declined.

Joe Collie worked long into the night getting his truck and flatbed trailer put back on their wheels and running again. One of the bulldozers was ruined. He had to call in some of the timber cutters he had working for him as Earl lit out for Ava where he came from, saying, "Linn Creek can go to hell, ever one of 'em," as he drove out of town.

Rose took supper to Joe and his workers and they ate by the headlights from the trucks. I was so mortified by my episode with Nita German I went straight to my room and fell asleep, sheepish and somewhat ashamed of what had occurred that afternoon.

Langston Beauchamp is in my dreams again.

There is no hole in his head this time. He sits slumped over in his brown chair, a wine bottle hanging from his hand, his head slumped on his chest. Mother shows up. She has a long-barreled dueling pistol with gold inlay in a solid walnut stock in her hand.

"You are a French son of a bitch," she says. "Damn you to hell."

A young boy is standing in the corner watching. I try to get him to yell, but he won't. His eyes are large and his mouth is open, but no words come out.

"Where is the slut? I'll kill her, too," Mother says.

But Langston Beauchamp isn't sleeping, he is laughing. He brings his head up and there is wine spilled all over his face and down on his ruffled front white shirt and gold lame vest.

"Madame, you could not hit a French whore in the middle of Pigale," he says. His laughter bounces off all the walls and blasts in the ears of the young boy so that he claps his hands over them.

She fires the dueling pistol and a lamp shatters a dozen feet away from Langston. He throws back his head and roars, his laughter rumbling until it turns into a high pitch shriek.

"You, Madame, are a disgrace to the human race. Look at you, behaving like a charwoman in a house of ill repute. Have you no pride?"

She brings the dueling pistol in line with him again and pulls the trigger over and over. The pistol discharges each time, but no bullets come out.

"You are such a stupid person," Langston Beauchamp says. "A dueling pistol only carries one bullet. Everyone knows that."

The boy begins to screech, but neither of them pay him any mind.

She looks at the pistol and tosses it lightly to him. He

catches it, sticks it in his belt and says, "Enough foolishness, now. Off to bed, both of you."

The woman takes the boy by the hand and leads him away.

"Good night," she says, and fades from the dream.

Morning brought a different day. Joe Collie dominated the conversation, expounding on his expenses to get his truck and flatbed trailer operating again and the lost time he had to make up. Not to mention the wrecked bulldozer.

"I've got a bunch of houses to level," he said.

Uncle Billy Jack said, "You ought to be ashamed of yourself."

"I got a job to do, Uncle Billy Jack. You ought to know that."

Leah asked, "How long before the town is leveled?"

"I get some help from the sheriff, won't take me a week," Joe Collie said. "I'm not goin out there with ever body in town heavin a rock at me."

"Sheriff's got two murders to solve," I said. "Hire you some bodyguards, Joe."

"Smith, how many properties you have left to buy out?" Leah asked, looking across at me with a smirk on her face. How could she know about Nita German?

"About a dozen. Lonnie, pass over that platter of bacon you don't mind."

"How many did you buy up yesterday, Smith?" Lonnie had the same smirk on his face as he handed the bacon around the table.

Oma Thornbush, next to me on the right, held the bacon in front of her and said, "How much did you end up paying the German tart?"

Trying not to choke, I turned to look at Oma.

"What? Tart? Oma, you talking about Nita German? She's a . . .you calling her a . . ."

"Whore," Leah said. "That's what I hear she is. Come on, Smith. How much did the electric company pay for your afternoon of *amore?*"

"Look," I said, my face feeling like I had a fire just under the skin, "She owns property. I'm buying property. I had to go see her."

"Took two hours, I hear," Lonnie said. "Lew Schneider said you bought him out in ten minutes."

"You got a dozen houses to buy and you buy one every other day, it'll be a month before you're done, Smith," Volly said. "Isn't that when the water's due to be in the streets?"

Oma passed the bacon and while I loaded some on my plate—though by now my appetite had fled along with any good humor—I tried to be calm and not show any of the guilt I was beginning to feel about yesterday's encounter with Nita.

"Ask Leah," I said, shoving my mouth full of bacon. "She's the dam expert," the words coming out garbled around the bacon.

Leah smelled blood of the wounded and went for the kill. "How much did your two hours with the town prostitute cost us?"

I chewed the bacon slowly, staring in Leah's eyes and I saw there corroboration of the parable about a woman scorned.

She hated me.

Everyone at the table had stopped eating, waiting for my answer. I was the only one chewing food. I drank coffee and felt the wad of bacon swelling up in my throat.

"She's entitled to some privacy," I said.

Leah grinned a wicked grin. "Privacy is something a person like her never wants. It would kill her business."

Comprehension of what was transpiring between me and

Leah passed around the table at gossip speed. Others abruptly resumed picking at their food and Rose got up from her chair and asked if anyone wanted more jam for their biscuits and Lonnie and Volly both put in an order for more. Oma talked with Jane McGann next to her in a low voice about the weather.

Leah's smile faded. She laid her napkin by her plate and excused herself. I watched her walk away from the table and regret for the state of our relationship swelled up inside of me.

Uncle Billy Jack said, "Six farms won't take her low price and are going to be flooded out, broke with no place to go."

Joe Collie said, "I just got a list of houses to knock down and burn next week and those six farms is on my list."

I said, "Who gave you the list, Joe?"

"Elmer Byron. He's in town now."

I was on the way to the Land Acquisition office when Sheriff Doyle Savoy stopped me.

"I drove over to Westphalia to assist with the investigation into Ruby Elam's accident yesterday," he said. "That's how come I missed Joe and Earl gettin stoned."

"He's going to be asking for your help today. Earl quit on him and he's in a bind with all the work he's got ahead of him. If he stopped using the bulldozers it wouldn't be so bad."

"How's he think me and Noah's going to stop a whole town from throwing rocks at him? Besides, I got other fish to fry. Looks like, near as the sheriff over in Maries County can figure it, a black vehicle ran into the left front fender of Ruby's car before it went over that bluff and crashed into the river."

"That was a black car tried to run me off the road," I said. "Doesn't Graves drive that black Packard around?"

Savoy was staring down Main Street. I followed his eyes, but the street was deserted.

"Smell that?" he asked.

"Uh, exactly what?"

"Ever fruit tree in town is in bloom. Smells like this ever year about this time. For about two weeks that smell is all over town. Then the blossoms fall off and the fruit sets on the tree. Best smell of the year except when people start smoking their hams in the fall."

"Joe's crew will start cutting those trees down before long, won't they."

"Yeah," he said. "Damn shame."

I had been too preoccupied with Leah and Nita German to pick up on the smell of the blossoming fruit trees. I was aware of what Savoy meant as the aroma hit me and I wondered how difficult it was for the people who owned those trees to pack up and leave them to the tree cutters.

I started on for the office when Savoy called to me. I turned back as he said, "This Elmer Byron, he's your boss isn't he?"

"Yeah. He heads up the Land Acquisition company."

"He's in town."

"I heard that."

"He's put in a claim for that twenty thousand dollars Ruby Elam had in his car."

"Elmer? How? Why?"

"He says him and Ruby had a business deal working."

"So, who decides about who gets the money?"

"I reckon the sheriff in Maries County."

"What's he say about it?"

"I think he's waitin to see how much of that twenty thousand dollars Elmer Byron is willin to part with."

Estelle Earnhardt carried a white linen umbrella with lace around the edges. I was thinking about the fruit trees in Linn

Creek when I saw her coming down the walk leading to her store. My first thought was Joe Collie might cut down every tree in town and tear down every building, but she was one object of beauty Joe couldn't destroy.

"Why, Mister Smith Beauchamp, good morning to you. My, you sure are getting around early. I expect you have a good deal of business to conduct today."

"Yes, I expect I do," I said. She wore that coquettish look on her face I had grown accustomed to seeing. "I'm enjoying the sights of beauty in town this morning."

"Well, a lady could take that as a compliment. I hear you were enjoying the sights of beauty in town yesterday, also."

"Are there no secrets in this town?"

"You're the most talked about man in town, Smith. Just everybody is watching what you do."

"I'll keep that in mind."

"Spending two hours with Miss Nita German makes me wonder if I was smart in turning my property over to Joel Dean Gregory instead of doing my own negotiating."

"We could re-open the negotiations if you like."

Her face, her soft, beautiful face lit up. "Do you play Mah Jongg, Smith?"

"As a matter of fact, I'm quite good at it."

"Good. Be at my house at seven tonight. I'm teaching Meren how to play. You can help."

Noah found me at a house owned by a family with eight kids. The father wanted four thousand dollars for his property which was about fifteen hundred dollars more than equivalent houses that I had purchased. Still, he had more mouths to feed.

The house had nearly a dozen fruit trees in the back, all in bloom. The pink peach blossoms caught the overhead sun and looked as if they were floating free in the air, apart from the leafing branches of the tree. The fragrance of the blooms reached me and poured persuasion into my head. Maybe the house was worth four thousand.

"Nice trees," I said. "Shame you won't get to enjoy the fruit this year."

"Can't take 'em with me," he said. "Have to start all over."

"Okay Mister Morrison," I told him. I shot a quick look at Noah who was waving for me to come over to the sheriff's car he was driving. "I'll come back. I'll bring a check."

"I gotta know about the movin," Morrison said. "And I got a possible buy on a place where the new town is goin in."

"You mean the new Linn Creek." I said. "Lane Lindall at the Missouri Bank is handling that."

"No, I mean the new town. I don't even think they've got a name for it yet."

"Well, last I heard, they were calling it Linn Creek," I told him.

"That town's just up the creek a ways. Where we used to call Easterville. I'm talkin about that one down the highway toward Lebanon. Where the Fergus farm is located."

I couldn't recall if I answered Morrison or not. The shock of what he said took some time to register. When I got to the sheriff's black Chevrolet, Noah leaned out the window and said, "Get in. Sheriff wants you over to the courthouse."

McDermott was there. And Graves. Standing in front of the podium where the three judges sat. Elmer was in the middle of the gathering with Leah. Joel Dean and Savoy stood aside, not participating in the camaraderie the others were enjoying. Leah glanced my way, but pretended she didn't see me. She did nudge Elmer in the ribs with her elbow and nod in my direction. Elmer pasted on a phony smile and offered his hand.

"Smith, glad you could come. Some great news taking place here."

"Where's Vincent?" I asked, looking around as I shook his hand. J.W. Vincent was the editor of the Linn Creek *Reveille* and an avid opponent of the dam. Elmer didn't know who I was talking about.

"The county's decided on a new county seat," Elmer said, sounding exactly as if he was the one who had made the decision. "The highway department has determined the most logical location for the two highways to meet and the judges have agreed that it is an ideal location for a new town. And the electric company is building a new courthouse there."

I looked straight at McDermott who was still looking flushed with victory, smiling and glad-handing the judges. "I hear it's going to be on the Fergus farm."

"We reached agreement with the Fergus's just yesterday," McDermott said. I really wanted to smash his lying tongue right through his lying teeth.

"Too bad you couldn't have reached agreement the day you kidnapped them and took them into Jefferson City," I said.

McDermott looked at me as if I wore a dunce cap. "They're lucky people," he said.

"The new town's going to be laid out like spokes on a wheel," Elmer said. "That idea came from the electric company. The courthouse will be right in the center of the wheel. Along with the cafe and some of the better houses in town. It's going to be the most modern town in America."

"Too bad Ruby Elam couldn't be with us," I said. "Instead of at the bottom of the Maries River." I looked at Graves when I said it. The smug bastard leaned against Judge Cargrove's podium, a smirk on his face.

"Don't you drive that big black Packard outside, Graves?"

Savoy asked. "The one I noticed had a wrinkle in the right front fender with some green paint rubbed off on it. Ruby Elam drove a green Nash."

"Some drunk run into me in Jeff," Graves said, the smirk still lingering on his fat lips.

"I guess the police up there will have an accident report," Savoy said.

"Didn't call 'em," Graves said, smiling at Savoy now. "Drunk was broke, wouldn't have done any good. So I got my money's worth another way."

"What're you trying to say, here, Sheriff?" McDermott asked. He shouldered himself in front of Graves. "Is this some kind of accusation?"

"I'm not tryin to say it," Savoy told him, his eyes cold, but his voice low and hard, like steel against rusty iron. "I said it. I think Graves had something to do with Ruby's accident."

McDermott whirled around to look at Judge Cargrove. "Why, that's slanderous, judge. I suggest you tell your sheriff he and the county's headed for a lawsuit if he continues his false charges."

Judge Cargrove drew himself up to his full six foot five, and leveled his steel gray eyes on Savoy and with all the authority he could muster, he said, "Sheriff, I believe you owe Mister McDermott and Mister Graves here an apology. And I suggest you hereinafter refrain from making baseless charges against honest, state employees."

Savoy's eyes sliced over to McDermott. "I guess I am sorry, Judge. I'm sorry I didn't arrest these two when they were down here at the Fergus farm. And I'm sorry, Judge, that you ever entered into any kind of agreement with people who kidnap and steal. This county deserves better."

Judge Cargrove suddenly had the appearance of a man with apoplexy. "Sheriff, I order you to stop accusing these men of any wrong doing. And I order you . . ."

"Judge," Savoy said, "you better brush up on the state constitution you took an oath to uphold. You don't have the authority to order me to do anything. And, if I remember right, I got a couple hundred more votes than you did last election."

Graves pushed McDermott aside and advanced on Savoy. His face was the color of a bandana, and the white splotches now showed like light bulbs.

"Let me handle this," he said.

He came right up to Savoy, threatening in manner. The sheriff pulled his revolver from the holster on his left side and in a blinding-fast move, clubbed Graves on the neck just below his ear. Graves' knees buckled, he let out a feeble groan, extended his hands and fell forward where Savoy and Joel Dean both stepped aside and let the body fall between them. The room became quiet as a tomb.

"How about you, McDermott?" Savoy asked.

McDermott's face was turning from white to red. His lips pursed and relaxed, pursed and relaxed, but no sound came from them. Judge Cargrove was the first to find his voice.

"My God, Savoy, you've assaulted the man. You're disgracing this county. Joel Dean, you're the prosecutor of this county. You witnessed that savage beating our sheriff gave that state employee."

Joel Dean, sounding very casual, said, "What I saw Judge was that man charging the sheriff in a threatening manner. What did you see Mister Beauchamp?"

"That's the way it looked to me."

Elmer stepped away from the judges' podium, stuck both elbows out like batwings and stared with lidded eyes right at me.

"Smith, what are you trying to do here? We've settled with the county, the judges have ordered Joel Dean to drop all the suits against the electric company and the ones in state and federal court, the electric company has agreed to construct a new courthouse and the new town is located strategically at the crossroads of two new highways, probably paved, and you and this . . .this Wyatt Earp sheriff are on the verge of splitting this agreement right in two."

"You're not worried about who murdered Happy Meens and Ruby Elam, Elmer?"

"Now listen, Smith . . ."

"No, you listen, Elmer. Two men are dead, the paint off this man's car is on Ruby Elam's car that was dragged out of the river and the two of them came out to the Fergus farm and took them to Jefferson City just so Ruby couldn't buy the land."

Graves was sitting up, a vacant look on his face, a hand to his neck and a moan escaping his lips.

McDermott said, "Are you arresting this man, sheriff?"

"I would, but we're vacating the jail house. I'm putting him on notice, if the paint on his fender matches that on Ruby Elam's car, I'll take him up to the jail in Maries County."

Elmer said, "Smith, I'll be wanting to see you in the office after this is over. We need to go over your records."

I looked at Leah. She wore a worried expression.

"Tomorrow, Elmer," I said. "First thing in the morning."

Estelle, in a pale, lilac chiffon dress with her hair swept up and a pearl-studded band around her head, threw the dice onto the table and squealed with delight.

"I'm East Wind first," she said. "I rolled a twelve."

Meren sat next to Estelle, across from me. She was different, a Meren I didn't know. Her hair was cut shorter and curled around her ears. She had a long, angular face with sharp cheek bones like Eleanor. Her eyes were larger than I had thought and they had been focused on me since the minute I came inside the door. Exactly how old was Meren? Sixteen? Seventeen? Was this supposed to be a date? A date I hadn't counted on. Joel Dean Gregory sat across from Estelle, a presence I hadn't counted on as well. I had been silly enough to think Estelle had invited me as . . .well, as her beau.

Meren was now a pretty girl, maybe a beautiful girl. Unexpected, true, compared to the ragged waif she had been on the Joost farm.

But Estelle was a beautiful woman.

And the best part, she wasn't married to Joel Dean Gregory yet.

Meren turned out to be extremely talented at the Mah Jongg game. she caught on to Chows and Pungs and Kongs and, though she didn't talk, her laughter, smiles and facial gestures were comical and infectious. I discovered something only Estelle knew: Meren had a personality.

Joel Dean seemed distracted, perhaps by the decisions the county had taken today on the new county seat. He kept watching his tiles as if he couldn't remember from one turn to the next. Meren ended the first hand when she went Mah Jongg with the right tiles. She became so excited she tried her best to say the name of the game, but it came out a coughing sound in her throat. We all joined in her laughter.

At one point before we completed the 16 hands that make a game, Estelle went to bring some refreshments to the table and called on me for help as Joel Dean was showing some point of the game to Meren.

As she handed me the glasses to take to the table, she asked if I was having an enjoyable evening.

"Very much so. I wasn't aware Joel Dean was coming. He was at the courthouse today when I was there and he didn't mention that he would be here tonight."

"It's the first time he's been here since Daddy was shot. I needed him back in my life. Daddy's almost gone now and a great big void is opening up. I need someone to love me."

"Loving you," I said, fixing her face in my eyes, "would be the easiest thing any man has ever done."

She didn't show surprise at my remark, just an easy smile before she leaned her head into my chest for just a moment, then pushed me toward the parlor and the playing table.

My heart hammered inside my ribs, the blood throbbed in my face and my knees could barely hold my weight. I set a glass in front of Meren and she looked up at me with a simple, schoolgirl smile.

A word came out in a whisper, "Smith."

Leah kept looking at me across the breakfast table, but I avoided her eyes. My feeling was as if I had lost something. Something I wanted very badly. Was Estelle telling me I had no chance with her? Was she saying that Joel Dean had already been chosen? Let me think, what had I been told about the two of them? All I could remember was they were lovers until Joel Dean shot her father. How did she feel about that? How did he feel about it?

Was I giving up? All hope lost? Was I really in love for the first time in my life? With a woman who had chosen another?

Leah was not welcome in my thoughts.

She barged in anyway. I tried to time my exit from the kitchen to avoid her, but on the porch, as I stepped off, she called.

Hurrying up to me, she held out an envelope. "Smith, I've been trying to catch you. Listen, this letter came for you yesterday. It's been forwarded several times, it was face down, I didn't notice your name on it, I opened it by mistake thinking it was a business letter and . . .well, I read it. I'm sorry."

I only half heard what she was saying. I took the envelope, my mind not on the letter, pulled it out and began reading.

Dear Mr. Beauchamp:
This is to inform you about the welfare of your
mother. Her health has taken a turn for the worse.
Pneumonia has set in and, although our medical
staff is doing everything possible, I'm afraid
there is very little hope for recovery. It would
be to the best of your interests to dispatch yourself with as much haste as your situation allows,
to her bedside. I hope sincerely you are in time.
Yours Truly,
Dr. Wilbert Segleman
Director, Normandy Sanitarium

When I looked up, Leah said, "Smith, I'm so sorry. You
need to leave right away. You can be in St. Louis before
nighttime."

"Elmer wanted to see me this morning. I'll go see what he
wants, then I'll head for St. Louis."

"Forget Elmer. That will keep. Go now, right away."

"He's the boss. He'll have to know where I am."

"I'll tell him."

"Thanks, Leah, but I'd better do the telling."

She took hold of my arm. "Smith, I want you to know I had
nothing to do with all this. With Elmer. With the new county
seat. I didn't know anything about it."

"What do you mean? What did Elmer have to do with the
new county seat?"

"I don't know exactly. But Elmer and Happy and Ruby
Elam . . . they were plotting to set up the county seat on Hayden Joost's farm. I saw some notes. And, well . . .they were
bribing, maybe, McDermott. But I don't have proof. I can't
prove anything. I just overheard a bit here, a bit there, saw
some notes. All I'm saying is stay out of it. There's been some

big money involved here. The county judges, McDermott, Elmer. The president of the electric company I think, I don't
know. Just walk away from it."

"Who killed Happy and Ruby?"

"I don't know. It's not my concern anymore. Nor yours. Let
that cowboy sheriff figure it out. Just go to St. Louis before
your mother dies. That's more important."

"Yes, it is. But I can't go without knowing if I have a job to
come back to."

"Quit. Just quit. I'll tell Elmer. I'll see that you get your
paycheck."

I walked off toward the bank and the Land Acquisition
office.

"I've got to know, Leah. I've just got to know."

Over my shoulder I saw her looking after me. Fright was all
over her face.

Elmer had papers spread all over the table inside the office.
Looking closer, I noticed they were contracts for sale of property. Even closer, I could see they were ones I had drawn up.

Ominously, I noted that Mary was not in the office.

"What's up, Elmer," I asked as if I didn't already know.

"I'm looking over these contracts, Smith." His hand was on
his bottom lip and he pulled it away from his face and let it
snap back into place.

"These aren't good. Not good at all."

"I think you'll find them to be in order, Elmer. That's my
specialty, writing contracts for people's property before we
flood them out."

He shot a look at me, stuck out his chest and drew himself
up and I knew then what he was going to say.

"I'm afraid we're going to have to let you go, Smith. You've
overpaid for every piece of property in this town. The electric

company isn't going to stand for this. We . . .you and I, Leah too, are in trouble. We may have to take money out of the contract we have with them to pay for the exorbitant prices you've paid here."

I felt the heat rising inside, but I knew I had to remain calm or else anything I said would come under the heading of a disgruntled employee.

"Well, why don't you show me one where I've overpaid. Let me hear your experience on this sort of thing. I'll listen."

He cleared his throat, shifted his shoulders around and started picking up the papers and laying them down. I was sure he had expected anger from me and resentment instead of compliments.

He picked up the contract with Estelle Earnhardt. "Look at this. We paid for lost business. Now you know that we were specifically instructed not to pay anyone for lost business."

"We were also told to avoid going to court. Joel Dean Gregory, the county prosecutor, represented the Earnhardt holdings. He already filed a suit in circuit court. I used my judgment, which would cost the electric company more, to go to court against the county's lead lawyer or to pay for lost business."

"Well, well, . . ." he tossed the contract back on the table. "How about this one. To a man named Bailey. To move his belongings. Another thing we talked about at the start. We can't pay these people just to move their belongings. The man doesn't even own any property, apparently. Why are we paying him anything at all?"

"The man is crippled. He can't work. He can't even walk. His wife died and left him with twin boys to care for. Yawley Earnhardt let them build a shack from scrap lumber on a piece he owned. I gave the boys two hundred dollars to move the lumber in the house after they dismantle it and to pay down

on another lot at the new Linn Creek. For crying out loud, Elmer, it's all they have. The electric company's causing them to
move, what's two hundred dollars to them."

"It all adds up, Smith. Here's another one. Ten thousand
dollars for a house owned by a Nita German. I went by that
address this morning on the way over here. You bought a
dozen houses in this town just like that one for two thousand
dollars. What's so special about that one?"

I shrugged, then I worked at getting a smile going. "She's the
town whore, Elmer. She knew Happy. She knows everybody.
She knows people who work for the electric company. I
thought it was a cheap price."

He sputtered and stammered, but he bought my lie. He
went on to question the price on the Morrison place.

"They own fruit trees, Elmer. You have any idea how long
it takes to get fruit trees to get to the bearing stage?"

He tossed the last of the contracts on the table. "It still
goes, Smith. You've overspent and you've left me to try and
explain your benevolence to the electric company. Pick up
your stuff. I'll get a paycheck made out to you for your time up
to today . . ."

"No, I'm not through, Elmer. I'm not quitting and you're not
firing me. I started this job, not just to buy property for the
electric company, but to help these people find a new home
and a new life. That's exactly what the electric company told
them they were going to do. Look at all the newspapers and
read what they told these people before we ever began buying
property."

"I don't give a damn. I'm in charge here . . ."

"Then you may end up with a lot of explaining to do, Elmer. About you and Happy and Ruby Elam. About the
twenty thousand dollars Ruby had with him when Graves ran
him off into the river. About Hayden Joost and about Happy
dying on Joost's farm. You don't want me with what I know

over there with Savoy and Gregory investigating all of your activities."

"Are you threatening me?" Elmer asked, his voice rising to a fever pitch.

"Maybe I am. Anyway, I'll be gone for several days. I'll be back to finish what I started. I have a few more properties to buy here in Linn Creek. I'll take care of that when I return."

Leah was waiting outside the office.

"I'll be back, Leah," I said. "If you don't want to get caught up in all the shenanigans that have been going on here, don't go back in there. Because if you do, you'll become part of it."

I crossed the street which was all powdery dust by now, and got in the Buick that I had parked in front of the Earnhardt General Store. I backed out, put it in gear and drove by the office just in time to see Leah going inside and closing the door behind her.

I felt something for Leah, then, for the first time. I pitied her.

NINE

The Normandy Sanitarium stood off the street surrounded by dozens of large elm trees. They formed a protective arch over the buildings where people existed who were not aware what was outside their windows. I had not been here for a year. It had been five years since she had even recognized me. Coming here was a hard thing to do.

Dr. Wilbert Segleman sat behind the oversized oak desk with a pious look on his face. He was a big man with big hands, blond hair being overtaken by gray and bags under his remorseless eyes that fell in folds and deep creases.

"Mister Beauchamp, your mother is heavily sedated at the moment, but in about an hour she should be conscious. At least, we hope that she is. She's very weak. And illusionary. Don't expect too much."

I nodded. Thousands of words were stored up inside me to be let out, but not to Segleman. I didn't like the man.

"There's no hope, then," I said, already knowing his answer.

"I'm afraid not. We've been treating her with the latest medications available, but nothing can help when her condition is as deteriorating as it is. Our staff . . ."

Segleman droned on and on trying to impress me with his

staff's efficiency and compassion. I was uninterested. This ending had been written fifteen years ago and the only surprise was the length of time it took to play out.

". . .and the amount you have been remitting is, I'm sorry to say, woefully inadequate."

"How much do I owe you?"

"Do I include the burial expenses?"

"Let's wait until she's dead."

"In that case, the amount comes to two thousand one hundred fifty dollars."

I hadn't expected it to be that much. "You're sure about the amount?" I said.

"Yes, quite sure. We've had your mother here for almost ten years. Since she was released from prison in 1921 for shooting . . ."

"I know, I know. I would just as soon not bring it up again. I'll get you the money as soon as I can, be assured of that. I would not want to have her life end with an unpaid bill."

"Well, we try to be as patient and understanding as we can, but ten years . . ."

"Yes, I understand. I think I'll go back to the room with her. I'll just wait in there for her to regain consciousness."

"I can only hope she does," Segleman said, sounding even more sanctimonious than usual. "At least, one more time."

I left because I felt like hitting him.

When I entered her room, she looked so frail I could see the life draining from her. Her chin was held high and even in her condition, she had about her that look of royalty she had always worn so well.

God, what a life she had suffered through. No one on earth deserved to be here less than she, but here she was, in a sanitarium for the feeble minded and the insane, life deserting her and no chance that the injustices she had suffered would ever be made right.

And all because of me.

I wanted to play the whole scene out right there, sitting by her bed, watching her die, but my mind rebelled. I focused on her still-smooth skin, the cheekbones that seemed to curve and form attractive cheeks that adorned a face perpetually young because the mind had stopped. Stopped at one terrible moment and died. The shell of a beautiful face, lovely hair and athletic body lived on, hollow inside and impenetrable.

I tried to turn my mind loose and let it think about whatever it desired, Linn Creek, Estelle Earnhardt, Happy Meens, Elmer Byron, but my mind was like a clock whose mainspring had unwound. Not enough energy remained in my body to corral a cogent thought. It remained fixed on a picture I had carried with me in the back of my head for fifteen years.

The light outside grew dim and disappeared into the darkness of oncoming nighttime. I slept for an indeterminable length of time and woke to two small lights burning over my mother's head. A large woman with all-gray hair came into the room twice, the last time to feel my mother's pulse, shake her head and leave.

Mother woke sometime in the night. I was awake instantly. She spoke my name.

"Mother?" I said as I took her hand and she squeezed it so slightly I barely felt it.

"So good of you to come, Smith." She paused to gain strength. "It's been what, two weeks since you were here?"

"Something like that."

"Is your father well?"

"Everything is okay, Mother. Don't worry about anything."

Her breathing was such an effort. Several times she tried to speak, but her strength betrayed her. I told her about me, about finishing school, about working in the Ozarks, about this pretty young girl I knew who couldn't talk—to myself, wondering if Meren's mind would turn out to be like my mother's—and when she managed to ask about the house, I merely told her it was still standing, smiling so she could see me, but her eyes were vacant and I wasn't sure whether she saw at all.

Then she asked about my father. "Is he dead?" she asked and she looked directly at me.

"Yes, Mother, he's dead."

"I knew that," she said, then turned her head and stared at the ceiling. "I didn't mean to kill him. I don't even remember doing it."

"Mother, it's all over. It's in the past. You didn't hurt any-one, believe me. Have you been comfortable here?"

Looking at me again she asked, "How long have I been here?"

"A long time. But, I want you to get well. Get strong so we can leave here. Would you like to see the house again."

"No," she said. "I never want to see that house again."

"Just get better . . ."

"I'm dying, Smith."

"I don't think so. Don't listen to the doctors . . ."

"Promise me one thing after I die. Bury me beside your father."

I couldn't answer. Tears were running down my cheeks and nothing was working in my mind, in my voice. I wanted to tell her all of it, repeat it as I had every time I came here so that this time she would hear me, understand me, and maybe some of the injustice would be washed away.

But speech did not come. Life did not go on. Wrongs were not righted. Justice did not prevail. Hope did not shine through, a brighter tomorrow never came, no prayers were an-swered, good did not triumph evil, the truth did not set me free.

My mother had left me all alone.

What is it that bonds one person to another so that no matter what fate befalls either of them, the other is similarly affected? And when one of those fades to a gossamer spirit, that invisible, bonding web, unrestrained by time and distance, stretches to the edge of another world, but cannot enter and is left hanging in space, unattached at one end with the nerves inside that web, raw, frayed and so worn they cannot be reattached at once to any other living creature.

My father had one brother and a bunch of cousins, none of whom I knew. I thought my mother might have some cousins out in Oregon, but I didn't know their names.

Francois Beauchamp said that I could not bury my mother beside my father.

"After all, she killed him," he said.

"No, she did not," I told him. But I knew he wouldn't hear the truth. The lie had been told too many times.

"So, who you think shot him? He shot himself between the eyes? What a fabrication. I understand you defending her. I'd probably do the same, but it does not justify what she did. No, no, no. You cannot bury that woman beside my brother, the man she killed fifteen years ago."

I took from my pocket the deed to the three cemetery plots where Langston Beauchamp was buried. "I only asked out of courtesy. I thought perhaps forgiveness was something that might have come to you in those fifteen years. But, your approval is not necessary. My father and mother owned the plots together. And so now, they belong to me. She will be buried where she asked to be buried. Beside my father."

Uncle Francois resorted to his native tongue and lashed me in language I chose not to remember.

"If you bury her there, I shall have my brother's body moved to a different cemetery," he said, some of it in English, some in French.

"Not without a court order," I said. "And only I can request it."

He damned me in French, in English, in Flemish, Italian and Spanish. I cut him off.

"My father was a cruel man at times," I said. "He was ill-tempered, abusive and controlling. He was entirely the wrong man for my mother. I don't know if what happened to her mind would have happened had she married someone with compassion and care, someone who would have nurtured her and shown her some love. I don't know that. But I do know my father never did any of those, anything for her benefit. Yet, her very last request was to be buried beside him. You see, Uncle Francois, she loved him. And she never harmed him, she never killed him. You believe what you want, but I know."

I left him standing there in his living room, his anger and his arrogance a barrier between us. It would be the last time I ever saw him.

A pity.

The day was a rare one, set in the middle of June. Few people attended the funeral. Some of the attendants from the sanitarium. A roommate of mine from college who had always read the obituaries first each morning in the *Globe-Democrat* and had recognized my name. I imagine he came not so much out of empathy as curiosity.

I lied to him about my unimportant job.

I left the cemetery to get something to eat, then came back after the grave was filled in. I stood before the handpainted marker. Evelyn Elaine Smith Beauchamp. I laid my hand on the loose dirt on top and told my Mother how I wished it could have been different and I told her how sorry I was she did not have a better life and how sorry I was for the things I had done and the things I hadn't done. How it wasn't her, but fate that had dealt her such a terrible hand.

It was, of course, too late to be saying those things, but what else could I say to her now?

I wasn't ready to leave yet. I stood at the foot of my father's grave, staring at his headstone. A moment passed before I could speak out loud, before I could say it.

"There she is. She's dead now. Are you satisfied, you son of a bitch?"

PART
3

ONE

The land was a solid mass of green that shocked your eyes and drove your mind to wondering how it came about so suddenly. The arrival of summer in the Ozarks was a phenomenon that had transpired before my very eyes over the last month, but the majesty and raw display of the foliage explosion was something that took more than a month to absorb.

I drove out of it with a suddenness I wasn't expecting. There before me as I came through a carved out roadway through a solid granite hillside was a gargantuan structure looming across the river. An eighth of a mile of solid concrete tapering down 75 feet below on either side to a sliver of water that was, or had been, the Osage River.

This was the completed and finished Bagnell Dam.

The sheer, massive immensity of it was impossible to comprehend. I could not stop the Buick on the concrete roadway across the dam as a long line of automobiles was strung out behind me, each full of people gawking out the windows, yelling and pointing. No one in this part of the world had ever seen anything like this, nor had they ever expected to see anything like this.

A parking place had been provided on the other side of the dam for the gawkers to pull in and express their wonder to each other. I found a place between two Model A Fords and I joined the group looking in amazement up the trickle of a river that was bumping up against all that concrete. The banks of the river up to where we stood had been denuded by a crew of tree cutters. What would they tell their children, these men who felled tree after tree all day long who left behind them the fallen giants who once soared over the valleys and the banks of this river which was scheduled to become a lake a thousand times the size of the puny river.

"Me? Oh, I cut trees all day. Beautiful oak trees and ash trees, willows and sycamores. Hickories and redbuds and dogwoods and every other thing that grew and got in the way of the lake. The glorious lake. The biggest one that man ever built. Bigger and better than trees and forests and all the woods in the valleys from here to Warsaw. Yessir, I was a part of progress and damn proud of it."

And might that child someday ask, "Daddy, what happened to all the people and all the towns down there when the lake filled up?"

The Land Acquisition office was full of men plus Mary and Leah. As I came through the door, I counted 11 men that I did not know and Elmer. Leah glanced at me, then down to the floor. Elmer saw me, but ignored me. I sidled up to Mary.

"What's going on here?"

"Oh, hi, Smith. All the new men from the electric company come in to close out the town. But who's going to help me?"

"Close out the town?"

"Yeah, you know, buy up the rest of the properties."

"But there's less than a dozen places left that haven't been bought out."

Mary shrugged and turned back to watch Elmer who had

an oversized map of the town mounted on an easel that sat on the table. With a pointer he was indicating each lot by number —instead of a more personal name—and lining up his pointer with a man in the crowd and calling him by name, instead of a less personal number. The men surely must have purchased their suits all at the same J.C. Penney store on Market Street. They wore hats unlike the one Estelle had sold me that looked like every man's hat in Linn Creek, and they all wore neckties and high collars. They might as well have been carrying a sign around their neck that said, "I just got in from St. Louis. I know everything."

I wondered if maybe Elmer might assign one of the proper-ties to me, but, of course, he didn't. Even acknowledg-ing me would have been nice, but, that too was a bit much to ask.

When Elmer had finished his little display, the men all snapped shut the little notebooks they carried and shoved them in their little pockets, put their pens away inside their jackets and turned to their neighbor and made some witty re-mark and they all laughed and made for the door. I elbowed my way through their midst until I stood before Elmer, folding up his oversized map.

"What's going on, Elmer?" I asked, wearing a lopsided grin to let him know I thought the whole affair was a charade of some kind.

Turning to me with a serious countenance, he fixed me with his intolerant stare and said, "I'm surprised you came back, Smith. I told you how things were before you left. There's nothing here for you now."

"Well," I said, "thanks a lot for your concern about the death of my mother. It speaks volumes to me about the heart in this company."

That shook him. Leah, I suppose, noticed his loss of com-posure and moved up beside me."

"Your mother died, Smith?"

"Yes, she did. Well, actually she died about fifteen years ago. I just now got around to burying her."

I didn't expect her to understand. If I had had the opportunity to explain it all to her, I was sure of her compas-sion, but at the moment I didn't want it.

"The lake is filling," Elmer said. "We've got to get these properties transferred and all the structures leveled."

"I just crossed the dam," I told him. "It's rising nine inches a day. Unless we have an abnormal amount of rain and runoff, it will be thirty days before the water reaches Main Street."

"It's going to be taken care of in the next two weeks," Elmer said, looking very much in charge. "Then we're closing this office because this building won't be here any longer."

"You didn't think I could finish the job, is that it?"

"We couldn't afford you, Smith. I told you that."

"And what's my job to be?"

He looked as if he didn't believe I had asked that question. Finally, with a shrug of resignation, he said, "Okay. All right. I'll give you two more week's pay. I owe you that. Just to show I'm not a heartless man."

"Gee, Elmer, I never thought you were."

Before I could say more, and probably for the better, Elmer followed his new crew out the door. I was left with Mary, who dove into a pile of paper, and with Leah.

"Did you get your family business squared away," she asked, looking sympathetic and sincere.

"Yeah, I did. There wasn't much to do. Put my mother in the ground. Leave her there alone."

"Maybe she's not alone."

"Maybe." I looked down at her, seeing yet another Leah. "It's tough, losing your mother."

"I wouldn't know. I'm an orphan."

Proving again that you never know what the other person has to bear.

The eleven men did indeed work for the electric company. They fanned out into the streets, notebooks in hand and began knocking on doors. I stood under the Judas tree by the jail house with Sheriff Doyle Savoy and watched them.

"Now there's a bunch of dumb asses for you," Savoy said. "It's bad enough to tear down the town, but to have a bunch like that doin it is almost too much to bear."

"You and Uncle Billy Jack," I said. "I'm not looking forward to supper at Rose's tonight and listening to him. I just hope he has a fresh jar of Ernest Raines whisky to share this evening."

"You know that's against the law, don't you?"

"Yeah."

Savoy inspected his fingernails. "I might drop by after dark," he said. "I haven't had a drink of Ernest's fine whisky for some time."

"Bring some blank warrants with you. Uncle Billy Jack'll be wanting to arrest somebody."

"I worry about what'll become of him," Savoy said. "He's the history of this town, you know. I sometimes doubt he wants to live longer than the town does."

"Rose is taking him under her wing. He'll be okay."

Savoy asked, "You goin to the funeral tomorrow?"

"Funeral? For whom?"

"Grant Joost stuck that rifle in his daddy's belly and pulled the trigger."

The shock of what he said jarred me. The biggest, strongest, roughest man in the Ozarks dead? I could think of nothing to say except, "Why?"

"Hayden imposed his will on the whole family until Grant left. Eldon stood up to him, Eleanor sent Meren away and then told him about me and her. I guess he decided to take it out on Grant, like he always did, and Grant wasn't having any more of it."

"What'll happen to Grant?"

"Reckon I'll have to go out and bring him in."

"Will they hang him?"

"Hell, yes, they'll hang him. That's a terrible thing to kill your own daddy."

I had to agree with him.

"Does Meren know?" I asked.

"I told Estelle. She told her. I don't know about Meren, if she'll understand what's happenin or not."

I thought of Meren and how quickly she learned the Mah Jongg game. "Meren will be okay,"

"I can't imagine that he would come, but just in case Grant shows up, you might want to stay close to Meren."

"You and Eleanor. How's that coming along?"

Savoy removed his hat and replaced it, tugging on the front brim. He rubbed his chin and said, "I'm givin her a job at the new jail house, we ever get one built. Who knows after that. Eldon's stayin with the Lewis family. They got a couple of pudgy little girls there to keep him busy."

"You know where Grant is?" I asked.

"He was seen earlier in Old Town. Joe Collie just tore down ever place over there while you were gone. Didn't find Grant."

"What happened with Graves?"

"That son of a bitch. He left town taking the Packard with him. Guess I won't be able to pin Ruby's murder on him."

"Well, I don't have a job. Elmer's going to pay me, but he doesn't trust me to do any more business for the electric company. Maybe I'll stick around and hang out my shingle in the new county seat."

"It ought to be a good town. I hear your boss paid top dollar for a new courthouse."

Hardly more than a dozen people attended Hayden Joost's funeral at the Baptist Church. Grant was not one of them. Noah came in at the last minute during the third hymn and told me that Savoy had gone out to the location of the new county seat. Someone told him McDermott and Graves were there.

Meren stood close to Eleanor. She kept her eyes downcast and it was difficult to read her mood. Eleanor stood firm, expressionless. Eldon had a blond-headed, plump girl of about sixteen beside him. He showed little emotion until the preacher, who admitted later that he had never met Hayden, started the eulogy. Eldon sniffled and showed some tears. I wondered how much guilt he and Eleanor felt for Hayden's death. Probably not much, after all, the man had been a tyrant at home.

Estelle was there, stunning in appearance with a black, knee-length dress and a little cape that spread over the shoulders. The small, black hat sat atop her pretty head and the netted veil would have obscured her beauty if I didn't have it ingrained in my mind. She held Meren's hand, and it was plain to see that she had selected Meren's dark dress and hat as well. Joel Dean Gregory stood beside Estelle and I have to admit he cut a handsome figure. I should have said to my self, 'Okay, that's it. Estelle has made her choice, Smith, and you're not it.' But then again, I thought, Yawley's not dead and she can't, or won't, marry Joel Dean until her father dies, so maybe Yawley will live a long time and maybe she'll get tired of waiting and maybe she'll see Smith Beauchamp hanging around town and . . .

And maybe horse flies will turn into eagles and mosquitos will start carrying the US mail.

Noah kept scanning the church sanctuary, watching for

Grant. I was surprised to see Elmer and Leah in attendance. I tried to figure why. I saw Meren's head turn to observe Elmer and Leah and was curious about that. Was it Leah who attracted her attention?

Uncle Billy Jack Cummins was there, smelling of moth balls. I could almost read his mind: Was this the last funeral in Linn Creek?

The few neighbors of the Joosts who attended lined up to express condolences to Eleanor and her children. She never smiled nor spoke, just nodded. Meren barely looked up from her fixed, downward stare. I was at the end of the line.

I stood before Meren, waiting for her to acknowledge my presence. When she looked up, there was fear in her eyes. They shot toward the departing line of sympathizers, then to my face. Her hand grabbed a fountain pen from my shirt pocket and she began fumbling for something in her pocket. I thought it might be a paper to write on, so I handed her the small notebook I carried in my trouser pocket. She fumbled at it, found a blank page, then began writing. She handed it to me, with Eleanor watching, and I turned the notebook so I could read what she had written. The writing was a childish scrawl that I had some trouble deciphering.

Man with woman he with man shoot by creek too men run off me two

I followed her eyes. Elmer Byron was going out the door.

The rocky road winding up to the dome was bracketed by dense growth of buckbrush and wild roses on both sides. I recognized the spot where Savoy's Chevrolet had mired in the red clay in the deluge we were caught in the day we drove out here to the Fergus farm.

The grass on the savanna was lush and green. The roadway blew up red dust behind the Buick and as I passed under a canopy of scalloped oak leaves that blocked out the sun, I saw a survey crew with transits, rods, chains and stakes. I seemed to be in the middle of a town to be.

I stopped to ask one of the surveyors if he had seen the sheriff or Mister McDermott.

He pointed toward the Fergus farmhouse. "Sheriff went that away. McDermott hasn't been around here today. Carl Graves came by checking up on what we're doing."

"What are you doing?" I asked.

"Staking out the highway," he said. "McDermott's awful anxious to get it started."

Before I got to the Fergus farmhouse, I met Savoy's Chevrolet. I stopped and waited for him to pull up beside me and asked if he'd seen McDermott and Graves.

"I saw McDermott earlier," He said. "Graves has been fired and he took the black Packard with him."

"I thought it was a state car with state license."

"McDermott hummed and hawed about that. Said he'd have to check with the legal department. Graves might be guilty of car theft."

"One of the survey crew said Graves was by checking up on their progress. Doesn't sound to me like he'd been fired."

"Yeah, told me that, too. I accused McDermott of lying. Didn't go over so good. What do I care. The bastard lied and got caught at it."

"So, what now?"

"I'm going back to Linn Creek and call the sheriff's office in Jefferson City. Before the day's over, I'm going to have somebody's ass in a sling."

"Something's come up," I said, anxious to tell him about Meren. "Meren talked."

His change in expression was dramatic. "What'd she say?"

"Elmer Byron and a redheaded man in a plaid coat was down by the creek with Happy Meens the day he was shot. I figure the redheaded man was Ruby Elam. Meren says somebody shot Happy, she doesn't know who. The others ran off and so did she."

"I'll be damned. She told you that?"

"She wrote it out."

"Why wouldn't she tell me that?"

"She's scared, Doyle. She's been scared since that day. Grant's looking for her and so is whoever shot Happy. Plus, Elmer and Ruby for sure didn't want her telling she saw them. She feels like everyone's looking to kill her."

"So she's been scared of whoever shot Happy and she doesn't know who it was?"

"Plus, she's scared of you, Doyle."

"Me?"

"She's scared you're going to arrest her? And she was scared of me for awhile. The girl's just plain scared."

"So, things are starting to come together. Let's see, we have Elmer Byron, who's probably speaking for the electric company, Happy Meens and Ruby Elam all acting together, offerin to make Yawley Earnhardt's property the new county seat if he'll cut them in. Yawley runs them off—he don't need them, he had lots of clout in Jefferson City—so they try to buy out Hayden Joost without lettin Hayden know why they want his property. Hayden runs Happy off. Meanwhile, McDermott and Graves are working on the Fergus's to run the highway through their farm for a cut. You can bet, somehow or other, those two have their fingers in that pie."

"So the prize is the county seat," I said. "Elmer and Happy can deliver the courthouse from the electric company, but McDermott and Graves can deliver the highways."

"Real convenient Yawley Earnhardt getting shot," Savoy said. "You know, there was some big bastard under one of those sheets that night I never did know who it was. He was the one blew my arm to pieces and he was the one eggin Yawley on. Maybe if Joel Dean hadn't shot Yawley, that big bastard would have. And I'm thinkin that was Graves."

"You think Graves shot you?"

"I've had an uneasy feelin about that pig-faced son of a bitch all along."

"So you figure McDermott and Graves had anything to do with shooting Happy?"

"It figures, don't it? I mean they get Yawley out of the picture, shoot Happy Meens on Hayden Joost's property so Hayden gets blamed for it and what's left? The Fergus farm."

"So McDermott kidnaps the Fergus's so Elmer can't get to them, but Elmer sends Ruby to Westphalia with twenty thousand dollars cash to buy out the Fergus property and Ruby ends up in the river."

"That's right," Savoy said. "And Graves puts him there. So, Elmer has no place to go except to join McDermott. Trade the county seat for some property on the Fergus farm."

"How you going to prove all that?" I asked.

"Meren can help."

"I don't think so, Doyle. She's too frightened."

Savoy removed his hat and slapped it against the door of the Chevrolet.

"I don't need proof. I find that goddamn Graves I'll kill him myself."

"I know you don't mean that."

"I mean it all right."

"Listen, Doyle, you can't go after this guy with the intention of killing him."

Savoy got out of his Chevrolet and began stomping up and down the road. I thought he was just going to keep on walking, but when he doubled back, I got out of the Buick and leaned against the front fender.

"You do understand that this is probably the guy who took away the use of my right arm don't you? I used to play the guitar, you know that? I was pretty damn good, too. I could lift my weight, I could handle any drunk or roughneck came along. Hell, I can't even do this job. People voted me in just because they took pity on me. Look at the goddamn useless arm."

He reached over with his left hand and took hold of his right arm and slammed it toward the ground. It swung back and forth from the shoulder for three or four swings, then hung motionless at his side.

"I don't believe, that, Doyle. Since I first met you I never had any pity on you. God, you would be the last guy I thought of to take pity on. You're a damn good sheriff and you probably would be even if you had no arms at all. Don't go throwing away that trust people put in you. They didn't elect you because of pity. They elected you because they thought you could do the job. Don't let them down."

"This happen to you and you found the guy who did it, what would you do?"

"That's a tough question."

Savoy stood by the hood of his Chevrolet, took out a sack of tobacco, pushed a paper out from under the label, laid it on the hood, tugged the strings of the sack with his teeth until it opened, shook tobacco out on the paper, laid the sack on the hood, rolled the cigarette clumsily with his left hand, licked it and stuck it in his mouth. I watched, knowing better than to offer my help.

He pulled a match out of his pocket, struck it against the fender and got the cigarette going. It was so comical, the cigarette hanging out of the corner of his mouth with a hump in the middle of it and a twist of paper on the end that flamed up as high as his eyebrows before it burned down to the tobacco. He squinted the one eye that smoke had entered and turned to me showing his twisted mouth, his squinting eye and I could not keep from laughing. I didn't know what to expect from this tough, wiry man who could take it as well as hand it out. Would it be a punch in the face or that lopsided grin of his.

"You think this is funny," he drawled, one corner of his lip curled, "you ought to see me eatin an ear of corn."

TWO

Savoy said he was driving over to the Millionaire's Castle at Ha Ha Tonka to see if Graves had been around there. I thought it unlikely, but then, what did I really know about the highway department's bully boy. Anyway it was a nice drive with sumac, oak and hickory bordering the roadway and the full color of spring and summer flowers that flowed through the timber, looking like colored lace around the stout trunks of the trees so numerous the sun never had a chance at drying the dew off the petals and leaves.

I followed along in the Buick, having a paying job, but no duties. The road was at best a one lane gravel thoroughfare. We came out of the woods at a relatively flat area and drove past a small stone building that said POST OFFICE on the front. I slowed to look around and when I glanced at the roadway again, I saw a large, black car coming at Savoy's Chevrolet head-on. And it looked like a Packard.

Savoy pulled his automobile across the road so that the oncoming car couldn't get by without driving out through the open field. He drew his gun and had it hanging by his side when the approaching car swerved off the roadway, bumped through the drainage ditch bordering the road and flew across the grassy flat.

Savoy aimed his pistol into the air and fired. I had stopped behind the Sheriff's Chevrolet by this time and from the window of the Buick I could make out Carl Graves face inside the Packard. Savoy aimed at the speeding car and shot once, the bullet missing by twenty or thirty yards. He ran back to get in his car and waved me out of the way. The black Packard was headed for what looked to be a break in the deep woods behind the Post Office. Savoy headed off to the left and it was then I saw that what Graves took to be a break in the timber, was actually just an offset and there was no way he was going to be able to go through.

He slid nearly into the trees before he could get headed off to the left which put him on course to collide with Savoy. Neither slowed.

I heard the metal crunching and saw Savoy's car bounce into the air and land on one side and remain there with the wheels on the upside spinning in the air. Graves' Packard continued with a mangled fender jabbing into the air and his radiator spewing steam.

Savoy clamored out of the door of his Chevrolet, the one now on the top of the car. He walked out into the open area firing at Graves. Graves whipped the steaming Packard around and came right at Savoy. Savoy stood calmly shucking the shells out of his revolver until Graves was practically on top of him and he dove to one side. Graves missed him by inches, zipped on by, turned and came back at him.

Savoy had lost his revolver in his dive and he was looking around on the ground when the Packard bore down on him again. Again he dove out of the way at the last moment and Graves whizzed by, yelling obscenities at Savoy.

Then, the Packard slid sideways on the grass and dirt, the radiator still steaming. Graves opened the door, got out, opened the back door and began searching around inside. He came out with a rifle.

He walked with a purpose across the knee-high grass carrying the rifle in one hand, grinning big as he came at Savoy who was now searching frantically for the revolver in the long grass.

The Buick jumped the drainage ditch like a bronco and as soon as I gained control of the wheel again, I pointed it at Graves and mashed the accelerator to the floorboard. He leveled the rifle at Savoy who looked up and said something to him and Graves laughed. That was when he heard the Buick.

He tried swinging the rifle toward me just as the Buick hit a dip in the ground and came up airborne. I flew over a ducking Graves, expecting to hear the underside of my car thumping his head, but instead it hit the ground and my head came in contact with the soft roof of the Buick and I felt the cloth tearing away. I jammed the brakes, turned the wheel and came whipping around facing Graves who was standing now.

Savoy had been running toward him when he saw the Buick coming and before Graves could retrieve the rifle, Savoy was on him, beating at his face with his one good fist.

I scrambled out of the Buick and started toward them. I saw Graves' rifle lying on the ground, picked it up and pointed it at them at about the same time that Graves hit Savoy with a swinging right hand punch that knocked Savoy backwards and to the ground.

I didn't know how to shoot the rifle, having never held one in my hands, but I did see that it had a hammer on it so figured that had to be cocked, which I did. Graves started walking toward me so I pulled the trigger, not even thinking about if I was killing a human being or not. The hammer made a metallic click when it snapped down, but nothing more. Graves got this crooked grin on his face and he held out his hand and said, "Just hand it over and I won't hurt you."

Savoy getting up off the ground, blood streaming from his nose, yelled, "Work the lever. Work the lever."

I looked down at the rifle, saw the lever and pushed it down and forward. When I brought it closed, the hammer was cocked and ready to fire. Graves stopped. Savoy came up behind him and kicked him in the leg right behind his knee. Graves' leg buckled and he went to one knee. Savoy was fronting him by this time and he slammed his fist into Graves face and blood splattered into a spray. Graves stumbled trying to get up, nearly ramming his head into the ground. Savoy took two steps toward him and drew back his fist again, his face a twisted picture of hatred. I stepped toward him and put myself in front of Graves.

"Don't do it, Doyle. He's not worth your job."

The rage was a fire in his eyes, then slowly it dissipated and he turned and walked toward his overturned car.

I had breakfast the next morning at the jail and Savoy looked happy, even when Noah brought Graves down from the cells upstairs. Eleanor set a pan of hot biscuits on the table followed by a pan of white flour gravy and a rasher of bacon. Graves had an X-shaped bandage over his broken nose and one black eye. Savoy had a purple and yellow lump under one eye, but he smiled at Graves.

Eleanor sat at the table, at Savoy's invitation, and Noah returned thanks before we started passing the food.

As he loaded his plate with bacon on top of the gravy on top of the biscuits, Savoy said, "Well, Graves, looks like you might swing for shoving Ruby Elam's car into the Maries River. Probably be up at the capitol where all your drinking buddies can watch. I'm goin to be there for sure."

"You ain't got nothin on me," Graves said. He fed his face without grace, shoving forkful after forkful into his mouth until his cheeks bulged.

"There's a Packard out there that you been drivin," Savoy

said. "And on one fender of that Packard is a dent and a splotch of paint that we can prove came from Ruby Elam's car."

Graves ugly face broke into a grin, biscuits and gravy still smeared on his crooked, uneven teeth.

"You look at that Packard again, Crip, you see a fender all smashed where it hit your Chevrolet."

Graves, proud of himself of a sudden, looked all around the table and his eyes settled on me. Recognition flashed through his snake-like eyes, whether from me pointing a rifle at him in the field or the incident in the highway office in Jefferson City, I couldn't be sure. But he knew me, all right. And the sight of me was not pleasing him.

"No," Savoy said, "It was the other fender you shoved Ruby in the river with, not the fender you rammed into me."

Graves put his fork down on his plate and his face turned scarlet. "The hell it was," he blurted out. "It was the same damn fender."

Savoy smiled as if he had found a gold nugget in his plate. "Well, well, Graves. Three witnesses besides me here at the table heard you confess you hit Ruby with the same fender you hit my car with. That'll hold up in any court."

Graves came to his feet with dishes crashing and coffee spilling on the tablecloth. He jabbed a finger at Doyle Savoy and roared in a voice he no longer had control of. "You ain't hangin that killin on me. I got an alibi. You ask McDermott."

"McDermott fired you. He'll turn on you like a brass penny. You be willin to tell about his part in this, the judge might go easy on you."

Graves' face turned to creases and frowns as he tried to fathom what was happening to him. He banged his fist on the table and said, "I ain't listenin to any more of this."

"You don't need to," Savoy said. "You want to swing alone, that's your business. You think McDermott's goin to jeopardize his commissioner's job to alibi for you, think again. Noah, take our guest back up to his cell."

As Noah was shoving Graves out the door into the main office, Joel Dean Gregory stepped aside to let them pass. Noah said, "Still lookin for a good deputy, Joel Dean."

The tall man smiled back at him. When he came inside, Joe Collie followed him.

Savoy said, "Welcome, Gents. Guess you heard I had a new cook and the jail house is back in use. At least for another week or so."

Eleanor got up from the table and set two more places.

Joel Dean said, "Nice to see you again, Eleanor. Sorry about all your trouble getting Hayden buried and all. Let me know if I can be of any help to you."

She nodded as she laid the utensils beside his plate and poured a cup of coffee for him.

"Heard you made an arrest, Doyle," he said, turning his attention to Savoy. "What's that all about?"

"Well, assault on a law officer for one thing," Savoy said. Eleanor was rolling a cigarette and handed it to him as he spoke. He lighted it with a sulfur match and said, "And we got a confession out of him this morning, right here at this table, that he ran Ruby Elam off the road into the Maries River where he drowned."

Joel Dean loaded up his plate with biscuits and gravy and laid several slices of bacon beside them and passed them on to Joe Collie before he said, "Pretty good work, I'd say, Doyle. Will that confession hold up in court?"

"Eleanor, Noah and Smith here all heard him. Solid as a rock, you ask me."

Joel Dean looked at me as he chewed. "How are you, Smith? See you got a new crew working the town."

"Not me," I said. "Elmer Byron thought I wasn't moving fast enough and thought I was wasting the electric company's money. Paying for things like lost business and moving expenses."

Joel Dean smiled at that. "Did you explain to him that it got you an invite to a Mah Jongg session?"

"Didn't bother. Elmer would be aghast that anyone should have a social life. Did it appear that I was buying an invitation?"

Joel Dean never lost his smile. "Some things aren't for sale. No matter how hard you try."

"Hmmm," I said. "In other words, you can't score points after the game is over."

"You could put it that way."

"Usually there's one person who decides when that game is over."

He tired of the game, I guess, because he turned back to Savoy. "What are you going to do with Graves? Understand the electric company wants the jail torn down. Isn't that right, Joe?"

Collie, scooping up gobs of biscuits and gravy, nodded his head. "Next week," he mumbled around his full mouth. "Soon's my crew gets done with the houses down the street."

"Joe," I said, "How does a nice guy like you get involved in a crummy job like tearing people's houses down?"

Joe looked at me with surprise showing in his face as if he couldn't understand what I was asking.

"We all got crummy jobs in here, Smith," Savoy said. "I arrest people, Joel Dean sends them to the penitentiary and you buy people's houses who don't want to sell."

He was right, of course. I finished my coffee and rose to leave, but Savoy motioned me to sit back down.

"Tell Joel Dean about Meren and what she told you," he said.

Joel Dean looked up at me, his fork stilled.

So I told him what she'd written for me to read.

He looked at Savoy. "What's that mean?"

"Means this Elmer Byron could shed a lot of light on who killed Happy Meens and why. One of us ought to have a talk with him."

Joel Dean said, "Why don't you see what he knows."

Savoy nodded. "Soon's he gets back to town."

Joel Dean looked at the scraps of biscuits and bacon left on his plate. "We can speculate on why. Sounds like the three of them were trying to lean on Hayden for a site for the county seat. You think Hayden shot Happy?"

Savoy shook his head. "Nope. I figure it was Graves. Him and McDermott whittling down the competition for a town site."

Joel Dean's turn to shake his head. "Couldn't be. Both of them were in the courthouse talking with the judges. I remember you coming by asking for volunteers to look for Happy. That was the day he was shot, right?"

Savoy looked thoughtful. "So, we can't pin Happy's murder on him. Don't matter. He'll swing for killing Ruby anyway. If I can get him to squeal on McDermott, we can hang that bastard, too."

"McDermott's too slick."

"Worth tryin," Savoy said. He rose from his chair. "Gotta go up to the new town and see about gettin a jail and an office. Don't need me to protect you today from the kids in town do you Joe?"

Collie looked embarrassed. "That's all over with."

"Guess I'll walk around town and see if I can get myself invited to something," I said, shooting a look at Joel Dean.

I was getting tired of that smile of his. "Maybe you can help Estelle pack. She's closing the store tomorrow."

On the way to the Earnhardt General Store I passed the courthouse and noticed a new posting on the front door. It read:

ELECTION NEXT TUESDAY
THIS IS A NOTICE OF AN ELECTION TO BE
HELD IN CAMDEN COUNTY ON THE
SECOND TUESDAY OF THIS MONTH TO
DECIDE IF THE NEWLY FORMED CITY
SHALL BE THE NEXT COUNTY SEAT OF
CAMDEN COUNTY. ALL REGISTERED
VOTERS OF THE COUNTY ARE ELIGIBLE
TO VOTE AT THE NEAREST PRECINCT.

So, McDermott had won. He had persuaded the county judges to locate the county seat in the middle of a farm pasture. Elmer was on board, too, leaving the voters as the only people to fight the location. I felt sure they would, at least the voters in Linn Creek who had re-located to the new Linn Creek where just about everyone had assumed the new county seat would be.

I turned to see Joel Dean Gregory reading the notice over my shoulder.

"Well, that does it, I guess," he said, to me and everyone in general.

"What do you know about this?" I asked.

"I know it's a dirty deal. I've been ordered by the county judges to drop all the lawsuits against the electric company. We've lost ten condemnation suits against the company by people here in Linn Creek. Every time I go into court against the electric company it's the same results. All the petitions have been denied."

"You were the people's last hope, Joel Dean. So it's over?"

"Well, there's the election. Linn Creek will vote against it, but I hear the rest of the county will go for it."

Without thinking it through, I said, "Things might have

been different if Yawley Earnhardt hadn't been shot."

He looked at me hard. "It's true, things changed in Linn Creek the night I shot Yawley. The night my sister died and Doyle lost his arm. But, this town died when the big money got behind the dam. And the big money is behind this new town. There is nothing we can do to change that. Not me, not you and not Yawley, even if he hadn't been shot."

"I didn't mean it was all your fault. I know what you've done to try and save the town. But are you just giving up?"

He opened the door to the courthouse to go inside. He turned back to say, "No, I've filed for Congress in the next election. I mean to see that big money can never do this to any town again."

When he closed the door in my face, I saw a look of grim determination to Joel Dean Gregory and the thought scared me. I would not want to be on the other side from him. And yet, I was. I realized the futility of trying to secure the hand of Estelle Earnhardt. My chances with her were as dead as Linn Creek.

I walked off in the opposite direction from the general store to where the sound of Joe Collie's bulldozer was spelling out the end of one little town and four hundred hopes and dreams.

They stood in a group, the owners and neighbors, in front of two small houses. Joe Collie on a green Holt bulldozer, raised the blade to a height of four feet and rammed it into the corner of the pale yellow house and groans went up from the group. The corner of the house collapsed and the roof teetered over the wreckage until it too crumpled into the pile of debris.

I recognized the man and woman who owned the house. I had purchased it from them and remembered the regret they shared when signing over the deed. The man acknowledged my presence and nodded.

"You gave me a fair price, enough to build a house in Richland, but it's hard seeing it tore down like that. We spent many a year inside there and never wanted to leave, but I reckon we'll get by."

Two of Elmer's new-hires stood watching, their city hats and city suits and ties looking strangely out of place. One pointed to a spot on the house and Joe Collie aimed his dozer blade at it and completed the demolition as the entire roof and sidewall construction crashed into a fallen heap of two by four wall studs with plaster and lath particles clinging to them, pointing into the air which was now filling with plaster powder that rose in a dusty, white cloud above the rubble that had moments before been someone's home.

One of the men walked briskly toward the ruins with a small kerosene can in his hands and began dousing the remains. The other man struck a match, tossed it on the kerosene and flames shot into the air and crackled across the boards and debris sending a black plume of oily-smelling smoke into the air. The man standing with the empty can in his hand smiled with approval at the man who had torched the house.

A job well done.

The owner turned to me. "I'm thankful you're the one bought my house," he said. "At least I didn't have to deal with the likes of them two."

The woman cried softly into her hands.

Crying day in Linn Creek.

Gloom and dismay were all around me. Might as well have some more. I headed for the Land Acquisition office in the bank. I'd seen Leah enter there a few minutes ago. And Elmer right behind her.

Leah gathered up papers and stuffed them into the satchel she carried with her everywhere.

"Leah," I said, coming up to stand across the table from her. "Are you leaving?"

"Yeah," she said, pausing long enough to flash a smile at me. "I just told Elmer it was time for me to move on. I'm not getting much satisfaction out of this job anymore."

"I made her the same deal I made you," Elmer said, a bit defensively I thought. "Two weeks pay. Neither of you need to stick around to collect it."

"Nothing for me here anymore, Smith," she said, She grasped the satchel in both hands and looked at me straight on. "Is there?"

I felt an overwhelming sense of compassion, friendship and sadness for Leah. Everything but love.

"I'll not forget you, Leah," I said. "Thank you for being my friend."

She held a hand over the table and I took it in mine and held it warmly. Like I said, it was crying time in Linn Creek. Tears formed in her eyes and just like with the woman who owned the destroyed house, I was touched where it hurts.

"Good luck, Smith." Turning swiftly to Elmer, she said, "You know where to send my check, Elmer."

She was gone, leaving me with a lump in my throat.

Elmer cleared his throat and said, "Well, it's always a little sad when a job is over. That's how it is."

"How is it, Elmer?" I asked, turning on him.

"Well, you know, you get attached to people you work with. Can't stay by their side forever. Time comes to move on."

"Leah was too good for this job, Elmer. So am I. This job was made for people like those cookie cutter flunkies you brought in here in their J.C. Penney suits and their Merchant Street hats. Men who like to tell people here's the offer, take it or we'll flood you out. Men who enjoy knocking down houses then setting them on fire. Men like you and Happy Meens and Ruby Elam who scheme to make money off the backs of people who have spent their lives making a home for their family, only to see it go up in smoke before their eyes."

Elmer got a fire going in his eyes. "What are you talking about, scheming to make money. I'll have you know . . ."

"What were you and Ruby Elam doing with Happy Meens the day he was shot?"

"What? What are you talking about?"

"You know what I'm talking about, Elmer. You and Ruby and Happy all got together to put the squeeze on Hayden Joost so you could build the county seat on his land. Only somebody shot Happy and you and Ruby took off running before you got it, too."

"Who says that?"

"A reliable witness, Elmer. And when the sheriff gets back in town, he wants to have a talk with you. This whole county seat business is going to get exposed. How McDermott and Graves ran Ruby off in the river and killed him. How you joined in with McDermott to put the pressure on the county judges to put the county seat on the land you were sending Ruby Elam to buy with $20,000 in cash."

Elmer's face was the color of red brick. He clinched and unclenched his hands as they trembled with anger.

"You've been nothing but a trouble maker since I hired you. There's a bad apple in every bushel and you're the one in ours. I should have fired you the first time Leah turned in a report on you. It's not too late. You're done with this company. And you can forget the two weeks pay I promised you. In view of your attitude, you'd best not come around here again. Leave town before I have you charged with obstruction with a lawful project."

I found myself laughing uncontrollably. Elmer had become

an object of derision, such a pathetic sight, a greedy, amateur crook whose small mind couldn't comprehend the grief and turbulence his actions were imposing on the people of this town.

"Elmer, you left too many tracks. You're small time. You'll never get away with it. If the sheriff doesn't get you, McDermott will eat you alive. He had Ruby Elam killed, maybe Happy and he won't hesitate to turn on you. You've made a deal with the devil. Try and stay alive. I pity you, Elmer, you're such a sorry case."

Walking out the door left me with the best feeling of the day. Eddie Bailey stood there looking as if he'd been waiting for me. I spoke to him and he said, "Mister Beauchamp, I got this note I'm supposed to give you," and he handed me a slip of paper, then turned and crossed the street.

I tried to figure who could be sending me a note as I watched Eddie walk away. At the time it seemed the sensible thing to do, try and figure out who's sending me a note instead of just opening it. Try not to be surprised, that was my motto.

Dear Smith,
I need you. Can you come right away?
Estelle Earnhardt
What a surprise.

Estelle Earnhardt looked as near to being disheveled as it was possible for such an attractive woman. Her hair strung down into her face and actual perspiration dotted her forehead and her upper lip. She had boxes strung out on the floor before her as she removed items from the glass front display case and placed them carefully into the storage boxes. Yawley Earnhardt sat ten feet away in a wheel chair, his face drawn and unhealthy in color. His eyes were frosted over and his mouth hung slack. Meren was at the back of the store, her back to me as she lifted items off shelves and placed them in boxes.

Estelle saw me and straightened, bringing her hand up to her hair and combing it into place with her fingers. A half smile was my greeting.

"I'm glad you could come, Smith," she said. "I hope I haven't imposed on you too much. Eddie Bailey said Doyle was gone and Joel Dean couldn't . . . " she looked at her father, "well, he just couldn't come so I thought of you."

"I'm glad you did," I said, then waited for her to explain.

The concern on her face was real, the first time I'd seen her without a smile there.

"It's Meren," she said. "I'd like for you to talk with her. She needs someone now. She seems to trust you and she likes you, I could see that. I want to tell her mother, too, but right now she needs someone she trusts who can protect her."

I was puzzled and I guess it showed. "Why? What has happened?"

"Didn't you know? Grant was just here."

As I walked toward Meren, she dropped a tin can on the floor and jumped back in fright. With her eyes still spread open and the look of fear on her face, she saw me. At first, I frightened her more than relieved her, then it came to her who I was. I held my hand out to her and she took it, then came to me in a rush and put her face in my chest and began to sob. Three women in one day crying to me. I had a new record.

I held her close and let her cry it out. When she looked up, the tears still glistening in her eyes, she mouthed, "Grant."

"I know," I told her. "Did he threaten you?"

Her head went up and down. She began to talk without a sound, but she was mouthing the words too fast for me to catch them all.

"Did he say he was going to kill you?" I asked.

Again her head went up and down.

"No," I said. "No, he's not going to hurt you. Doyle will be back this afternoon. He'll find Grant and place him in jail. His days of hurting people are over. He won't hurt anyone ever again."

She poked a finger into my chest and began talking again. The sound was no more than a whisper of air, but she said the words slowly and this time I understood her.

"You, too, Smith. He's going to kill you, too."

PART
4

ONE

Against the bright, full moon and one lonely house light down the street, a cloud of no-see-ums fluttered aimlessly, interspersed with a light-seeking moth here and there, and round bodied June bugs, bent on suicide, thumping their brainless bodies against obstacles and falling to the ground to lie there upside down, legs churning soundlessly and futilely in the still night air. The smell of Uncle Billy Jack's pipe tobacco collided with my olfactory senses while the last taste of Ernest Raines smooth whisky lingered on my tongue.

This was a special summer night, meant for memory and joy; a night the likes of which we would not experience again. It was our last night at Rose Minton's boarding house.

"You say Doyle has a guard at the Earnhardt place for Grant?" Uncle Billy Jack asked, breaking a lull in conversation.

"Noah's keeping an eye out for any trouble. Provided he stays awake."

Uncle Billy Jack grunted. "Noah's due retirement. Let's see, he's pushing on towards sixty-something. Been about thirty five years since his baby boy and wife died. Surprised he never remarried. Been a good deputy."

"So you're moving down to Lebanon with Rose tomorrow, huh? Got everything packed?"

"Rose helped me. That friend of yours, what was her name, Leah? She up and moved out yesterday. I always thought she was fond of you."

"We were pretty good friends, that's all."

"Uh-huh. You don't have your cap set for Estelle Earnhardt by any chance do you? Not that it's any of my business."

"She's just about the most beautiful woman I've ever met, Uncle Billy Jack."

"She could be a movie star, that's true. Like her mother, maybe."

That surprised me. I tried to think of a way to ask about her mother without breaking Estelle's confidence.

"Tell me about her mother." I said.

"Some say she's a movie star." At least, that's part of the myth. The part about Champ Gowan's daddy running off with Yawley Earnhardt's wife. It's become a part of the history of this town now, and it don't matter if it's true or not. People believe what they believe and it don't matter much what the facts are."

"Except to Estelle. It matters to her."

"Yes, it does. I admire that girl. She's become a woman since that night Joel Dean shot Yawley. I'm not so sure she needs anybody now. Her mother, Yawley, maybe not even Joel Dean."

I worked up the nerve to ask the next question. "You think she'll marry Joel Dean after Yawley dies?"

I don't know why I was so apprehensive about hearing his answer. As if Uncle Billy Jack Cummins was not just the historian of Linn Creek, it was as if he also controlled the future.

He said what I didn't want to hear. "Yes, they will. Those two clinched their relationship a long time ago, at a place, a time and a way that only they know about. It would take a miracle to break that."

A miracle? Well, miracles still happen.

"I don't reckon there's anything we can do about that bunch that the electric company brought in here, is there? They're a cold hearted group of people, nothing like you at all, Smith. It's tough seeing the town torn down, but those people are tearing things down right in front of the ones who spent years building it up. Then burning it and walking away. I see people standing there looking into the ashes as if they could salvage some part of their lives. It's a cruel ending for the town. I hadn't planned on it happening this way."

"I wasn't sure how it was going to end, Uncle Billy Jack. I wasn't sure how it *could* end. I got fired, I'm all through with it. Time for me to be moving on, I guess."

"Where will you go?"

"I'm not sure. I feel like I have an obligation to Meren. She's going to be staying on with Estelle, helping at the new store. But, until Grant's found, her life will continue to be unsettled. I wish I knew a way to help her."

"I hear she's very fond of you. Doesn't talk with anyone— even her mother—except you and Estelle."

"Well, that's another problem. I'm afraid she regards me too highly."

"She's a very pretty young woman."

"That she is."

"Would take a special person to take care of her the rest of her life. Very special indeed."

"What are you suggesting?"

"Nothing. Nothing at all. I'm just saying you're a very special person, Smith. I saw that the first time I met you."

I felt objection rising all over me. The temporary anger at Uncle Billy Jack passed swiftly and my thoughts went to a place and time I wasn't anxious to revisit.

"I can't look after Meren," I said. I noticed a tremor in my voice, but I went on. "I took care of my mother for as many years as I could until the state institutionalized her. Some days she was normal, some days she was somewhere else. It wears on you, Uncle Billy Jack. It wears on you and leaves a scar that won't go away and you don't ever want to live through it again."

"Meren's a normal person if people would let her be normal. She's got a lot to forget, too, Smith. The fact she talks with you, well, that's pretty special if you ask me."

"What do you know about what happened to her?"

He took so long to answer I leaned toward him to make sure he hadn't fallen asleep. His rocker was moving back and forth and I could see the slight glow from the bowl of his pipe.

"What I know I swore I'd never tell. But maybe it would help her if I told you."

"I do want to help her. I just don't know how."

"Hayden Joost was a mean and cruel man. And secretive. You know the verse in the Bible? John 3:18 or 3:19 I think it is. About the light coming into the world, but men preferred darkness because their deeds were evil?"

"I've read the Bible. Several times."

"That was Hayden Joost. He had a reason to be secretive. His deeds were evil."

I was surprised at what he was getting at. "You mean . . . you don't mean Meren do you?"

"I'm afraid I do. The reason he and Grant never got along was because of the rivalry between the two of them over an innocent little girl not more than twelve years old."

"My God. How long did this go on?"

"Far too long for her sake. When she fought Hayden and screamed too loud, he liked to choked her to death. Damaged her vocal chords. Doc Hardesty doesn't think she'll ever talk again. She was near death for weeks. But when she recovered, the two of them went back at her again."

"Where was Eleanor? Why didn't she stop it?"

"She tried. Doc Hardesty could tell you what happened to her if it wasn't for his professional ethics. When Ora Mitchell was sheriff, he suspected something and he went out there and beat Hayden to within an inch of his life. Only man to ever best Hayden Joost until his own son shot him. It stopped for awhile, then Ora got killed. It started all over again."

What Uncle Billy Jack told me was a horror story. And one thing I didn't want in my life was another horror story.

"I don't know what I could do about all that, Uncle Billy Jack. I'm not a person equipped to handle something like that."

"Maybe you're more than you think you are."

"No, I've been tested and found wanting. I'm not very proud of myself in that area. I want to help people, I just don't seem to be able to. Leah was a very nice person. She was an orphan, she just wanted someone to love her. I rejected her."

"How do you feel about Meren?"

"What do you mean? I feel, well, she's pretty. She's a woman, though she is childish in many ways."

"How do you feel when you meet her?"

"I, well, good, I suppose. I mean, she's warm and she kind of reaches out to you."

"You don't pity her, do you?"

"I used to. At first I thought, 'Oh, you poor little thing.' But she's more grown up than I thought. She changes day by day, living with Estelle."

"I always use the test of what I feel whenever a person walks into the room where I am. If I'm glad, if they light up the room, if it's like sunshine breaking through the clouds, then I find I like that person. If gloom sets in the minute they walk in the door, chances are I won't be too fond of them."

"Meren lights up the room," I said, thinking about it. "I go out of my way to meet her."

"Hmm."

"Maybe not as much as I go out of my way to meet Estelle.

Whenever I see Estelle Earnhardt, it's like one of those big sky rockets they shoot off at the Fourth of July. You know, the ones that explode into the sky, then they spread softly all over with little sparkly things dancing down to earth. But Meren, well, she's sort of like a candle being lit and a warm glow reaching out to you."

"You have a way of putting things, Smith."

"You ever been in love, Uncle Billy Jack?"

I could hear him puffing on his pipe and against the full moon I saw a fresh fog of smoke drifting by. He probably wasn't going to answer and perhaps I shouldn't have asked. But, finally he told me.

"I went south to Arkansas in the eighties. There were several gold rushes down there, most of them false alarms. In a little town called Bear, down near Hot Springs National Park, I got shot on a creek where I was doing some prospecting. Never found out who did it. I spent a couple of weeks in the hospital there and the most beautiful young woman in the world nursed me back to health. I was so in love I would have done anything to have her hand."

I waited, sure he would continue, then decided maybe he wasn't going to.

"So, what did you do?"

"Nothing. She was married, but she loved me, too. I was torn, you see, between being the kind of person I didn't want to be by taking her away from her husband who loved her too, or losing her."

"So you gave her up?"

"Yes, I did."

"And you lived to regret it."

"I did."

"That's the way I feel about Estelle Earnhardt."

"I was afraid of that."

Little swirls of dust danced in the street as we watched in awe at the work of Joe Collie's bulldozers. Most of the town had moved away, but word reached out that this would be the day the business section and the courthouse were coming down. That was enough to pull everyone back to town.

Already Linn Creek looked like some of the French towns you saw in the old Look magazines showing the destruction the Kaiser's German artillery had inflicted on the small towns that stood in their way. Houses only dotted the streets instead of lining them and at the rate Joe Collie's crew was moving, Linn Creek had about another three or four days before being nothing. The river, backed up by the mammoth dam, had swollen until the water was lapping against the short wall around the courthouse.

Doyle Savoy, standing beside me, said, "I suppose they'll get the jail tomorrow or the next day. Guess I'll see if Maries County will keep Graves, the bastard. Ought to shoot him."

"How long is Noah going to be able to watch the Earnhardt place?"

"Just till tomorrow."

"What happens then?"

"I'm goin out to look for Grant again today. Drop by the old Joost place then hit some drinkin places he's been known to frequent. Maybe you could break the news to Estelle."

"Grant's already threatened to kill Meren. She's scared to death. What if he shows up here while you're in the new town up the creek?"

"We'll be taking turns drivin by to check on her at night. Best I can do until I hire some more deputies."

"You could deputize me. I could keep watch on the place."

He grinned his crooked grin and slapped me on the shoulder. "Smith, if my job was buyin houses, you'd be the first person I would hire."

I watched him leave the crowd, resentment growing in me. I didn't have long to dwell on what I considered his dereliction of duty when the Missouri State Bank crumpled into the street with a thundering roar and the dust rose over the site in the shape of a mushroom. The dynamite blast we had been warned about was more punishing to the ears than we had anticipated. Women ducked away from the blast, kids held their hands over their ears and the men waved their hands in front of their faces to drive away the dust.

One by one the buildings fell, most of them done in by the bulldozers, the occasional brick building blasted by well placed dynamite sticks. Fires set by the men Elmer had hired— my, those slickers sure enjoyed setting fire to things— consumed the debris. Smoke and clouds of dust rolled skyward and soot gathered on the onlookers' faces and clothes.

People wiped at their faces and dark streaks appeared like the war paint on Apaches. Under the eyes of most of the women, tears had washed the skin clean of soot and the wipe of the women's hands could be tracked by the curling stripes of soot going back towards their ears.

Between the sound of the buildings collapsing we could hear the rip-rip, rip-rip of the two-man crosscut saws that were felling the Linn wood and Cottonwood trees that lined the creek across from the business site. A shout of "Timberrr," was followed by a building crescendo of cracking limbs and trunk and a final earth-shaking thud as another big tree hit the ground.

"Ate many an apple under that old tree," one man said. "Sparked my wife there thirty year ago."

A woman, still with an apron tied around her waist, turned to the man beside her and pulled on his arm. Tears ran freely down her face and puddled about her firmly set mouth. "C'mon Arly, I've seen about all of this I can stand," she said, tugging the man to the edge of the crowd.

As the bulldozers moved toward the Earnhardt businesses, Estelle, with Meren beside her, appeared next to me. Remembering my conversation with Uncle Billy Jack the night before, sky rockets went off and after the sparkling dots disappeared, a small candle glowed in the face of Meren. She smiled a bright little smile and opened her eyes larger.

"I said I wasn't going to watch it," Estelle said, grabbing me by the arm, "but I couldn't stay away. It's like watching yourself die."

"Your father didn't want to see it?"

"I didn't tell him. It would finish killing him for sure."

We watched it, Estelle's jaw set firmly, Meren's eyes blazing fire at the bulldozers. When all the buildings were down we stood silently, all the people gathered here to see the town die, and one after another the men removed their hats in tribute and the women stood stern-faced, some holding back tears, others letting them stream down to drip off their chins while the kids stood enthralled and stunned.

The bulldozers moved toward the courthouse and the crowd dispersed, seeing all they had come to see and more. As I walked away, flanked by Estelle and Meren, I told Estelle that Doyle Savoy would not be watching her house anymore. She was piqued.

"Well, that doesn't please me." She turned so that Meren could not see her. "Don't tell Meren. She's scared out of her wits at night. She has started sleeping with me in my bed."

"Doyle said he would be driving by the house," I told her.

"Won't do. I can't ask Joel Dean to stay, Daddy might wake up in the night."

We reached the end of the street where the bank building had finally stopped smoking with just small ribbons rising like the smoke from a cigarette.

"Smith," Estelle said, her grip on my arm tightening, "how about you. Could you stay over? I'll fix you a bed on the sofa

in the parlor. Nell will cook for you. We can play some Mah
Jongg or maybe some gin rummy."

The request floored me. I couldn't believe it, Estelle Earnhardt asking me to stay in her house.

So as not to appear too eager, I took my time answering.
"Sure, I could do that. Anyway that I can help. Besides, I'm
out of a place to stay. Rose is leaving the boarding house
today."

"Good," she said, patting my arm with her other hand. "It's
settled then. Come by in time for dinner. Six o'clock."

As they walked away from me, Estelle talked to Meren
who watched her lips intently. She must have understood because she turned back to me and smiled, waving her hand.

Was I lucky? Time would tell.

The courthouse fell next. I'm not sure how many sticks of dynamite it took, but the series of explosions rumbled through
the ruins of the town and shook windows in the jail house. All
of the offices in the courthouse had been closed for a week
now and the furnishings stripped and carted off or sold. The
election was over, the new town plotted by McDermott and
his highway crew was now officially the county seat. People
said the town was building fast, that two men were selling lots
and surveying streets, though, those who had been at the site
recently admitted nothing was there but mud and grass and a
sea of stakes.

A lot of people watched the courthouse go down. It surprised me that so little conversation took place among the
throng that had gathered to watch the demolition. When the
courthouse was down it was as if the town was now officially
gone. All of the businesses lay in rubble, only a few homes
were standing and the jail house looked like a lonesome spire
against a sky filled with cumulus clouds with dust and smoke

boiling up from the debris that lay scattered like the ruins of battle.

I was surprised to see Joel Dean Gregory on one end of a two-man crosscut saw that was taking down the large redbud tree between the courthouse and the jail. It fell awkwardly, splitting and splintering into the burning rubble of the courthouse. Someone grabbed a burning timber from the courthouse wreckage and threw it on the tree and it smoked and smoldered amongst the green, heart-shaped leaves, then the bark on the trunk and limbs began to burn. Joel Dean still standing there, holding the saw upright, watched the tree burn. He had the look of standing by the bedside of a friend, watching the last breath. Uncle Billy Jack Cummins stood ten feet behind Joel Dean, his eyes glued to the back of the younger man. What coursed through the mind of both men, I could not say.

They pulled over the tower on the Methodist Church in early afternoon, then moved on to Rose Minton's house. Uncle Billy Jack had walked from site to site watching his town being destroyed as if his intent was to commit each incident to permanent memory. All the boarders from Rose's stood with arms linked as we watched the destruction of the house we all called home. Rose could not stem the flow of tears, letting them run freely down both cheeks without wiping them. Oma Thornbush sobbed softly with dry eyes while Jane McGann closed her eyes and would not look. Volly kept saying, "Damn, damn, damn," and Lonnie stood straight and silent, his lower lip trembling. Uncle Billy Jack watched stoically.

When the building collapsed and Elmer's boys had the fire going pretty strong, Rose said loudly, "Oh, my God, I must have left the biscuits in the oven," and the lot of us busted out laughing in relief. We hugged, said goodbyes and a chapter in all our lives closed.

I wandered aimlessly around the destroyed town. Soot and ashes were falling like rain. Craters in the earth marked where foundations had been just hours before. The creek bank was nude of trees, just the charred remains of what had once been a peaceful border of leaves and trunks and a tangle of limbs.

No birds sang in town. They had no trees to sit in, no roofs to perch on. The barrier of smoke kept them away; the hot earth left them no place to forage. Life seemed strangely barren without them.

Only a half dozen houses still stood. And the jail across from Volly's Shell station which he had closed for the day. I watched him walk around his building looking for something he might want to save from tomorrow's destruction. The Bailey twins worked feverishly removing the siding on the house and leaning the boards in a stack against the wall. Smoke curled up from the chimney of Granny Harris' small home. She sat rocking on the front porch, her pipe clinched tightly in her mouth.

Doyle Savoy's Chevrolet came along the street, threading through the smoldering timbers which had spilled out into the thoroughfare. I walked toward the jail to meet him. After he stopped and got out, he stood looking at the courthouse, or where it had been.

"They did it, didn't they?" he said as I came up to his car. "Never thought I would see it, but there it is. First thing I noticed when we came to this town. Big old courthouse."

He shut the door on his Chevrolet. "Had to drive all the way over to Maries County. Glad I didn't take Graves with me. The prosecutor over there didn't sound much like he wants to charge Graves with Ruby Elam's murder. Said Graves confession wouldn't hold up in court."

"So he's going to get away with it?"

"I'm going to lock him up in a house I rented up the creek in the new town. At least we can charge him with assault. That'll get him fifteen years in the pen."

"I was looking forward to a hanging."

"Yeah, well, take what we can get, I reckon." He started toward the jail. "Come in and have supper with me and Eleanor. Noah's probably already fed Graves by now. Stay the night if you want. You can sleep in one of the cells. I see Rose's place was taken down today."

"I'm staying in the Earnhardt house tonight. Having supper there, too. Estelle is putting me up on her sofa since you can't provide a guard for tonight."

Savoy stopped, put his good hand on his hip and said, "Doing the best I can with one deputy. What're you going to do if Grant shows up?"

I shrugged. "I'll think of something. Throw a skillet at him maybe."

"Nell could do that."

I flushed in embarrassment. "I think I can handle Grant."

He turned and walked on toward the jail, jutting alone into the treeless sky. "Call me if the skillet misses."

From the Earnhardt front porch, I looked across the hazy valley where a town once stood, at a sun, hidden by smoke, and off to the north where the river widened and the water, relentless, would be nine inches deeper tomorrow and two feet closer to Volly's station and the jail house.

Estelle and Meren both greeted me at the door. Meren all smiles, took my hand and said in a voice nearly audible, "Smith. Hello." She clapped her hand over her mouth to cover her huge grin and Estelle laughed along with her.

"She's been like this ever since I told her you were spending the night on the sofa," Estelle said.

Nell called us to dinner and throughout the meal Meren,

across the table from me, kept me constantly in her stare. We chatted about what Estelle and Meren had read in the latest copy of the *St. Louis Globe Democrat* and Meren explained to me, with whispered words and hand gestures, what latest women's styles were being advertised in the newspaper. I was somewhat astonished at the change in her and how easily we were communicating.

Nell made up the fourth hand in a Mah Jongg game after dinner and was quite good at it until it was time for her to take care of Yawley. She laid pillows and blankets on the sofa for my bed and Estelle joined her as the two bid us goodnight and left up the stairs.

The night was young and I asked Meren to sit in the swing on the front porch with me and look at what had been a town just a few days ago.

"I'm sorry about Estelle's stores," Meren said, her voice tailing off in an inaudible whisper. But, I knew what she was saying, even the part I couldn't hear.

"You're doing well with your speech, Meren," I told her. "You look happy here."

She nodded enthusiastically. "I love Estelle," she said. "She's my sister."

We laughed together. "Are you going to work with Estelle in her new store?" I asked.

She nodded again. "I want a store," she said. "My store."

"You? You want a store? What kind of store?"

She took her dress in her hands. "For dresses. A store for dresses."

"That would be a good idea."

"I could sell a lot of dresses."

"If you think you could, then you could."

"People buy more when you don't talk to them," she said, then made a talking motion by opening and closing her thumb and fingers. She laughed and I laughed with her.

Stars twinkled through the drifting smoke over the town and frogs in the creek croaked even louder as if they were the town criers and had a lot of news to tell up and down the creek tonight about the fires and the rising water.

The night was cool and Meren clasped her arms in front of her and said, "Cold, tonight." She scooted closer to me.

Her body was warm against mine and her smell was pleasant. I put my arm around her shoulders and drew her to me and she lay her head against me. She said something, but the whisper was weak and her head was turned so that I could not understand.

She brought her upturned face around to within inches of my face and said, "I said, you could kiss me."

So I did. Her lips were warm and tender and her hand behind my head kept us engaged for several minutes.

"Will you come to my store?" she asked when the kiss ended.

"What? To buy a dress?"

She nodded. "For your wife."

"I don't have a wife."

"Will you have a wife soon?"

"I don't know. I haven't been thinking about it. I mean, maybe I have, but, well, I'm afraid I wouldn't make a very good husband."

"No, no. You make a good husband."

"How do you know?"

"I know. What kind of wife do you want?"

"I don't know. A pretty one, I guess."

She shook her head. "More than that."

"Yes, more than that."

"Smart?"

"Yes, smarter than me."

"A wife who doesn't talk too much?"

I couldn't help laughing and she laughed with me. We

heard the door open and Estelle stepped out onto the porch.

"Doyle just telephoned from the jail house. Thank goodness they didn't burn the Henderson house and the phone office yet."

I waited a moment. "Any problem?"

"No," she said. She turned so that her profile was lined up against the nearly full moon and I was struck again by the beauty of the woman. I could not help comparing her beauty to that of Meren's and realized then for the first time I was considering Meren as a woman, not a girl any longer, not a victim nor someone to pity or patronize.

"Noah's sick," Estelle continued. "Doyle sent him home. He said he would be driving by later on tonight, but he wouldn't stop."

She turned to me and saw Meren still cuddled up to my side. "He said for you to be careful."

I lay awake on the sofa thinking about the night behind me. The feelings I had about Meren were new. And different. They conflicted with the feelings I had for Estelle.

I was pleased to have feelings about two women at the same time. It was something new for me. And exciting.

Suppose I had to choose between them. Suppose they both wanted me. Which would I choose. For the first time in my life my thoughts were on marriage. I was sweating and I turned restlessly from side to side.

Marriage? Me? Now?

No, maybe later. Much later.

I made the mistake of trying to solve all my problems, all the problems of the town, all the problems of everyone I knew, all while my brain was operating at half speed, slipping in and out of sleep, and I came up with the usual results.

Nothing.

I woke in the morning at the sound of Nell in the kitchen. I had finally fallen into such sound sleep that I heard nothing during the night. If Savoy had indeed come by, I didn't know it. He had been right, Nell would have made a better guard.

I joined Nell in the kitchen and she fixed me a hurried breakfast. She said Estelle and Meren would be down soon, but I wanted to leave before they were. Nell didn't understand —or maybe she understood more than I did—but she placed a full plate in front of me and I made short work of eating it all.

The sun had barely shown when I made my way down the hill toward the town. I saw someone walking around the jail placing objects against the walls and stringing wires away from it. I realized then they were preparing to dynamite the jail house and supposed that Savoy had already taken Graves to the house in new Linn Creek. But, then, I saw his Chevrolet parked not far away. He must still be inside.

The jail was too far away from me to shout a warning at the man who had been placing the charges around the building. I began to run toward the jail. I saw no one else up and moving in the town. It was eerie. The low sun barely peeped above the hill behind me. Small curls of smoke still rose from the craters here and there.

I started shouting, though I saw no one to hear me. I was in the street, even with where Estelle's store had been when the jail exploded. The sidewalls came inward, the roof came down and the back wall crumbled and fell in on the roof. The front wall stood, though it was soon obscured by the dust and flying debris. When I reached the building, I could see nothing but total destruction.

"Doyle," I yelled. "Savoy."

Someone was beside me. Billy Bross.

"Billy, what the hell are you doing here?" I yelled.

"It was me," he said and he laughed. "I got the job. I blew up the damn jail."

"You fool. You killed Savoy. You damn fool."

"I didn't kill him. He ain't in there."

"His car's here. He's in the damn jail house."

"No he ain't. They told me he wasn't. They hired me to blow her up and I did it, by God. I told old Doyle I was going to blow 'er and I did."

I was in the wreckage now, moving timbers and calling Savoy's name. Billy was right behind me, laughing at me, saying Savoy wasn't in here, but I knew he was.

"Who told you to do this, Billy? Who the hell told you to blow up the jail?"

"He hired me last night. Said to meet him by the courthouse this morning. He works for the state. He said nobody was in here now and it would be a good time to do it."

"He works for the state? McDermott? Tall, bulky guy with sandy hair. Gold-rimmed glasses?"

"Yep, that's the guy. Works for the state."

"That's McDermott, Billy, you fool," I shouted. Then I shoved him. "God dammit, Billy, you just killed Savoy and Graves and that's what he hired you to do."

Billy was stunned. It was as if I had hit him over the head. He was having trouble comprehending what I was talking about.

"They're in here," I yelled at him. "Savoy and Graves and Eleanor Joost. You probably killed them all."

"I didn't," he said. "I couldn't. I never killed anybody."

"Shut up and help me look for them," We started moving timbers and I kept calling. Joe Collie and several other men showed up.

"What's going on here," Joe Collie asked. "Who did this. I was supposed to blow the jail. Who set the charges?"

"Billy, here," I said, "but it was a mistake. Doyle's in here and Eleanor Joost. There was a prisoner upstairs, he's in here, too. Let's find them."

Joe Collie and his crew began moving the timbers faster than I could. A dozen men or so were working and searching when we found Eleanor. Her skull had been crushed. Billy began sobbing and bleating like a goat. He was no use to us after seeing Eleanor.

Graves had been in one of the iron cells upstairs and would have survived the blast as the cell never collapsed, but a wall stud had splintered and shot through him like a spear. He was dead when we uncovered him.

Doyle was unconscious, but breathing when we found him. Some ceiling joists had crossed over his head as he sat at the desk in his office and they had prevented the rest of the upstairs and the roof from smashing him.

He came around after we leaned him up against the front wall that was still standing. His right leg appeared to be broken and he had cuts and bruises all over him. I explained to him about Billy. And McDermott. Billy was walking around in a daze talking to himself and apologizing to everyone, tears still raining down his face.

Doyle asked about Eleanor and when we didn't answer, he looked up at me. I shook my head.

"Graves?"

Again I shook my head.

"That damn McDermott had him killed, didn't he. Had poor simple Billy do it. Tried to kill me, too, I guess. Didn't give a damn about Eleanor."

"Looks that way," I said.

"You goin to tell the girl?" he asked. "Meren?"

"Yeah, I'll tell her."

"Eleanor never had a chance in life," he said. "I thought I could make up for what I did to her, but she wasn't even inter-

282 ROBERT DEAN ANDERSON

ested. Told me last night she messed up everything and she wanted to die."

"Why would she feel like that?"

"Cause she thought the girl was possessed by the devil, she said. She was afraid of her own daughter. I don't know, it's crazy as hell. Guess she got her wish."

"What about McDermott?" I asked.

Savoy shook his head. "Man, five people dead over a new county seat. I sure as hell hope it's a good one

TWO

I had no passion left, none at all. Life without passion is no life, like the no-life I'd experienced before coming to Linn Creek. Two dreams occurred, both with Langston Beauchamp rambling and raving with a hole in his forehead and a slow dribble of blood oozing out. My mother sat cowered in the corner and I stood straight and tall with the abuse sloughing off me like a bag of garbage dumped on my head.

I sleep walked through the next three days. The demolition project stopped. Estelle did not open her new store. Meren was so distraught over the death of her mother, following so closely the death of her father, that she stayed secluded inside the house.

I continued to sleep on Estelle's sofa in the parlor each night, but my mind never focused on a possible visit from Grant. He could have walked into the house any time I was there and I doubt I would have noticed him.

A hearse came down from Jefferson City to transport Graves body back to that city. Eleanor's body was taken to Richland for embalming and was brought back to the cemetery on the hill at Linn Creek for burial. There was no service except at the grave site as there were no churches in town in which to hold them.

I held Meren's hand during the services. She was in a trance and had stopped speaking altogether. Telling her that her mother was dead after all she'd been through was the hardest thing I'd had to do in Linn Creek. I wanted so much to say and do the right thing, but what the right thing was, I did not know.

I stayed with her throughout the afternoon and sat with her in the swing that evening, but all of my attempts to get her to talk with me about her mother, her fears or anything at all were met with silence. She held my hand until the time Estelle came outside to tell her that she should come to bed. Meren kissed me softly on the cheek and followed Estelle up the stairs. I lay awake most of the night on the sofa, my mind a vacuum.

Joel Dean was still in the capitol so during the next couple of days I helped Savoy retrieve what records we could from the jail wreckage, then I helped him get an office established in the new Linn Creek town site. He wasn't much help. His broken leg was in a cast and, from the look on his face, I could tell it was hurting him. He couldn't get around easily with the cast. Noah helped some, but he didn't look well enough to be shoveling through the debris.

We said very little to each other. Savoy stopped sifting through the ashes once, leaned on his crutch and looked off into the distance as he said, "Dammit, I can't figure out if I ever loved her or not."

I wanted so very much to leave this town. The whole affair, purchasing people's houses, watching them move, seeing the houses and businesses torn down and burned was too depressing to put me in any thing but a foul mood.

But, I couldn't leave just yet and I knew it and I knew why. Estelle was going to have to tell me she didn't want me. But, what if she didn't tell me? What if she made me believe I was the one man just for her. The thought of getting married came to mind once again and I nearly strangled. I was not husband material.

If I was depressed, what about Meren? Or Billy Bross? He wandered the empty streets all day long and came to the jail house site where Doyle Savoy and I searched through the ashes and told Doyle he was ready to go back to jail for killing those people and wished the state would hurry up and hang him so he could feel good again. Doyle didn't know what to tell him. He said he would talk with Joel Dean about what to do. Maybe if Billy signed a statement, they could shift the blame onto McDermott. After all, it was really his fault.

Billy felt some better. He asked me if he could see Meren and apologize for killing her mother. I said I would ask and let him know. I told Meren that evening, but she just shook her head no and looked away.

It took three days for her to speak again. Early on the morning of the fourth day she came downstairs while I was still eating the breakfast Nell had fixed for me and she told me in a very quiet whisper that she was sorry for the way she had acted.

"I don't think you have anything to apologize for," I told her. "You've had too much sadness lately. I'm sorry for you."

She joined me at breakfast. She said, her voice still so low that I needed to watch her lips to understand, that Billy could come to apologize to her if he wanted.

I heard the sound of Joe Collie's bulldozers echoing up the side of the hill where we were. I finished my breakfast quickly and left Meren smiling. For some unknown reason, I wanted to witness the final destruction of Linn Creek.

The Rasher brothers were putting the skids under Granny Harris' house in preparation to move it up the creek. Jack Rasher came over to where Joe Collie and I were standing and told Joe that Granny Harris wouldn't leave the porch of her house where she sat rocking, puffing on her clay pipe.

"Hell's fire, Joe, we can't move that house with her settin there. You're goin to have to tell her to move. The way that house is goin to bounce around while we're movin it, she'll be throwed off and run over," Jack said.

Joe said, "Well, she's never had much use for me or my bulldozer. Maybe Smith here can convince her to move."

I thought about Granny and her house of memories. I knew why she wouldn't leave her post on the porch. It was her symbolic way of saying she was staying with her house no matter what. And if the house was wrecked, then so be it. So would she be wrecked. Life to her without her house was like life to me without a passion. It was no life at all.

"What's it going to hurt?" I asked and Joe Collie and Jack Rasher looked at each other and shrugged. Jack walked to the truck that was to move Granny Harris' house to the new Linn Creek, got in and started the truck down the road. As the house faded out of sight I saw smoke from her cooking fire twisting in a swirl out her chimney and Granny rocking away on her porch.

The Morrisons were in front of their modest house engaged in loud conversation with three of Elmer's handpicked St. Louis men. I went over to see the cause of the dispute.

Morrison saw me coming and came forward to meet me. "Smith, these men are for burning my house down right now, before we've had an opportunity to walk around a bit and say goodbye to 'er. They say they own the house now and I've got to get out of it right now."

I went over to one of the men, a pug-nosed, red faced man whose ill fitting suit was three inches too short for him in the sleeves and a size too small through the shoulders.

"Move on," I said. "I'll take care of the Morrison place."

"Who the hell are you," Pug Nose asked in a belligerent tone.

"I'm the guy who bought it from them. Now, move on and

leave them be. They want some private moments before they leave the house."

"Well, I ain't got time for private moments. I got work to do."

He turned his back to me and strode toward the house, searching in his pockets for matches.

I said to his back, "You torch that house and I'll have you arrested."

He stopped, waited a moment for his brain to catch up and he turned and said, "What are you going to have me arrested for?"

"Arson," I said. "I haven't finished writing up the deed, yet."

He thought about my lie, thinking that it was, not knowing for sure, but deciding not to test me. He walked off down the street past the piles of ashes that had all been houses a few days ago.

I told Morrison to take all the time he wanted and left the two of them alone in their house as I walked away to where Joe Collie's bulldozer was ripping another house to the ground. Pug Nose and a couple of his friends ran to the pile of lumber that Joe's bulldozer had left and soon had a smoking, flaming fire going in the pieces that had been a home to someone.

There were two houses left, the German's and the Bailey twins. The twins worked feverishly to finish taking their house apart so that the Rasher Brothers could move the pieces when they returned from moving Granny Harris' house.

The German argued with Joe Collie.

"It's still my house. I don't sell it. I go to court. Joel Dean Gregory, he take you people to court. You can't touch my house. It's mine."

Joe said, "The court cases are all over. Some won, some lost. But it don't matter whether the house is up or down. And it's going down. Today."

"No, by God," the German roared. "She stays up. The judge, he sends somebody to look at her. He says what she's worth. Then the judge he tells you people what you have to pay me. Then you can tear her down."

"Sorry," Joe Collie said. "But you'll have to step aside. The house is going down."

"Have you moved your stuff?" I asked.

"Ya, I move. The house, she's empty. But she's mine."

"No," I said. "It doesn't belong to you any more. It belongs to the electric company. It's called Eminent Domain. The court has already ruled on that issue and said the electric company can take your property for the common good. The court rules on how much the electric company has to pay you for it. Joel Dean will be back from the capitol today or tomorrow and he'll tell you what the court decided."

The German looked confused. "How I know all this to be true?"

"You know me. You know I tried to buy your house. You know I worked for the electric company. What I have told you is true. Maybe it's not fair, but it's true. The electric company owns the house."

Joe Collie and the bulldozer rumbled toward the German's house. He watched in dread.

"But it is my house," he said, just as the sound of the bulldozer splintering the corner of the house and the sound of the roof caving in drowned out the sound of his voice.

Joe took two more swipes with the bulldozer, then the St. Louis men rushed in to start the fire in the debris. As the flames licked at the broken parts of the house, then roared to life, the German said again, "But, it is my house."

The Morrisons were getting into their car when I went back to their house. Morrison said, "Thanks, Smith. If you wouldn't mind, don't start her to burning till we're out of sight. And don't let Joe and his bulldozer knock 'er down. I left a fire in the fireplace. Burned some stuff we didn't want to take with us. Just scatter it out on the floor, she'll burn pretty fast."

"Sure," I said. "I'll do that."

Morrison took one last look around at the fallen fruit trees that dotted his lot, shut the car door and drove off. When I could not see their car any longer, I went inside and scattered the fire from the fireplace onto the floor of the house in a large circle and threw some newspapers on top of the coals. I waited until the floorboards were burning good before I left the house. I saw Joe coming with his bulldozer. I walked toward him and held up my hand.

"Just let it burn," I said. "Morrison didn't want the bull-dozer knocking it down."

Joe nodded and we watched the house burn until the flames were on the roof.

When I got far enough away from the Morrison house, I heard the sound of the Bailey twins yelling loudly. When I got closer to their house I saw that Pug Nose had set fire to the piles of siding and the flames were spreading to what re-mained of the main structure of the house. I ran as fast as I could.

"My dad, my dad," Eddie was yelling and jumping into the air and pointing.

"Is he inside?" I shouted at him.

"Tommy went in after him," Eddie said, and followed me into the burning house.

Smoke filled the house. Tommy had found his father and was trying to carry him outside, both of them coughing from the smoke. I grabbed the father from Tommy and leaned him over my shoulder. I knew Mr. Bailey outweighed me, but at the moment didn't consider it. I got out the door with him, pushing Tom and Eddie ahead of me.

I dropped him on the ground and fell beside him. Tom be-gan talking to his father who coughed without stopping.

Sitting on the ground, I saw Pug Nose standing with his hands on his hips staring with disdain at the four of us. I couldn't stand him any longer. I came up off the ground with a roar and I hit him in his pudgy gut with the point of my shoulder. He grunted hard and went over backward. Before he could struggle up, I was on him, pounding away with my fists. I felt the pain and the jolts from my blows all the way up to my shoulders, but it didn't stop me.

I felt someone's hands under my arms pulling me off Pug Nose. I discovered then I had been growling some animal sound and mucous was coming out of my nose and drool was dripping from my mouth.

"Smith," Joe Collie said, "What the hell you doin?"

"That St. Louis son of a bitch was trying to burn up the Bailey twins' dad inside their house. That house wasn't supposed to be burned. The twins were going to rebuild it on a lot in new Linn Creek."

"Uh huh," Joe said. "Well, damn, you bout killed the guy."

"I should of killed him," I said, "The sorry son of a bitch."

Pug Nose was sitting up now, his face a bloody mess. Doyle Savoy leaned on his crutch and looked down at him with disgust, "Who told you to burn that house?"

"That's my job," Pug Nose said.

"No, no it ain't. Your job is to burn the buildings you're told to burn and not to burn the buildings that you aren't told to burn. Now, you owe these boys for burning their house."

"Hell, I do. They've been paid for it once."

"No, they haven't," Savoy said. "How much money you have on you?"

"Why?"

"I'm trying to keep you out of jail. I'm a little short on jail space right now and I'd like to not to have to arrest anyone. How much you have on you?"

"What the hell is this, a holdup?"

"I already told you what it was. Let's see your billfold."

"You can't get by with this," Pug Nose said.

Savoy leaned forward so that his face was closer to Pug Nose's face.

"Am I going to have trouble with you?"

Pug Nose reached inside his coat and extracted a leather billfold and tossed it on the ground.

"Take the money out of it," Savoy said.

"Jesus Christ," Pug Nose whined. "It's all the money I have. It's my whole pay for my work here."

He took some bills out of his billfold.

"How much?" Savoy asked.

"A hundred and thirty dollars," Pug Nose answered.

"Give it to the boys." Savoy called Tom and Eddie over to him and Pug Nose held out the money. "It's okay, take it," Savoy said.

When they left with the money, Pug Nose said, "By God, I'm reporting this."

Savoy pulled his pistol, cocked it and pointed it inches away from the man's terrified face.

"I could have shot you to stop you from burning a house with a cripple man inside. You see any witnesses around here that would say it was a crime if I did?"

Pug Nose looked around, then brought his eyes back to Savoy. He shook his head. His eyes twice the normal size.

Savoy said, "Now you get your fat ass up off the ground and you get it moving in the direction of St. Louis and don't you stop until you get there. Because if I see you around here in ten minutes, I'm goin to shoot you where you won't ever sit down again."

Doyle, with the pistol dangling from his hand, watched Pug Nose leaving in his car. "Man's got a hard head," he said.

I looked at my bruised and cut knuckles on both hands.

"Tell me about it," I said.

THREE

I hadn't slept for four nights. I don't know what kept me going. As I lay awake on the Earnhardt sofa in the parlor, I decided to leave tomorrow. I didn't know what else to do. I couldn't marry Estelle. I couldn't help Meren. The whole town was gone except for Volly's Shell station. I needed to help myself. The dreams were coming more frequently. The agony inside my head, lodged in my memory, had taken me over.

A shadow, so slight, moving so quickly that it could have been a cloud passing over the moon, shot past the window. I waited. No sound. Nothing else outside the window. It was probably my imagination. Or nothing.

Then a sound, a slight scuffing noise like a shoe moving over a board in the floor of the porch. Either my imagination and my fear had increased or something, someone was out there.

I slipped into my trousers, went over to the fireplace and grabbed a poker then headed for the back door in the kitchen. I had no trouble going through the rooms to the door with moonlight and the beginnings of early morning lighting my way. I opened the door cautiously, slipped outside after looking around, then moved off the small back porch to head around the house so that I would come up behind whoever, or whatever it was I thought I had seen that had moved past the window.

I moved slowly, silently, until I was at the front of the house. I waited for a full two minutes, looking for movement, shadows, anything. I stepped silently onto the porch, crouching low. I tried to determine if anyone else was on the porch, but saw nothing except the swing and the rockers. I moved past them, came to the front door, tried the knob which was still locked, then felt a shock of fear run up my spine when I heard the voice behind me.

"Take it easy with that poker, Smith."

Joel Dean Gregory stepped up onto the porch.

"Damn," I said, expelling the pent up breath I'd been holding, "what are you doing sneaking around here, Joel Dean?"

"Doyle said you were staying here. Said he'd been driving by to check every night. So, I told him I'd come by instead."

"I thought you were Grant," I said.

"Long as you're out here, let's have a talk," Joel Dean said.

"You sure as hell picked an odd time for a talk," I said. "What would you like to talk about while we're waiting for morning to get here?"

"What are you doing still here?"

"Me? Estelle asked me to stay over. Sleep on the sofa, watch for Grant."

"Grant's gone. Doyle's got posters out for him for killing his father. He's not going to stick around here. The posters are everywhere. Someone would have spotted him by now."

"Uh huh. Well, why don't you see if you can convince Meren of that."

"What I mean," he said, hesitating. "What I was asking was what are you still doing in Linn Creek? All the properties have been bought up. Doyle says the last of the electric company men left yesterday. Joe Collie is gone. Why aren't you ? "

I didn't like what he was implying. My first reaction, none

294 ROBERT DEAN ANDERSON

of your damn business, Joel Dean Gregory. Mister Big Shot.

What I said was, "Are you afraid Estelle might start to care for me?"

"Listen," he said, "everybody says what a nice guy you are, so I'm taking their word for it. Thing is, Estelle Earnhardt and I are going to be married. Soon."

"I haven't heard her say that."

"I filed for Congress at the capitol today. If I'm elected, we'll be moving to Washington. Do something for Meren. Estelle says she thinks Meren's in love with you. She needs help."

"Sounds to me like you're trying to tell me who I can marry and who I can't."

"No, I'm trying to tell you that if you're sticking around here thinking you've got a chance with Estelle, you can go ahead and leave because you don't."

He left then, going down the front walk to where his car was parked, partially hidden by some bushes. I watched him drive away, the anger building inside me.

Well, by God, if Estelle wanted me, if Estelle would have me, I would marry her. I would show Joel Dean Gregory he couldn't tell me whom I could marry.

Volly's station went up in balls of flame from the fire he, Lonnie and Joel Dean started. The water from the backed up river lapped at the edge of the station. Streets turned to mud and ashes that had once been houses floated and bobbed in the rising lake.

It was over. My job had ended long ago. One thing was unsettled and I was on my way up the hill to the Earnhardt house to finish that.

Estelle greeted me on the front porch with tears in her eyes.

"It's over, isn't it?" she asked. "That was Volly's station."

"Yes," I said. "It's over."

"Well," she said, "it's time to move on. What's next in your life, Smith?"

"I was hoping you could tell me that, Estelle."

She turned fully toward me and I could see that I had taken her by surprise. Her usual stunning smile was not there, but the rest of her beauty was. As if she could hide it.

"Do I know what you mean?"

"I think you do, " I said. "Joel Dean was by in the middle of the night. We talked. He thinks there is no reason for me to stay."

What was going through her mind as she waited? She didn't look down, she didn't look away, but, instead, she fastened her eyes on mine and we stared at the other and we waited. It was up to her, there was nothing more I could say, was there?

"Maybe you better tell me what you think," Estelle said, her face now perfectly calm with maybe a bit of expectation there.

The moment had arrived when I could confess my love for her, but as I opened my mouth, I was suddenly unsure what I was going to say. In front of me was one of the loveliest creations God had ever put on earth, but a vision kept blurring my mind of a tall, slender girl in a sackcloth dress with tears in her eyes and whispering my name.

I took too long. We both knew it. The much anticipated moment had come and gone and I stood mired in place, mute as a mule.

When finally she spoke her voice was unusually soft, even for her. "I guess that leaves us something we will both wonder about doesn't it? I know I will. Was it possible that I could love two men?"

My mind took a hit. I was a comic strip Katzenjammer Kid with an empty speech bubble positioned over my head.

"You see, dearest Smith, I do love Joel Dean. I can't help

myself. Oh, I flirted with you. What fun it was. I began to think. . . well, like now I wondered. This I know, Joel Dean and I will be married, there was never any doubt in my mind about that. But there is no doubt in my mind that I won't forget you either. Is that fair? I don't know. Could I . . . would it be all right if I kissed you?"

I didn't have a chance to answer. She had her warm, moist mouth on mine and the smell of her overwhelmed me. She held me around the neck and my arms encircled her and my head grew light.

She pulled away and lowered her head. Over her shoulder I saw Meren standing inside the screen door staring out at us.

After I had gathered my things from the parlor and placed them on the front porch, I searched the house for Meren, but she was nowhere to be found. Nell was in the kitchen, but she hadn't seen Meren. Estelle was in with her father. I put my belongings in the Buick and drove down to the burning remains of Volly's station. He and Lonnie stood with Joel Dean staring into the flames. I walked up to Joel Dean and stuck my hand out.

"Estelle and I had that talk," I said. "I'm moving on. I wish you both good luck."

He nodded. "I think you were good for the town," he said. "Thanks for everything you did. What does Meren think about you leaving?"

"She was gone from the house. I don't know where she is. "

"Meren needs a friend."

"She has one. And she has Estelle."

"Yes, she does. Where can we get in touch with you?"

"I'll write."

I shook hands with Volly and Lonnie, they in a somber mood with the destroyed station burning behind them.

I drove away from the little town that used to be. Everything was flattened now, looking very much like I imagine a war zone would look. My future was as bleak as most of my life had been. Except for the few weeks in Linn Creek.

I took a road that led to the top of a promontory overlooking the river and the valley it passed through. I saw the swollen size of the Osage River and I imagined what the lake would be when it was full. I could see a cleared area around the river on both sides where Joe Collie's men had downed the trees. The size of the lake to be was not difficult to imagine. I thought it would be a good thing, but what about the people in Linn Creek? What would happen to them. I spent several hours at the spot, eating the lunch Nell had handed me when she said goodbye.

In the late afternoon I stopped in the new town and drove to the house Doyle Savoy had rented for his sheriff's office. When I came through the door, Savoy had his injured foot up on another chair while he sat in the oak, swivel chair that had been salvaged from the jail house. He had a cranky look on his face like my high school principal used to wear. I couldn't tell what he was thinking, his mind always cleverly hidden behind a grinning face. But the grin had been lost since the time there'd been a real jail and an office.

"Well, well," he said. "Look who just walked in. Mister Smith Beauchamp."

"Came to say goodbye, Doyle."

"Not quite yet. Noah just came back from the Earnhardts. Seems Meren has run away."

"Run away? What do you mean, run away?"

"She left a note. Told Estelle she couldn't live with her any longer. Didn't say why. Nobody seen Grant in the area so I don't guess he made her leave. You got any ideas?"

I saw Meren's eyes through the screen door after she had watched Estelle kissing me.

"Who's looking for her?" I asked.

"Noah's driving around. Joel Dean's down at the new county seat. Nobody else around to do any lookin."

"Where would she go?" I asked, more to myself than to Savoy.

"Noah said Estelle wanted him to look in the new store, maybe Meren had gone there. He looked, didn't find anything. Except, maybe a rifle gone. And some shells."

"Would she go back to the Joost farm?"

"Don't know," he said. "Nobody's been out there for a week or so, as far as I know. Eldon's stayin with the Lewis family."

"What if Grant's hiding out there?"

"Wasn't there when I looked. Why would he go back there?"

"Maybe he still wants to kill Meren. And me."

"I think it more likely he'd want to save his own hide. He ain't around here any more, I'd bet on that."

"I'm not so sure. Want to take a drive out there with me?"

"Look, Smith, I can't get out and do any tracking after Meren or Grant. Noah's out asking around. Places like Stoutland and Roach and Mack's Creek. Up where Zebra used to be. Somebody'll see one of them, maybe, and we can deputize a posse if it turns out to be Grant."

"What happens if Grant finds Meren?"

"She took a rifle."

"Remember the speech you made to Hayden. The one about how you do the protecting and arresting. How people like Happy's wife and Meren aren't supposed to have to carry guns around to protect themselves or catch killers."

"In about two days I'll be able to ride a horse. I'm going to search every inch of ground between here and the Glaize. Way I figure, that's where she's bound to be?"

"You actually think she'll go back to the Joost farm, to the place where she shot Grant?"

I spoke too sharply and he didn't like it. He squared around in his chair and narrowed his eyes when he spoke, sounding like he was chastising a child. "Well, yeah, that's possible. The girl don't know the country. She's never been off that farm since she was a little girl. Where else would she go."

"Well, that's the way I figure it, too. Now guess who else is going to think that way."

He squirmed some more and picked his hat up off the unusable leg and lightly, but firmly punched the crown in with his fist.

"I know, I know. That's the way Grant will see it too, if he's still around. Which I maintain he ain't. But she's no dummy. She'll watch for him. In another day we'll have some people out there."

"Not soon enough."

"I can't help it. Noah's already gone . . ."

"In the wrong direction."

He swung his bad leg off the chair where it was propped and with his one good arm and one good leg, he attempted to stand. But he couldn't.

He collapsed back into the swivel chair, a smaller man. A beaten one.

"I can't help it, Smith. I shouldn't have been out there goin through the wreckage. Doc had to reset my leg and I'm half drunk from the whisky I been drinkin to kill the pain. I'm prayin hard, real hard, that Grant ain't here and if he is, he won't find her before we do. I called the capitol and they promised help tomorrow. I called the sheriff up at Miller County and he's off chasing some bootleggers. I can't find any help for her. I can't . . ."

He left his sentence hanging, unfinished, like his search for Meren and Grant. Savoy never looked smaller or more impotent. He knew that and it was killing him.

"I'll go find them," I said. I walked around him to the desk and opened the center drawer. I clawed through the contents until I found what I was looking for. I pinned the deputy's badge on the front of my shirt.

"You want to make it official or do I wear it as an ornament?"

His brow creased in a dozen wrinkles and his eyes drew together as if pulled by a thread.

"Smith, I can't make you a deputy. You ever own a gun? Have you even shot a gun."

"Yes, I have."

"What kind of gun," with scorn.

"A pistol."

"You own a pistol?"

"Yes, I do."

"Where'd you get a pistol? What kind is it?"

"My father's dueling pistol."

The lines in his face disappeared, he put a hand behind his neck, threw his head back and laughed.

"A duelin pistol? Hell's fire, Smith, a damn duelin pistol only holds one shot."

"I don't need but one."

"Jesus, you can't be serious."

I stood and watched him laugh until the humor had left him.

"Listen, I deputize a greenhorn like you, you go out there looking for a man ready to kill somebody and lookin for his half-sister to kill and what chance you think you'd have against Grant Joost."

"Better than you would have. One arm, one leg."

His face turned the color of raw meat and he squared around in the swivel chair and with Herculean effort pushed himself erect on his one good leg.

Before he could say anything, I said, "I didn't mean that.

I've never met more of a man than you, Doyle. One arm or two. But I can't wait until tomorrow. Surely you see that. If you think so little of me, I'll take the damn badge off."

I unpinned it and laid it on his desk.

"All right, all right," he said. "You think I don't worry about her, too. Pin the damn badge on and repeat after me."

I replaced the badge on my shirt, raised my right hand and repeated the oath.

"Take the shotgun," he said, barking the command at me. "Leave that damn duelin pistol here."

"Doyle, if I carried the shotgun and I saw Grant, I'd throw it away and go for the dueling pistol. I know how to shoot that."

"What was your daddy doin with a duelin pistol?"

"He was Langston Beauchamp (pronouncing it the French way) a Frenchman. He owned a LePage-Moutier Dueling pistol. The finest French-made pistol ever. He shot a man with it in a duel in 1885 on an island in the Mississippi River between Missouri and Illinois. Neither state knew what to do about it."

"So your daddy goes around challenging people to a duel?"

"Used to. He's been dead since I was ten years old."

"Killed in a duel?"

"No. He was shot with the LePage-Moutier."

He was silent for a minute.

"Well, who did that?"

I felt suddenly tired. Secrets and guilt had piled up on me like bags of rocks on my shoulders. I could no longer bear their weight. I needed a rest. I needed relief. I needed confession. I pulled up the other lone chair and sat.

"All right," I said. "You confessed all your skeletons hanging around inside your mind to me. About Eleanor and the guy you shot. So guess it's only turn about I tell you mine."

I wasn't sure I wanted to do this. I mean, I'd never said

any of this out loud since the trial fifteen years ago when they put my mother in prison. But, what the hell. Nothing that had ever happened in my life occupied such a front row seat in my mind as this. Might as well tell it. Couldn't be any worse, could it?

"Langston Beauchamp was a descendant of French royalty. So he said. He certainly acted the part. He was a brilliant man, schooled, mannerly, worldly. He was handsome and was a great presence in any gathering. Trouble was, he was arrogant, abusive, controlling, an aggressive bully and a horrible father. An even worse husband."

I rested. Savoy was an attentive listener. He said nothing, showed no expression except interest. I drew a deep breath and went on.

"I grew up watching him berate my mother day after day. She was a proud and beautiful woman, but to him, just someone to show to his acquaintances. Night after night I listened as he ticked off her faults and how she should comport herself. She started taking up the dueling pistol and threatening him with it. He laughed at her. Even at ten years old I could see her mind going. Maybe she would have ended up that way no matter what he did, but I hold him to blame for it.

"On this one night, a night so brilliantly lit with the full moon I can't forget it. The lights inside the house were off, but the room was as bright as day because of the conservatory roof that let the moon shine inside. She threatened him again with the pistol. I had gotten out of bed and I stood in the hallway watching. I was ten years old. I saw her put a bullet into the pistol and aim it. I was glad, I remember that. I was happy that she was at last going to kill him and his taunting and overbearing presence would be gone forever and it would just be me and my mother. He laughed at her, saying she didn't have the nerve or the courage to do it. Telling her she was a coward, 'Just like your damn kid.' I knew he meant me, of course. When she dropped the pistol on the rug and went weeping from the room, I walked over, picked up the LePage-Moutier and shot my father between the eyes."

"Damn," Savoy said. "Ten years old?"

There, I'd said it. The secret I'd hidden since the day I told it in the courtroom where they sentenced my mother to ten years in prison because they thought I was just trying to protect her. And because she confessed to a crime her tormented mind actually thought she'd committed.

I told Savoy the rest of it. About the trial where no one believed me. About my mother spending years in the criminally insane ward, then being released to the Normandy Sanitarium to save the state some money.

What I didn't tell him, what I kept for me only, was about the years that followed. About the guilt I'd lived with and had slapping me in the face every time I went to see her. But, somehow, he already knew that. Or guessed it.

"Must have been hard carryin that around with you."

"I got over it. Sort of. She never did. She died in a sanitarium."

"That's where you went in St. Louis? To bury your mother."

"Yeah. She actually knew me for awhile before she died."

"Guess we don't always know what the other person had to go through."

I started for the door, opened it and turned back. "Keep praying for Meren," I said. "She needs it more than I do."

"Smith, do me one favor. Don't get shot."

I pulled up to the spot on the Glaize Creek where Savoy had parked his Chevrolet the first time I'd ever seen the Joost home. The rocks where we'd crossed were no longer visible, the dam having raised the level of the Glaize enough to hide them.

Fact is, I didn't see a way of crossing the creek without getting my feet wet.

I waded across, carrying my shoes with my pants rolled up to my knees. They still got wet as the water was now thigh-deep. The day was sunny and warm so I figured they would dry soon enough.

After I dried my feet with a handkerchief and put my shoes back on, I made my way to the Joost cabin, calling Meren's name as I walked. No one answered my knock on the door, nor did I expect anyone. I felt an uneasiness about entering the cabin, mostly because Grant might be inside, but also because it was trespassing. The electric company had bought the Joost land, but only up to the 660 foot mark which didn't include the land where Happy Meens and Elmer Byron had intended to build a new county seat, where now the cabin and the other outbuildings stood.

The inside of the house was an untidy mess and it was obvious someone had been living here since Eleanor had moved out. Scraps of food were left on soiled dishes and one of the beds had been slept in. The cooking stove was cold, so I couldn't tell how long it had been since someone had been here. It had to be Grant. Meren wouldn't have left the place messed up like it was. Besides, she had only been gone one day.

The thought of Grant being here was a disturbing one. I believed that Meren might come back here. Where else would she go? And what did she intend to do here, live out the rest of her life as a hermit because she saw the man she believed herself to be in love with, kissing another woman?

I did a calculation in my mind about how long it would take someone to walk here from Linn Creek. If she had chosen a direct route that would have taken her across several high ridges, past the promontory where I had lunched, she could have been here several hours before I got here. Or she could have walked the edge of the Osage that had all been cleared of trees until she came to the Glaize Creek. But she would have been seen by the people living along the river and she would not have wanted that.

She was here, I was sure of it.

The barn yielded few clues about Grant's presence. I checked the tool rack and noticed one tool missing. It could have been any tool or none at all. My imagination pictured one of those long, sharp blades farmers keep to chop brush.

Under the tree where the flower garden grew, I noticed that a number of weeds had been pulled recently enough that the soil that had been disturbed was still moist. Meren was here and she had visited her flower garden.

But how to find her? And was Grant still around?

I took the trail through the brush down to the creek where Happy Meens' body had been found. The trail had been worn smooth before, but since Eleanor had left the farm, no one would have used the trail and grass and weeds would have grown back on the pathway. A sparse growth was present and closely examining the path, it looked as if someone had been walking here recently. I never had a chance to be a Boy Scout as I grew up and reading signs in the forest was strictly guess work.

The creek was considerably higher than when I had last been here. The spot where I had first seen Happy Meens' body was now under water so that I wasn't even sure exactly where it had been. The whole area had changed enough that I was beginning to think I was wrong about where I was.

The growth along the creek was thick, so I knew this had to be above the magic 660 mark. Down the creek and around the bend would be where Meren had taken her baths and where Grant had spied on her and ended up getting shot. Below me was the spot where I had first seen her across the creek from me, staring with her big eyes, tears running from them, and whispering "Goodbye," to me before she fled.

I made my way through briars and brush until I stood about where she had stood that day I met her. Only now, the creek was about fifteen feet wide instead of six. I studied the soil along the water's edge, but there was too much growth there to find any kind of footprint. I sat on the ground and thought about how I could go about contacting Meren. I had a feeling she might even be watching me as I sat there.

I thought about a lot of things sitting there. About how the beauty of Estelle Earnhardt had blinded me to the way Meren had behaved when she was around me. She clearly had an elevated opinion of me, but whether that would hold when she knew everything about me, I couldn't say. I could tell by the light in the trees that the day was about to end. I decided I would not see Meren this day, but I had no intention of leaving until I did find her. What I would say to her I could not decide. What a fool I had been.

The frogs were starting to croak upstream, but the singing of the birds grew silent. At first I thought night was coming on, but then I sensed that someone else was at the creek. I could only hope it was Meren.

She came out of the trees some twenty or thirty feet downstream from me. When I saw her I rose. She carried the rifle in her hand as she had that first time, and she wore the same brown, sackcloth, shapeless dress.

She came close, three feet away, and looked hard into my eyes. The close feeling I had always felt with Meren was back. I remembered what Uncle Billy Jack had said about deciding how you feel about a person by how you feel when they walked into the room.

"Meren, why did you leave? Why are you here?"

She didn't answer right away and I thought perhaps she

had reverted to not speaking. After a minute or so, she whispered, "Why are you here?"

I was surprised to find that the answer was as easy as any I had ever given anyone. "Because I love you, Meren. Because I need you."

She showed surprise at that. Several times she mouthed one word, the same word. On the third time I made it out: "Estelle?"

"My friend. Your friend. She kissed me because I was saying goodbye. She is going to marry Joel Dean."

"You don't love her?" The whispers grew louder.

"I might have thought I did. She's very beautiful. But, she talks too much."

She tried not to smile, but the smile came and she looked away.

"You joke with me," she said, looking back.

"Because you are so easy to talk with. There are a lot of things about me you should know. I'd like to tell you all about them."

She said nothing.

"Is Grant here?"

Her face turned dark and her eyes narrowed.

"I feel him," she said.

"Have you seen him?"

She shook her head.

"Let's go back to my car. We'll send the sheriff out here, they can arrest him."

She shook her head again.

"He's wanted for killing Hayden," I said. "He's going to be arrested and sent to jail."

There was no response from her.

"I know about the bad things he did to you, Meren. Terrible things. Things he has to pay for. He took your life from you the last five or six years. Now, the law will take his. That's justice. That's the way it has to be."

There was a look on her face now that I hadn't seen before. She was somewhere else. Another time. Another place. I looked down at her hands that were gripping the rifle so tightly her knuckles were white.

"Don't do it," I said. "That"s what you came here for, isn't it? Don't let him ruin the rest of your life."

She stared.

"I know about killing someone, Meren. It stays in your mind and becomes part of you forever. Don't let him do that to you."

Her mouth formed the words. "Kill him."

"No. No, don't do that. I killed my father. That's what I wanted to tell you. That's why I need you, to help me forget. There's no satisfaction in killing. You only go from one sad world to another."

"Got to die," she said with no sound coming from her mouth. No change in the dead expression on her face.

"My family," she said. "All bad. All gone but him. And Eldon. I'm bad, too."

"No, you're not bad. Remember how it was with Estelle. You deserve that life, not this life. It's over with Grant. Try to forget that time."

She looked down. "Can't. I've been bad. Not over till Grant is dead."

"You haven't been bad. Bad things have happened to you. Things you couldn't control. But it's over. You're going back to live with Estelle."

She looked into my eyes again, her face softer now. "You?"

"I was going to leave," I told her. "I didn't think I had anything to stay for. Do I? I won't be able to marry you if you're in jail for killing Grant."

Her features took on a look of pleading. "Understand, Smith, he has to die or I can't live."

"Then let some one kill him who has already killed. I want to marry the woman I knew at Estelle's. That's the woman I fell in love with."

She looked up so that I could see her mouth. "I'm ashamed. And afraid"

"No, no. Don't ever be ashamed. You did nothing wrong. People wronged you. And you'll never have to be afraid again."

I took the rifle from her hand and laid it on the ground. I took her in my arms and I knew what I should have known all along: this was the woman I wanted to spend the rest of my life with. The woman who was already such a part of me that I knew I would never be whole without her.

We kissed and I held her and finally we sat on the ground. With everything that had happened to her, I wasn't sure how easily we could make love when the time came, but it would work out, I was sure of that.

The evening had grown so dim I didn't see him when he first came out of the woods. He came over and picked up the rifle I had laid on the ground and stood there holding it, not saying a word. Meren had not seen him yet and I hated to tell her, But I had to.

"Grant's here," I said.

She jumped with a start, getting to her feet quickly and looking on the ground for the rifle before she saw it in his hands.

"The two people I been waitin around to see again," Grant said. "I figured I wait long enough, I'd get to see you both. I's lucky enough for the two of you to be together. Lovebirds, are you?"

He laughed, a loud, irritating laugh. "I got me some money and I s'pect you got some on you. And thanks for bringin a car for me. I'll be out in Kansas or someplace this time tomorrow."

"Anything happens to us, you'll be dead this time tomorrow," I said. "The sheriff knows you're here. He's out there somewhere."

"I don't think so," Grant said. He levered a shell into the chamber of the rifle and the clacking of metal against metal sent chills through me.

"Look," I said, "take the car. Take what money I have and leave. If you don't shoot us, they won't be so anxious to catch you. You kill us, every lawman between here and Kansas will be stopping every car and looking inside. You wouldn't even get out of the county."

He laughed again. "Got something to settle with little Miss High and Mighty first. Thinks she's too good for me. We'll see. You can watch, see if you want her after I get through with her. Maybe I will let you live. Or maybe not."

Meren watched Grant with loathing on her face. Her eyes shot between his face and the rifle. He didn't miss that.

"Thanks for bringin it, Missy. Wasn't nothin left at the house or barn except Pa's old brush knife."

With the barrel of the rifle he lifted Meren's dress to her waist. She still wore the stylish underwear Estelle had picked out for her.

"My, my, look at them drawers," Grant said, gawking at her. "Now I ain't never had me no woman with drawers like that. Take that there dress off and let's see what else you got underneath there."

Meren stood locked in place. Grant showed some anger. "Hey, you hear me all right. Or you want me to put some lead in your boyfriend over there?"

He threw the rifle to his shoulder and pointed the barrel directly at me. My heart went cold. Meren took her dress off quickly and Grant cackled at her and lowered the rifle.

"My, my, look at all them lacy things. Now that's plum pretty."

He leaned toward her. "Go ahead and take them off, too."

Meren stripped her underpants and her brassiere off and stood naked before Grant. She turned so that I could no longer see the look on her face.

Grant leered. "Now, that there's more like it. Get down there on the ground, now. You know how you're supposed to do."

Meren dropped to her knees and leaned over backward and spread her knees apart. Grant moved closer, trying to unbuckle his belt and unbutton his pants with one hand. He found it too difficult and looked over at me. He couldn't have liked the look I gave him.

He leaned over slowly, keeping his eyes on me, then laid the rifle on the ground, straightened slightly and started lowering his trousers.

"Grant," I said, my voice full of anger and disgust.

He looked. "What the hell's that?" he asked, eyeing the dueling pistol I'd pulled from my jacket.

"It's a LePage-Moutier," I said. "The finest dueling pistol ever made."

"What the hell's a dueling pistol?"

"A pistol used by gentlemen. You wouldn't have any reason to know about that."

"Watch your damn tongue. You put your toy away or I'll use this rifle on you."

I rose slowly and, once erect, I positioned myself exactly as Langston Beauchamp had so many times when he toyed with my mother. I never knew if that was the time he was going to put a bullet in the LePage-Moutier and kill her, or if the pistol would only emit the metallic click that sent her body into spastic shudders.

I could see that Grant was not impressed with either the LePage-Moutier nor my stance. I moved sideways so that Meren was no longer between us. I saw in his eyes when he decided he could grab the rifle and kill me before I shot him. My heart beat so loudly it was like a steel drum inside my head. At the time I don't recall thinking that I was about to get myself and Meren killed. I just knew what was going to happen.

I fired the LePage-Moutier as Grant's hand closed on the rifle. He came up with it, but went over backwards and sat down. There was no little round hole in the middle of his forehead as there was supposed to be. Grant smiled as if he had just heard a great joke, then he began to shake his head sadly as if he actually pitied me.

Meren raised up on her elbows, facing Grant and just as he was about to pull the trigger on the rifle, she shouted in a voice as loud as my own, "Grant, you hurt me."

He looked at her in surprise. His forehead wrinkled and his eyes squinted nearly closed. He seemed unable to discern what she was saying and why she was saying it.

Everything stopped. The LePage-Moutier dangled from my hand, Grant stared in complete puzzlement at Meren as she remained on her elbows, her face darkened. Her breath came loudly and with great effort.

Grant leaned slowly over onto his side and it was then I saw the hole in his shirt and the blood leaking out and running down his front. He died still trying to figure out what Meren had said to him and why.

EPILOGUE

Meren and I were married a few weeks after that fateful day when Grant died. I was really scared that I would let her down as I had my mother. But Meren seemed so happy it was infectious. I was happy, too.

Months would pass before Estelle and Joel Dean could marry. By that time, Joel Dean was already in Congress and Estelle had her new store open. Next door, she opened a small dress shop and turned it over to Meren. Down the street a few doors away, I opened a law office. Not many customers came. Doyle Savoy put me on as a reserve deputy sheriff, but I never learned how to use the shotgun. Without the revenue from the dress shop we probably couldn't have paid all our bills, but that didn't matter to me and it didn't matter to Meren.

We had many friends and that mattered a lot to Meren. Her progression from a recluse of a child to a mature woman was such a pleasure to witness. Her voice, though it did get stronger, never again reached the volume it had that night when she shouted at Grant and probably saved both of our lives. At times, she would appear lost in thought and I suspected it was sadness about her family and the things that had happened to her. We spent one day of our lives talking about our past and what we had lived through. We closed the book on all that once we'd shed our conscience of the events. Afterwards, for the most part, considering the life we'd had, we were both supremely happy.

Days after we were married, we got word from Rose Minton in Lebanon that Uncle Billy Jack was failing and would like to speak with me. We drove down and found him in the hospital. Rose said the doctor told her that Uncle Billy Jack probably wouldn't last more than a few days. She gave me a bottle of Ernest Raines' fine mash whisky to take to him.

I was surprised and saddened when I saw his condition. He was barely able to hold his hand out to me.

I told him how events had turned out for me and for Meren. He smiled weakly. After we had talked for a few minutes, he asked me to take a box out of the small cabinet for personal effects. The box, a foot-square of corrugated cardboard, was wrapped with a heavy piece of twine wound around and around and tied. It took me some minutes to untie it and get it open. Inside was an expensive looking notebook with leather cover and a name in gold on the front. The name was Happy Meens.

I looked at Uncle Billy Jack with all kinds of questions rising up inside me. He waved his hand at me to open the notebook and look inside, which I did.

Details of all of Happy's land transactions for the electrical company were listed with dates, names and dollar figures. It went all the way back to the amount of money Happy, Elmer and Ruby Elam had offered Yawley Earnhardt for a piece of the county seat in the new Linn Creek. The phony transactions that Happy and Elmer had made and the kickbacks involved were listed. Happy had bought Hayden Joost's land for five hundred dollars, then reneged on the deal when McDermott and Fergus seemed to have the inside track for the county seat. There was enough evidence in here to send Elmer to jail and McDermott too.

When I had finished reading the book, I looked at Uncle Billy Jack, my mind full of questions.

"Found it," he said. "Read it. Knew what was going to happen to Linn Creek. My town. Couldn't let it happen. Borrowed a car. And a rifle. Followed those three to Joost place.

Happy told Hayden deal was off. Hayden got mad, ran Happy off."

He had to stop here to let his breathing catch up. I thought I knew the rest of what he had to say, but I waited for him to say it.

"Three of them argued. I shot Happy, but the other two ran off. Meren saw me. She knew who did it, but she never told anyone. I would have told Savoy before I would have let him arrest her."

"Why didn't you just turn it over to Doyle Savoy or Joel Dean Gregory?"

"I couldn't explain how I got the book without going to jail. I wanted to stick around and see what happened to the town."

"I understand your anger, Uncle Billy Jack, but it didn't help anything. The dam came in, the town was destroyed, everything that would have happened anyway, happened."

"No," he said. "You were a kind man. You treated people fairly. He didn't. It was worth killing him."

"No, it couldn't have been. Now you've killed a man. So did I, Uncle Billy Jack. I killed a man once and I have regretted it every day."

"Maybe the good Lord will have mercy on us both, then," he said.

When I came out of the room and saw Meren, she knew what he had told me.

"You knew," I said.

She nodded.

Uncle Billy Jack died the next day. What happened to his soul was not revealed to me. We attended the funeral for him and went back to Linn Creek. On the way, we went through the new county seat. It was going to be a fine town. It seems that once the Fergus's were free from the influence of McDermott and Elmer Byron, they sold the site to the two men who actually developed the town.

Everyone who was re-settled from old Linn Creek seemed fairly happy in their new surroundings. They began talking about the lake with pride when it was filled up.

But when old Linn Creek was mentioned, their eyes took on a far-away look and in some cases misted over. Granny Harris said it best: "It was home and it's a terrible thing when you have to leave your home."

Author's Note

On January 16, 1930, Clint Webb contracted to purchase 160 acres of land, then known as the Chipman Farm, from R. S. Dhority of Mystic, IA. The purchase price was $2750. Webb and his partner, Jim Banner, cleared the land and surveyed it into parcels. On May 29, 1931, the town of Camdenton was approved by the Camden County Court. Rumors notwithstanding, no evidence has ever been discovered of illegal activities concerning the naming of the county seat to replace Linn Creek nor in the re-routing of Highways 54 and 5 which previously had passed through Linn Creek.

In the Spring of 1931, well over a hundred houses, churches and businesses in Linn Creek were torn to the ground and burned to make way for the Lake of the Ozarks. Within months the waters of the lake were thirty feet deep over the remains of the town. Every tree in the town had been sawn down.

Those are the facts. But the facts do not speak of the wrenching agony of the residents as they watched their homes burned and their town destroyed house by house, church by church, business by business. I hope that this fictional story will serve to illuminate the truth of the despair of the people of Linn Creek because it is there that the real tragedy struck, and lives on today in the memories of the few who remain that were there, and by the descendants who listened as their parents, grandparents, uncles and aunts told endless stories of the destruction of Linn Creek and the peaceful and quiet lives they had lived in that little town now lying under the water.

THE DOOMED VALLEY

When a boy of nine, I traveled
With my parents, now grown gray
To a valley in the Ozarks
Which they're taking now away

With my sisters and my brothers
Playing round that kitchen door
We could hear the sweetest murmur
Of a spring we'll hear no more.

It was there I grew to manhood,
Childhood seemed as short as night,
There I wooed and won a maiden,
And we settled down for life.

Many summers have gone fleeting,
Since the year of ninety-six,
When I came into the Ozarks,
Where the river waters mix.

Yes the great old silent Osage,
Creeps along in silent dream,
But the clear Niangua waters
In the sunshine makes a gleam.

Time! O no has not been backward,
It has left its trace of toil,
Two sisters and two brothers,
Sleep beneath this Ozark soil.

When the bright sunshine of springtime,
Tends to rise from up above,
We can see the violets blooming,
In the valley that we love.

ASHES 319

Now has come the Union Electric
In the year of thirty-one
Forcing us to leave this valley,
That was home to old and young.

Yes we'll have to leave our homestead,
And our eyes with tears grow dim,
They are filling up this valley
Of the Ozarks to the brim.

They say they paid in money,
All that any man could ask.
For the best part of the Ozarks
Where the beauty always lasts.

Little do they know our feeling,
Or they care not for the pain,
That they created in the Ozarks,
Just to help St. Louis gain.

Oh! a great corporation,
Drives out people from their door,
Just as it has in the Ozarks,
And they'll have a home no more.

Time alone has told its story,
And our hearts are very sad,
As we have to leave this homestead,
That was a homestead of our Dad.

By Ray Libby
Originally Printed in the *Reveille*.
Reprinted here with permission from
The Lake Sun Leader